PENGUIN BOOKS

Crusade

Stewart Binns began his professional life as an academic. He then pursued several adventures, including that of a schoolteacher, specializing in history, before becoming an award-winning documentary-maker and latterly an author. His television credits include the 'In-Colour' genre of historical documentaries, notably the BAFTA and Grierson winner *Britain at War in Colour* and the Peabody winner *The Second World War in Colour*.

He also launched *Trans World Sport* in 1987, *Futbol Mundial* in 1993, the International Olympic Commitee *Camera of Record* in 1994 and the Olympic Television Archive Bureau in 1996.

Currently Chief Executive and co-founder, with his wife Lucy, of the independent production and distribution company Big Ape Media International. His first novel, *Conquest,* was published in 2011 and is available in Penguin paperback. *Crusade* is the sequel.

Stewart's passion is English history, especially its origins and folklore. His home is in Somerset, where he lives with his wife Lucy and twin boys, Charlie and Jack.

www.stewartbinns.com

Crusade

STEWART BINNS

PENGUIN BOOKS

PENGUIN BOOKS

Published by the Penguin Group

Penguin Books Ltd, 80 Strand, London WC2R ORL, England

Penguin Group (USA) Inc., 375 Hudson Street, New York, New York 10014, USA

Penguin Group (Canada), 90 Eglinton Avenue East, Suite 700, Toronto, Ontario, Canada M4P 2Y3
(a division of Pearson Penguin Canada Inc.)

Penguin Ireland, 25 St Stephen's Green, Dublin 2, Ireland (a division of Penguin Books Ltd)

Penguin Group (Australia), 250 Camberwell Road, Camberwell, Victoria 3124, Australia
(a division of Pearson Australia Group Pty Ltd)

Penguin Books India Pvt Ltd, 11 Community Centre,
Panchsheel Park, New Delhi – 110 017, India

Penguin Group (NZ), 67 Apollo Drive, Rosedale, Auckland 0632, New Zealand
(a division of Pearson New Zealand Ltd)

Penguin Books (South Africa) (Pty) Ltd, Block D, Rosebank Office Park, 181 Jan Smuts Avenue,
Parktown North, Gauteng 2193, South Africa

Penguin Books Ltd, Registered Offices: 80 Strand, London WC2R ORL, England

www.penguin.com

First published 2012

001

Set in 12.5/14.75 Garamond MT Std

Typeset by Palimpsest Book Production Limited, Falkirk, Stirlingshire

Printed in Great Britain by Clays Ltd, St Ives plc

ISBN: 978-0-241-95757-8

www.greenpenguin.co.uk

Penguin Books is committed to a sustainable
future for our business, our readers and our planet.
This book is made from Forest Stewardship
Council™ certified paper.

ALWAYS LEARNING   **PEARSON**

To Edgar

A forgotten prince, the last of his dynasty, but one of
the builders of a new England

To Edward Grant-Ives, 1926–2010
My father-in-law, a true Englishman

Contents

Introduction

The year is 1126, the twentieth year of the reign of Henry Beauclerc, the fourth son of William the Conqueror. He will be the last Norman King of England.

Norman rule in England remains resolute and the country is prospering. However, endless feuds within the Norman hierarchy, especially between the Conqueror's sons, have brought much strife and bloodshed to England, the British Isles and Europe.

Elsewhere, Christian Europe has become obsessed by Jerusalem and the Islamic lordship of the Holy Land. The First Crusade had been launched in 1095 and, amidst much brutality, led to the capture of Jerusalem in July 1099. After 700 years of slumber, a new Europe is asserting itself and the price paid for this by many tens of thousands is exacted in blood.

And yet, even in the midst of the worst of the mayhem of internecine bloodletting and religious fanaticism, the hope still flickers among many that peace and liberty are attainable.

A new code of ethical behaviour begins to emerge, in part influenced by the moral qualities of Islam, known as the Mos Militum – the Code of Knights. Honour, truthfulness, courage, martial prowess, pride in the face of superiors, humility in the face of inferiors and protection of the weak – women, children and the old –

all are becoming cherished virtues among the warrior classes.

Epic sagas of heroic feats from the past flourish. The highly popular *Chansons de Geste* and *1001 Arabian Nights* tell of great and worthy deeds and inspire young warriors to lead better lives. There is even the beginning of a highly romanticized view of women. Previously excluded from military ideals, the notion of Courtly Love has emerged, where women are idealized and knights strive to impress them rather than possess them.

It is the dawn of the Age of Chivalry.

PART ONE
The Forgotten Prince

1. Beyond the Eye of God

The scriptorium of Malmesbury Abbey is in the middle of a long working day, a day that begins at five in the morning and does not end until vespers in the evening. Over twenty monks are zealously transcribing and illustrating the great books of the day, including those of Abbot William, the leader of Malmesbury's Benedictine community and widely regarded as the wisest man in England.

Although the scene is a picture of intense toil, except for the gentle scratch of quill on vellum, it is conducted in reverential silence.

The monks of Malmesbury are the guardians of the finest library in northern Europe. They are engaged in the vital work of transcribing the precious word of God and the entire fruits of human knowledge. Their labours will become a major part of the heritage of these times.

Outside the abbey cloisters the burgh of Malmesbury bustles and flourishes noisily with the din of the commerce of urban life. An ancient settlement resting on an easily defended flat-topped hill, its celebrated springs have attracted settlers for hundreds of years.

In the heart of Wessex, Malmesbury had been a jewel in the crown of Anglo-Saxon England. With the arrival of the Normans sixty years ago it was one of the first English burghs to come under direct Norman rule. In 1118, Roger of Salisbury, Chancellor to King Henry I, seized Malmesbury and brought it under his bishopric at Salisbury. He immediately began to rebuild the abbey and the burgh's walls in stone, a process which is still much in evidence.

The burgh is typical of England under the Normans – at least, in the prosperous southern earldoms. It is thriving in an uneasy, pragmatic truce between the ruling Normans and the defeated and dispossessed English. As is often the case in conquered lands, the victors offer sufficient wealth and opportunity to important parts of the native community to persuade them to cooperate with the new regime. Some call it treason, others cowardice, yet others common sense.

William of Malmesbury's great work, *Gesta Regum Anglorum*, a history of the kings of England, had been completed in 1122, but he is still adding accounts, anecdotes and stories to the vast wealth of knowledge in the abbey.

Sadly, his eyesight is failing him and he relies more and more on the support of the brightest of his young acolytes, Roger of Caen, an intellectually gifted and enthusiastic young Norman, the second son of a nobleman.

William, a tall, stooping figure looking every inch a learned ecclesiast in his black habit, summons Roger into the cloister.

'We must journey to the North.'

'Why, Abbot? It is a wasteland . . .'

'Recently, a Norse trader from Northumbria brought me an interesting story. What do you think became of Prince Edgar the Atheling?'

'He must be dead by now.'

'Well, the Norseman tells me he's alive and living in a remote hamlet, high in the Pennines.'

'Do you think such a journey is wise when winter is well nigh upon us?'

'Perhaps not . . . but the chance to meet the rightful heir to the English throne is a rare opportunity, and too fortuitous to miss.'

'You English, you never give in! His time passed him by sixty years ago. If he is still alive he must be in his dotage by now.'

'Nevertheless . . . Choose three or four good men, and make sure they are handy with a sword. We leave after prayers in the morning.'

As William's small party of monks journeys northwards, England's countryside changes from a thriving kingdom of southern shires, where another rich harvest has been safely gathered in, to mile upon mile of grim desolation.

At Gloucester, Worcester and Chester they see new Norman strongholds in all their grandeur. Massive stone keeps are replacing wooden mottes and baileys, modest Saxon cathedrals are being rebuilt on impressive Romanesque lines. Normans and Englishmen mix freely; this new England is a land transformed. However, north of Chester, settlements become more and more sporadic and in places where people are to be found, they live in little more than hovels and endure a pitiful existence.

In the southern earldoms, people speak only of the memories of the massacres committed by William the Conqueror in his Harrying of the North of nearly sixty years ago. But in the North, the nightmare is still real.

After crossing the Mersey, William decides to make several detours down minor routes, both east and west. Away from the main road to Scotland, a route which runs north through Preston and Lancaster where a thin band of normal life is upheld by the vigilance of Norman garrisons, lie huge tracts of ravaged land. Rapidly being consumed by nature, decades of backbreaking toil to clear forests, plough fields and build villages will, in another generation, be wasted. Prime farming land will become nothing more than wilderness.

The western side of the Pennines is the most impoverished of all. In the east, the strategic route to Scotland and the importance of York and Durham mean that the Normans have been careful to rebuild and resettle. In the west, little has changed since the murder and destruction of 1069.

So complete is the devastation and killing in the remote parts of the hinterland that no one is left to bury the dead. Bodies, now no more than sun-bleached skeletons wrapped in rotting fragments of clothing, are still lying where tens of thousands of people were massacred in their villages.

William is deep in thought; there are tears in his eyes, his knuckles white as he grasps his reins in anguish.

'I have read all the accounts of the Conqueror's dreadful deeds in this land, but words cannot describe the true horror of this. It is to be hoped that he is now suffering at the hand of God for what he has done here.'

Roger has been fortunate in life. His has been the

sheltered existence of a cleric since childhood; he has never witnessed anything like this before.

'So, it is true. He really was a monster.'

'Yes, he was a ruthless tyrant, like many of your countrymen.'

'We are not all like him.'

'I know, my son, but my father was a Norman, so I know that a love of war and a penchant for avarice fire the Norman blood.'

Both men say silent prayers as they pass every example of the brutality committed a lifetime ago.

There is still a small community on the hill at Lancaster, where a heavily armed garrison of the King's men is overseeing the building of a stone keep, but the only civilians are a few souls marooned in service to the garrison and the masons. Most of the old burgh is in ruins, its simple wooden buildings burned to the ground, its small Saxon stone church gutted, its roof timbers charred and decaying.

William and Roger make camp beneath the walls of Lancaster's keep. It is a cold night and their men build a large fire for them.

Roger is in pensive mood.

'Abbot, why is it always the innocent who suffer?'

'War is like a tempest; no one is safe. When a storm rages in the hearts of men, it consumes everything in its path. Like peasants' hovels in a gale, it is the little people who are the most vulnerable.'

'I'm glad we have the walls of Malmesbury and our Holy Orders to protect us.'

'Don't be too complacent, my young friend. If the winds are powerful enough, neither stout walls nor a monk's heavy cassock will keep you safe. Both can prove flimsy in the midst of the tumults made by men.'

'Thank you for that comforting thought, Abbot.' Roger smiles wryly before another blast of cold air reminds him how uncomfortable he is. 'This prince, Edgar . . . what kind of man is he?'

'He is intriguing – enigmatic, shrewd, obviously a survivor. He has lived a very long life and is the only senior figure from the time of the Conquest still alive. He knew two Kings of England – Edward and Harold – and he was at York with Hereward of Bourne when the great English rebellion looked like it might succeed. And that was only the beginning of his story.

'He befriended King William's firstborn, Robert Curthose. He fought in Sicily and the Crusades, and stood with Robert at the Battle of Tinchebrai. What stories he can tell us!'

Roger stares at his mentor admiringly.

'Well, if you put it like that, I suppose it's a journey worth making.' Then he adds, with rather less enthusiasm, 'I just wish it wasn't so far north and so bitterly cold.'

When they reach the settlement of Sedbergh, they find another tiny enclave of normality. Previously a flourishing village, it is now no more than a few makeshift shelters; the once-proud Anglo-Norse inhabitants have been reduced to a wretched vestige of humanity. Many are sick, some are lame, and all look pale and undernourished.

Their clothes are little better than rags, few wear leggings and most walk barefoot.

William decides to stay for a while to help the community find some purpose. He puts his men to work, trying to make the meagre dwellings more habitable, while he and Roger strive to inspire the locals to help themselves. One young man, no more than a boy of sixteen or seventeen, seems the most vigorous, and William takes him to one side.

'How many people are there here?'

'Sire, about twenty in the village and another dozen or so in the hills around us.'

'Where is your priest, or your thegn? Don't you have a lord?'

'There is no one. We are all from different villages. Our parents settled here a few years ago, after spending years hiding in the forests and on the fells. No one has claimed the village, so we came here to try to rebuild it.'

'What is your name?'

'Aldric, Abbot.'

'Where are your parents now?'

'They are dead. All the original settlers are dead. Last winter was very harsh, and many died. A group of younger men went down the valley in the spring to look for work, but we never saw them again. So, this is all that's left – old men and women, a few children and four or five of us who are reasonably fit and well.'

'Why haven't you left?'

'Because it's our duty to stay; they would all die if we left.'

'I admire your courage and sacrifice. Gather together

the fit members of the community; I want to talk to them.'

Young Aldric summons two other young men, as well as three girls in their teens. William sits them down in the middle of the village and addresses them.

'I am claiming possession of this village under the ownership of the Abbey of Malmesbury.'

There is an immediate look of horror on the faces of Aldric and his companions, but William is quick to reassure them.

'My abbey will not be taxing you – at least, not until you can easily afford it. I will give you silver to buy seed, a couple of oxen and a plough, and sufficient to buy some sheep and cows. Tomorrow, Roger and one of my men will ride back to Lancaster to buy food to get you through the approaching winter.'

William is heartened when he sees the horror on the faces in front of him transformed into an expression of astonishment.

'I am appointing Aldric as Thegn of Sedbergh, which I will have confirmed by King Henry at Winchester upon my return to Malmesbury. The rest of you are appointed elders of the village on my authority. Are there any questions?'

There is a stunned silence.

'Tomorrow we will help you build a longhouse for the village, where you can all stay warm together in the winter. We won't leave until it is finished. When it is complete, I will bless it and we will say mass together. In a few months' time, when I find the right candidate, I will send you a priest from Malmesbury and together you can build him a church.'

Aldric bends down to kiss William's ring, but the Abbot pulls him up, embarrassed at the overt show of gratitude. However, he's not agile enough to prevent the girls, overcome by emotion, kneeling at his feet to bury their heads in his cassock.

Roger, seeing William's unease at this outpouring of gratitude, catches William's eye and grins at him mockingly.

'Away to Lancaster with you,' roars the Abbot. 'And be quick about it!'

Ten days later, the longhouse finished and the village given a spark of life, William and his party head north to Appleby on the river Eden and begin to ascend the fells of the high Pennines towards Kirby Thore and the old Roman fort of Bravoniacum.

As they leave Sedbergh behind, Roger turns to Abbot William.

'Will they prosper?' he asks.

'I think so. They've been through a lot and are strong people; they just needed a little bit of inspiration. We will keep an eye on them.'

Roger smiles to himself. He knows he has a lot to learn and that William will be an inspiring teacher.

There is a similar scene of poverty and destitution in Appleby. The old village is in ruins, save for a single ale and mead house run by Wotus, a crusty old Northumbrian, and his family, whose Anglo-Norse language William has difficulty understanding. Wotus makes just enough to survive by serving the itinerant charcoal-burners and lead-miners who come to his house once a week to drink themselves stupid and stare longingly at his comely daughters.

After a couple of days' rest, William's men conclude that, although the Northumbrian's daughters are worthy of a modest detour, his ale and mead are far less endearing, his beds are in desperate need of fresh straw and his midden not fit for pigs.

And so, they move further north. The chill wind of winter begins to bite and snow falls from the gull-grey clouds above them. They lose touch with humanity. All signs of life – or death – disappear. Roger looks out across the bleak scene.

'What kind of man would choose to live up here?'

'One who has many memories to dwell upon, and perhaps a few regrets. When people who have lived a turbulent life come to face the end of it, it's often the case that they seek solitude in which to reflect.'

William and Roger spend many hours speculating on the long and fascinating life of Edgar the Atheling, all of which only increases William's impatience to meet him. But their idle musings are brought to an end by the increasing remoteness of their route.

Their men-at-arms look tense; they are not easily unnerved but are not accustomed to such hostile terrain. The boundless swathes of primordial forest, untouched by the hand of man, are dense and dark, and above them the high fells rise like menacing shadows. Only on the very crests of the fells is the ground clear, where relentless wind and bitter cold make it difficult for anything to grow except moss and heather.

*

On the third day north of Sedbergh, their sergeant rides back from his lead position to speak to William.

'My Lord Abbot, is it wise to go on? This place is wild.'

'Sergeant, the man we seek will have chosen this place deliberately. He is a prince of the realm – if he can venture here, so can we.'

'I fear we are being watched . . . perhaps for the last couple of hours. I'm not certain, but I think I can see movement in the trees.'

'Be vigilant, Sergeant. Send your best man to higher ground to see if we're being followed. And tell the men to stay alert.'

The sergeant sends out his senior man, Eadmer, with instructions to work his way around to the back of the small party and check if anyone is following them.

They eventually find the key to their passage: the Maiden Way, an ancient Roman route, cut over the fells a millennium earlier to link the lead and silver mines of the northern hills to the routes heading south and to the fort at Carvoran on the Great North Wall of the Emperor Hadrian.

William has often reflected on Rome and its achievements. When writing his chronicles of the English kings, there were many monarchs he admired, such as the great and noble Alfred. He has marvelled at their courage, wisdom and triumphs. But if only he had been a scholar in Ancient Rome, then he could have been the chronicler of men who had conquered the known world; those who built a civilization so sophisticated and powerful that it endured for hundreds of years.

Now he is approaching the last outpost of their empire.

He shivers, partly in awe at contemplating their triumphs and partly in dread at what he is getting himself into in this fearful place. He wonders what the intrepid Romans must have thought as they trudged northwards. Rugged and resolute, no doubt, they were men from the Mediterranean, southern Gaul; perhaps as far as Anatolia, North Africa, or Phoenicia. They must have been as anxious as he is now. What men they must have been!

The Maiden Way is little used and difficult to negotiate, but at least it cuts through the forests, fords the rivers and points true north.

'Abbot, do you know the route?'

'I do; the Norseman's instructions were very clear.'

'May a young monk, who is perhaps often too sure of himself for his own good, confess to an overwhelming feeling of terror at his current circumstances?'

William smiles and turns to his young companion.

'There is much to fear in this world: nature and its wild and unpredictable habits; man and his bestial depravities. But it is God we should respect the most, for He controls everything. Pray to Him and ask for His protection.'

Roger kicks on, not at all reassured, scanning the trees intently and twitching at the slightest sound. After a while, he blurts out another question with an anxious tremor.

'I know Edgar is the last English claimant to the kingdom, and I know what you said . . . But are you really sure he is worth such a perilous journey? He's probably nothing but an incoherent old fool by now.'

'Far from it, my young friend. The Norseman said he was not only lucid but a fount of stories. Remember, Edgar was announced as King of England after Harold's slaughter on Senlac Ridge. He had powerful friends, including the Kings of Scotland and France. After being reconciled with the Conqueror and befriending Robert Curthose, he went to the Great Crusade with him – and both men came back in one piece, an outcome not afforded to many.'

'I have been doing my arithmetic. He was too young to succeed the saintly Edward in 1066 – fifteen or sixteen, I think – so, he must be in his mid-seventies. I hope he keeps warm in this miserable place.'

'I think we will find a man of some resolve. He fought in the wars between the Conqueror's sons and must have gained their respect, otherwise King Henry would have had him killed or thrown into an oubliette.'

'And you think this abode any better!'

'My son, you have obviously never been in one of the King's dungeons.'

2. Kingdom of Rheged

They are now approaching the high moorland and the trees are thinning. Roger stops suddenly and crosses himself.

'God bless and save us! It is Eadmer.'

He points to the last tree before the open moor. Hanging from it, severed from his body and tied by his hair, is Eadmer's head, blood still oozing on to the ground. Bizarrely, despite the gruesome scene and the horror of his death – perhaps only moments ago – his eyes are closed and at peace, and he looks strangely serene. Nearby, his body has been propped upright in his saddle and his horse carefully tethered.

'It is a warning to turn back.'

The sergeant is already turning his horse as he speaks.

'Where are you going, man? You are a soldier; your father was a housecarl in King Harold's army. Get a grip of yourself! We will cut him down and give him a Christian burial.'

With that, the renowned scribe of Malmesbury takes the sergeant's sword and removes Eadmer's head from the tree, placing it on the ground. They then pull his body from the horse, lay his corpse in a shallow grave and hold a short service.

A piercing wind shrieks at them as William reads from his Bible. The skies darken and the snow begins to fall more heavily, swirling around them in wild flurries. William seems oblivious to everything that has happened; the others are in a state of terror.

It is Roger who voices their fears.

'Abbot, the men want to turn back. So do I.'

'Roger, calm yourself. We haven't come all this way to turn back now. We'll find a place to camp over there in the trees and see what the morning brings.'

'This is madness. We are in the middle of the wilderness and someone has just beheaded one of our men!'

In silence, and with grim determination, William leads his group to a small copse of trees barely a hundred yards away. As they enter the grove, looming above them, far off in the distance, they can see the mighty crest of Cross Fell.

Then the Druid appears.

He is standing alone on a small rocky knoll, no more than ten yards away. He wears a simple grey robe of washed wool tied at the waist with a pleated cord. His untied hair and beard are long and hoary and he has a heavy silver chain and amulet around his neck decorated with pagan images. His right hand holds a long oak staff topped by a ram's skull replete with enormous horns, and around the wrist of his left hand is a small garland of mistletoe. His dark, piercing eyes are fixed on them in an unblinking stare. William assumes he is a druid, for he has exactly the mien and bearing that legend describes.

The sergeant-at-arms makes for his sword, but before he can draw it more than six inches from its scabbard an arrow cuts through the air and lodges in his throat, the tip of its head exiting close to his spine. A second hits him square in the chest near his heart, and a third lands inches away from the second. Both are deeply embedded. He is silent and motionless for a moment before reaching desperately for his throat, uttering a muted cry that turns into a sickening splutter as a stream of blood cascades from his mouth. His futile grasp of his gullet soon relaxes and he tumbles off his horse, hitting the ground with a heavy thud.

In that instance, at least thirty heavily armed men appear, as if out of nowhere. They make no sound, not even the faintest rustle underfoot.

William begs his remaining companions in a hiss, 'Do not move. Stay silent.'

They are clearly Celts, but resemble a breed William has only read about, never seen.

The Druid speaks in excellent English, but with a strong accent that confirms it is not his first language.

'You are a monk and, I think, an important one. What brings you to our land?'

'You have committed murder here.'

'Your bodyguards are not welcome here, and neither are you. This is our land.'

'Is this not the land of the Earl of Bamburgh?'

'It is not. Our tribe has owned this land since before the legions of Rome came here. I asked you a question.'

William is thinking quickly.

Could it be possible for a tribe of Celts to have remained here, undisturbed since antiquity? To have avoided or repelled the attentions of Rome's legions and of Saxon, Dane and Norman?

They certainly look like the ancient Celts of the

chronicles. Their bearded faces and bodies are adorned with swirls of pagan imagery, but not in the blue woad of legend – theirs are an ochre colour, not painted on to their skin, but cut in and permanent. Their dress is like the Celts' of Wales and Cornwall: woollen leggings dyed red; heavy cloaks over their shoulders – the only covering for their bare chests. Their weapons are similar to the seax, spear and shield of a Saxon housecarl, but they do not carry the housecarl's main weapon, the axe, preferring a short but powerful Celtic bow and quiver of arrows.

'I will see to it that your crime is dealt with by the Earl.'

'The Earl? I know no such man. I rule here. Your guard strayed from the Roman path; that means he had to die. This one drew his weapon, which cost him his life. We let people pass, but if they stray into our domain or raise their weapons, they pay with their lives. It has always been so. I ask you for the final time, what brings you to our land?'

William decides that it is wise to acquiesce.

'I am on a journey with my cleric, Roger of Malmesbury –' he chooses not to mention Roger's Norman origins '– to meet a man I am told lives near here. I am William, Abbot of Malmesbury, a chronicler. These are my men-at-arms.'

The Druid does not respond. He looks at his men, then closes his eyes and prays out loud in a language that is unrecognizable. He finishes his invocations by raising his staff with its ram's head and pointing it at Cross Fell. He then looks at William, but more benignly than before.

'We respect you. You chose to bury your man and pray over him; few men would have done that, preferring to scurry off the fells as quickly as their horses would carry them.' He stares at William intently. 'So, you are a story-teller. Storytellers are welcome here, but your warriors are not. They must go back to Appleby and wait for you there.'

'But they are here for our protection.'

'You have no need of them now. You are safe with us.'

William knows immediately that the Druid is right. Whoever these people are, it is certainly their realm. He nods to his two remaining warriors to depart. The older one, visibly terrified, questions the wisdom of William's decision.

'Are you sure, Abbot?'

'I am sure. We are not far from our destination and these people will give us safe passage.'

The man-at-arms leans forward in his saddle to whisper, 'They are heathens, murderous savages.'

'They are heathens, and there is no doubting their savagery. But I have travelled a long way for the man I seek and I am not turning back now. Wait at Appleby for ten days. If we do not return, go to the garrison at Lancaster and tell them what you have seen here. In the meantime, say nothing of this to anyone – especially not to Wotus and his family.'

As his men turn and leave, William impatiently begins to ask the first of many questions to which he wants answers.

'Do I address you as a priest, or are you lord of these people?'

'I am Lord of the Gul. We do not have priests, or a god, as you would understand them; we worship the earth, moon and stars and follow what nature teaches us. You may call me Owain, for that is my name.'

'And you are Celts?'

'We are. Before I take you to the man you seek, I will tell you a little about us. We are the Gul, the last tribe of the great Kingdom of Rheged, a land that once stretched from the Picts of the mountains of Scotland all the way to the end of the fells of Hen Ogledd – what you call the "Old North" of England. Our southern boundary was the marshland where the waters of the Derventi, the Trenti, the Soori and the Irre Wiscce meet. Beyond lived the Coritani people, in what you now call Mercia. We speak Cumbric, which is like the Welsh you know in the south. I am a direct descendant of Urien Rheged, the most famous of our leaders; he ruled here many generations ago.'

'How do you preserve your traditions? Do you trade with the other people in the area?'

'That is all you may know about us. You are a story-teller, are you not? Read the poems of Taliesin; you will find them in the chronicles of the Welsh bards.'

'You must tell me more. You are part of the great history of our land.'

'I must? Indeed, I will not. We are not part of the history of "your" land. This is our land!'

Owain spits his answer at the Abbot, who realizes he has been given all the information the Druid is prepared to impart.

'We must leave. The day is moving on and the snow will fall into the night. No man would want to be on these fells at night, blizzard or otherwise. We will help you bury your man. The Prince lives a few miles from here, next to the

Water that Roars, near the Norse settlements of Alston and Garrigyll.'

'How do you know we seek Prince Edgar?'

'You surely haven't come here to mine for lead. Why else would an English storyteller be high in the mountains of Rheged, stepping over the corpses of ill-begotten Saxons and Norse?'

William presides over another interment, for the sergeant-at-arms. Then, after several hours of struggle over difficult ground with driven snow increasingly obscuring the track, Owain Rheged and his band of warriors leave William and Roger at the top of a steep gorge. He beckons them towards a raging waterfall that spews its innards angrily into the valley below.

'The Prince's hall lies beyond the falls to the south, next to the Grue Water. There is a safe place to ford further upstream. You must show respect here; this place is sacred to us.'

William nods his assent.

Before he departs, Owain moves closer to William. He speaks gently, the ferocity of his demeanour suddenly assuaged.

'Have you told all the stories you want to tell?'

'Most of them, Owain Rheged.'

'That is good. When you pray to your god, save a prayer for yourself.'

'I always do. Are you concerned for me?'

'You will soon be like the blacksmith without his strong arms . . .' He pauses. 'You will be blind by Midsummer's Day.'

'How do you know this?'

'I have seen it before. You have what the Ancients called *nazul-i-ah*, "the descent of the water". In Latin it is called *cataracta*. It means "waterfall".'

'How do you know this?'

'I have seen it in the infirmaries of Constantinople. Prince Edgar believes I have never left these fells and that when he came here, he taught me English and the ways of Christendom. He doesn't know that before my face was decorated my father sent me into the world to learn its ways. I was away for a dozen years and travelled across Europe and into the great empire of Byzantium.'

William hesitates, shocked by the Druid's pronouncement about his eyes.

'Is there anything that can be done about my sight?'

'No . . . but keep that boy close to you. You will need him.'

'You are a fascinating man, Owain Rheged. I would like to hear more of your story one day.'

The Druid doesn't answer.

In an instant, he is gone – he and his warriors melting into the forest as unobtrusively as they had appeared.

3. All Hallows

William and his men travel for some distance to find the crossing point of the Pennine beck, shallow enough for their horses, before doubling back on themselves to reach the settlement where the Druid had said they would find their quarry.

William's next Northumbrian revelation is the humble nature of the Prince's settlement.

The main hall is not much bigger than a freeman's two-room cottage, and the two smaller buildings are about the size of a peasant's simple one-room dwelling. The cluster of buildings, which appears to be deserted, cannot be home to more than ten or twelve people.

They search for a few minutes, but no one can be found. The fire in the hall is just a cool ember and has not been tended for several hours. Roger seizes his chance to bid for a rapid retreat to Malmesbury.

'So, Abbot, the bird has flown; there is no point in wasting our time here. I will feed the horses and we can begin our journey home.'

'Not at this time, I fear. It will be dark soon.'

'I suppose I must bow to your judgement – if we can't start tonight, I'll find us a place to sleep.'

William gazes into the dense wall of trees surrounding the settlement.

'Let's bed down in the hall. I don't think our host is far away.'

William and Roger enter the modest hall and start to pile wood on to the ashes of the smouldering fire.

'Roger, hand me those bellows.'

As the young monk reaches for the means to bring the fire to life, a gruff voice speaks to them from the shadows.

'What do you want here?'

William, startled, turns sharply.

'Show yourself, we have had enough shocks for one day.'

'We are the ones who should be shocked. You have entered our hall uninvited.'

'I am William of Malmesbury, and this is my cleric, Roger of Caen. We seek Edgar, Prince of this realm.'

'There are no princes here, priest. Are you mad? Why would a royal prince be living in this godforsaken place?'

'I am sorry; we have been told that Prince Edgar lives here. In fact, it was your neighbours, the Gul, who escorted us here.'

With that, another much gentler voice speaks.

'Welcome to Ashgyll, William of Malmesbury. I'm afraid we will not be able to offer you the many comforts of the dormitories in your great abbey, but our settlement suffices for our simple needs.'

William and Roger turn to their right as the man they seek steps from the shadows with his steward. At the same time, the first man also steps forward; he is a large battle-scarred man, who is clearly Edgar's sergeant-at-arms.

William bows and says, 'My Lord, I am honoured to meet the Atheling Prince of England. You knew of our coming?'

'Of course, my friends the Gul keep me informed. But none of that "Atheling" formality, that was a long time ago. I am now Edgar, Lord of Ashgyll, but my realm is no more than what you see around you. You must call me Edgar.'

The Prince tells his steward to take care of the horses, then gestures to William and Roger to move closer to the fire.

'You must forgive my furtiveness when you appeared. I like to remain as anonymous as possible up here. I have chosen a quiet and contemplative end to my life. As a monk, I'm sure you will understand that.'

'Indeed, although life at Malmesbury can sometimes be far more hectic than I would wish.'

'How did you know where to find me?'

'A Norseman. He came to the abbey to sell linen.'

Edgar smiles ruefully.

'I thought as much. I recall he just appeared one day. He recognized me at Durham and must have followed me here. I don't know how he avoided the Gul; perhaps he paid them off. I suppose you made it worth his while to tell you where I lived?'

'Well, we did buy rather a lot of linen from him.'

'Yes, he was a good salesman – very persuasive; he carried some excellent Norse mead. He probably got me drunk. Anyway, he had already guessed my identity, so there was no point in denying it.'

Edgar shrugs his shoulders, sits himself down by the fire and changes the subject.

'You are a Norman, young Roger. I know Caen; it is a fine city. And I know the Normans well – especially a very noble one called Robert.'

After a pause, Edgar turns to William and stares at him pointedly.

'Are you here to hear my confession?'

'Not exactly, but I would like to hear the account of your many trials and tribulations. My life is devoted to the chronicles of the past.'

'I know your work and that you have just completed your *Deeds of the Kings of the English*. The monks at Durham have a copy, which they are very proud of.'

'You flatter me. How often do you visit the cathedral?'

'I used to go occasionally, but now the stiffness of old age prevents any travel beyond my weekly trip to Alston, an old Norse settlement nearby. Like so much of the North, it's not much more than a ruin where the few locals who survive hold a weekly market.'

'Does that include the mysterious Owain Rheged and his band of Celts?'

'No, indeed. No one ever sees them. They live deep in the forest – high up, near the open fells. Owain comes here from time to time. I like to drink, he likes to talk; he tells me endless stories about his ancestors and the great Urien Rheged.'

'He killed two of my men; beheaded one and hanged his head from a tree like an animal. The other he butchered in front of us like a deer in the forest.'

'I'm surprised he didn't do that to all of you; he is guarding the safety of his tribe. He still holds human sacrifices, or so I am told. He's getting old, though, so perhaps he was curious about you. Maybe he was tempted to tell you his story? He must know the end is close for his people. It's one thing keeping superstitious Saxons and Danes at bay with his sorcery, but quite another to resist the Normans. He knows their brutal reputation.'

'I don't suppose there is any point in trying to seek redress for what he has done?'

'No, he is the law here. The Earl doesn't venture up here; no one in their right mind does – except you, of course.'

Recalling the Druid's account of his early life, William asks, 'Where did he learn English?'

'From me, although I suspect I wasn't the first to teach him. I came here nearly fifteen years ago; I chose this place to be close to my friends in Scotland and because Ashgyll Force cleanses me. I like to wash away the dust of Palestine and the memory of Jerusalem every day. I also came here because I once had a very traumatic experience high in the fells of the Pennines. It changed my life.'

'May I ask about the circumstances?'

'You may. My life was saved by a man called Hereward of Bourne. You know of him?'

'I do. He has become a legend, but I would like to hear about him from you.'

Edgar appears to ignore William's request.

'Let me tell you about Owain Rheged. He is a remarkable man and his people are a lost tribe, full of strange rituals. He started to appear in the distance after I had been here for about a year and we had finished building our home. Then one day, as I was admiring the endless cascade of the Force, he appeared behind me, shouting and cursing in his language and pointing his ram's-head staff at me. Eventually, I realized he was telling me the ground was sacred, so I fell to my knees and bowed my head. I felt certain I would be struck down, but he saw my gold ring and seal and relented. He just stared at me, then walked away.

'I didn't cast eyes on him again for several months. Then, one bright spring morning, he appeared with an oak sapling, their sacred tree. It stands over there, taller than my hall now. We have been friends ever since. I am very meek with him; he is a king, after all, and I'm only a prince.'

William observes Edgar intently as he speaks about Owain, King of Rheged, and of the land of Hen Ogledd.

He is tall and, although now stooped with the ravages of age, still has the bearing of a nobleman. His clothes are modest, no better than those of a minor thegn, and his only adornment is the gold ring of the House of Wessex, the royal Cerdician lineage of the ancient kings of England. Although its many wrinkles suggest much anguish in the past, his face has a kindly demeanour. His grey hair is cut short, as is his neat beard; only his dark eyebrows hint at his previous colouring. His steel-grey eyes are clear and alert; he carries no visible scars, and his aged hands are delicate and soft like those of a scholar.

'Do you know there are still bears up here?'

'That cannot be. The last bears in England died out hundreds of years ago.'

'So, you don't know everything, William of Malmesbury.'

Edgar then asks his steward to bring him his winter cloak.

'It's cold enough for this today. Here, try it.'

William takes the bearskin cloak and drapes it over his shoulders.

'Well, it's certainly a bearskin – ideal for your Pennine eyrie.'

'Owain's people know where the bears are. There are only a few dozen left, but they're here all right. And lots of hungry wolves to keep them company. The Anglo-Danes who lived in the valleys – before King William butchered them – used to say that Owain could change himself into a bear or a wolf at will.'

'Edgar, it is your life I have come to hear about. The mysteries of Owain Rheged can wait for another time.'

Again, Edgar ignores William's request.

'He has a Roman centurion's helmet and sword, hundreds of years old. He brought them here once; he's very proud of them. They were passed down to him from his ancestors. The helmet still has some of its horsehair crest, a remarkable thing. He says he also has the head of the Roman who once wore the helmet. It wouldn't surprise me. The Gul keep the skulls of their victims as trophies.'

'Edgar, your story please.'

'Let's discuss it in the morning. We must build up the fire now, and drink some mead; tonight will be cold.'

'It is already cold! Does that wind never stop howling? And how do you sleep with that thundering waterfall?'

'You'll get used to the waterfall. As for the wind, that happens often. It comes off Cross Fell, which the locals call Fiends' Fell. It is the Helm Wind and it shrieks like a banshee. The Gul say it is their gods speaking to them.'

*

The next day, Edgar the Atheling, the 74-year-old rightful heir to the throne of England, is still reluctant to give his account of his turbulent life. He asks William to walk with him to Ashgyll Force, so that he can talk to him beyond the earshot of others.

The deafening roar of the Force makes it hard to hear, and Edgar's words fight against nature's resounding presence.

'William, I am sure you are as sympathetic a man as you are learned. But if I were to tell you my story, it would be painful for me. Few men have been as blessed by birth as I have, but I doubt that many have had their blessings so cursed. When I first came to England as a boy, I spoke only broken English; I knew several of the Slavic languages of Europe and some local Magyar, but English was very foreign to me. My father died within days of setting foot on our ancestral soil, and I immediately became a target for the ambitions and greed of others. I lived in fear and, despite all that has happened to me, I am still haunted by my formative years. Even now, I often wake in the night, disturbed by some nightmare or other. That's when the Force comforts me, or the Helm Wind takes away the hot sweats. Do you live with fear, my learned scribe?'

'I live with my anxieties, like every man. Perhaps the telling of your story will bring you peace, as well as enlightenment to others.'

'I have already found a sort of peace here. I have learned to live with my past. And I think, when my life is weighed in the balance, the favourable will outweigh the unfavourable – at least, that is my hope. There is a thread which weaves its way through my story and makes some sense of it all.'

'Will you at least reveal that to me?'

'The thread connects four old men. I am one, and my good friend Robert, Duke of Normandy, now languishing in the King's keep at Cardiff, is the second.'

Edgar hesitates; he looks wistful, sad even.

'And the other two?' William prompts.

Edgar turns away and sighs before continuing, clearly in two minds about whether to trust William with his story.

'The third is Hereward of Bourne, a man whose heroic deeds are known to us all, and the fourth is the seer, the Old Man of the Wildwood and father of Hereward's remarkable wife Torfida, who set Hereward on the path that changed his life. We all lived into old age and, I hope, acquired some contentment and a little wisdom from what we had experienced. I know three of us did, and I only hope the same is true for Robert – I have had no contact with him for twenty years.'

William takes a deep breath. He is about to make the move that he hopes will convince Edgar to tell his story.

'I have been to see Robert, in Cardiff.'

'How . . .?'

'I have been asking the King for permission for several years. When I heard of your whereabouts, it became much more urgent, so I went to Winchester to plead my case and he relented. He's getting old himself and softening a bit.'

'How is Robert?'

'He's frail, but well. He is well taken care of – confined,

of course, but he can walk about the keep freely and his chamber is warm and comfortable.'

'Did he tell you his story?'

'No, he wasn't really strong enough for that and he said you would be a much better storyteller.'

'Did he, indeed? He had a habit of getting me to do the things he didn't like to do.'

'He gave me this parchment.'

William hands Edgar a small scroll, sealed with Robert's ducal ring. The Prince's thin, bony fingers carefully break the seal and he begins to read. At first he smiles, then his eyes fill with tears. The message is only brief and William has no idea what it says. But it has a profound effect on Edgar, who turns and walks closer to the Force.

After a while, he walks back towards William, pushing the scroll up into the sleeve of his shirt.

'He must be very frail; his writing is tentative, like the scrawl of a child.'

'I'm sorry. He was a little shaky when we met; he's a very old man.'

'He says I can trust you, that your chronicles are fair and accurate, but I knew that already. When I heard that you had arrived on these fells, I knew what you had come for. I have had time to think. The mighty Hereward once told me that the lives of men move in great circles and that at the end of a long journey there should be time for reflection. I have had plenty of time to reflect here in the Pennines. It's a place for penance, as in Purgatory. Perhaps I am purged; I will tell you my tale. As you say, it may do some good, and Robert seems content that I should let people know more of his life.'

*

33

Later that morning, Edgar settles by his fire to begin his account. William of Malmesbury reminds young Roger of the date. It is 31 October, All Hallows, the Feast of the Dead, in the year 1126.

Roger's responsibility will be to help William remember as much of the detail as possible. It is fortunate that he does not have to commit quill to vellum, as his hand still quivers from the horrors of the previous day and the menacing environment in which they find themselves, with the chilling cold of an approaching winter at over 1,000 feet in the Pennines, the thunder of Ashgyll Force and the screams of the Helm Wind off Fiends' Fell.

PART TWO
The Rightful Heir

4. Abernethy

The years following the Conquest were a living hell for me and the people of England. Its army, once so potent behind its legendary shield wall, never recovered from the gruesome battle of Stamford Bridge against Harald Hardrada's formidable Norwegians and the slaughter of Senlac Ridge, where the courageous King Harold and most of the English aristocracy were massacred by William, Duke of Normandy, and his merciless clan.

Some brave souls rose in rebellion but were quickly annihilated. One by one, village by village, burgh by burgh, the English acquiesced. The last great rising came in the North, in the earldoms of Edwin and Morcar. When Svein Estrithson, the King of Denmark, landed with his army, there was a glimmer of hope. But Estrithson was easily bought off by William – his treasury was full with the spoils of his prosperous new domain – and the English rebels, now just a handful of valiant men, were left to their fate.

I played a part in the rebellion, but was too young to lead it; I was no more than a boy and had lived a confined life under the watchful eye of old King Edward. As I was the true heir of the Cerdician line of England's Kings, the last thing he would have let me do was prepare to be a leader of men and learn how to wield a sword like any other in the realm.

I will always believe that it was King Edward who had

my father poisoned when we arrived in England from exile in Hungary in 1057. My father was also called Edward; he would have been fifty-one years old at the old King's death and the undisputed successor to the throne. None of the events we will speak of would have happened had my father not been poisoned. Ironically, the King placed the blame at the door of Harold Godwinson, the Earl of Wessex, the future King Harold, who had travelled to Budapest to bring us home.

But I digress. The real hero of those final days of England's resistance was the man who saved my life in Swaledale, Hereward of Bourne. He was a great warrior and almost reclaimed this land.

He had stood with Harold on Senlac Ridge and was badly wounded, but his companions got him away and he escaped to Aquitaine. Edith Swan-Neck, Harold's widow, persuaded him to return. In a long campaign in the North, he came close to killing the King by his own hand, but he had neither good fortune nor enough loyal supporters. William was a cunning, ruthless and formidable opponent and, in due course, prevailed.

I admired Hereward enormously, and wanted so much to be like him. When the campaign became too dangerous, he sent me with a small force high into the Pennines, into Upper Swaledale, a remote and harsh place, to see out the winter. But it proved disastrous – I wasn't strong enough, and the morale of my men disintegrated.

When William and his Normans began their massacres in the North, it looked as though we were trapped. My men had lost the will to fight. Then, when all seemed lost, Hereward and a small squadron of his redoubtable followers appeared from the top of the fells, as if from nowhere, their horses sinking to their chests in deep snow. It was a miracle – a moment I will never forget.

Hereward breathed new life into us, just by his presence and sense of purpose. I vowed then to find a way to follow his example.

He sent me to Malcolm Canmore, King of the Scots, for my protection and organized a last redoubt on the Isle of Ely. Hundreds flocked to his standard, including all the prominent men of England who still had the courage to resist. These included, to their ultimate credit, the last two English earls, Edwin of Mercia and Morcar of Northumbria, who had previously disgraced themselves by not joining Harold at Senlac Ridge and then by submitting to William at his court. A Brotherhood in honour of St Etheldreda was sworn and word was sent to all corners of the land proclaiming the right of the people to be ruled justly by common law.

It was the bravest act I have ever known. I should have been there, but Hereward wanted me to survive as the embodiment of England's past and to remain a symbol of resistance for the future. For many years I asked myself if I had given in too readily to Hereward's insistence. Did I take the easy way out? In my heart I know I did not, but, again, I grew stronger from the experience.

It took the King several months to break the besieged city. The end came in October 1071, almost five years to the day from Senlac Ridge. Few survived the Norman vengeance. Those who did were mutilated; most died from their wounds or, unable to care for themselves, starved to death. Morcar was the only one spared and left whole, but was imprisoned for the rest of his life.

Hereward's loyal companions – Martin Lightfoot, Einar of Northumbria and Alphonso of Granada – were also killed, but some of his family escaped to the home they had made in Aquitaine. However, the fate of his twin daughters, Gunnhild and Estrith, only became known to me many years later.

As for Hereward himself, that became an even greater mystery. It was rumoured he had been taken alive, but then flogged to death by William's men. Others believed he was killed by William's own hand in the Chapel of St Etheldreda and buried in secret at Crowland Abbey. A few even believed he escaped into the Bruneswald and lived a long life away from England. Some even believe that he is still alive now. Sadly, that is not possible, as he would be almost 100 years old, but he deserved a long and contented life for all he did in leading our fight against the Normans. The Siege of Ely may have ended when the rebels' resistance was broken, but he made sure our spirit never was.

My memory of him is still vivid. He was an extraordinary man, very tall, with great strength and courage. He carried a mighty double-headed battle-axe, the Great Axe of Göteborg, with which he slew countless victims. He also wore a mystical talisman given to him by his wife, the seer, Torfida. She too was said to be a remarkable woman, but I never met her. Sadly, she died in strange circumstances a few months after Senlac Ridge.

I hope that one day, despite what the Norman scribes may write, the heroism of Hereward and all those who fought for freedom and justice with him at Ely will be remembered for generations to come.

*

I spent the years after the fall of Ely at the court of Malcolm Canmore in Scotland with my sisters Margaret and Christina, feeling sorry for myself and for England. Canmore was good to me but he could be a brute. He had little learning of any kind – he was a thug, on a par with the harshest of his housecarls. He sent Christina to the nuns in England and demanded that my beloved sister Margaret marry him. She was not only beautiful and kind, she also carried the bloodline of England's kings stretching back to Alfred the Great, which was very appealing to Canmore. The poor woman had no choice if we were to have the safety of his kingdom.

She, on the other hand, was a saint. She produced a large brood of children for him, brought culture and sophistication to the court and worked tirelessly for the poor and the Church. She was everything he was not, and much loved for it. Happily, she was a good influence on him and he began to moderate his ways. Eventually, she became fond of him – perhaps she felt it was her duty to bring a woeful sinner back into God's fold.

In many ways, Malcolm and Margaret became my surrogate parents – he the powerful, domineering father, but one to be respected and admired, and she the kindly and confiding mother every boy should have.

King William loomed prominently in my life throughout the years I spent at the Scottish court. I loathed him for many reasons, not the least of which was that he wore the crown that rightly belonged to me. He was also a brute, not like Canmore – who was a simple soul with some redeeming features – but a brilliant, remorseless monster of a man. The time Margaret and I were held hostage by him after Senlac Ridge was a terrifying experience that I would never want to repeat. It was during this ordeal that I learned how to deal with my anger, how to deal with the Normans and how to survive.

As he had shown in his conquest of England, William lacked neither audacious ambition nor astonishing military aptitude. In 1072, he launched a brilliant attack on Scotland with both a large army and a huge fleet.

He marched more than 3,000 of his finest cavalry from Durham, crossed the Forth at Stirling and met with his fleet on the banks of the Tay. He had assembled 200 ships carrying 3,000 infantry and butescarls up the east coast. It was a mighty invasion force, not quite on the scale of the host that had crossed the Channel in 1066, but large enough to put the fear of God into Canmore.

While William sat and waited by the Tay, Canmore pondered his response. Not the most intelligent of men, he nevertheless had the cunning of a warrior and carefully weighed his options.

'I will go to him and negotiate. I have no choice. Edgar, you will come with me.'

His judicious decision was applauded by my dear sister.

'That is a wise choice, my husband. Let Edgar help you; he will give you good advice. Do what is best for Scotland and don't let your pride get in the way. I will pray for your safe return.'

I was overawed by the sight of William's army. He was camped around the old Pictish tower at the settlement of Abernethy, his tents in neat rows, his destriers tethered on ordered picket lines in the meadows. His massive fleet was in sight to the north, the ships lashed together in long rows by the banks of the Tay. This was the work of a leader of armies second to none. When he greeted Canmore he was at the head of his Matilda Conroi, the finest cavalry in Europe. He was a large, imposing man with a considerable girth and a deep, growling voice.

Canmore also looked impressive at the head of his hearthtroop. I was to his left, his son Duncan, a boy of twelve, to his right. He tried to remain calm as he addressed his doughty opponent.

'You are a long way from home, William of England. With so many men, I assume this is not a hunting party.'

'I will come to the point, Malcolm of the Scots. You attack my northern realm as far as Bamburgh and Durham in the east and Carlisle and Penrith in the west. This must cease forthwith.'

'The border between our kingdoms has never been agreed, so who are you to say whose realm it is? Besides, what my men may have done is nothing compared to the slaughter you meted out to the English, a people you now call your own.'

'What I do in my own domain is my business. You will stay out of it, south of a border we will agree here and now at the line of the Wall of Hadrian.'

'That is an insult. Cumbria has been part of Scotland for centuries.'

'Not any more. I will take your son as hostage to our agreement and I also require you to send Prince Edgar from your court. He may go to Europe, but I do not want him on this island fomenting trouble among my people.'

At that, I felt compelled to assert myself.

'My Lord Duke, they are my people too and I have a stronger claim to be their lord than you.'

'You offend me, Prince Edgar. I am your King; even the rebels at Ely acknowledged it.'

'But I do not!'

'Enough, Edgar.'

My brief spat with William had given Canmore time to think. Forthright though he was in his verbal sparring with William, he knew he had to concede.

'It is a hard bargain, but I agree to your terms; your army gives me no choice. I will not let them do here what they did in Northumbria. I will bow to you this day; but take your men back over the border where they belong. Duncan will join your court in England and Edgar will leave these shores directly.'

Canmore and William dismounted and entered the base of the tower. In circumstances that William had contrived with great symbolism and with Walchere, the new Bishop of Durham and Earl of Northumbria, presiding, the two Kings swore their agreement on the ancient Bible of Bede, brought especially for the occasion from Durham. Two monks had to hold the giant book so that Malcolm could place his hand on it. Then, to make the obedience complete, William laid his hand over Malcolm's and rested his baculus, the fabled Viking mace of his ancestors, on his forearm.

The deed was done. William had secured his northern border, and Canmore could be at peace in his Alban realm – for a while, at least.

My blood ran cold as I contemplated the circumstances. Malcolm and his Scottish warriors were a formidable force, but he stood there humbled by the overwhelming strength and ambition of William and the Normans. As for me, I remained the embodiment of the defeated English, a mere witness to yet another Norman conquest.

Even so, my determination to find my own destiny grew ever stronger.

On hearing the outcome upon our return to Dunfermline, the Queen was relieved that Malcolm had acted with such restraint, but greatly upset that part of the price was the loss of her son and brother.

Duncan took a small retinue and left within hours to reach William's army before it had gone too far. I left two days later to make my way to William's neighbours and enemies in Flanders and France. However, I would be back far earlier than I anticipated.

I travelled with only a dozen men and two stewards, and moved quickly through England's ravaged North.

It was a difficult journey for me. The Great North Road was a hive of activity with cartloads of provisions of all sorts going backwards and forwards. York and Durham and the burghs towards the southern part of Northumbria were alive with masons and carpenters about their work, but it was a different story away from the routes under the watchful eye of the Norman overlords and their garrisons.

Ragged little children would often appear at the side of the road, begging for food. Sometimes, half hidden by the trees, the remnants of abandoned villages could be seen. There was fear and loathing just beneath the surface. It was well disguised, but it was there – as was the deep-seated melancholy of a once proud people, now vanquished and forlorn.

When we got to Mercia, I left my men at Peterborough and, disguised as a monk, rode to Ely to find out more about what had happened there a year earlier.

What I found filled me with a heartfelt sorrow. The burgh of Ely, although small, was thriving. The causeway across the Fens, which King William had built to break Hereward's resistance, was thronged with merchants and farmers. There was a considerable garrison of Normans at work on a huge motte and bailey, their work almost complete. Although all trace of the bloody encounter of thirteen months ago – which had seen England's final capitulation to the Normans and the deaths of so many brave men – had gone, I shuddered at the thought of it.

Few would speak about the events of 1071, and those who did merely repeated the oft-told myths and rumours. The new abbot, a man called Theodwin, was not a Benedictine monk but a secular governor, placed there by the King to keep order and oversee the garrison and the building of the fortifications. I was told that the King also intended to tear down the abbey and St Etheldreda's Chapel to build an enormous cathedral, modelled on the ones in his homeland. The door of her chapel was still barred and had not been opened since the King ordered it to be sealed at the end of the siege. Many believed that it had become Hereward's tomb, his body still lying where it had been left after his execution at William's own hand.

Outside the abbey I did find a man who would speak to me. I did not recognize him – perhaps I should have done, as he was one of the few survivors of Ely and had campaigned with us in the North. But he was only a wretched shell of his former self.

His name was Wolnatius. He had been blinded after being captured at the collapse of the final redoubt and had barely survived the following winter. But when a new community of monks arrived, they took him in and cared for him. He was reluctant to speak to me until I gave him details, which only I could have known, about events in York during the rising and he was able to feel the Cerdician seal on my ring.

He had been close to Einar when he fell, had seen Martin brutally slain by the King and confirmed that Hereward had been taken alive – and flogged, he assumed, to death. Like many others, he thought his body had been buried by the Normans in a secret location to prevent it becoming a shrine to the English cause.

'Like King Harold?'

'Not exactly, my Lord Prince. Harold lies in an unmarked tomb in Waltham Abbey.'

'How did he get there?'

'Sire, it is said that Edith Swan-Neck returned to his makeshift grave on the beach near Senlac and took him to Waltham. The monks loyal to his memory keep his resting place a closely guarded secret. I am sure they will let you visit it.'

'I will indeed visit him there and pray to his memory.'

Brave Wolnatius had little more detail to add. He wished me well and promised to be at my coronation when it happened. In return, I guaranteed him a place in my honour guard on that propitious day. As I left, I gave him a little silver to help with his care. He grabbed my arm and buried his face in my sleeve, sobbing like a child.

So this is what had become of one of our bravest housecarls: reduced to poverty. I resolved there and then to do all I could to help restore the pride of men like Wolnatius.

My first act was to rejoin my men at Peterborough and make my pilgrimage to Waltham to pay my respects to Harold's remains.

I have never resented Harold's decision to claim the throne. He was the right choice for England's future security. With foes like Hardrada and William threatening our shores, my prospects as King would not have been promising. I would have been lucky to survive Stamford Bridge, let alone Senlac Ridge.

I knelt by Harold's unmarked crypt for a long time, thinking about the desperate and brave decisions he had made. Should he have waited for more men to arrive in London in those fateful days before the battle, before heading for the coast? Perhaps he did act too quickly, but he was fearless; that was his strength. He took a gamble, as daring men do, and although it was a close-run thing, he paid with his life.

I knew I could never be like Harold or Hereward, but I also knew that their example could be a guiding light for me, which, coupled with my own gift for thoughtful and considered decisions, might allow me to find a way to lead others and make my mark.

As I left, I placed my hand on the plain, cold slab of his sarcophagus and vowed that one day I would pay homage in the same way to England's other noble warrior, Hereward of Bourne.

The canons of Waltham, ever loyal to Harold's and England's memory, agreed that I could stay in Waltham for a while to plan my next move. I needed new allies; they were not difficult to find. William had many enemies, and my claim to the English throne made me a useful asset. I sent word to Flanders and to France and soon had a response.

Young King Philip of France had emerged from his weakened position as a boy-king to become a young ruler of great skill and tenacity and was keen to challenge William for control of Normandy. He offered me the formidable castle of Montreuil on the French coast, from where I could harass the Normans.

I took a ship from Maldon, but fortune once more deserted me. Not far off the coast of Essex, a ferocious easterly gale got up and pushed us relentlessly towards the sandbanks off Foulness. We ran aground and, within minutes, were in the water, losing most of my men and all of my silver.

I eventually made it back to Dunfermline, exhausted and thwarted once more. I was in my twenty-first year, but I felt like a boy again.

'You can't stay here,' was Canmore's blunt response when he received me. 'I will give you a chest of silver, but you can't stay in Scotland.'

Margaret pleaded my case.

'William has gone to Normandy and taken Duncan with him. He won't hear of Edgar's return for months.

Besides, when did you ever care about upsetting the King of England?'

'I need time to build my forces. This Norman bastard is building castles all over England, and he can put navies to sea and cavalry on the march in great numbers; what I saw on the Tay was a force a Roman emperor would have been proud of. I fear no man, but I can't let him take Scotland like he took England. As soon as he knows Edgar is here, he will be at my gates within the month.'

Margaret held me. She had tears in her eyes.

'What will you do?'

I was desperate but knew I had to leave. My next decision was the making of me. Had I stayed in the King's comfortable fortress at Dunfermline, I would have withered away, consumed by my own anger and regrets.

'I am going to submit to William.'

'No, Edgar! We tried that; you remember what it was like.'

'I know, but I'm older and wiser now. I have to find a life for myself. I will submit, gain his trust and bide my time. I will learn from the Normans. They are all-conquering; I have to understand why.'

Canmore looked at me curiously.

'That's a clever move. I am not done with William yet. Learn from him – and when the time is right, we will meet again to see what can be gained for both of us.'

'My Lord King, you have given me a refuge here. I will always be in your debt. Please take care of Margaret.'

The Queen rode with me all the way to the Forth, where one of Canmore's ships was made ready to take me to France. He had granted me a small retinue and a not inconsiderable purse. I would travel well.

Margaret understood me better than anybody. Like many women who live obscured by the larger shadows of their menfolk, she knew that beneath the aura of masculinity that men are required to show, they are often vulnerable and anxious. She knew my weaknesses and had helped me overcome them throughout my childhood.

She used our journey together to help me even more.

'You are not a mighty warlord like Malcolm, but you have great courage, a clever mind and excellent judgement. Have faith in yourself and trust your instincts.'

'What will I do without you, Margaret?'

'You will do well; I know it. You have great gifts and are decent and loyal. Those precious things are not given to many.'

Margaret's words were a source of great strength to me. I knew she was not just being kind; she was a good judge of character and too thoughtful to fill me with false hopes.

When we parted, I held her tightly as she sobbed at the renewed pain of losing both a brother and a son and begged me to keep an eye on young Duncan in the Normans' lair.

I wondered if I would ever see her again.

I left Scotland knowing I had to put the past behind me and abandon the fight to become the rightful King of England. That hope had been extinguished when Hereward and the Brotherhood accepted William as King in their struggle for liberty at Ely.

On that long voyage to Flanders, I steeled myself to the future and began to find a tenacity that had eluded me for so long.

5. Robert Shortboots

Robert Curthose had to live with the sobriquet 'Short-boots' all his life. The Normans like to attach monikers, either in mirth or ridicule, and, in truth, Robert was not very tall, so 'Shortboots' he became. Robert did not get on well with his father, or his father with him. They could not have been more different – Robert took after his diminutive and taciturn mother rather than his towering and domineering father.

He was King William's firstborn and, even as a young man, became de facto Duke of Normandy while his father was busy massacring the English in his new domain.

I had liked him when I was taken as hostage to Normandy after William took the throne. Our friendship blossomed and he soon became the salvation of my second submission to the King after I had decided to swallow my pride and let self-preservation rule my emotions. I faced the prospect with dread, but William was unusually gracious when I humbled myself before him at Caen.

He allowed me to keep a retinue and gave me enough land and titles to maintain my status as a royal prince. It was a far better deal than I could have hoped for, but one made by him not through generosity, but by way of expediency. I still represented a beacon of hope to any disgruntled Englishman and anyone else with a grudge against him – and there were many of those – so it was significantly in his interest to keep me close by and for me to declare my fealty to him.

He still seemed fit, but his hair was turning grey and his girth much expanded. As for his temper, it was much the same – simmering some of the time and frequently volcanic in his outbursts.

Robert held the title Count of Normandy and I was fortunate to travel with him throughout the domain he ruled in his father's absence. He was the perfect teacher of Norman ways. Although he was much calmer and more considerate than his father, he was forthright and disciplined; he expected obedience from his subjects and dealt firmly with miscreants. I learned quickly.

The months passed and I became more contented than I had ever been in my life. We hunted well and I ate and drank like a Norman lord – in large quantities, with only a modest regard for quality. Their appetite for women was similarly less than discerning, the priority being the frequency of the conquests rather than their worth.

But I did not complain too much. His father denied Robert the chance to take a wife, fearing that an alliance with another royal house would make his son too powerful, so I chose to stay single also; consequently, we could debauch ourselves as much as we liked.

William still styled himself as 'Duke' when in Normandy, and when he returned from England – which was usually two or three times a year – his relationship with Robert worsened. Only the intervention of Robert's mother, the formidable Matilda, kept the peace.

To Robert's great dismay, his father seemed to favour his thirdborn, William Rufus, especially after his second son, Richard, died in a hunting accident in 1074. His name was the clue to William's preference. Rufus 'the Red' was tall and fair – like his father and their Viking ancestors – whereas Robert took after his mother, whose stature was so meagre it became the subject of common jests.

Robert and I were both in our mid-twenties, Rufus nineteen. Understandably, he wanted to join us on our drinking and whoring excursions, but Robert would not hear of it and Rufus became more and more annoyed at the rejections. I tried to reason with Robert.

'He's your brother and good company, let him come.'

'No, I'll not have him running to my father or, more importantly, my mother with exaggerated stories of our adventures. He's a prick, that's all that needs to be said.'

Robert's increasing distance from his father threatened to explode into violence in 1077. It was also the year when a boy called Sweyn appeared at Robert's court in Rouen – a boy who later, as a man, would be as influential in my life as Hereward of Bourne. By coincidence, he was also a son of Bourne.

I had not met him before but I recognized the knight who brought him to court. They rode into Rouen's keep together, the knight carrying the colours of Toulouse. The boy, although far too young, was dressed as a sergeant-at-arms. I strode over to greet them.

'You must be Edwin of Glastonbury; you stood with Hereward during the revolt.'

'I am, my Lord Prince. It is good to see you again; a few years have passed.'

'Indeed. And who is the young man?'

'Let me introduce Sweyn of Bourne. Sweyn, it is your privilege to meet Prince Edgar, the rightful heir to the English throne.'

Sweyn looked confident, spoke clearly and bowed deferentially to Edgar.

'My Lord Prince, it is an honour to meet you at long last. Our paths almost crossed in England, but I was only a boy then and you would not have remembered me.'

I smiled to myself. Sweyn, so obviously still a boy, clearly thought of himself as a grown man. He was of average height and not particularly broad, but was lean and had a determined look about him. His clothes were plain but good quality, as were his weapons. He was dark-haired and tanned, and could well have passed for a man from Aquitaine rather than an Englishman.

'Stewards, take the horses of our noble guests. Edwin, Sweyn, come into the hall and rest. Count Robert is out hunting. He will be delighted to meet you later.'

I ushered them both to the fire, eager to hear their news.

'So, you are in training to be a knight?'

'I am trying, sire. But I am not of high birth, so I must train as a soldier first and then hope I can win the right to carry a knight's pennon.'

'You are not related to Hereward?'

'No, my Lord. My father was a humble villein, bonded to Hereward's father, Thegn Leofric. He was killed when Ogier the Breton and his thugs came to our village. I was the only one who got away. My mother hid me in the hayloft where I waited until nightfall, when I crept away.

Three girls survived as well; they were taken as playthings by Ogier and his men and defiled until Hereward came and saved us.'

'He had a habit of doing that. He saved my life too.'

'Sire, I try to be like him every day.'

'That is a very noble ambition. Edwin, I have so many questions for you about Ely ... But first, why are you here?'

'I am Sweyn's guardian, and his care and future matter to me more than anything. I had heard that you were at Count Robert's court, so now that Sweyn is old enough, I hope to be able to place myself at your service as a knight and begin Sweyn's training and education.'

'You are both welcome. The Count will be pleased to have two sturdy Englishmen in his retinue, especially ones who stood with Hereward of Bourne. But tell me how you got away from Ely.'

Sweyn, with a self-confident air beyond his years, answered in Edwin's stead.

'The King spared us in circumstances we still don't understand. We were all captured as we tried to escape. We know that Martin, Einar and Alphonso died in the siege and that Hereward was almost the last man standing when he was overpowered. He was bound and flogged to the point of death and then taken into the Chapel of St Etheldreda by the King, who summoned Hereward's daughters, Gunnhild and Estrith. What happened after that is a mystery. We never saw them again.'

'William must have had them killed.'

Edwin resumed the account.

'We assume so, but, as you can imagine, there are many stories, some more plausible than others.'

'They are not dead.' Sweyn spoke with firmness, verging on ferocity, a fire burning in his eyes.

'Sweyn, you are addressing a prince,' Edwin reminded him.

'I am sorry, sire, but I am sure they live. I will find Hereward and his daughters. Perhaps then I can repay the debt I owe them.'

'My Prince, of Sweyn's many passions that is his most ardent, closely followed by his loathing of Normans.'

'Well, both are not without reason, but you have brought him to the court of the Count of Normandy, who is, *pro tempore*, Duke of all Normans.'

'That, sire, will be part of his education. He will learn that there is good and bad in all men – and good and bad men in all places.'

Sweyn looked at Edwin sullenly, clearly not convinced.

'So, Edwin, where is your home?'

'We are from a place called St Cirq Lapopie on the Lot, close to Cahors, in the realm of Geoffrey, Count of Toulouse. Hereward's family settled there after Senlac Ridge. I first met them when King Harold's widow, Edith Swan-Neck, sent me there to ask Hereward to come back to England to lead the English revolt. Sadly, when the revolt failed and King William released us after the stand of the Brotherhood at Ely, we returned there. The King was surprisingly magnanimous and let us keep all our silver and possessions. Our land had been well managed while we were away, so we wanted for nothing – except of course those we loved, who we left behind in England. Since then, we've prospered.'

'I'm glad you found some comfort after all your trials in England.'

Sweyn spoke up again.

'When we returned from England, the first few months were awful. The girls had lost mothers and fathers and the women had lost their husbands. Alphonso's wife, Cristina, couldn't get over his death and soon returned to her home in Oviedo. After a while, the anguish subsided a little and life became more settled. Martin and Einar's daughters, Gwyneth and Wulfhild, married local men and both have children of their own now, as have Emma and Edgiva, two of the three girls from Bourne.

'Now that Edwin and I have left, there are just three members of the family still there: Martin's wife, Ingigerd, and Einar's wife, Maria – who run the estate between them – and Adela, the third girl from Bourne.'

'She has not found a husband?'

'No, sire. There are not many men worthy enough. She is full of passions and causes. She fights like a housecarl and doesn't suffer fools. It was a mighty struggle to persuade her to stay in the Lot. She begged Edwin to be allowed to come with us, but he forbade it.'

'Interesting; there must be something in the soil of Bourne. Three fearsome warriors from one village.' I decided that one day I would travel there to see what had become of Hereward's village. 'Let us eat, you must be famished. It doesn't look like the Count will be back tonight.'

After dinner, when Sweyn had gone to his bed, Edwin and I talked.

'I'm glad you are here. It is good to have an English knight among all these Normans.'

'What are they like?'

'Good soldiers, strong-willed; some can be ruthless, even vicious. But that's true of all people. I like your young protégé; he seems to be a fine young man.'

'He's a very special boy. But I am desperate for him to make the step to manhood and to become a warrior in the right place with the right people. He wouldn't be happy with Count Geoffrey in Toulouse. He's a good man, but his men are ill-disciplined and lazy.'

'Training with the English housecarls is no longer possible, but the Normans are the next best thing. And, most importantly, you're here. He wants to finish what Hereward started and put you on the throne of England.'

'The boy needs a lesson in harsh reality. Sometimes caution can be more effective than haste.'

'I know, but he's young. I am trying hard with him, but he is so determined. I hope you will help me.'

'Of course.' I reassured Edwin. 'But harsh reality may be here sooner than you think. Robert has gone hunting to calm down. He and the King have been at loggerheads for years, and it's getting worse. Robert now thinks his father favours his younger brother, William Rufus, who he dislikes intensely. . .'

I paused before voicing for the first time the conclusion to which I was inevitably drawn.

'I think Robert will rebel and bring us civil war.'

I was right. Events moved quickly in the next few weeks. William had already been annoyed by a revolt by several of his Breton earls in his kingdom in England. Even the Danes had stirred again. The old King, Svein Estrithson, who had abandoned Hereward to his fate at Ely, had died, but his son, Cnut, had sailed with a fleet of 200 warships and plundered York and the east coast. William's dukedom in Normandy was also under threat, surrounded by increasingly powerful and fractious neighbours. None of this did much good for William's temper, an ire that usually found a victim in Count Robert.

In the autumn of 1076, William had suffered his first military setback in twenty years when he was forced to retreat from an attack on Dol on Normandy's western frontier. He had been besieging two of his enemies, Geoffrey Granon, Count of Brittany, and Ralph de Gael, the rebel Earl of Norfolk, in their castle at Dol, the same fortress that he had taken so memorably with Harold Godwinson at his side in 1064.

This time, the defenders were more resolute and the castle held.

Significantly, it was young Philip, King of France, who came to the aid of the Bretons. William tried to stand his ground, but Philip's military prowess was becoming more and more pronounced, and he deployed his large army to good effect.

William, the mighty warrior, victor of many battles, had been complacent. He had left a significant part of his elite cavalry behind and had not roused his men quite as vigorously as usual. Philip, on the other hand, was young and dynamic and had something to prove.

When Philip's force appeared to the Normans' rear, instead of turning his entire force to meet the threat,

William split his corps of archers in two, leaving half to carry on the assault on the city, while the other half tried to halt the French attack. But Philip's cavalry were too numerous and disciplined to be blunted by a small force of archers. William delayed committing his cavalry, thinking that their role would be to cut into the French horsemen after his archers had inflicted heavy losses on them. As a consequence, his infantry was overrun and his cavalry had no time to form up properly for a counter-attack.

From the Norman perspective, it was a shambles. William had made the sort of mistake one might expect from a novice on the battlefield.

When I heard the details, I could not stop myself from thinking how different history would have been had William made the same errors of judgement at Senlac Ridge.

William lost many of his finest men and suffered a massive dent to his pride. It was a crucial turning point for him; his aura of invincibility had been shattered. Normandy suddenly looked vulnerable. Its powerful neighbours began to grow in confidence and act in concert: in the west, Geoffrey Granon, Count of Brittany; in the south-west, Fulk le Rechin, Count of Anjou; in the south-east, Philip, King of France; and in the east, Robert, Count of Flanders.

Not surprisingly, these developments were also followed with great interest by the Danish King, Cnut, sniffing the chance of more Danegeld, and by my former protector in Scotland, Malcolm Canmore.

However, the next challenge came not from William's circle of enemies or his neighbours, but from his own son.

*

It was February 1078 and winter still held its grip on Normandy. However, William, as usual, had little regard for the hardships of the season and had billeted us in L'Aigle on Normandy's southern border to begin the strengthening of the defences of the dukedom against the many threats it faced.

For the first time in a long while, William and his three sons were together. Young Henry, still only ten, was precocious and clever and relentlessly pestered his father to be allowed to travel with him. As usual, Rufus was loud and obnoxious and constantly aimed insults at Robert.

I had appointed Edwin to my hearthtroop as a knight and made young Sweyn my page. Robert liked them both, but on this expedition he was not particularly pleasant to anyone.

'I am going to see my father. Enough is enough; I am going to demand that he grants me the dukedom in my own right. He's got his own bloody kingdom in England, which should be enough for the old bastard!'

'Don't you think you should request rather than demand?'

'No, I don't! I'm tired of his bullying. I'm going to stand up to him. When I'm Duke, I'll send that arsehole Rufus off to England, and his insufferable little brother will go with him. And if I hear of anyone calling me "Short-boots", I'll have his tongue out at its root.'

No amount of persuasion could stop him, and he duly confronted the King. It did not go well. It was unwise and ill-timed, with several courtiers within earshot.

William looked at his son impassively at first, and answered calmly.

'I suppose you would want me to include Maine as well? It would be of no use to me in England.'

'Of course.'

William's volcanic temper began to growl.

'And how do you propose to deal with our Breton friends and the Angevins? And that French upstart, Philip?'

'Better than you did at Dol.'

That caused the volcano to erupt.

'Do you know how long it took me to quell our troublesome neighbours? How many campaigns I had to fight? And now you want me to give it all to you so that you can call it yours! You snivelling little bastard!'

'You're the bastard, remember. Your mother was the whore, Herleve. My mother is a queen, a descendant of Charlemagne and Alfred the Great!'

William flew at his diminutive son, grabbed him by the scruff of the neck and, while aiming several hefty kicks at his arse, threw him out of his tent.

Robert landed in a heap in full view of the King's men and his two brothers, who roared with laughter – a signal for everyone else to do the same.

When we heard the commotion, I and Robert's entire retinue rushed to his aid. A mass brawl ensued, with all three sons at the heart of it, until the King brought it to halt in that unmistakable voice of his.

'Enough! Enough! I will not have brawling in my camp! If there is another example, an insult spoken or even an aside uttered, I'll have the culprit flogged. And that includes the three of you.

'The sons of the King of England and Duke of

Normandy do not fight with their fists like peasants. Get out of my sight!'

Robert took his father at his word and we were many miles from L'Aigle by midday the next day. It took Robert until the middle of the afternoon to calm down and to tell me his intentions.

'We are going to seize Rouen, from where I will declare myself Duke.'

'Robert, that's insane, it's your father's ducal citadel.'

'Not any more.'

He kicked on with his horse.

'I have sent for Ives and Aubrey of Grandmesnil, Ralph of Mortemer and Hugh of Percy. In a couple of days we'll have five hundred men.'

It was obvious to me that Robert's temper had got the better of him and I rode hard to catch up with him. As soon as I had, I grabbed his horse's bridle and forced him to pull up.

'Robert, use your head, act calmly and with a clear plan; what you're doing now is driven by your injured pride. Think about the consequences!'

Robert did not respond. But the look on his face made me realize that my advice was falling on deaf ears, and so I let him go.

Despite my pleadings, four days later Robert had assembled his men at the gates of Rouen, but he faced a dilemma he had not envisaged. His father had heard of his plan and had sent word to Roger of Ivry, who was the guardian of the city in his absence, to call out the garrison and bar the city gates. Robert had sent Hugh Percy into the city to warn the Count that if he did not lift the bars, the city would be attacked.

Edwin and Sweyn were at my side as we watched Robert contemplate the impasse.

'This is not the most auspicious of military adventures, my Lord.'

'It is not, Edwin. Robert does tend to act before he thinks.'

'Sire, may I make a point?'

'Yes, of course, Sweyn.'

'Well, sire, doesn't anger sometimes serve a man well? When we're angry, we fight better, and Count Robert certainly has a lot to feel angry about.'

'You are right about anger in the heat of combat, but battles are won as a result of calm calculations by leaders before the contest commences. If tactics need to change during the encounter, again, it is the wise general who thinks of all the consequences of his actions, weighs them carefully, then makes his decision. Do you play chess?'

'I do not, sire.'

'Do you, Edwin?'

'I do, my Lord.'

'Then you must teach young Sweyn. There is no finer teacher of the military art than the game of chess.'

'Thank you, sire. I will learn this evening.'

Edgar laughed.

'I think it might take a little longer than that. I will get one of the Count's carpenters to make a set and board for you.'

Hugh Percy returned from the city with the news that I feared. Robert was forced to listen to the unwelcome outcome of his rash plans.

'My Lord, Roger of Ivry has refused your request, and not in the politest of terms.'

'Spit it out, man.'

'He said that I should tell "Shortboots" to run home to his father where he will get his arse kicked again . . . I'm sorry, sire.'

Robert seethed.

'Who does he think he is, to refuse me? I am his Lord, the Count of Normandy!'

I tried to reason with Robert.

'Remember, he will be more frightened of your father than of us. Let's withdraw and plan a more careful strategy. We will go to Philip of France.'

Robert eventually calmed down, realizing he had overplayed his hand and that his bluff had been called. As we withdrew, he rode next to me.

'You were right, Edgar; I've made a fool of myself. Next time I will use your wise counsel and think before I act.'

It was gratifying to know that Robert had begun to realize that my advice was worth listening to. I remembered Margaret's words when I left Scotland, and took comfort in thinking that she may have been right. In time, I might find a niche in the dangerous world of intrigue and war in which my birthright had placed me.

6. Battle of Gerberoi

Philip, King of the French, cut a dashing figure. A handsome man in his mid-twenties, he offered us not only excellent advice, but also men, weapons and silver. Like his nemesis, William of Normandy, Philip had inherited his domain as a child, his mother acting as co-regent with Count Baldwin of Flanders until his full accession as the fourth Capetian King of the Franks in 1066 at the age of fourteen.

He had inherited his good looks from his mother, Anna of Kiev, the daughter of Yaroslav, Prince of Kiev, and his wife Ingegerd, Princess of Sweden. It was his mother who, it was said, had given him his Greek name in honour of antiquity's Philip of Macedon. Her choice was inspired, as Philip had developed into a strong leader of his people and a superb general of his army.

We travelled to Philip's seat at Melun on the Seine, south-east of Paris. He greeted us with lavish ceremony and, after an extravagant feast in his great hall attended by his many allies and knights, offered us a plan of campaign.

'Gentlemen, we have an opportunity to bloody the nose of England's new King, the fat Duke William. Now that my friend Robert, Count of Normandy, has decided he has had enough of his father's behaviour, we have, if we act in unison, the strength to meet him on the battlefield and deal him a mortal blow. We will build our forces here, harass his lands on his borders and, when we have vexed him sufficiently, we will strike.'

I was impressed, and so were Edwin and Sweyn. Philip had great charm and a commanding presence.

Towards the end of the feast, Robert and I introduced Edwin and Sweyn to the King, who was thoughtful and appeared to be genuinely interested in them.

'Gentlemen, you have chosen well in giving your allegiance to Prince Edgar and Count Robert.'

Philip turned to me and embraced me like a long-lost friend. He then put his arm around Robert and began to tease him.

'Edgar, I see you have found one of the few Normans worthy of being called a noble friend.'

'Indeed, sire, he is rare creature – a Norman with a few redeeming features!'

The banter between the three of us continued as we drank copious amounts of the King's excellent wine. The three of us were in our prime, with the world at our feet. I felt invigorated. While it was true that Philip already had his kingdom and Robert was a de facto duke, whereas my kingdom was an impossible dream, I nevertheless let my mind wander. What a powerful triumvirate we would make: Robert in Rouen, Philip in Paris, I in Westminster! There would be no greater power in Europe – not even the Emperor in Cologne, nor the Pope in Rome. However, I soon put an end to such vainglorious fantasies, content that I was being treated as an equal at a King's high table.

Robert's cause and the colours of the gallant young King of France attracted many supporters, mostly men of a similar age whose fathers had made their fortunes and won their titles fighting to acquire England's riches with William. Their fathers were now ageing, wealthy and content. Their sons, on the other hand, were ambitious, virile and restless for their own adventures. Ives and Aubrey of Grandmesnil, Ralph of Mortemer and Hugh of Percy were soon joined by Robert of Bellême, son of Roger of Montgomery, Earl of Shrewsbury, Hugh of Châteauneuf-en-Thymerais, William of Breteuil, son of William Fitz Osbern and Roger, son of Richard Fitz Gilbert, Lord of Tonbridge and Clare.

They were a fearsome group, the rising cream of Normandy's warrior elite.

At the end of 1078, Philip and Robert decided that the time was right to launch an attack on William and word was sent to all their allies to gather their forces. By the end of January 1079, a force of over 300 knights and an army of 4,000 cavalry, infantry and archers entered Normandy. We camped at the formidable fortress of Gerberoi in the Oise, situated in the disputed border area between Normandy and France, a stronghold that had been fought over for years.

It did not take long for William to answer the challenge. A week later, he appeared on the opposite bank of the River Thérain, a tributary of the Oise, with an army at least the match of ours. After making camp, he asked for a parley on neutral ground, which was granted. He brought two of his Matilda Conroi, but not Rufus, who usually accompanied his father on his campaigns.

'So, my son and heir is now my adversary and recruiting help from my lifelong enemies.'

'You give me no choice, Father.'

'Of course you have a choice! You could serve your father and Normandy instead of dishonouring me and siding with my rivals.'

'You talk of honour, yet you insult me at every opportunity. And now you encourage my brothers to do the same.'

'I have entrusted you with Normandy and this is how you repay me.'

'I have served you well in Normandy. But what of England? I suppose you have promised it to that red-faced brother of mine.'

'What would you prefer me to do? Give it to you, so that you can give it back to Prince Edgar and the English?'

William then turned to me with a look of contempt.

'I suppose that's why you sniff at my son's backside, hoping that when he passes wind you will get a whiff of England?'

'Sire, your insult is not worthy of you. My friendship with Robert is not at odds with my loyalty to you as King of England. The issue here is between you and your son.'

'You speak like an ambassador. Do you fight like one? Or like a warrior?'

I chose to ignore the new insult – as I had said, this was a dispute between a father and his son.

William, seeing that his provocation was not working, turned back to Robert.

'I will make my decision about England in due course. For now, your rights and privileges in Normandy are forfeit and I would advise you to return to Melun with your lackeys.'

That insult prompted Philip to intervene. Despite his

relative youth and the towering presence of William, he was calm and self-assured.

'I will not trade insults with you, William of Normandy. We will settle this on the field of battle. Shall we say tomorrow morning, on the meadows by the Thérain?'

'Agreed.'

With a crushing look of scorn for his son, William turned and rode back to his camp. Philip turned to Robert and me.

'There is much to do. Tomorrow we face a formidable foe.'

The evening was spent in animated conversation about how to defeat William.

We all agreed that a solid wall of infantry and well-positioned archers and crossbowmen was vital. Philip had heard the accounts of Senlac Ridge and how the mighty English shield wall had been breached only by the crucial intervention of a withering hail of arrows. For years, he had been recruiting the best archers and bowmen he could find and was confident that they were the key to victory against William's renowned destriers.

After the Council of War, Edwin, Sweyn and I returned to our tents.

'Sire, may I be in your conroi tomorrow?'

I was not surprised by young Sweyn's plea. He was an impeccable trainee warrior. His sword arm was strong and he was excellent in the saddle, but his greatest gift was his speed of thought and reflexes. On the training ground, he could outwit far bigger opponents and use guile and feint to overcome them in combat.

'How is your chess coming along?'

'Good, my Lord. Edwin is a good teacher, although I am yet to beat him.'

'Edwin?'

'He learns quickly. He has learned to open solidly, but is still too rash in the middle game.'

'That's not good, Sweyn.'

'I know, sire, I am still impetuous. But in combat I am stronger and wiser by the day, and I am sixteen now – old enough to fight.'

'Are you sure?'

'Well, I am not sure of the month of my birth, but I am sure I am sixteen this year.'

'Yes, but it's only January.'

Edwin and I both smiled; Sweyn scowled.

'What do you think, Edwin?'

'Well, if he stays close to me, he should be fine.'

'Then it is agreed. But, Sweyn, think on this tonight. Tomorrow the contest will be for real, and death will be commonplace. You must stay away from the carnage unless the situation is dire and you are fighting for your life. Do you understand?'

'I do, sire. Thank you. I will not let you down.'

By late morning both armies were in position. The vibrant mingling of kings' standards, lords' gonfalons and knights' pennons along neat rows of men and horses made a vivid spectacle, the pageantry of which was only a masquerade for the mayhem that was about to ensue. Soon there would be but a single dominant colour – the red blood of the fallen.

As Robert of Normandy and Philip of France rode along the lines encouraging their men, I checked on my companions. Edwin was steadfast on his mount, while Sweyn gripped his reins tightly and looked around confidently.

It was then that a sentry appeared and addressed me.

'My Lord Prince, there is young knight at the picket lines. He asks to join your retinue.'

'Does he have a name?'

'He calls himself Alan of St Cirq Lapopie, my Lord. But he is clean-shaven and can't be much more than a boy.'

Unable to resist the sarcasm, I smiled at Sweyn before replying.

'Let him pass. I am always happy to have knights at my side, even if they haven't started shaving.'

He and Edwin looked mortified, but did not say anything.

When, moments later, the knight appeared, I knew why. The knight in question presented himself with the usual courtesy of removing his helmet, only to reveal the tender skin and the soft, flowing locks of a young woman.

'My Lord, forgive my deception, but I needed to get beyond your picket lines. I am Adela of Bourne.'

Edwin was furious.

'Adela, this is unforgivable! I forbade you to come. Yet you appear, and in the garb of a knight.'

I was intrigued but, even so, this was not the time and certainly not the place to start recruiting women to the Order of Knights.

'Madam, I am honoured that you would consider join-ing my retinue, but a more formal introduction, and in more relaxed circumstances than on the cusp of battle, might be more appropriate. May we discuss your request tomorrow? Sergeant, take our guest to the rear and see that no harm comes to her.'

The sergeant grabbed the bridle of Adela's horse. As he did so, Adela drew her seax and had it at his throat in an instant.

'Take your hand off my horse.'

Seeing the tenacity in her eyes, the sergeant relented.

'Prince Edgar, I will leave the field at your request, but only if Sweyn leaves with me. He is like my little brother; we have been very close since our village was massacred. I will not see him in battle unless I am at his side. We learned to fight together and I am as good as he is.'

'I have heard of the wretched circumstances of your encounter with Hereward and his companions.'

'Sire, I was only a baby when Hereward left our village but, many years later, he saved me after my innocence was so cruelly stolen. I watched with delight as he exacted a terrible revenge on the Normans who defiled me. Ever since Ely, I have lived with his memory. Now, like Sweyn, I model my life on his. I am not a man and will never equal the feats of Hereward of Bourne, but I can follow his example.'

Edwin's demeanour softened, and Sweyn looked proud of his sister-in-arms. I admired her resolve.

'Very well, the battle will soon be upon us. Stay close to Edwin. Sweyn is under strict instructions not to engage the enemy unless his life is threatened. The same applies to you, is that clear?'

'It is, my Prince. Thank you.'

'Edwin, unfurl my standard.'

As he did so, tears welled in the eyes of Sweyn and Adela. My standard was the Wyvern of Wessex, the emblem of Harold at Senlac Ridge and of all the Cerdician Kings of England as far back as Alfred the Great.

A most bizarre sight then appeared on the battlefield. The Pythoness of Gisors was a peculiar creature, quite frail and slight, but with a shock of silver-grey hair and startling bright-green eyes which never seemed to blink. She wore a plain black cassock tied at the waist by a woven leather cord and carried a large staff elaborately carved in the shape of a serpent, replete with inset rubies for eyes and a forked tongue painted blood red. Around her forehead was a richly chased band of silver, also in the form of a serpent, the head of which ran down between her eyes and finished just above the bridge of her very large nose. She had marched out beyond William's front line by at least twenty yards.

Philip looked bemused. It was left to Robert to provide an explanation.

'She is a local sorceress from the Bastide of Gisors. Among my father's many increasingly odd habits, resorting to seers and witches is one of the more harmless.'

'Is she going to win the battle for him?'

'Yes, she will cast a spell on us and damn us to Hell for eternity.'

The Pythoness began to chant and moan in what she called her 'diabolic' – her language of the dead – before scattering charms and potions on the ground.

'Do you think my archers could put an end to this farce?'

'Possibly . . . It's worth a try.'

Philip summoned his master bowman and a company of his finest archers and gave the order.

To loud cheering from William's army, the end of the witch's performance saw her raise her python staff and damn us all to Hell, after which she turned her back, pulled up her cassock to bare her buttocks and proceeded to urinate profusely on the meadow.

But Philip's archers had already taken deadly aim and their arrows were in flight, plummeting from the sky at a steep angle. From a distance of almost 200 yards, the arrows started to land all around her, striking deep into the ground. To the great amusement of our army, just as the old crone was concluding her stream of insults, one of the archers scored a bull's-eye, impaling her in the top of her rump with a four-ounce arrow. Another struck home moments later, hitting her between the shoulder blades. It was the last spell she would ever work.

William, in a rage at the skewering of his favourite enchantress, ordered his cavalry to advance at the gallop and the infamous thunder of his conroi of destriers began. I gulped and prepared myself for the onslaught, casting one last glance at my companions. The Norman cavalry was a chilling sight, their ordered lines broken only by the dashing knights who led the charge, a glistening brown phalanx of equine muscle topped by armoured killers wielding finely honed swords and spears and massive cudgels and maces.

Robert knew his father's tactics well and saw that on

this occasion he had chosen the brute force of a massed attack by his horsemen. This played into the hands of Philip and his bowmen. Relying on Robert – who had ridden in many of his father's charges – to judge the timing, Philip ordered his archers to launch their first onslaught on his ally's signal. Many more followed in rapid volleys.

The missiles came out of the sun like hailstones, landing in lethal rhythmic waves; most hit the soft earth, penetrating to half their length, but tens of dozens hit human or horse flesh with devastating consequences. The tightly packed conroi was reduced to a mass of stricken bodies as horses and men hit the ground and careened into one another. The din was terrifying as men screamed and horses screeched in agony.

William had underestimated the power of Philip's aerial assault, but instead of ordering a withdrawal to count his losses, he let his anger get the better of him. With himself at its vanguard, he called up his elite Matilda Conroi, committed his reserves of cavalry, ordered his infantry to attack in support and signalled his own archers to begin their onslaught. His entire force hurtled headlong into the fray.

For once, he had acted rashly and had seriously miscalculated.

Robert and I smiled at Philip. The French arrowsmiths and fletchers were busily unloading cartloads of arrows to replenish the spent quivers of the bowmen and archers, in order to continue the relentless barrage against the Normans. Philip offered Robert the chance to lead the allies' charge, which he accepted with relish.

So, with Robert's flamboyant battle cry ringing in our

ears, we were off at a gallop. I stayed close to Robert, with Edwin close behind me. To our rear, only seconds later, Sweyn and Adela looked at one another and barely hesitated before donning their helmets in anticipation and joining the attack.

Our force was much more colourful than the Normans'. Philip had attracted knights from many parts of France, Flanders, Anjou, Brittany and beyond. In the bright sun of a clear winter's morning, their standards were a rich medley of colours, their shields an array of fanciful designs. It was a stirring sight, and exhilarating to ride in the midst of it.

William's archers were much less effective than Philip's and by the time the two vanguards of cavalry met, our force outnumbered the Normans three to one. We scythed through the Matilda Conroi with ease, scattering men across the battlefield. Many were caught by the French infantry, pulled from their mounts and cut to pieces.

For my part, my only encounter with bloodshed was brief but fortuitous. Edwin and I and several of Robert's knights were in pursuit of a group of William's cavalry when they suddenly turned to make a stand. My pace took me into the midst of them, slightly ahead of the others, and for a few moments I was heavily outnumbered. Blows were aimed at me from left and right and my sword and shield had to parry several assaults. Thankfully, Edwin and the others soon joined the fray, easing the pressure. However, just at the moment when I began to think the worst was over, a Norman lance whistled past my ear and struck one of Robert's knights behind me full in the face.

Vinbald, a young man from Évreux much admired by

his peers, was killed instantly. Hurled with venom from only a few feet away, the lance was meant for me, but a slight movement of my head had been sufficient to remove me from its deadly trajectory. Even so, I felt it cut through the air next to my cheek before it smashed into Vinbald's skull, entering through his eye socket. The impact was such that, when the missile exploded from the back of his head, it took his helmet with it. It was one of the worst things I ever saw on a battlefield.

The horror of Vinbald's demise filled us with rage and we waded into William's cavalry in a frenzy. For the first time in battle, the dread of injury or death left me and I went about the business of war like a savage beast.

William, a small group of his knights and his personal conroi tried to form a phalanx to force a way through our onslaught, but they were too few to make an impact.

His elite horsemen had never been punished like this before. As he surveyed the field, all he could see was his army in disarray. Finally, he issued the order to retreat.

Robert heard the horn sound the withdrawal and saw his father pull his war horse round. His blood was up and he meant to rub yet more salt into his father's already painful wounds. He signalled to us with his sword and we were off in pursuit.

When William saw that it was his own son giving chase, he turned to face him, but few of his knights and only a handful of his conroi were able to halt their stampede and turn with him. He was soon engulfed by our cavalry and fighting for his life. Robert managed to grab the reins of his father's horse and called on his men to sheathe their swords.

It was only then that I saw that two of the knights in the midst of it and at the forefront of the duel with William were Sweyn and Adela, still with their blades drawn.

'Your Lord has ordered you to sheathe your weapons!'

Edwin could not have been firmer. They both – reluctantly – did as they were bidden.

William had been wounded. A spear or sword had cut through the mail on his right arm, which was soaked in blood, and the gauntlet on his left hand had been split open, revealing a deep gash. His check was gouged from below his eye to his jaw by the slash of a blade. He seemed confused and hardly able to speak.

Robert spoke to the few remaining knights who had stayed with his father.

'Take him back to Rouen. When he is coherent, tell him to go back to England and leave Normandy to me. He will not be welcome on this side of the Sleeve until he installs me as Duke of this realm.'

William started to mutter something, but, wisely, his men drew him away at a canter. I watched as he was led away, noticing him swaying unsteadily in his saddle. I felt sorry for him – the once all-conquering warlord – now humbled in battle by his own son.

There were wild celebrations that night in the allied camp. Philip and Robert addressed their army to great cheers and raucous applause.

When the revelries were in full swing, Edwin and I took Sweyn and Adela to one side. I let Edwin give the reprimand.

'You were given a clear order.'

Adela answered first.

'Yes, we were.'

'You disobeyed that order.'

Sweyn was next.

'No, we did not. Our orders were to stay close to you and not to fight unless our lives were in danger. We did stay close to you and we were in mortal danger. The King came within a yard of us, swinging the baculus wildly. I was only defending myself.'

I took over the interrogation.

'Does that mean that you actually engaged the King?'

'Yes, my Lord. I was the one who slashed his face; his helmet saved his life. If I had been closer, I would have killed him.'

'And I was the one who smashed his gauntlet. I too would have killed him if I had been given the chance. We both have a debt to collect.'

Edwin looked at me, astonished and exasperated, but without an immediate answer to their bravado. I could not decide whether to embrace them for their daring or admonish them for their defiance. I thought the latter the wiser option – at least, for the time being.

'This conversation must remain with the four of us. If anyone discovers that you were responsible, at least in part, for the King's wounds – and bear in mind, we don't know what the consequences of them will be – you will be in mortal danger. Lauded as avenging warriors by some, derided as committing regicide by others; either way, you will be marked for life. Apart from that, I find it hard to believe that you just happened to stumble into the

King's path. Everything you have said leads me to believe that you sought him out and thus flagrantly ignored Edwin's direct order. Sweyn, you are rusticated for a period of three months. You must return to your home in the Lot and think about the value of discipline and the importance of obedience. If you are to become a knight, you must embrace these values.

'Adela, you are to go with him and you may accompany him on his return. You too should think of these things. If you want to fight in the company of knights, you must learn to act like one.'

Sweyn was furious, his eyes burning with rage.

'Sire, this is not just, we did nothing wrong.'

'Your further disobedience serves only to discredit you. I have spoken, now go! We will talk again when you return. I do not want to see you again until Easter has passed.'

With that, they relented and strode away. Even though Sweyn had his back to me, I could almost feel his rage.

'I hope I have done the right thing. I have to admire them both; although the circumstances were fortuitous, they came closer to killing the King than anyone ever has. It almost defies belief.'

Edwin was shaking his head in bewilderment.

'My Lord, I can't quite believe it. They continue to astonish me; he's a slip of a boy, she's no more than a hundredweight wet through, but they have a strength about them like fine-tempered blades. I suppose they were forged in the same furnace – in the horror that was Bourne.'

'I am impressed. They remind me so much of Hereward.'

'You are right to send them away; they will come back

stronger for it. I'm sorry Adela suddenly imposed on you, but I did warn you she was obstinate.'

'Don't apologize, Edwin. She is remarkable; her inner resolve is so striking. Not a word of this. They are too young to be lionized or to be the quarry for those seeking revenge for a stricken king. Let's hope his wounds are not severe.'

My personal experience on the battlefield and the deeds of Sweyn and Adela left me with much to think about. Up until then, my motives in contemplating a fight, or in the heat of battle, had always been focused on myself. Either I, as an Atheling Prince, had been the cause of the conflict, or else I stood to gain significantly from the outcome. But this time, I was peripheral to the cause.

Vinbald's sudden, horrendous death and my response to it made me realize why people fight with such courage – even though they may not benefit directly from victory, or suffer overmuch from defeat. Sweyn and Adela had shown the same resolve in their passion to enter the fray and to influence the outcome of the battle.

In essence, I had learned how to fight.

7. Brothers-in-Arms

King William's injuries at Gerberoi were not severe enough to immobilize a young warrior for long, but at the age of forty-four his recuperation took some time. This did not improve his humour and only added to the acceleration of his corpulence. The damage to his morale was also significant – enough to suggest that he might never fully recover from it.

In the summer of 1079, Robert's bravado in challenging his father reaped a bountiful harvest. The King's magnates, both in England and Normandy, gathered in Rouen, steeled themselves to the task and confronted William. They were led by men whose own sons had joined the cause of William's prodigal son.

Their words hardly needed saying: Normandy and England's neighbours were now too strong, Malcolm of Scotland too opportunistic, the Danes too avaricious, for William's large and difficult-to-defend domain. Therefore, it was imperative that he treat with his firstborn, offer concessions to him and make peace in his realm.

They were not easy words to say, nor were they palatable for William to listen to, but after the customary bellowing and blustering, hear them he did. So, in the middle of August 1079, we accompanied Robert and his followers after he was invited to Rouen to negotiate with his father.

I had sent intelligence to King Malcolm in Dunfermline

throughout the internecine squabbles in Normandy. He had been poised to act since the spring and now his timing was perfect. Two weeks before the negotiations, he launched a major offensive, ravaging a huge area from the Tweed to the Tees and filling his barns, granaries and treasury with plunder. It was a major card for Robert to play in the haggling to come.

Sweyn and Adela had returned to us by then, much chastened by the experience of being stalled in pursuing their ambitions. I agreed that they could accompany us to Rouen, in part because I wanted to see how they would react when they were again close to the King. We did not discuss their return to their home in the Lot but, for some reason, I sensed that they had not gone there, but had journeyed elsewhere. There was a diffidence about them which I suspected disguised a secret; one day I would come to know what it was.

The confabulation with the King was tense. He was accompanied by Queen Matilda, Roger of Montgomery, Hugh of Grandmesnil and the ageing Roger of Beaumont. Besides me, Robert chose Robert of Bellême and Ives and Aubrey of Grandmesnil, all sons of the men they were facing.

As I watched the polite formalities and courtesies, I felt uncomfortable – an outsider privy to what was, in truth, a family feud which just happened to be among the most powerful men in northern Europe. I was also ill at ease in being in the confidence of one party to the quarrel. Even these Normans, who had become my friends, were the very same people who had stolen my birthright and were oppressing my kinsmen. I also had the same anxieties that everyone else must feel. The fate of kingdoms often hinges on the outcome of battles, but this time the future of England and Normandy rested on the settlement of a family quarrel. But this was no ordinary family, this was the brood of an extraordinary warlord.

I was deep in those thoughts when the King, who was on his best behaviour, made the same observation that had occurred to me.

'Why do we have an English prince in our midst, a man who repeatedly bows to me and then chooses to be my enemy?'

'Father, he is my ally, wise counsel and good friend. He is no enemy of Normandy.'

On any other occasion that would have sent William into a tirade, but the circumstances made him relent and, with a sneer aimed at me and a dismissive grunt, he signalled for the parley to begin.

It did not take long to reach an agreement. Two crucial factors were in play. William's humiliation at Gerberoi had put Robert in a powerful position, especially because of the support he could now draw on, both inside Normandy and among its enemies. This meant that, if William were to placate his son, he would also placate his enemies, especially Philip of France. Secondly, Robert had saved his father's life on the battlefield. This meant that not only was the King in his personal debt, but he also had an obligation in the eyes of the entire Norman aristocracy to reward his son for his magnanimity in victory.

'My son, let our differences stay in the past. Your prowess in the field at Gerberoi and your exemplary behaviour towards me have taught me to understand that my regard for you fell far short of what it should have been and that my deeds and words, and those of your brothers, were ill-judged and hurtful. All that will now be put right and the wrongs of the past will not happen again.'

They were astonishing words, such that I had to pinch myself to be sure I was hearing them, uttered by the same man who in the past had conceded nothing to any man, under any circumstances.

'Thank you, Father, I am content that you now feel you can give me the respect that I have deserved for a very long time.'

Robert was visibly moved by his father's contrition. Although he was short-tempered, impetuous and some-times indolent, Robert was good company and generous and had become a close friend. I was delighted that the burden of half a lifetime of disrespect and bullying by his father appeared to have been lifted from his shoulders.

The King solemnly granted to Robert his succession to the Dukedom of Normandy and made recompense for all his son's costs during the rebellion, which were substantial. Tactfully, Robert did not raise the subject of the English throne, or the inheritance of his brothers; those quarrel-some subjects would have be resolved, or otherwise, in due course. The Queen sat and beamed, there were com-radely hugs all round, and food and drink began to appear for a celebratory feast.

During the merriment, the King delivered a shock. Although William was not as imperious as he had been, he was still capable of flashes of highly astute manoeuvring. It was not a trap for Robert – indeed, for him, it was a gen-erous gesture – but, for me, it was certainly a move that would test my diplomacy and force me to examine my loyalties. The King delivered his surprise with a hint of mischief in his eyes.

'Robert, I am concerned about our northern borders. As you know, Malcolm of Scotland has flagrantly ridden roughshod over the pact we made at Abernethy. I would like you to lead our army on a campaign to remind him of his manners.'

Robert was beside himself. Not only was it a tangible affirmation of his reconciliation with his father, but it was also a major blow to Rufus, who would read into the mission the suggestion that Robert may well inherit England as well as Normandy.

William delivered his devious ploy with a smile and with cunningly chosen words.

'Prince Edgar, perhaps you would accompany Robert? You know the Scots well; you can be of great service to us in helping to put them in their place.'

Robert looked concerned for me. I just about mustered a smile in response.

'My Lord King, I would be honoured to accompany Count Robert. Thank you for entrusting me with the task.'

The King's request made me wonder whether my friendship with Robert, while I continued to support the cause of my brother-in-law in Scotland, had made me a hypocrite. Here I was, the trusted friend of the Normans – at least, of Robert and his followers – while at the same time sharing my allegiance with King Malcolm and the Scots. While peace reigned the charade seemed inconsequential, but it was always Malcolm's intention to take advantage of any Norman weakness. Not only had I been complicit in that, I had also aided and abetted Malcolm's exploitation of the situation, the result of which was great mayhem and carnage on the English–Scottish borders.

I needed to resolve the predicament. My thoughts turned to Harold and Hereward, and the inspiration I had felt while at Harold's tomb at Waltham Abbey. I knew what they would have done: acted courageously and truthfully.

And thus, I knew what I had to do.

We reported the outcome of the negotiations to King Philip at Melun. He was delighted that he had ensured one of two outcomes: either England and Normandy would be separated and weakened upon William's death, or his friend Robert would rule both realms, thus bringing peace and harmony to all concerned.

We then returned to Rouen to prepare for our expedition to Scotland. There I decided to confide in Edwin, explain my dilemma and seek his confirmation that my way of resolving it was wise.

'If we are to support Count Robert's expedition to challenge King Malcolm, it is likely there will be a fight, where we oppose Malcolm, but I have been in contact with him ever since I left Dunfermline and have frequently sent him intelligence to his advantage. But now, there is a direct conflict of loyalties. I cannot support both sides in a war.'

'I agree, my Prince, so you must declare yourself to both sides as neutral. I'm sure Count Robert will understand and will respect your candour. Perhaps in that way you can prevent bloodshed.'

'That is wise counsel; I appreciate it. Will you travel with me on those terms? It means you will no longer be in the

Count's service, but serving me directly. As you know, my retinue is but a few men and I have limited funds – especially as I am likely to lose both my current benefactors.'

'Sire, I could not think of any other place I would rather be than at your side.'

'Thank you. We are only two – a small band of English exiles – but perhaps we will grow in number.'

'My Prince, have you given up all hope of claiming the throne?'

'Yes, that ambition is a millstone around my neck. If I am to find my path in life, I need to cast that dream into the midden where it belongs.'

'Sire, if this is the beginnings of a band of brothers-in-arms, may I suggest two more recruits?'

'Of course. But I am ahead of you. I had already thought that two Englishmen were hardly a formidable posse; Sweyn and Adela would be fine additions to our crew. And I'm sure Adela would be happy to be called our "brother".'

Edwin and I were eager to tell Sweyn and Adela of our intentions, and we were gratified to see that their elation was almost boundless.

For the first time, the near constant expression of sullen anger on Sweyn's face lifted, while Adela's feminine emotions nearly got the better of her. At one point, I thought she was going to kiss me! But her sturdy resolve regained control and she kept command of herself.

I pointed out to her that there could be few concessions to her womanhood while on campaign. Her answer, as always, was forthright.

'My Lord, with Emma and Edgiva, I was the plaything of nine Norman thugs for nearly a week. Nothing that could happen to me, now or in the future, would come close to the horrors and indignities of that.'

Sweyn put his arm around her.

'Nothing like that will ever happen to you again. I will make sure of it.'

'We both will,' she said resolutely.

Edwin was smiling broadly at the pair of them.

'Does this remind you of anything?'

'Of course,' said Sweyn in an almost blasé way, 'the beginnings of Hereward's family.'

I often think back to the moment Edwin and I began our band of followers – brothers-in-arms, as he liked to call us. I was in my twenty-ninth year, Edwin was thirty-one, Adela twenty-six and Sweyn about sixteen – or so he claimed. Our pedigrees were so different: Edwin was a second cousin of King Harold of Wessex and England and carried the same Cerdician royal blood as I did, while Adela and Sweyn were the children of peasants. But I had little doubt, even then, that circumstances had made them of sterner stuff than Edwin or myself.

We were hardly an intimidating group, but we had something in common that would lend us great strength: the legacy of Hereward of Bourne. As I steeled myself for my difficult conversation with Robert, I wondered, as I did almost every day, where England's great hero might lie and what he would think of us now, trying to cast ourselves in his image.

Robert was, as usual, generous when I explained my dilemma. I asked him if he would like me to withdraw from the expedition.

'I will not hear of it. In the affairs of kings and princes, loyalty often changes like the wind. One day, I am confronting my father on the battlefield, the next day I am reconciled with him and leading his army into battle. But our friendship is one between men and goes deeper than treaties and alliances. Let us keep it that way.'

I then suggested to Robert the role I could play in Scotland.

'King Malcolm is an opportunist, like all leaders of men. When we cross Scotland's border, I will go on ahead to Malcolm's court and talk to him, tell him of our friendship and see if we can reason with him without bloodshed.'

Robert happily agreed to my plan.

'You have never deceived me and, like the man you are, have chosen not to hide your relationship with Malcolm. Let's turn it to our advantage and make our journey to Scotland a successful one.'

With a substantial force drawn from Normandy, we set sail for England in late summer 1080. More men would be gathered in England from William's Norman landlords and his permanent garrisons. Robert was hugely excited about the journey; not only was he to lead his father's army in a major campaign, but it was his first visit to England, a realm he had heard so much about. He was like a child with a new toy from the moment we made landfall at Dover, gawping at every landmark and building we passed and greeting everyone we met enthusiastically. The Normans were effusive towards him and even the English – or, at least, most of them – were polite and friendly.

We spent more time than was scheduled in London, a place that particularly fascinated Robert. Its buildings were not as grand as those in Normandy's cities, but it was changing rapidly and the amount of building work being done was astonishing. He was particularly taken by old King Edward's beautiful cathedral at Westminster, completed just before his death. It was modelled on the great cathedrals of Normandy and France and reminded him of home.

But it was what was being built on the eastern side of London that made us all gaze in wonder. Close to the edge of the Thames and bound on two sides by the old Roman city walls, William was building a huge tower, the scale of which I had never seen before.

Robert had heard his father talk about it and showed it to us with a sense of self-satisfaction which said, 'See what miracles we Normans can work!'

It was almost complete; its walls, dazzling white limestone, were forty paces long and it was almost as tall. It could be seen from every part of the burgh and for miles around, a reminder – visible at every turn and each minute of the day – of who ruled this land, and a statement, etched permanently into the skyline, which said that they intended to do so for a very long time. If I had not realized it before, the sight of this mighty fortress was confirmation that abandoning any hope of regaining my kingdom was a wise judgement.

Inside the great tower was an elegant chapel which had been completed and consecrated to St John the Evangelist only a few weeks earlier. We stayed for a while and prayed for our safe return from Scotland.

With the great oak door closed and the din of the masons' mallets and chisels all but stifled, it was a place of immense charm and serenity. The chapel's sturdy columns, plain Roman arches and solid, unadorned stonework spoke volumes about its builders: powerful, determined and austere, this was indeed a Norman place of worship. Our footsteps echoed and we hushed our voices to a whisper, making the place resonate with its symbolic power.

I watched Edwin, Adela and Sweyn, English kinsmen and now brothers-in-arms, to see if they too admired the handiwork of their Norman lords. If they did, they did not show it. Edwin was too chivalrous to disclose any disdain, Adela, as always, was impassive, while Sweyn looked stern, as a young knight should.

There we were, four progeny of England, in the company of Normandy's military elite, admiring their icon of the oppression of our homeland. It was a perplexing experience.

Sweyn spoke to me as we left the great tower.

'Sire, they do things on a massive scale. No army, no matter how big, could breach these walls.'

'Never underestimate them, Sweyn. You don't have to like them, but you must respect them and learn from them.'

'Should we not also fear them, my Lord Prince?'

'Yes, we should fear them; they are capable of inflicting terrible retribution on those who cross them.'

'I can't see how we can ever loosen their grip on England.'

'Neither can I. They are here to stay, and we have to come to terms with that.'

Adela had been listening and reacted angrily. 'I will never accept that.'

I tried to mollify her forceful stance. 'One day you will.

Eventually, the whole of these islands will belong to them. There is no one to stop them.'

'That's not true. I, for one, will never give up!'

'Adela, it's now more than ten years since Senlac Ridge; there are tens of thousands of Normans here. Look at this fortress, this beautiful chapel. We can't make the sand in an hourglass fall upwards.'

'But what will become of us, if we don't fight?'

'England will evolve. It is already changing, and what was fought for at Ely is vital. Everyone deserves to be treated according to the law and with respect; that is something I hope the four of us can strive for.'

'But the rule of law, and respect for all people, must be just as difficult to achieve as freeing England from the Normans.'

'Perhaps . . . but, like those who died at Ely, we can each find our own destiny in fighting for a cause – even if the cause seems impossible to achieve. Because nothing is truly impossible.'

'Do you really believe that?'

'Yes, I do. Hereward taught me that when I watched him lead a few hundred men against William and the entire Norman army.'

8. Atrocity at Gateshead

As we travelled north our welcome was less enthusiastic, but still courteous. Beyond Peterborough, the population was far more Anglo-Dane than Saxon and their loyalty to England had always been meagre, so it was hardly surprising that they should be lukewarm in their greeting to the Normans.

In the north and west, the Norman marcher barons ruled largely hostile territory from the safety of their redoubtable donjons, many of which were having their original timber structures replaced by massive stone keeps, deep ditches and high curtain walls. There was still unease in those parts of the country; the people looked cowed, their Norman lords apprehensive.

Almost no one recognized me, which was a relief. I had been a clean-shaven boy when I left England, now I sported cropped whiskers, fashionable in Europe, rather than the full beard of Britain and Scandinavia, and wore the garb of a Norman lord; to all intents and purposes, I appeared to be one of them.

For Adela and Sweyn, the journey through Northumbria was a trying time. Although they had witnessed the brutality at the end of the Siege of Ely, the enormous scale of the horrors of the Harrying of the North was almost too much to comprehend. Each devastated village, with its hideous corpses and decaying fragments of buildings, was a glaring reminder of the massacre at Bourne and what they had suffered there. I watched them carefully, fearing that at any moment they might leap on to the nearest of our Norman comrades and slit his throat!

We reached York in time for the celebration of a very singular day for the burgh. Although the north-west was still a wasteland, a few people were returning to the major eastern burghs of the past, such as York and Durham, where a modicum of normality was beginning to return.

Not only were the Normans building mighty fortresses in praise of their military prowess, they were also erecting great cathedrals in homage to God. Thomas of Bayeux, who had been appointed Archbishop of York by the King, had taken ten years to gather the resources to begin a new cathedral to replace the derelict Saxon minster. When he heard of our journey to the North, he decided that it was a perfect opportunity for Robert to lay the foundation stone. So, amidst great panoply, yet another Norman monument began on the site of a place of worship that was centuries old.

Thomas of Bayeux was that other type of Norman – not the marauding warlord intent on building a military empire, but the builder of cultural empires, a man devoted to creating places of learning and for the worship of God. He had a kindly demeanour, but still had the gleam of the zealot in his eyes.

He greeted Robert like a prodigal son, overjoyed that such a prominent Norman would anoint his new project. A man of at least forty years of age, Thomas would of course never see his homage to God completed, but it mattered little to him; it would be his legacy to future generations and his gift to God. Those were the only things that were important. This was the power of the Normans – their desire to create a lasting legacy based on their immense martial prowess and their unshakeable faith in themselves and in God.

As we watched the masons and churchwrights busy themselves in preparation for laying the foundation stone, I tried to explain to Adela and Sweyn why I respected our Norman conquerors.

'Look at them – like ants, relentless. It's little wonder that Normans are sought after everywhere as soldiers and builders.'

Adela seized on my analogy.

'More like pigs, to my mind – and it is our trough they're feeding from. This church will be built with the sweat of thousands of English peasants, and thousands more will be made to pay unfair tithes to support it.'

'I concede that it will not be built without sacrifice, but I wager that when the common people of Northumbria see their church rise to the heavens, they will be proud of it and claim it as their own.'

Sweyn added his own voice to Adela's argument.

'But they won't have a choice.'

'I agree, and that is to be regretted. But one day people will have choices – even the lowliest villein. I am committed to that.'

'Indeed, sire, we know you are. That is why Adela and I have sworn our allegiance to you and Edwin.'

'I am delighted that you have. This is only the beginning of a long road together; let us hope our path is not too arduous and that at the end of it we will feel that the journey has been worth it.'

When it came to the time for the ceremony, Thomas of Bayeux blessed the huge cornerstone as it hung over its position in the south-east corner of what would be the nave of the new church. The remains of the old Saxon minster had been cleared away and a deep trench for the footings of the new nave had been dug. The trench seemed to go on for ever, suggesting a building of huge proportions. The cornerstone was a cube, half the height and width of a man, and had to be lowered into position by block and tackle and a team of oxen. Before it was set down, Robert placed a pouch of silver and a small crucifix in the trench beneath the stone. When it was in place, the masons backfilled the trench with rubble and the first of the thousands of pieces of finely dressed limestone that would be fashioned into the new church was laid.

Robert turned to us and smiled.

'The silver is from my own mint in Rouen; the coins have my head on them. When they were clearing the site, they found coins minted with the head of Alfred the Great. I had them melted down; I think my image will last a lot longer.'

We all smiled at Robert. He was not being arrogant; he meant what he said. Such was the bravado of the Normans, he knew that the churches his countrymen were building would be substantial enough to stand much longer than those of the Saxons.

York also brought the final additions to our army. The contingents from William's northern magnates joined us there, giving us a formidable force over 5,000 strong. As usual it was a highly disciplined, well-provisioned professional army capable of putting the fear of God into its enemies and able to deliver a mighty blow should the intimidation not work.

Like his father, Robert had created four conroi of elite cavalry, 100 horsemen in total, as his own hearthtroop. I had the honour of commanding the second of those, composed largely of men from my own retinue. It was named the Cerdician Conroi in honour of my royal lineage – a great irony, under the circumstances, but only one of many anomalies, oddities and absurdities in England in those early days of Norman rule.

Edwin continued to be my standard-bearer, and Sweyn and Adela rode behind me as page knights-in-waiting.

As soon as we left York, I unfurled my war banner and the Wyvern of Wessex flew over English soil once more, another incongruity in bewildering times. Robert did not mind in the slightest. In fact, he said he was proud to have King Harold's famous ensign in his ranks.

We reached Durham in the second week of September. It was a bleak and desolate place. The iron fist of the Normans did not rule as firmly that far north, and in the spring there had been a gruesome massacre.

Walchere of Liège, both Bishop of Durham and Earl of Northumbria, had become yet another victim of the lawlessness of the far reaches of England's northern wilderness. Many of the Northumbrian nobles and thegns had found refuge in Scotland or escaped to the high fells during William's onslaught of the winter of 1069. Now they were returning to their estates and villages and attempting to rebuild them. It did not take long for tensions to surface with the new Norman rulers.

In trying to settle a dispute between his Norman retinue and the local Northumbrian knights, Walchere had agreed to travel to Gateshead with a large force of his household knights to meet the local aristocratic families. Old enmities arose at the meeting and boiled over into violence. Walchere and his men were overpowered and locked in the church, which was then torched. Many died in the flames and any who escaped were butchered as they left. Over a hundred men were killed, almost all of them Normans.

When Robert heard the details of the slaughter, he acted with the ruthless efficiency that was the hallmark of Norman rule. Like the Roman disciplines of the past, the tenet was simple: work hard, pay your tithes, stay on the right side of the law and you will prosper; become idle, avoid your taxes or break the law and you will be punished with a ferocity that you will never forget.

Like his father's Harrying of the North ten years earlier, Robert ordered his conroi to travel far and wide to find the perpetrators of the atrocity at Gateshead. For understandable reasons, my conroi was spared this odious task, but within two weeks the patrols had returned.

Their reports made my blood run cold. In total, 251 men had been killed in the chase or executed. Each arrested man had been tortured to extract the names of all who were involved in the massacre until the Normans were satisfied that all the culprits had been dealt with.

Where a man had been hiding in a village or farm, all the buildings were torched, livestock killed and the people cast out. The execution of the leading figure in the outrage, Eadulf Rus, a local nobleman related to the powerful Earls of Bamburgh, was saved until last and carried out in full view of the entire population of Durham, who had been ordered to attend.

With Normandy's finest standing sentinel on their huge destriers, Eadulf Rus was dragged from the cage in which he had been incarcerated since his capture. He was in a bad way; he had been blinded, his tongue ripped out and his legs and arms broken by repeated blows from Norman maces.

He was still conscious as his body was hauled across the grassy bailey beneath the newly reinforced wooden keep being built above it. The crowd, mainly Anglo-Danes and kinsmen of Eadulf who had returned to their homes to try to rebuild their lives, was silent.

Robert sat on his destrier, his helmet set down, his face stern; he addressed the crowd in Latin.

'I am Robert, Count of Normandy, son of William, King of England and Duke of Normandy. Let those who would slaughter a bishop of Christ and an earl of England, and over a hundred of his kin, understand that this will be their retribution.'

He then signalled to the execution party and Eadulf's limp body was laid beside a mounting block, his head raised by its hair and his neck stretched to give the executioner a clear strike. One of the Normans' most formidable sergeants-at-arms stepped forward, bowed to his lord and took Robert's sword.

It took three blows to sever Eadulf's head from his body, but it was done. There were a few gasps from the crowd and sobbing could be heard from some of the women, but in the main there was silence. The Northumbrian's head was stuck on a spike above the gates of the castle and his body thrown into the River Wear. The crowd shuffled away dispassionately, hiding their true feelings from their Norman masters.

It was difficult to comprehend what they must have felt about the cruelty they had just witnessed. They had seen so much killing and knew only too well what the Normans were capable of.

Were they intimidated by what they had witnessed?

Probably not.

Were they angered and yet more emboldened to continue their resistance?

Unlikely.

Were they overwhelmed by the volume of suffering endured in over ten years of hardship, so as to be almost numb to any further pain?

Almost certainly.

I spent the evening with Edwin, Adela and Sweyn.

'No one deserves to die like that.'

It was the first time I had heard Adela speak with a tremor of emotion in her voice.

'Adela, it was a horrific punishment. But remember, he was a man who burned to death over 100 men.'

'The execution fitted the crime, but to torture him like that is no better than the bestial act that he committed. Justice has to be greater than that.'

Sweyn concurred with Adela.

'I agree. If a man has killed or raped, then he deserves

to die. But his death should be just that – he forfeits his life, it is enough.'

Edwin looked at his young friends admiringly.

'Those are wise words. How did you come to such a judgement?'

Sweyn looked at Edwin and me purposefully.

'We remember what Hereward often said: "Let others make mayhem, we will make the peace."'

I sensed that Adela and Sweyn had come to a new and profound view of the world and its traumas.

'You two have become wise beyond your years.'

I was proud of them and honoured, like them, to be part of Hereward's heritage. His principles were always unequivocal and yet he knew that it wasn't always possible to make principled judgements in the real world; sometimes decisions had to be pragmatic and swayed by circumstances. Watching Robert mete out the punishment of the Normans was a case in point. Knowing him as I did, I felt sure he would have acknowledged that his justice was horrific. But did it match the bestial crime that had been committed?

When I pushed Adela on the point, she admitted that it was perhaps easier for her, as a bystander, to answer that question, rather than if she were the Duke of Normandy.

Sweyn also conceded that actions were often easier to judge when one did not have the responsibility of making them. He then paused, looking a little sheepish.

'Sire, when you rusticated us from Normandy, we did return to Aquitaine, but only briefly. We didn't want to fester in the Lot for three months; our short lives are too precious to waste a quarter of a year in limbo.'

'It is strange, but I sensed that there was more to your time away from Normandy than you admitted to.'

Adela continued the admission.

'We travelled much further south, to Spain and the Taifa of Zaragoza, to meet an old friend of Hereward: the Cid, Rodrigo Diaz of Bivar, Armiger to Ahmad ibn Sulayman al-Muqtadir, the Lord of Zaragoza. Hereward often talked about Rodrigo's prowess as a soldier, and he described the beauty of his wife, Doña Jimena –'

Sweyn interrupted.

'Hereward went to Spain at a crucial point in his life, when Edith Swan-Neck asked him to lead the English resistance. Adela and I felt we were at the same crossroads in our lives.'

I had heard talk of Doña Jimena's great beauty and was intrigued to know how true it was.

'She is everything that is said about her and more. She is in her mid-twenties, with three young children – Maria, Cristina and the newly born Diego Rodriguez – but she still looks like a young girl, exactly as Hereward used to describe her, "as perfect as a black pearl".'

Adela, irritated at the men dwelling on Doña Jimena's loveliness, continued their account.

'We were given a warm reception in Zaragoza. Hereward's name was enough to get us an audience with the Cid – although I, as a woman dressed in the garb of a knight, did raise a few eyebrows!'

Adela was now in full flow.

'Rodrigo has lost favour with the Christian King, Alfonso VI of León and Castile, and has offered his services to the Moors of southern Spain. There he finds much more justice and honour than among his kinsmen in Christian Spain. Rodrigo introduced us to the Muslim knights of Valencia and in particular to al-Muqtadir's son, Yusuf al-Mu'taman. They are a remarkable family and it is obvious why the Cid would want to serve them.

'They have just completed their gleaming new palace, the Aljaferia, and Prince Yusuf is visited constantly by scholars from all over Europe. His book *Kitab al-Istikmal* – *The Book of Perfection* – we were told is a wonder of mathematical calculation. If only Torfida were alive, I'm sure she would have understood it and been able to discuss it with him for hours.'

Sweyn was just as effusive.

'Yusuf and Rodrigo told us about the Mos Militum, the Code of Knights, which is spreading in southern Europe. It is a code of honour based on the Futuwwa, the Way of the Spiritual Warrior, as written in the holy book of Islam, the Quran, and the Mos Maiorum, the code of honour of Ancient Rome. Young knights are adopting it throughout Spain, Italy and France. The code requires us to be honourable, truthful, courageous and humble, and to protect the weak – women, children and the old. Adela and I have both sworn to adopt the Mos Militum for the rest of our lives.'

It felt as if I were listening to visionaries or zealots who had found an eternal truth. Adela continued the sermon.

'Hereward often talked about the Talisman of Truth, the ancient amulet they carried, and its messages of truth and courage. We also remember the Oath of the Brotherhood, the principles they fought for. The Mos Militum is an extension of that, but it's not an amulet or an oath, it's a way of life.'

I was fascinated, and I could see that Edwin was also intrigued.

'It sounds like a worthy standard to follow; we must talk more about it. But first, you both need to be granted the title of knight and be given your own pennons. That is something only Count Robert can do, as I no longer have a domain to call my own. In your case, Adela, it is a highly unusual step for which I do not think there is a precedent.'

'Then I will have to prove myself as better than the men.'

It was unusual for the trial of knighthood to be attempted at Sweyn's age, but there was little doubt he was ready. Adela was old enough, but – as far as I knew – no woman had ever attempted it.

I looked at Edwin, who had been listening to the account of the trip to Zaragoza with mixed feelings. He was angry that, yet again, we had been disobeyed, but his admiration for our young companions' conviction was all too evident. He just shrugged his shoulders.

'So be it. Let's talk to Count Robert and ask for them to be put to the test.'

9. Knighthood

While final preparations for the army's attack on Scotland were made, Robert agreed that Sweyn could undergo the trial of knighthood as practised in Normandy for generations. However, he was adamant that Adela could not be admitted to the Order of Knights. His argument, although a massive disappointment for her, was compelling – even though I told him that she was formally a brother-in-arms to Edwin, Sweyn and myself.

'That is your choice and has nothing to do with me, but no one has ever heard of a woman being admitted to the knighthood. If I were to be the first to sanction it, I would be ridiculed far and wide. And besides, it's just wrong – she's a woman, and women shouldn't fight on the battlefield, let alone be knights.'

'Many women have fought in battle and many have died.'

'I know, and they have died well, but it has usually been in extremis to defend their homes and children. It still doesn't make it right in my eyes, or in the eyes of God. Let that be my final word on the matter.'

Few men would disagree with Robert and there was little point in pressing him further, so I had to give Adela the bad news. I had one crumb of comfort for her, which was that Robert had agreed that she could undertake the test on the strict understanding that, no matter how well she performed, it would not qualify her to join the Order of Knights.

Edwin helped me break the news to her.

'I will speak to the Count myself,' she vowed.

'You will not, Adela. That would be countermanding my authority and I will not allow it.'

'I am the equal of all of them – and better than most. It is not just.'

Edwin intervened.

'Remember who you are speaking to.'

'My Lord, I'm sorry, but I want to be treated according to my talents, not constrained by traditions that men created to keep women as slaves.'

'You have my sympathy, but you can't fight the way the world is.'

'On the contrary, sire, I can and I will.'

'I understand but, on this occasion, I can't help you.'

'My Lord, I realize how much you have supported Sweyn and myself, and we will always be grateful. So, if I accept this, what will become of me? Will I be able to accompany you on campaigns?'

'I don't see why you can't carry on as page in my retinue – and, indeed, bear arms. Let me talk to the Count after the trial.'

The trial was undertaken with the help of several of Robert's senior knights, in a series of tests supervised by Hugh Percy. A large crowd gathered when word spread around the camp that Adela had been allowed to take the challenge.

There were many emotions and opinions about Adela

within Robert's army, both among the fighting men and the men and women who made up the baggage train. All assumed she would have preferred to be a man and that her sexual desires favoured women rather than men. That was understandable, given her appearance and demeanour, and most men – and many of the women – were adamant that a long night with a well-endowed, vigorous young man would solve all her problems. A few were more sympathetic, admiring her fortitude as well as her martial skills and courage.

The tests were arduous: target practice with longbow, crossbow and javelin; tilts at dummy targets and personal jousts with some of Robert's finest horsemen; duels on foot and on horseback with sword, mace and seax; various tests of horsemanship, including a long-distance gallop through the forest and heath; and the final challenge, a foot-race around the camp where, at several points, they had to run a gauntlet of abuse, blows, traps and obstacles.

The test was scored by Hugh Percy and both passed handsomely. Sweyn's score was one of the highest anyone could remember, while Adela's would have put her close to the elite bracket of candidates had she not suffered the misfortune of being taken clean out of her saddle in one of her three jousts, which lost her several points. However, accompanied by much cheering, her sheer determination, desperate scrambling and instinctive cunning meant she beat Sweyn by ten yards in the foot-race, even though he had the physique of a hunting dog.

The camp was delighted at the outcome and had been thoroughly entertained for an afternoon.

It was a very special moment for Sweyn when he stood

before Count Robert to be dubbed a Knight of Normandy. He bowed to his lord and, with the only blow to which Sweyn was required not to retaliate, Robert struck him hard across the side of his face with the mailed side of his gauntlet, drawing blood from his cheek and nose. He then handed him his pennon, placed his sword in his hand and raised it to the assembled crowd. The army cheered enthusiastically and his fellow knights raised their swords in the time-honoured salute.

Sweyn had got his wish. He was a member of the Order of Knights at the tender age of sixteen, an honour usually bestowed at a boy's coming of age at twenty-one. Only members of the higher nobility or warriors of exceptional ability were given such an accolade so young.

The most significant gesture, one that I will remember for the rest of my days, was embodied in the colours of Sweyn's pennon. Robert had sought advice from me and, despite what the three colours represented, was magnanimous enough to grant Sweyn the crimson, gold and black of Hereward's war banner, the colours chosen to represent the Talisman of Truth by the noble Einar in 1069.

Sweyn tied the pennon to his lance and held it high in the air. It was yet another huge paradox for me to contemplate: it was less than ten years since Ely; we were in the wild and forsaken burgh of Durham, still not recovered from Norman brutality; and once more Hereward's colours flew proudly over English soil, this time in front of William's firstborn son and heir and the cream of Normandy's army.

Robert then addressed Adela directly.

'Adela of Bourne, you have acquitted yourself with great distinction here today, you have performed as well as the best of my knights. I hope you understand why I cannot dub you as knight today – but rest assured, you have won our respect.'

Robert nodded and a steward brought forward a magnificent black destrier of the size, quality and colour reserved for the elite Matilda Conroi.

'Please accept this mount. It reflects our regard for you and especially your outstanding skill as a horsewoman.'

Adela, despite the disappointment of being denied knighthood, seemed overawed. She did not curtsy of course, but bowed deeply, smiled broadly and took the reins of the horse. The crowd responded warmly – most seemed won over by her impressive performance in the trial.

'Count Robert, I am very grateful and appreciate all the support you have given Sweyn and myself. We are in your debt and will serve in whatever capacity you wish. The mount is a fine specimen and a more than generous gift. I will put him to good use, sufficient to be worthy of such largesse. As for convention, I hope to prove to you that although some traditions are worth keeping, many are not.'

Adela's combative spirit could not be quashed.

I was much relieved that Robert appeared to take it in good part.

Later that night, Robert asked to see me.

'I have been thinking about Adela. Do you want her to stay with this campaign and any others we go on together?'

'Yes, I do.'

'I think that's a problem. There is much disquiet among

the knights, and innuendo and banter among the men. Many of the women are suspicious or jealous of her. I had not given it a thought but, after the trial, Hugh, Yves and Aubrey came to me with the gossip. They are set against her staying – they say she will cause trouble, and that's the last thing we want when we're about to set out for Scotland.'

'What are you saying?'

'I assume she likes women rather than men?' Robert asked bluntly.

'It is never discussed. She has never taken any interest in men – except to be very protective of Sweyn, whom she treats like a younger brother. I know of no evidence to suggest that she's inclined to either men or women, which must be a consequence of her trauma as a girl.'

I then told Robert what I knew of the events in her village. However, the information, although eliciting much sympathy, did not dispel his concerns.

'There are many in the Church and in the nobility who would have her flogged – or worse – if there were any suggestion of her fornicating with another woman.'

'There is no suggestion of that.'

'That may be so, but I can't stop the rumours and I can't have disquiet in the army or the baggage train. Hell, in my naivety, I gave her a stallion today. When she said she'd put him to good use, you can imagine the insinuations that echoed around the camp!'

I despaired.

'Robert, please, this will break her heart. She knows nothing else, has no other dreams; she just wants to fight.'

'Someone is going to have to wed her. It will stop all

the rumours and she can accompany you on as many campaigns as she likes; sometimes, the wives of knights not blessed with children accompany their men.'

'That is preposterous. Who do you suggest takes her in marriage?'

'I've no idea, but you must find someone. We can give him a small estate as an inducement, and I understand she is not without her own dowry.'

'She wouldn't accept it; I would wager a Danegeld on it.'

'What about the boy, Sweyn? Or Edwin? That might be a good match.'

'Robert, this is a shock. I need time to think.'

'You have twenty-four hours. We march at dawn the day after tomorrow.'

I had to act quickly, and immediately sought Edwin's advice.

'Count Robert is adamant that someone must take her as a wife if she is to continue in his service.'

'Sire, I thought he was an admirer.'

'He is, but Hugh Percy and the others have spoken to him and are set against it. They say it will cause trouble and that many of the knights are opposed, claiming that she prefers to be the ram doing the tupping rather than the ewe being tupped.'

'It is unfair, my Lord, she has done nothing wrong. I think I know why the knights are causing trouble. Some time ago, I woke early one morning to find her alone by the horses and very pensive. Eventually, she told me that during the night she had been disturbed by two knights from Avranches, naked, drunk and egged on by others, who were fondling her and pulling down her leggings. As you might guess, her seax was at the throat of one and her foot in the balls of the other within moments. I suspect both were humiliated. She told me that it was not the first time it had happened.'

'Does she prefer women, as the rumours suggest?'

'My Lord, I don't know. She never has any suitors because she never encourages anyone – Emma and Edgiva seemed to be able to subdue the memory of Bourne, but Adela never could. They are now happily married with children, whereas Adela has chosen the life of a warrior. I suspect vengeance still burns in her heart.'

'So, what are we to do? Robert is being generous and suggesting that he will offer a small landholding to a suitable candidate.'

'Sire, I suspect that steed won't gallop. Adela is not without funds of her own, and the thought of her marrying a stranger would be out of the question.'

'Then you'll have to marry her.'

Edwin looked stunned.

'You'll make a handsome couple. You're close enough in age; it's perfect.'

'With respect, my Lord, it is not perfect. My regard for her is like that of a brother. I can't marry her.'

'Well, someone is going to have to marry her, or she will be using the gift of a steed from Count Robert for a long ride home. He's given me twenty-four hours to resolve it.'

I sent Edwin to get Adela and Sweyn the next morning. The encounter was not one I relished.

'So, that's the situation. I'm sorry, Adela, but the Count is adamant. I think he's very sympathetic, but there are many in his retinue who are set against you continuing to Scotland. This expedition is crucial to his future and he can't afford doubts about his judgement getting back to the King.'

Adela tried to grit her teeth, but her eyes filled with tears and there was nothing she could do to stop them streaming down her face. Her chest began to heave and she bit her lip to try to contain her emotions, to no avail.

'They think I am queer, I know that. But that's not the real reason – the real reason is, I frighten them. Weak men fear strong women, and weak women are jealous of those who stand up for themselves in a man's world.'

'Adela, forgive me . . .' I hesitated. 'But I have to ask you this – remember, we are comrades, brothers-in-arms – is it women you desire, rather than men?'

'My Lord, I desire neither.' She shrugged. 'All that was extinguished in Bourne a long time ago.'

'Would you consider a marriage proposal from an upstanding knight in the Count's retinue? That would give the Count a way to let you stay with his army.'

'No, sire, I would not.'

'Adela, the army marches in the morning and you will have to return to Aquitaine if we cannot resolve this.'

'So be it. I will find another way to follow the Code of Knights and fulfil my destiny.'

She had now regained control of her emotions and the look of steely resolve had returned to her face.

'I will marry you.'

Sweyn had said nothing until this point, but his sudden intervention stunned all three of us.

'If you'll have me.'

Adela did not respond; her face remained set, free of emotion. It was Edwin who broke the silence.

'Sweyn, you're not yet seventeen and only just dubbed a knight.'

'On the contrary, Edwin, I am an ideal suitor; I am a knight of Normandy and I have land and money in Aquitaine. I think I'm a pretty good catch for any lady, even someone as discerning as Adela.'

'But you're like brother and sister.'

When it came, Adela's blunt reply was as astonishing as Sweyn's offer had been.

'I accept. You're right; you are a fine catch, any woman would be proud to have you as a husband.'

'Then it is agreed, we will be married today. I'm sure one of the Count's clerics will conduct the service.'

I was rendered speechless; I just sat and listened.

Adela took Sweyn by the hand, her expression still stern.

'I know why you are doing this and I'm very grateful, but this marriage can only be a cloak. If I ever see your little prick poking out of your smock with an evil look in its eye, I'll dice it up like minced meat!'

'Thank you, my beloved. Worry not, I will try to keep my "little prick" under control. If its needs become too great, I'll take comfort in one of the baggage girls; that's what they're there for.'

Edwin and I looked at one another, not entirely sure how much of the exchange was serious and how much was banter. Either way, although not exactly made in heaven, it seemed to be a match that served its purpose.

The four of us agreed that the terms of the marriage would be known only to us, to be kept in the strictest confidence.

I went to Robert to give him the extraordinary news.

The wedding ceremony was organized within hours. Adela managed to borrow a linen dress from one of the few Norman women in Durham and made for herself a lovely circlet of wild flowers. The overall effect was very fetching, and she looked like any other bride on her wedding day – serene and striking. Her dress was an abrupt reminder of her femininity. The pleasing curves of her sexuality, previously hidden by the smock, leggings and hauberk of a warrior, were plain to see. Her hair, washed and brushed, fell in gentle ash-blond waves and her skin shone with the rosy glow typical of her Englishness. She seemed smaller – indeed, petite – without her male garb and weapons. It was an image that must have challenged many prejudices about her sexual preferences.

Sweyn stood by her side, proud and handsome, a young man who had, within just two days, become a knight and a husband. Not surprisingly, he now looked older than his years. He had always had the bearing and manner of a knight, but now he was one. With his dark-brown hair and tanned skin, in contrast to his fair English bride, he could easily have been the haughty son of a Count of Aquitaine; he looked the part and had the self-confidence of a young man born to wield power. I was proud of my brother- and now my 'sister'-in-arms. They were, to everyone's agreement, an eye-catching couple.

Sadly, that was not the end of the matter. Even before the happy couple could retire for the non-consummation of their marriage, several of Sweyn's fellow knights were determined to cause trouble.

The taunts were predictable. Sweyn was ten years younger than Adela so, inevitably, the mocking suggested that she was the real 'man' of the partnership and that at the bedroom 'tilt' it would be Adela who would do the 'tilting' and Sweyn who would be 'speared' in the joust.

Adela tried to pull him away from the insults, but Sweyn's anger could not be assuaged and pandemonium broke out. He drew his sword with lightning speed and lunged at his barrackers before any of them could unsheathe their weapons. They retreated rapidly, some falling over one another as they did so. Sweyn managed to get his blade firmly under the chin of one of them, who happened to be Alan of Sées, the youngest son of one of King William's most powerful allies and one of Count Robert's most capable young knights.

As Sweyn spoke, the razor-sharp tip of his sword drew blood, which began to trickle down the blade.

'If you ever insult my wife or me again, I'll kill you. And that applies to any other man here.'

Adela was at his side in an instant. She had hitched up her dress beyond her knees and pulled out the seax concealed inside the ankle straps of her leather shoe. Now she was holding it towards their goaders, crouched in the pose of a knife-fighter. Suddenly, she was a warrior again.

Sweyn glared at them all with a fiery look in his eye that

had real menace in it, then calmly put his sword in its scabbard, took Adela by the hand and walked away.

She, in turn, sheathed her dagger in its improvised scabbard, dropped the hem of her dress, smoothed out its wrinkles and curtsied sweetly to Count Robert, who had arrived to see what the commotion was. Their assailants dispersed sheepishly as the many onlookers began to mutter to themselves.

The speed and ferocity of Sweyn's reaction had certainly mesmerized me. Whether it had won him respect among his and Adela's detractors, or created enemies for life, was difficult to tell. Notwithstanding that, he had certainly made an impression.

At dinner that night, Robert was full of admiration for Sweyn.

'That boy put the fear of God into Alan of Sées today.'

'Yes, he did. It was quite extraordinary.'

'Let's hope he can break Adela as easily as he can tame my knights.'

I smiled to myself, remembering the terms of the marriage, and thought, 'If only you knew, my friend.'

For a long time after the wedding, I pondered on the wisdom of what the four of us had contrived. Old-fashioned ways and simple prejudice had led us to create a perverse mock marriage and a deceit that we all had to live with – in particular, Sweyn and Adela. It was a clever disguise to solve a problem, but a disguise all the same. As with all subterfuges, it ran the risk of ridicule for all concerned should the ruse ever be discovered.

Much as Sweyn and Adela's well-being was a great

concern for me, my anxiety about our expedition to Scotland was growing. Although I was delighted at the prospect of seeing Margaret again, I feared that Malcolm would be much more difficult to deal with than in the past.

I was compromised in more than one respect. Not only did I have a high regard for both sides, but they both knew of my split loyalties, suggesting little room for manoeuvre when trying to steer them away from conflict. However, I resolved to use my openness as a strength, rather than a weakness, and to appeal to both sides to use me as an intermediary.

It sounded like a good approach, in theory. I prayed that it would work out that way, in practice.

10. Grief at Launceston

At the end of September we crossed the Tyne at the ruins of Hadrian's ancient wall and moved rapidly towards the Tweed. As Robert and I had agreed in Rouen, once we crossed into Lothian I took my conroi on the shorter but more difficult route north across the hills of Lammermuir to begin the negotiation with King Malcolm. Robert took the long way round, along the old coastal road, laying waste to everything he found.

Unfortunately, the Lord of Dunbar, Gospatric, one of Malcolm's major allies, decided to make a fight of it. Robert was ruthless, the garrison was destroyed, his heavily fortified tower by the sea burned to the ground and Gospatric taken prisoner.

Robert considered executing him, but decided it would be a more powerful message to use Gospatric as a courier to Malcolm. He was stripped of his armour and fine clothes, had his head shaved, was dressed in the crude woollen smock of a peasant and given charge of an ox wagon. Robert's men then loaded the wagon with two dozen severed heads from the Dunbar garrison and told Gospatric to deliver them to Malcolm's forces at Musselburgh.

It had the desired effect. By the time we reached Dunfermline, Malcolm was in a rage.

My conroi was billeted outside the King's keep. His steward took us through his great hall, where Edwin,

Sweyn and Adela were required to wait, while I was taken to a small private hall next to his and Margaret's chamber.

Autumn was beginning to come in on the westerly winds and a large fire roared in the hearth. Malcolm swung round when I entered and was about to launch into his tirade when Margaret stopped him.

'Let me greet my brother, Malcolm!' She rushed towards me and enfolded me in a warm embrace. 'How are you, Edgar? And how is Duncan?'

'I am well and so is your son. The Normans are good to him and he prospers at court in Rouen. He speaks the language well – although, to the amusement of everyone, still with a heavy Scottish lilt – and he thrives. I don't see him often, but he sends his love to you both.'

Only the last part of my account was untrue. I had hardly seen the boy, but I knew him to be well and treated with respect.

Malcolm could not contain himself any longer and launched into his onslaught, an attack only made worse by my admission.

'You know I am loyal to Count Robert.'

'And that includes leading his army to ravage my kingdom?'

'I came to explain the situation and to try to avoid bloodshed.'

'Then you're too late! Dunbar has been destroyed and its lord is sitting in Musselburgh with only the heads of his garrison for company. The misbegotten son of that Norman bastard is marauding all over my kingdom.'

'Because you've been plundering his.'

'It's not his kingdom, it's mine!'

'That's not what you agreed at Abernethy.'

'So, whose side are you on?'

'In this instance, neither. Robert has allowed me to come here as a neutral party, out of respect for the friendship you have shown me for many years.'

Queen Margaret tried to soothe her husband.

'Malcolm, listen to Edgar, instead of shouting at him. The situation is just as it was eight years ago at Abernethy. You broke the agreement with William by rampaging over the border. It's your own fault.'

'Be quiet, woman, and go and tend to your sick and needy!'

'Indeed, I am – you're the one in need of help! For pity's sake, listen to Edgar.'

'Margaret is right; Robert's army is too powerful for you. You will have to concede.'

'I will not! I will send this upstart home with his head in a cart, just as he did with the men of Dunbar!'

Malcolm then stormed off, shouting at his stewards to summon a Council of War.

Margaret looked just I remembered her, perhaps even more serene and beautiful. How lucky Malcolm was to have her as his queen; and how lucky were her people to have her benign influence on their tempestuous monarch.

'Don't worry, Margaret, I'll talk to him later when he's calmed down.'

'He's been much better recently, but he gets restless and likes nothing better than riding south with a band of cutthroats intent on plunder and savagery. All I can do is pray for him.'

'You're too good for him, Margaret. Why do you put up with his boorish ways?'

'It's my lot. He's the father of my children and it is my calling to redeem his soul from eternal damnation. Besides, he's not all bad. He can be good company and is very generous. He also warms my bed at night.' She smiled mischievously. 'He's very good at that too.'

So, as I had always suspected, beneath that saintly facade, hot blood did run in my sister's veins.

'Who are the young people you have brought with you?' she asked.

'They are interesting. I am going to present them to both of you when Malcolm has faced up to what you and I know is inevitable.'

It did not take long for Malcolm to compose himself sufficiently for me to talk to him, especially after his senior lords and allies told him that they had no stomach for a fight with Robert and his Norman cavalry. His Council of War had not gone well and he had retreated to the battlements of his tower to ponder his dilemma.

Darkness was settling over the hillsides to the east of his royal burgh as I clambered through the trapdoor to the top of the tower.

'They won't fight.'

'They are very wise, you should listen to them.'

'I am their Lord, they should listen to me.'

'I'm sure they hold you in the greatest esteem, but without their support you can't put more than 1,000 men in the field. Even if you had their warbands, you would be no match for Robert. They know that – and I'm sure you do. It's just that you don't want to accept it.'

'You play a clever game, Edgar. Do you also tell Robert what he "knows" and what he "won't accept"?'

'Sometimes, but he and I have also become friends. I have not been disloyal to you or to him. I sent you information to your advantage when Robert rebelled against his father. You took advantage of that to try to reassert your claims in the Borders. When he and his father became reconciled, my loyalties became compromised. I explained my dilemma to Robert, and he accepted it. Now I am explaining it to you.'

'And you expect me to accept it?'

'Yes.'

'You speak like a papal legate – full of fine words and crafty thinking. But I'm suspicious of men who won't settle their differences on the battlefield. Words are easier said than deeds done.'

'Robert is not a man to avoid a fight. Believe me, he would like nothing better than to defeat you in battle, take your head back to London and claim a vast new kingdom. But the Normans know they are not yet ready to try to impose their rule this far north. So, the compromise you should consider is for you to guarantee stability on the border so that they can continue to consolidate their power in England and allow you to have peace in Scotland – at least, for the time being.'

'On the understanding that it is only a matter of time before the Normans bring a vast army here to take my domain.'

'You're right, it is only a matter of time, but I don't think it will happen in William's reign. He is getting weaker and his neighbours are getting stronger, especially Philip of France. So, you have time to make Scotland stronger. Take it! Build your alliances with the Norse in the Highlands and Islands, and with the Danes. Make preparations so that your sons have a better chance to resist when the onslaught comes.'

Malcolm pondered for some time, pacing up and down.

'I am relieved that Duncan is well and that the Normans treat him with respect.'

'He is indeed well. He is kept close to the King, but he is well cared for and flourishes, perhaps a little too well. I didn't mention this to Margaret, but I hear that many a fair maiden at the court of Rouen has fond memories of the boy's Scottish vigour.'

'Good boy!' Malcolm smiled for the first time. 'I'm glad he's sowing his wild Scottish oats. I wouldn't expect anything else from a Canmore.' Growing serious once more, he said, 'I suppose you are right. Perhaps Duncan will have a better chance of dealing with the Normans – at least, he'll know them well. Perhaps your fine words are wise words.'

'Scotland could prosper for a long time yet. If William splits his legacy between Robert and Rufus, sooner or later they will fight and the Norman Empire will be severely weakened.'

'So, I must bow to the Normans once more?'

'Yes, but it will be the action of a wise king, not a weak one.'

Malcolm reflected for a while. Although he dreaded the prospect and the humiliation of it, he knew what he had to do.

'Will you make the arrangements?'

'I suggest Abernethy Tower again. Robert will like that; it will make him look good in his father's eyes.'

So, eight years after Malcolm's first submission to the Normans at Abernethy Tower, the ceremony was repeated. Once more, Malcolm, King of the Scots, placed his hand on Bede's mighty Bible and swore his fealty to William, King of England and Duke of Normandy.

Robert was gentler with Malcolm than his father had been, and the two men showed one another a mutual respect.

As Robert prepared his army to march south, we returned to Dunfermline so that I could say goodbye to my sister and to Scotland yet again. It was also an opportunity to introduce my brothers-in-arms formally to Malcolm and Margaret.

After the courtesies, during which Adela and Sweyn behaved impeccably – just like the young courtiers they had become – the four of us sat at the King's high table for dinner and enjoyed a typical Scottish banquet, heavy on meat and game and even heavier on mead, beer and wine.

Although it was not apparent from their behaviour, I thought about how Adela and Sweyn must be feeling, seated within a few feet of a king at his high table. They had become part of the lesser gentry of Aquitaine – nonetheless, their life had been lived a long way from the tables of kings.

After the banquet, I sat with Malcolm and Margaret to discuss the future and tell them of my fears for the Celtic peoples of Britain.

'The Welsh princes are already in awe of the Normans. They have few natural defences and the Norman lords are building huge castles everywhere. William Fitz Osbern, Earl of Hereford, has taken Chepstow and Monmouth; Hugh of Avranches, Earl of Chester, is in control as far as Denbigh; and Roger Montgomery, Earl of Shrewsbury, has pushed deep into the heartland of the Welsh tribes along the Vale of Powys. Scotland's time will come and, in due course, Ireland will also face the Norman threat. For the moment, they are lucky; they have the great Western Sea to protect them, but it won't keep them safe for ever.'

As always, Margaret's thoughts were for me rather than the affairs of kings and their realms.

'Your advice to Malcolm to count our blessings and prepare for the future is much appreciated, but what will you do now?'

'Well, I have my small band and we've sworn allegiance to one another. We may stay with Robert, or go in search of adventures of our own.'

Malcolm laughed out loud.

'You are wise in the affairs of others, but a fool to yourself. Your "band" is one knight of good birth, a boy who has the beard of an old crone and a girl who thinks she's a man!'

'Malcolm, please don't be unkind to Edgar,' Margaret remonstrated. 'We owe him a lot, don't forget that.'

'I think our debts balance in the pan now! But I still maintain it's ridiculous for a royal prince to have a retinue of three – two of whom should not even be in the same room as him.'

Malcolm's boorish comments were beginning to irk me.

'Please don't goad me; their origins are way behind them. They are exceptional people who have been brought up in very special circumstances and fully deserve my allegiance.'

Whether Malcolm agreed with her or not, I felt that Margaret spoke for both of them as the evening drew to a close.

'Go with our prayers and blessing. God's speed, until we meet again.'

It was painful to think that I had to leave Margaret yet again. She had such strength and had managed to make a life – indeed, to find happiness – in a place not of her choosing and with a man she had resisted for a long time. She had been the anchor in my life as a boy and in many ways her inspiration still guided me.

I took comfort from the fact that Malcolm's new treaty with the Normans should keep her and Scotland safe for the time being, but I remained concerned that, sooner or later, Malcolm's temperament, coupled with the inevitable burgeoning of Norman ambitions in the North, would eventually lead to another crisis.

We caught up with Robert's army encamped next to the ruins of a Roman fort on the north bank of the River Tyne where, because it was significantly further north than his bastion at Durham, he had decided to delay in order to build a new fortress as a strategic stronghold. As the ruins marked the eastern limit of Hadrian's great wall, the new castle would act as a very tangible reminder to Malcolm of William's insistence that the old Roman wall was to become the new boundary between the two kingdoms.

For now, his men were building the huge walls from timber felled from the forests in the west, but it would only be a temporary structure to keep the new garrison safe. Eventually, a great stone keep would rise to intimidate all-comers.

Our small band decided to use Robert's building project as an opportunity to discuss our future plans. Edwin picked out half a dozen men as an escort and we travelled along the bank of the Tyne for a few miles until we found a secure place to make camp in the ruins of another large Roman fort.

After a supper of boar and beer, and much debate about the Normans' ability to impose their will on the Scots, it was Sweyn who was the first to make his preference clear.

'I would prefer to go to Italy. Hereward and the family often talked about it. They once lived happily in Melfi, serving the Guiscards, the Norman rulers of the south. He spoke very highly of Roger Guiscard, Count of Sicily, who, Hereward often said, was a great soldier and a noble knight. We were told in Zaragoza that he is still fighting for control of the western part of the island from Muslim and Byzantine warlords.'

Adela spoke next.

'I too would like to journey to the south, but first I would like to see if we can find some trace of what became of Hereward, Gunnhild and Estrith.'

Edwin agreed with her.

I suggested that, given the likelihood of Robert spending a lot more time in England consolidating the success of his Scottish campaign, we should continue in the service of Robert until we felt the time was right to travel to

Italy. I liked the sound of Roger of Sicily – and the warm Mediterranean seemed very appealing as we huddled around the fire on a chilly autumn night by the Tyne.

And so, we returned to London with Robert's army before the worst of winter began to bite, leaving his garrison on the Tyne to continue their work. I did not envy them their task.

We spent the long winter of 1080 amidst the intense activity of a burgeoning Norman capital. Only in January, when it became so cold that the Thames froze for three days, did the work stop.

Our time there was full of mixed emotions for me. It was a thriving, boisterous place, full of old money and new. The Norman aristocracy passed through on their way to and from their estates in England and Normandy. The merchants, innkeepers and craftsmen benefited hugely as a result and some of these were rapidly becoming the new English elite. They adopted Norman ways, spoke their language and were starting to accumulate wealth.

The areas around Westminster, Southwark and along the ancient route between the old Roman city and Westminster were all being transformed by new homes, churches and warehouses. The Thames, busy enough when I was boy, was now so crowded you could have forded the river just by stepping from one boat to the next. The vessels came from all over Europe and the Mediterranean. The sights and smells were intoxicating: leather, spices and wine were among the more appealing, with human and animal waste the most pungent of the less edifying aromas.

With the rich citizens in their finery came those who fed on them – serving them and doing their bidding – and also the poor, hoping to acquire a morsel just to survive on, who were regularly abused by them. The Normans had healthy appetites for all of life's pleasures and were more relaxed about moral turpitude than their Saxon predecessors. On both sides, and almost for its entire length, Ludgate Hill was the haunt of harlots and beggars, as were most of the taverns serving the wharfmen and stevedores along the river.

As in all places where there are large gatherings of humanity, London exhibited much that was to be admired in my fellow man, and much that illustrated his frailties only too well. As for me, I was just like the rest of them – frail, most of the time – occasionally redeeming myself with moments of kindness or contrition.

I resolved to improve.

Sweyn and Adela made several journeys throughout southern England during this time in search of clues to the fate of Hereward and his daughters.

They discovered nothing about Hereward, but did learn that after Ely the two girls had been placed under the protection of the Norman lord, Robert Mortain, Earl of Cornwall, at his keep in Launceston.

Assuming that my status would be required to gain an audience with the Earl, Edwin and I were persuaded by Adela and Sweyn to ride with them to Cornwall as soon as the worst of the winter had lifted. We set out in late February 1081.

It was another melancholy journey. Wessex was flourishing; its estates were prospering, its farms thriving, its burghs burgeoning. But it was a new Wessex. The quiet slumber that had been Saxon England was now a brash bustle of toil and energy. Many of the people were being handsomely rewarded, but most were not.

The old Saxon lords and thegns had gone, their modest halls and longhouses replaced by huge fortified towers, earthworks, keeps and mottes. Norman soldiers were everywhere, jittery, belligerent, glowering. The realm was at peace and prospering, but this had come at a heavy price, paid in the rivers of blood that had been spilled in the past and the ever-present odour of oppression and brooding resentment.

Adela and Sweyn took everything in, trying to come to terms with their own part in England's traumas. They practised their weapons routines twice a day, every day – two hours in the morning, two hours in the evening – sword and seax, lance and bow, mounted and on foot. They ran and swam, climbed, crawled and clambered through woods, across heaths and along beaches.

Their routines were like those of the devout monks, performed with the regularity of an hourglass, the dedication of a pilgrim and the intensity of a zealot. It was exhausting to watch.

Edwin and I joined them in many of their exercises and routines, but never with the same ferocity of purpose. Edwin was as fit and strong as any warrior and I maintained good health and followed strict military disciplines, but Sweyn and Adela were relentless. Typically, if I felt sore or feverish, I would take a break, or if I had over-indulged in one of the many pleasures of the flesh available to a nobleman, I would let lethargy get the better of me.

Not so, Sweyn and Adela. Pain or discomfort seemed to drive them on – and if they were diverted by worldly desires, they kept them well disguised.

As I observed them day after day, my admiration for them grew. They were so agile and strong and their close-quarters skills with a seax or dagger were a sight to behold. They often described how they had watched Alphonso of Granada in training at their home in St Cirq Lapopie. He was Hereward's friend – the man he had admired more than anybody in single combat – and so they copied all his moves and routines.

Passing in the shadow of the wilderness of Dartmoor, it reminded me of the North. It was a forbidding place, much of it still covered in snow. Its practically impenetrable forests stretched high up, almost to the crests of the moors, where the trees gave way to the bogs and mires that could swallow a horse and rider in minutes.

The further west we went the more Celts we saw, still with their own language and ways, until we found only the occasional Saxon settlement close to the rivers.

The Earl of Cornwall's Launceston was like the rest of this Norman land. There was a huge wooden keep atop a towering motte, with the stone walls of a new fortress being built around it.

The Earl's greeting and hospitality were generous. A man in his mid-forties, he was typical of his warrior breed: forthright, strong and disciplined. He appeared to carry more Frankish blood than that of his Viking ancestors, for he was short and dark with a girth that reflected his age.

'I am sorry to tell you that Gunnhild died two years ago. She developed appalling swellings and became very ill.

Estrith nursed her for several weeks but she just wasted away. My physician said she was consumed by black bile, which produced terrible tumours that eventually killed her. Her pain was great, but she bore it with fortitude. When she died, Estrith took her to a secret place where Torfida, her mother, is buried. She then decided to leave Launceston. I had to seek permission from the King, which he granted. She left here about a year ago.'

Adela got the question out just before me.

'My Lord, may we know where she has gone?'

'You may not, young lady. First of all, the King forbade the girls any more than passing contact with anybody outside my immediate jurisdiction until they married. And secondly, Estrith left specific instructions that no one was to know her whereabouts.'

'But, my Lord, we're her family.'

'She made no exceptions. Even though her father was a mortal enemy, I was charged with the girls' care and would not betray Estrith's trust to anyone.'

'You were at Ely, Earl Robert?'

'I was, Prince Edgar.'

'So, you were a witness to Hereward's demise?'

'I was, but the account of the events after the end of the siege is known only to the King and to me. My recollection will go with me to my grave. As for the King –' he gave a short laugh '– I wouldn't recommend that you ask him.'

Sweyn then stepped forward.

'My Lord, did the girls not marry?'

'They chose not to, although there were many suitors. They were beautiful – indeed, Estrith remains so – and very learned and charming; perfect wives for Norman lords looking for English brides to charm their tenants. But they chose to spend their days helping in the local communities with the sick and the poor; in the evenings they would talk and write, read and draw. Estrith is exceptionally talented with calculation and would seek out any churchwright or mason in the area to talk about the techniques of construction. She said that her mother had seen the great buildings of Rome and Greece and understood how they were built.'

Adela and Sweyn looked at one another warmly, clearly enjoying fond memories from the past. It was obvious that the Earl had become very fond of the girls and remained fiercely loyal to their wishes. It was pointless to press him further.

We made a detour during our return to London in order to visit the nuns at Hereford, feeling certain that that was where we would find Estrith. Hereward had first met Torfida there, and that was where she had gone shortly before her tragic death.

To our surprise and disappointment, Estrith was not there, nor had she been there.

Our trail had gone cold.

Short of visiting every ecclesiastical house in the country, we had no choice but to return to London, leaving me saddened to think that our hopes of ever finding her had all but gone.

11. This Turbulent Priest

We spent the next few months on a grand tour of England as Robert undertook an inspection of the rapidly growing Norman fortifications which seemed to loom over every burgh in the realm. The monotony was broken only in the spring of 1082, when Robert asked me to take my conroi and four of his own to Rochester on a mission of some delicacy.

Odo of Bayeux, apart from being Earl of Kent and a bishop of Normandy, was King William's half-brother and closest confidant. He was also unrelentingly ambitious and had his eyes set on the papacy itself. He had begun to recruit supporters from the Norman hierarchy for an expedition to Rome to press his claim to be Pontiff by force of arms. It was a naive plan at best; the last thing the King wanted was for England and Normandy to become embroiled in the politics of Rome and in military campaigns in southern Europe, where other powerful Normans with friends and allies in Normandy ruled most of the Italian peninsula.

Odo had committed a cardinal sin – he had begun to act in a way that threatened the authority of the King. William ordered his immediate arrest. Robert gave me the task, thinking that it would only add to the ignominy of Odo's seizure that his captor should be an English prince.

Even though my escort of 120 men was significantly

outnumbered by Odo's garrison, he rode out to meet us with a small group of knights. Most of the population of Rochester had gathered to watch the confrontation.

I asked Sweyn to read out the charges.

'Sweyn of Bourne, read the King's warrant!'

He delivered it in perfect Norman French.

'Odo of Bayeux, you have plotted sedition against the throne and impugned the King's honour in the eyes of his lords. William, King of England and Duke of Normandy, commands that you be taken under arrest to his donjon in Rouen, where you will be held at the King's pleasure. Your lands and titles are forfeited to the King forthwith.'

Sweyn then took the bridle of Odo's horse and made to lead him away.

'Take your hands off my horse, boy.'

Sweyn's response was immediate and authoritative.

'You are in no position to issue orders to me.'

He then pulled hard on the horse, making Odo jolt back in his saddle.

'What is your name? You disgrace a fellow Norman in front of these English peasants?'

I could see that Sweyn was seething at Odo's contemptuous attitude towards his English subjects. I glanced at Edwin to be sure he was aware of the potential flashpoint.

'I am not Norman, I am English; these "peasants" are my people and yours. You are under arrest by royal warrant of the King of England.'

Sweyn tugged once more on the horse and made to lead the once mighty lord away in disgrace, at which point Odo's knights drew their swords. My men reciprocated immediately and a vicious melee ensued with men hacking at one another in a frenzy.

Sweyn had the eminent good sense to pull Odo and his mount away, with Edwin and Adela protecting his rear. Odo seized the opportunity to dismount, and ran for the protection of his keep. A large man, he was no match for Sweyn, who jumped from his horse and ran him down within ten yards.

As Sweyn closed in on Odo, the cleric drew his seax and lunged at his young pursuer. But Sweyn was too quick for him and kicked the blade from his hand with a deft swing of his boot. At the same time, he smashed his mailed glove into Odo's face, inflicting considerable damage to the Bishop's noble features. His nose was broken and blood poured from his mouth. He staggered backwards before Sweyn put him on his back with another heavy blow, dislodging several of his teeth.

As Sweyn stepped over him, sword in hand ready to strike, Odo raised his hand in meek submission, wiping the blood from his mouth as he did so.

I had stayed with the melee to make sure it could be contained, but as soon as Odo raised his hand his men relented.

Edwin and Adela helped Odo to his feet and led him to his keep to get help for his battered face. He said nothing, but he stared long and hard at Sweyn with a look that was a blend of fear and respect.

We gave Odo time to gather some belongings and bid farewell to his family before Sweyn led my conroi and escorted Odo's to Rouen. As the disgraced Bishop left for

Dover, he gave me a gift for Robert. Looking like a butt of wine wrapped in cloth, it was put into one of the carts in my baggage train.

'Give it to the young Count. It is embroidery, the finest you will ever see, a record of his father's great victory at Senlac Ridge. It has taken the fine seamsters of Kent over a year to make. I was going to present it to the King myself, but that is no longer possible. When Robert is King of England, he should hang it around his hall at Westminster to remind him of what our generation did to win this kingdom for him. You can also tell that young knight of yours that when I have settled my differences with the King, he will face me again in very different circumstances.'

'My Lord Bishop, he was only doing his duty.'

'Perhaps so, but not with any measure of respect.'

Despite the rebuke from Odo, I was proud of Sweyn. He was now eighteen and no longer looked like a callow youth, but had the bearing of a mature knight and nobleman. He had acted firmly, as he was required to do, and had not been intimidated by the second most important man in the kingdom. Odo was in disgrace and could expect no courtesies – thus, none had been given. The swift and ruthless way in which Sweyn had dealt with Odo's physical challenge impressed all who witnessed it and word spread quickly about his adroitness at close quarters and the power of his punch.

Bishop Odo, imposing warrior of Normandy, one of the most fearsome of William's supporters, left England for seclusion in Normandy. He would not be released from captivity during the King's lifetime. William had acted decisively against his closest ally – but it was the act of a king whose power was in rapid decline and who feared everyone around him.

'Our boy did well, did he not, Edwin?'

'He did, sire.'

'Adela, you must be proud of your husband?'

'I am, my Lord. It is a shame the King had not ordered his execution; if he had, I could have been the one to deliver the fatal blow!'

Our tour of duty of the King's fortifications continued throughout the spring. England, as always at that time of year, was resplendent. We travelled to the south-west, to Montacute in Somerset and on to Exeter, Wells and Glastonbury. As we progressed, at every turn we witnessed a land beginning to prosper. Fields which the farmers had brought under their care were full of wheat and barley, and meadows that remained untamed were carpeted with wild flowers. There was game aplenty in the forests and the rivers teemed with fish.

It felt good to be alive.

Sweyn returned from Rouen in the summer and we continued our duties with Robert and his inspections around his father's realm. As time went by, Robert took more and more opportunities to go hunting, taking time to explore each new forest, saying that England had the finest hunting he had ever encountered.

I was left to undertake the detail of the assessments and make regular reports to him. It was an ideal opportunity for me and for my companions to understand the meticulous attention to detail of Norman architecture and military planning, and we thus became absorbed by our work for many months.

Another major setback befell King William in November of 1083. His beloved wife, the diminutive yet formidable Matilda, died in Caen.

The King was inconsolable; he had been faithful to her throughout the entire thirty years of their marriage, while she had borne him ten children. It was Matilda who had held the family together, especially the ever-fractious Robert and Rufus.

We escorted Robert to the interment at his mother's convent in Caen. The epitaph on her tomb was a perfect summary of what she meant to William and to Normandy:

> The lofty structure of this splendid tomb
> Hides great Matilda, sprung from royal stem.
> Child of a Flemish duke, her mother was
> Adela, a daughter of a King of France,
> Sister of Henry, Robert's royal son.
> Married to William, most illustrious King,
> She gave this site and raised this noble house,
> With many hands and many goods endowed,
> Given by her, or by her toil procured.
> Comforter of the needy, duty's friend,
> Her wealth enriched the poor, left in her need.
> At daybreak on November's second day
> She won her share of everlasting joy.

Throughout the entire service, William's head remained bowed, his shoulders hunched. When he looked up, his eyes had the haunted look of a broken man.

There was much irony in the setting: where once William had towered over his acolytes, he now seemed to exist in their shadow. Their once doting eyes were insincere and, behind them, their machinations to bring about his imminent downfall and likely successor were almost palpable.

At the end, he had to be led away.

Robert announced that he would stay with his father in Rouen for the time being, so we decided that now was the time for us to undertake our journey to southern Italy.

We had become close friends – but while it was important for Robert to stay in Normandy, it was equally vital for me to seek a new challenge.

We parted like brothers.

'Go well, Edgar. When we meet again, I expect to hear all the stories in detail and anticipate that they will include many tales of conquest – over fearsome warriors and dark, lusty maidens.'

'I will try my best, Robert,' I answered with a laugh, before turning to weightier matters. 'Try and humour your father a little. The loss of your mother may make his temper even more difficult to control, but he is becoming increasingly isolated and will need your wise counsel and support.'

'Perhaps, my friend . . . I'll make the same pledge as you've just made to me – I'll try my best.'

PART THREE

Roger the Great

12. Adela's Scars

Yet again, Robert was generous in allowing me to recruit a sturdy captain, six men-at-arms and sufficient silver for our expedition to Italy.

We travelled slowly, paying our respects along the way to all those to whom it would be an insult not to – and to many more who may, one day, be useful to us. We were treated with the greatest respect, much of it a result of understandable curiosity about the events we had lived through and witnessed.

Along the way, Sweyn and Adela repeated many times the stories they had heard about the impressive castle at Melfi in Apulia and of the worthy deeds of Hereward's good friend Roger Guiscard, Count of Sicily.

The Guiscards were typical of the Normans of their day. Roger's father, Tancred de Hauteville, had been a minor noble with a small estate near Coutances in the Cotentin Peninsula of western Normandy. His only real claim to fame was that, by two wives, over a period of almost thirty years, he sired a large brood of fearsome warriors and beautiful daughters – fifteen offspring in all. His daughters married well above their station in the Norman aristocracy, and no fewer than eight of his sons became counts. Roger was the youngest of them all.

Roger's older brothers – William Iron Arm, Drogo and Humphrey – led the Norman mercenaries who gained control in southern Italy in the 1040s and, in turn, became Counts of Apulia.

Robert Guiscard, the ferocious sixth son of Tancred, still ruled in Melfi, where his reputation as an intimidating host even to his friends and allies persuaded us to continue on to Sicily, where we knew we would receive a much warmer welcome from his younger brother, Count Roger.

Sicily was unlike anything we had witnessed before. We had seen the wonders of Italy in Turin, Florence and Rome, where the ancient buildings made everything in northern Europe seem so new and brash. But Sicily had, until Robert brought it back under Christian rule only ten years earlier, been occupied by Islamic rulers for 250 years. The architecture was breathtaking, the food exotic, the languages incomprehensible and the customs mystifying.

We wallowed in it – especially Sweyn and Adela, who had during their childhood heard so much about the intoxicating world of Islam and the ancient cultures the Muslim people cherished.

Apart from Sicily's more intriguing qualities, it was also as hot as a blacksmith's furnace. We arrived in July 1084 with the temperatures soaring to the point where much of the middle of the day had to be spent in the shade with the necessity for minimal effort of any kind.

Roger's court was at Palermo, a vast city of great wealth and antiquity. We had never seen so many people; it was much bigger than the great cities of Normandy and France and made Rome look like a small town. The buildings – the Ancient Greek and Roman temples and amphitheatres, the Moorish palaces and mosques of the Muslims and the new

Norman fortresses and churches – were so numerous and on such a grand scale that it was impossible to count them or to appreciate their grandeur fully.

Palermo was like a crossroads of all the cultures of the world. Its cuisines, languages, religions and races were so varied, its people so diverse, it was difficult to imagine that they could live happily side by side, but they seemed to. We spent several days gawping at the dark-skinned Muslims and their veiled women, enjoying food rich in spices and exotic herbs and vegetables, and listening to strange tongues such as Arabic, Greek, Hebrew and Berber. Some traders by the port had skin as black as charcoal and came from lands far to the south. They had brought spices so pungent their aroma hung in the air for miles around.

We were soon told that Count Roger had left Palermo to inspect his new castle at Mazara, an important port on the south-west tip of the island. Palermo's garrison commander advised us not to travel, as the route was treacherous and under threat from Muslim warlords still resisting the Norman presence. As Roger was not due to return to Palermo for several weeks, we decided to make the journey. We had the comfort of seven highly trained men and felt secure in being able either to defend ourselves or to outrun any adversary.

As we left Palermo behind and climbed steadily into the hills of the island's interior, our journey south began uneventfully. Lower down the hillsides were miles upon miles of citrus and olive groves and the vineyards that produced Sicily's highly regarded wine. Higher up, the land had been turned to arable use, and higher still it became pasture, providing grazing for goats and sheep.

The Muslim lords of Sicily had introduced elaborate irrigation systems and new farming techniques to the island and, as a consequence, its agriculture had blossomed.

We only travelled early in the morning and late in the afternoon, and spent the hours in the middle of the day sheltering under trees, as near as possible to the small rivers that cut through the hills. There were still thick forests on the highest slopes where the hum of insects was incessant and the peppery smell of pine overpowering.

The first settlement of any significance we came across was the hilltop Muslim fortress of Calatafimi, lying about forty miles south-west of Palermo. The Muslim lords and their garrison had abandoned the stronghold and its interior had been destroyed by fire, leaving only the peasants – Christian and Muslim – to tend their fields, as they had always done.

Nearby was the ruin of a large Roman temple and theatre on the hill of Segesta. The temple seemed to be complete, except for the roof, but its heavy columns provided excellent shade and we decided to camp there.

It was at the end of one of these long afternoons of rest that I found Adela sitting alone, high on the terraced seating of the theatre. I had been thinking about her strange existence, alone in a man's world, in a contrived marriage to a young man whom she regarded as a little brother and trying to succeed as a warrior when her ambition was well nigh impossible to achieve.

She looked forlorn, but smiled when she saw me.

'Lord Edgar, do you remember the Roman ruins on the Tyne?'

'I do – it was where the four of us decided to travel here.'

'Sire, the Romans must have been like the Normans – warriors, conquerors, builders – their empire was huge and we haven't yet got to the end of it. They achieved so much. I am nearly thirty years of age and my life has come to nothing.'

'Adela, please call me Edgar when we are alone. We have been comrades for three years now.'

'I cannot, sire, you are a royal prince, the heir to the throne of my homeland, and I am the daughter of a peasant.'

'That is of no consequence any more. My royalty doesn't mean much now. You, on the other hand, have achieved so much in life and become a knight in all but name.'

'Not really, my Lord, think of what Hereward and Torfida had done at our age.'

'You cannot compare yourself with others, especially two people like Hereward and Torfida. They were exceptional, and also propelled by a remarkable destiny whereby the circumstances of history took them on a unique journey. Your fate will be what it will be; there is a limit to how much you can change it.'

'I don't accept that, sire. If challenges and adventures won't come to me, I will seek them out until I find my calling.'

'And what do you think that is?'

'I don't know, but I know it's out there.'

For once, she failed to answer me formally but just turned away to watch the sun dip behind the hills beyond the temple. There were tears in her eyes. She suddenly seemed feminine and vulnerable. I sensed something I had never felt before: she was no longer the driven warrior; she looked lost, almost childlike. I wanted to help her with the immense burden she carried.

'Do you not have desires like other women, and want to have children?'

'Yes, but my desires and dreams are so damaged by my memories. I will confide in you because you are so kind, like an older brother, but please keep my confessions private, just between us.'

'Of course, you have my word.'

'I occasionally comfort myself, but never with a man, nor, despite the rumours, with a woman. I have to live with what happened to me in Bourne, and so I do.'

'And what of Sweyn? You share his tent . . .'

'Yes, but he never touches me – that would be wrong, he is like my younger brother.'

'You know I will always be here.'

'You are very kind, but a simple life is not for me. Since Ely, my dreams have become nightmares, my desires violated, my emotions corrupted; you don't want to share in any of that.'

'I have my own nightmares and burdens to live with. I didn't suffer the kind of ordeal that you had to endure, but I have to face the fact that I should have fought harder for my rightful inheritance and perhaps even died trying to claim the throne, like so many others who sacrificed themselves in my name.'

'I know that can't be easy for a man, but we all respect you for your wisdom and strength. You can always look to us for support – just as we, in turn, can rely on you.'

'Thank you, Adela.'

She wiped the tears from her eyes, kissed me on the cheek and hurried to her tent. As I watched her go, I thought about the burden she carried – the scars of an ordeal that would haunt her for the rest of her life – and was glad that I had at least let her know that I cared about her so deeply.

She was close to the Temple of Segesta, beginning to disappear into the long shadows of the setting sun, when the attack began. I saw her fall and heard her cry out, but there was no other sound or movement. I looked north and south towards the two sentries we had posted, but there was no sign or signal.

As I got to my feet, I saw our mounted assailants stream down the hillside towards us. Their recurved eastern bows were pulled taut as they unleashed volley after volley at our tents. Although the men were on horseback, their aim was lethally accurate. I saw at least three of our men fall before I had taken three paces. I shouted orders but I was too far away to be heard over the din of their horses' hooves clattering on the hard ground.

I ran towards the temple as quickly as I could. As I did so, Sweyn appeared from behind one of the columns and brought down a horseman with a sweep of his sword across the steed's fetlocks. He was on top of the rider before he could regain his feet and impaled him through the chest with his lance. Blood spewed out of the wound and the man spat and spluttered in his death throes as Sweyn put his foot on his chest to recover his lance. Just as he did so, looming above on horseback, two more adversaries were on top of him. The first he despatched easily by hurling his lance at him, impaling him through the right shoulder. The second one he brought to the ground by skewering his mount through its throat with his seax, then running him through with his sword as the horse rolled on top of him.

Sweyn then tried to run towards Adela, but he was hit on the back of his helmet by a Saracen's latt. He collapsed in a heap and did not move. I then saw Edwin and two of our men surrounded by cavalrymen, desperately trying to defend themselves before they disappeared behind a wall of men and horses.

By the time I reached the temple, sword drawn, all was still – the fight was over. I had passed Adela, but she did not move or utter a sound.

As I approached the horsemen, I heard an order issued which was obviously a call to sheathe weapons. I looked around and put my sword in its scabbard. I was surrounded by more than forty black-bearded, swarthy warriors, all clad in lamellar-mail hauberks not unlike Norman armour. Their clothing was black, as were the turbans they wore around their conical helmets. Their shields were smaller than the northern European designs and bore no emblems other than simple geometric patterns. Their horses were small, agile, grey beasts – very different from our heavy bay destriers.

'You must be lost, Christian.'

Their leader addressed me in good Norman French. I was trying to remain calm, but the speed and ferocity of the attack had left me shaking and very concerned for the welfare of my comrades. I had never encountered Saracens before, but I knew of their formidable reputation as soldiers.

'I am Edgar, a prince of England. We are travelling to Mazara to meet Roger Guiscard, Count of Sicily.'

'I am Ibn Hamed, Emir of Calatafimi. Have not the Normans conquered your land?'

'Yes, my inheritance has been taken from me.'

'So, why do you travel all the way to my homeland to visit the people who have taken your birthright?'

'I am no longer heir to a throne, but I am still a prince. Now I am in search of a life beyond England.'

The Saracen lord looked at me curiously.

'My comrades are in need of help. Will you permit me to see to them?'

'Of course. I am forgetting my manners; my physician will help you.'

He then barked some orders in Arabic and his men started to move quickly to assess the aftermath of the skirmish.

'We were driven from Calatafimi by Roger Guiscard three years ago. We now live in the hills, trying to defend our land. Like you, we have been dispossessed.'

Ibn Hamed's men then began to bring bodies towards us and lay them on the ground. Both sentries had had their throats cut and had been dead for some time, and three more of our men had been killed by the Saracens' arrows. Edwin, our sergeant-at-arms and our other cavalryman were all bloodied but able to walk. They were bound hand and foot, but did not appear to be badly injured.

'The two knights are alive. This one will have a sore head for a few days and the one over there will need the arrows removing and the wounds cauterizing. My physician will see to it.'

I checked that Sweyn was still breathing. He was very fortunate that he had managed to get his helmet on –

otherwise, the blow would have certainly killed him. I could hear him groaning and beginning to come round as I hurried over to Adela. She was moaning in pain, her eyes closed tightly, fighting against the discomfort. She had not been wearing her armour and an arrow had struck her in the back of her left thigh, just below her buttock, while another arrow, which had come from the same direction, had entered her chest just below her shoulder.

'Prince Edgar, the one in my leg has only caught flesh, but I think the other has shattered my collarbone.' She grimaced in agony. 'That one really hurts. Tell them to be especially careful.'

'Adela, your clothes will have to be cut from you.'

'I know. Let's get on with it.'

I turned to the Emir.

'This knight is a woman. Please tell your physician.'

'You have women in English armies!'

'Not usually, but this woman is an exceptional warrior.'

A debate then began between Ibn Hamed and his physician, which obviously had something to do with him treating a woman. Adela had also worked out what the debate was about.

'You do it, my Prince. You've seen a woman's body before.'

I managed to get Adela's leather jerkin off without causing her too much pain, but I had to cut away her smock and leggings with my seax, a process that exacerbated her pain greatly. To the horror of the physician, I also had to cut away her cotton undergarment, fragments of which had been taken into her wound by the arrowhead.

The whole of the left side of her body was now exposed, but Adela was much more concerned about her pain than her nakedness. She beckoned the physician to begin his work by turning her thigh towards him. He took the hint and got on with his work.

The physician summoned three men and, between us, we held her down. He gave her a thick piece of leather to bite on and then began to heave the arrow from its resting place. It had gone in deeply; its three triangular blades, barbed halfway down, caused much tearing of flesh as it came out. To the admiration of those attending her, Adela cried out only at the end, more out of relief than anguish.

The next indignity was that she had to open her legs to allow the physician to bind the wound, which was now gushing blood profusely. Again, she dealt with the embarrassment as something of little consequence and helped him put the bandage in place.

He called for a fire to be lit and two blades to be made hot, poured some kind of lotion on to the wound, covered it with a poultice, and then dressed it with a heavy cotton bandage. He was clearly a man who had dealt with countless battlefield injuries.

Her shoulder was a more complex challenge. The arrow looked like it had broken on impact and its tip was lodged behind her shattered collarbone. The physician gestured to me to turn her head away, and as I did so he immediately plunged his fingers into the long gash in her shoulder and started to retrieve the tip of the arrow and bits of bone. This time Adela spat out the lump of leather in her mouth and screamed in agony, cursing all of us and heaving and kicking to try to get free.

The pain must have been excruciating as the physician spent at least a minute making sure he had collected all the bone fragments with a pair of small bronze tongs before calling for the first hot dagger. Adela asked for the piece of leather as he signalled to me to push both sides of the wound together with my fingers. As I did so, he seared and sealed the gash with the hot blade. There is very little worse than the stench of burning flesh, but when it is someone you care for very much, it is almost unbearable. Adela tried not move this time, knowing that it was important to get the blade in the right place.

When he had finished, she had a huge black and bloodied wound the colour of burned pork running from the top of her shoulder to the beginnings of the mound of her breast. Once again, after the pain of the treatment, she had to face the indignity of the wound being dressed. She leaned forward so that the physician's bandage could be securely wrapped under and between her breasts and over her left shoulder, leaving her breasts exposed and taut either side of the dressing.

For the first time, she smiled – if only weakly.

'I chose this calling; I've lived with knights for three years . . . it's not the first time my tits have been on full view to a group of men.'

Her thigh was then unbandaged so that her leg wound could be cauterized by the second blade and re-strapped. Thankfully, the bleeding had stopped.

Finally, the ordeal was over. Adela looked deathly pale and was shaking, her teeth chattering. She thanked the physician, who touched her forehead and nodded his head in appreciation of her resolve. One of the Saracens brought her a blanket and placed it over her, smiling warmly as he did so.

The Emir dismounted and knelt down by Adela, placing his hand on her forehead.

'My physician says you must stay warm and eat and drink. You have lost a lot of blood and the pain will have exhausted you. Your body could react badly to everything that has happened to it. You must rest. We will prepare food, and the physician will make you a potion to help you sleep. It is fortunate that it is your left shoulder; the surgeon says the collarbone will never heal. You will be badly scarred and will carry the pain always. You are very brave, worthy of the brotherhood of knights.'

'Thank you, my Lord, and please thank your physician and your men.' Adela grasped my hand and pulled me towards her. 'Sire, where is Sweyn?'

'He is over there, coming round from a blow to the head; I think he will be fine.'

'I need a piss. Will you carry me to somewhere discreet?'

It was not the most polite request anyone had ever made of me but, under the circumstances, Adela's forthrightness brought a wide grin to my face.

By the time I brought Adela back to her tent, Ibn Hamed had ordered his men to release Edwin and the two survivors of our retinue, who rushed over to us.

The physician was now attending to Sweyn, wafting some foul-smelling substance under his nose to bring him round. After a while, it began to work and he started to ask questions.

'We are being held by Ibn Hamed, Lord of Calatafimi, who is in conflict with Count Roger,' I explained.

'Where is Adela, my Lord?'

'She is in your tent. She has been well taken care of but has suffered two bad arrow wounds, one to her leg and one to her shoulder.'

'I must go to her.'

'Of course, but let her sleep – she needs to rest, and so do you. Try to get some sleep also. Edwin, have the Moor's physician dress your wounds and those of our men.'

The Emir was talking to his men. He was a tall, dignified-looking man. His armour and weapons were more elaborately decorated than those of his men and he wore fine gold wristlets, gold rings on four of his fingers and a padded, pale-blue silk smock under his armour.

I was calmer now, but my anger was beginning to rise at the senseless violence of the attack.

'Ibn Hamed, we are visitors to this land. You have attacked us for no reason and killed five of my men. What is your explanation?'

'We are at war with the Normans. My family has ruled here for many generations, but now our home has been destroyed and many have been killed, including two of my sons. You look like Normans, act like them and speak like them. Even if, as you say, you are English, you are allied to the Normans and so are still our enemy.'

'We are nobody's enemy; we are knights in search of a new future away from our homeland. We too have lost many who are close to us. Tens of thousands of our people have died.'

'I am sorry for your losses, both here and in your homeland. If you will accept, you may now enjoy our hospitality until your knights are healed.'

'I accept, with gratitude. Adela will need time to recover. She cannot travel easily with those wounds, and there is the danger of infection.'

'I think infection is probable. My physician is highly trained, but even he doesn't know how to stop it – although he does know how to treat it. Tell me, why does the girl choose to be a knight?'

'It is a long story, but there is no doubt she is a warrior.'

'Has she no shame, living with men, exposing her body? In Islam, our holy book, the Quran, forbids it.'

'Our Bible certainly doesn't encourage women to fight, or to be naked! Adela is very unusual – but, I can assure you, she is worthy of your respect.'

'And the boy, the one who fights so well? He killed three of my finest soldiers, veterans of many years' service.'

'Sweyn is an exceptional knight. He is highly disciplined and motivated, with the physique of a hunting dog. In a fight he is quicker and more agile than anyone I've ever seen.'

'I look forward to getting to know them. Come, let us bury your dead; my imam will read over them. When the young woman is rested, we can travel to my camp. There you can meet my family and the survivors of our community.'

13. Mos Militum

The Emir's camp was high in the heavily wooded Sicilian hills. It was a difficult ride for Adela, who could only manage it side-saddle on a sturdy Moorish saddle cushioned with sacks of straw and with heavy strapping to her shoulder. Ibn Hamed's men showed enormous respect for her. They treated her like royal princess and helped her on and off her horse as if she were a piece of delicate pottery.

Sweyn watched over her like a hawk, still wary of our Muslim hosts. I now felt more like a guest than a captor, but Sweyn's warrior instincts led him to be much more cautious. Edwin was also chary and had told our men to be vigilant – not that there was much we could have done, had the Saracens decided to do something untoward.

The camp, well hidden in a clearing in the forest, was home to about 250 people. They had clearly left their homes in a hurry, bringing with them only what they could carry. Although ordered and clean, the settlement was a ramshackle assortment of lean-to shelters, canvas tents and temporary wooden huts with palm roofs.

Children ran around wearing brightly coloured baggy trousers and shirts while their mothers, grandmothers and some older men sat around in groups preparing food, doing their chores or chatting idly.

At the top end of the camp, standing a little apart and surrounded by the neat rows of his soldiers' bivouacs, was the large tent of the Emir. All men of military age appeared to be soldiers, and all were heavily armed, armoured and resolute. We were invited to make camp close to the Emir, and that night a feast was given to welcome us.

From that day forward, the hospitality shown to us was unprecedented. Sweyn and Adela became increasingly friendly with the young knights, and any anger about the ferocious welcome we had been given to Sicily was mollified by our acceptance of the simple fact that it was an understandable deduction on the Emir's part that we were a Norman patrol in hostile territory and therefore fair game.

Sweyn became effusive in his praise of our hosts.

'Most of Ibn Hamed's knights adhere to the Mos Militum; they put courage, loyalty and honour above all things. They are fine soldiers and good men and accept Adela as an equal. Some of the older men do not accept the code and reject Adela, but they are few in number.'

I also liked and respected the Muslims, but advised caution.

'We must be careful. We came here to join the campaigns of Count Roger. Now we are camped with his enemy.'

'I know, my Lord, but it is hard to tell whether we are captives or guests.'

'We are being well treated, but we must be clear about the fact that we were attacked by Ibn Hamed's men and we are his prisoners.'

Edwin agreed.

'Be careful, Sweyn. All seems at ease up here in the mountains, but these people are at war with the Normans – and, sooner or later, Count Roger will hunt them down.'

'I understand, but I want to carry on training with them and, when she's fit, so does Adela. Sire, do we have your permission?'

'Very well – but remember, the same men you are becoming friendly with may one day oppose you in deadly combat.'

I felt increasingly ill at ease with the situation as time passed. The Emir's hospitality seemed to be limitless, but Edwin and I felt we were abusing it, knowing that soon we must ask for permission to continue our journey to meet Count Roger.

Our honeymoon with Ibn Hamed ended when Adela was strong enough to travel.

She had made a good recovery and, although she still walked with a limp and moved her shoulder warily, she was able to ride in moderate comfort and mount and dismount from her horse without help. I was not looking forward to my conversation with the Emir, a proud and forthright leader of his people and a generous and sincere host. I had grown to respect and like him.

'My Lord Emir, I know that in truth we are your prisoners here, but I must ask you for permission to move on. Your hospitality has been overwhelming and we will always be grateful to you.'

'Prince Edgar, you are free to go whenever you wish. I would just ask for one act of kindness from you.'

'Of course. It is the least I could do.'

'I want to hold you to ransom.'

'At what price?'

'A parlay with Count Roger.'

'And your objective in the parlay?'

'To negotiate safe passage to the south. There are several of my Saracen brothers with much stronger defences in the south – at Enna in the mountains, and at Noto on the coast. If we can get there, we have a much better chance of resisting the Normans.'

'Have you not considered submitting to Count Roger? I hear he is a man worthy of respect.'

'I hear that also, but when he first came here with his brother, Robert Guiscard, they were dark days. Many were killed and Robert showed no mercy to anyone. My people are terrified of the Normans, and I am reluctant to trust Count Roger until I am convinced he is not like his brother.'

'I can understand that. I will stay here as your hostage. I appreciate that you had no need to ask me, but could have just imposed your will. Your gesture is a reflection of your genuine chivalry. When the time comes, if you will permit it, I will happily lend my voice to your request for safe passage.'

'Thank you. I will make preparations for an escort to take your retinue down the mountain to join the road to Mazara.'

When I told the others about the Emir's plan, they were reluctant to go and suggested that we send the sergeant-at-arms and the surviving cavalryman.

I pointed out that the Emir's request would come better from a knight and that they would be able to emphasize to Count Roger that we had been well treated and that the Emir was an honourable man.

After some discussion, it was agreed that Edwin would travel to Mazara with our men and that Sweyn and Adela would stay with me.

Adela had now begun her training with Sweyn and Ibn Hamed's knights. They had both become firm friends with the Emir's men and it was fascinating to watch them develop their skills in the various Saracen practice routines. One particular skill they started to master – an expertise unknown in the armies of Europe – was the use of the recurved eastern bow, a powerful, accurate weapon at close quarters and small enough to be used on horseback.

Sweyn ultimately became so proficient with the bow at a gallop that he could outscore all the Saracen knights. Adela did not yet have the strength on her left side to steady the bow, but she began to impress everyone with the speed of her footwork and her dexterity with a sword in duels. She adapted well to the curved sabre of the Saracens and soon exchanged her straight European blade for the slashing Arab scimitar. Even with her left hand in a sling to protect her shoulder, and hampered by the weakness in her left leg, she was still able to practise duelling with the Emir's best swordsmen.

Hassan Taleb, the Emir's finest warrior, took Sweyn and Adela under his wing and helped them hone their skills.

It was a particular delight to see him tutor Adela in the art of the sword: advance and retreat, thrust and parry, strike and deflect. Their movements flowed with a poise that belied their purpose – they looked more like the elegant moves of a graceful dance than the crude paces of a ruthless slaying. She was only ever outdone in a routine against far stronger men, or against the finest swordsmen – and then only after putting up a ferocious defence.

It was obvious that Hassan had designs on Adela. Clearly

a man used to getting what he wanted, he was big and powerful, charming and chivalrous. He flirted with her, fussed over her and fed her ego. Sweyn became less and less happy with the overt attention.

A clash seemed imminent, so I decided to raise the subject with him.

'Will you speak to Adela about Hassan?'

'I already have, my Lord. She knows it is a problem, but doesn't know how to deal with it. Adela told me that she had confided in you about us . . . and about her situation.'

'Do you mind that?'

'No, she needs someone to speak to besides me. She sees me as her younger brother and you as her elder brother.'

'That makes me your elder brother also.'

'I know, sire. So, may I also share something with you?'

'Yes, you may . . . as long as you stop calling me "sire" while doing so.'

'Adela has told me that she finds Hassan attractive, but only in outline. When her thoughts go beyond the superficial, she sees only Ogier the Breton, the monster from Bourne, and all the memories from those terrible days come flooding back. It is a curse that denies her so much.'

'I fear it is a burden she will carry all her life.'

'I want to help her.'

'We all want to help her.'

'But I am her husband.'

'In name only.'

'Yes . . . but the truth is, I yearn for her. I lie next to her night after night and all I want to do is comfort her, make love to her and make her memories go away.'

I suddenly realized that in the midst of all my anguish

about Adela's predicament I had ignored Sweyn and his inner thoughts and anxieties. Quite apart from his own childhood traumas, he was now telling me that he had nightly suffered the purgatory of lying next to a woman who was, in the eyes of the outside world, his wife but who treated him like a brother in a marriage of convenience when, all along, he desired her with a hunger.

'It is an impossible situation for both of you. Can you not find comfort with someone else? Adela would understand and give you her blessing.'

'She would, and she encourages me all the time. But I have two problems. How do I find someone in this nomadic life we lead? And, more importantly, no other woman comes close to Adela in my mind. All I want is her.'

'Have you told her this?'

'No, I cannot. If she knew, it would ruin everything. She would either feel sorry for me and let me take her out of pity, or she would leave me in order to prevent the agony continuing. I couldn't bear either.'

'I am so sorry. How can I help?'

'You cannot. It is my cross to bear.'

Sweyn walked away despondently, leaving me to reflect on two lives which, like so many others, had been devastated by the savagery of the Norman Conquest of our homeland.

The inevitable confrontation with Hassan Taleb took place a few days later. Adela had been practising her swordplay with him when she slipped and fell to the ground, hurting her damaged shoulder in the process. He had helped to her feet, but lingered too long and too suggestively with his arm around her. She had pulled away angrily and marched from the practice ground, muttering to herself and shaking her head.

Sweyn arrived moments later. Adela refused to say what had happened, but Sweyn realized immediately who had caused her distress.

His sword was drawn within two paces as he attacked the Saracen with lightning speed. Hassan Taleb was an outstanding swordsman and parried all Sweyn's blows with great dexterity, but Sweyn was relentless, driven by a burning fury.

I remembered what he had said to me when we first met – that anger in battle is a powerful ally.

Hassan began to look concerned, realizing that he was facing a man who not only had the fortitude to kill him, but also the ability.

Sweyn began to get the upper hand and Hassan Taleb started to tire. He took a gash to his forearm, and only his heavily mailed hauberk prevented Sweyn's blade from inflicting a deep wound to his chest. Even so, blood began to seep into his cotton tunic.

I tried to put an end to it and shouted at Sweyn to stop, but to no avail.

He was deaf to all pleading. Only when Adela reappeared and walked in between them did they relent. She started to push Sweyn away, repeating over and over again that the incident was a misunderstanding and unimportant.

I rushed to help her.

By now the Emir had appeared, beside himself with anger. When he heard what had happened, he ordered that Hassan Taleb be restrained to await a trail by his fellow knights. However, before any of his men could detain him,

Hassan lunged at Sweyn with his sabre. Alert to the attack, Sweyn pushed us away, ducked under the Saracen's wild swing and plunged his seax into Hassan's neck. The blade entered his throat on the left and exited next to his spine on the right. Both men were motionless for a second and the onlookers frozen in shock before Sweyn put his left hand on the Saracen's shoulder and wrenched out his weapon. Blood spurted everywhere and splashed to the ground.

Death came almost instantly for the Saracen but, before it did, he was able to lift his hands to his throat in a futile attempt to stem the cascade and momentarily stare at Sweyn with wide-eyed incredulity. He then toppled to the ground and was dead within moments.

It was an astonishingly quick reaction from Sweyn, the adroitness and accuracy of which had made all who saw it gasp.

After ordering the removal of the body, the Emir spoke to him.

'I apologize for the behaviour of a man I thought was my most noble knight. He has brought shame to me and my community. You have done me a great service by killing him; he deserved to die.'

'My Lord, he was but one man. You and your people have been more than generous and courteous.'

'I am still in your debt, young knight. How may I repay you?'

'Sire, the debt is easily paid. Allow Adela and me to join your order of knights so that we may follow the Mos Militum, as they do.'

'It is a small price to pay. We would be honoured to have you. I have not heard of a woman ever being made a knight before, in either Islam or Christianity, but as I answer to no one here, I will permit it, if my knights will agree.'

I did not want to embarrass Sweyn or upset the Emir, but I was tempted to intervene. I felt certain that membership of a Saracen order of knights would create problems if and when we ever made contact with Count Roger.

The next day, with much fanfare and flourish in front of the entire community, Adela and Sweyn were dubbed as knights by Ibn Hamed.

They swore to uphold the principles of the Mos Militum.

Honour
Truthfulness
Courage
Martial prowess
Pride in the face of superiors
Humility in the face of inferiors
Protection of the weak: women, children and the
  old

A few of the Emir's knights had been opposed to Adela becoming one of their number, but most had agreed readily. Adela and Sweyn both knelt in front of the Emir as he gave them short, curved jewel-encrusted Arabian daggers. He then placed his hand on their heads in turn and blessed them.

Several sheep and goats were slaughtered, and tables were heaped high with fowl and game. Deep baskets of bread, fruit and vegetables were prepared for a grand feast of celebration, the only disappointing part being the lack of alcohol – an indulgence strictly forbidden by Islam.

There were drums and horns to accompany the knights as they performed the precise choreography of their ritual warriors' dance. The women wailed encouragement as the children copied the adults, and the entire community shared in the joy of the occasion.

Adela and Sweyn sat with broad smiles on their faces, as did I. We were all charmed by the warmth of our Muslim hosts.

Edwin returned a few days later, not just with an answer from Count Roger, but with the Count in person. In a remarkable gesture of goodwill, and with considerable fortitude, Count Roger of Sicily rode into Ibn Hamed's camp with only Edwin and our two men for company.

His appearance – he was tall and fair and elegantly dressed, with fine weapons and armour – suggested he was a man of high status. When he announced himself to the Emir, there was a stunned silence.

'My noble Lord, Ibn Hamed, Emir of Calatafimi, I am Roger, Count of Sicily. I have come to offer myself as a hostage in place of Edgar, Prince of England.'

The Emir was dumbfounded, as was I. If Roger had prepared a devious trap, I could not see how it could be sprung. Ibn Hamed stood and walked up to the Count to offer his hand. I stepped up and did the same and introduced myself.

I could sense that Ibn Hamed was at a loss to know how to react, but eventually he replied.

'Courtesy demands that I welcome you to my camp, but

I must confess to you, I am taken aback by your presence here. You are either a very brave man, or a very foolish one.'

The Count, a man who must have been in his mid-fifties but who looked fit and lean, spoke calmly and with great self-confidence.

'I hope I am not foolhardy, and it does not require an act of bravery to seek the ear of an honourable man like you.'

'If I were to cut you down here and now, it would not be without considerable justification, given that you have killed many of my people and destroyed our homes, leaving us to skulk in the woods like frightened animals.'

'That was war, Ibn Hamed, but now we have peace. My family came here many years ago with a mission to remove southern Italy from the influence of the Emperor of Constantinople and the Grand Caliph of Cairo. We have achieved that ambition; now we want peace.'

'Peace on your terms.'

'Yes, of course. But my terms are very different from my brother's. He has returned to Apulia and rules there with an iron fist. My rule in Sicily is with a much more gentle touch.'

'But this will be the touch of a Christian, with no tolerance for men of my faith.'

'Not so. I have learned a good deal about the ways of Islam over the years – how Christians are allowed to worship openly in the Muslim world, and how you tolerate people of many colours and creeds. This is how it will be in Sicily.'

'Those are fine words, but your past deeds still leave me and my people burning with anger.'

'I understand. That is why I came here alone, to convince you of my sincerity. Except for a few enclaves in the south, all the Muslim and Greek people of Sicily have accepted my lordship. All our faiths are protected – Christians both Roman and Orthodox, Jews and Muslims – we trade together, our communities mix together and everyone pays the same taxes.'

'That all sounds very laudable, but at the moment we have only our faith. We have nothing to trade with, possess no silver to pay taxes and are barely able to feed ourselves.'

'I offer you two choices. I will give you and your people safe passage to one of the emirates in the south, as you requested, or you can return to Calatafimi and I will restore your lands and titles and help you rebuild everything that has been destroyed.'

'And in return?'

'My freedom and that of Prince Edgar and his English knights. In due course, when you are able, I will levy you for knightly service and taxes like any other lord. I will relish the service of your knights, as I know them to be fine warriors and honourable men.'

I stood, open-mouthed in amazement at what I had just heard. Roger of Sicily was everything that had been said about him and more.

'Think about my offer, talk to your people. I will return to my escort in the valley and come back tomorrow for your answer.'

'Very well, you will have my answer tomorrow.'

The Emir immediately called his senior knights, household and imams together to discuss the Count's offer.

Before they gathered, he asked me for my opinion.

'There is no doubting his sincerity. Edwin led him to

your camp only because he chose to come alone. That is the act of a man of great resolve. Roger's reputation for decency and tolerance is well known, and what we saw in Palermo confirms everything he said. The place is alive with the bustle of commerce and its people are a rich medley of colours, creeds and tongues.'

'That is how it was under Muslim rule.'

'Then you will be relieved to know that nothing has changed.'

That evening, the four of us had dinner alone, but within earshot of the long and heated debate in the Emir's tent.

I took the opportunity to talk to Sweyn and Adela about their decision to join the Emir's order of knights.

'Before the Count's remarkable appearance, I had doubted the wisdom of your decision to join the order of knights. I thought it might cause us problems with our Norman hosts. Now, I don't suppose it matters. In fact, it may stand us in good stead. Edwin, perhaps you and I should join too?'

'Why not? They have good discipline and fine principles –'

'As does Count Roger.' Adela did not offer praise too readily, especially of Normans. 'That was one of the most audacious things I have ever witnessed. Hereward was right about him, he is remarkable. When he returns tomorrow, I want to meet him.'

'So do I.' Sweyn was also fulsome in his praise. 'Any man who can do what Count Roger did here today is worthy of anyone's respect. It's a shame there aren't more Normans like him.'

The debate lasted late into the night, but eventually those of the Emir's retinue who wanted to submit to Count Roger and return to their homes in Calatafimi held sway.

Some of the younger knights refused to accept the decision, and Ibn Hamed gave them permission to leave to join their Muslim brothers in the hilltop fortress at Enna.

When Count Roger arrived, far earlier than expected, his demeanour was considerably less calm than it had been the previous day.

'Ibn Hamed, Emir of Calatafimi, you and your people are welcome in this new Sicily, a land where all can live in peace and share in a new prosperity. When I return to Palermo, I will send masons, carpenters and blacksmiths to help you rebuild Calatafimi. But now you must forgive me, for I must make haste. I have just received news that a large Byzantine fleet is anchored off the coast at Mazara and that several themes have already disembarked.'

'Go, Count Roger, you must organize your forces.'

Count Roger's news was alarming, but it offered us an ideal opportunity to make a mark with the Norman lord of Sicily. I did not hesitate in seizing it.

'My Lord, Emir, with your permission, we would like to join Count Roger in meeting the Byzantines.'

'Of course. We will join him also. We have no love of Byzantines either, and if we are to accept the Count as our sovereign Lord here in Sicily then we must fight at his side.'

Count Roger was grateful for the support.

'Thank you. When this is done, you will all be my guests in Palermo, where you can meet the other lords and emirs of my new Sicily. And now, my Lord Emir, I must hurry.'

As Roger rode off at a gallop, I turned to Ibn Hamed.

'It will have cost Count Roger several hours to return here this morning. He could have sent one of his knights to get your answer, but he must have wanted to show you how sincere he is.'

'I know, and I think we have made the right decision. I like the sound of this new Sicily. But we must hurry – Byzantine themes can be formidable, and the Count is going to need our help.'

The Emir gave instructions to his stewards to break camp, and for the community to return to Calatafimi to begin its new life. Within the hour, he was leading us down to the valley and the road to Mazara.

His men were a mixed bunch. The elite Faris were freemen and led small squadrons of Mamluks, who had begun life as slaves but had trained as professional soldiers. Most were Arabs, with their ancestral roots in Egypt, but there were also small numbers of Berbers, Kurds, Turks and Christian Armenians among their ranks.

The Turks and Kurds came from families with military traditions going back many generations, while the Armenians, highly adept cavalrymen, chose to live in a Muslim community because their belief that Christ had only divine form, not a parallel human form, made them heretics to both Roman and Orthodox Christians.

The Emir also had Nubian servants, both male and female – very tall, dark people from beyond the great southern desert – and a Bedouin personal bodyguard, a fierce-looking man who rarely spoke and whose people lived in the deserts of Arabia.

The four of us, English knights many miles from home and about to join forces with a Norman lord against a Byzantine army, added a little northern flavour to the Emir's exotic blend of warriors. We numbered only a few more than fifty, but all were professional soldiers of the highest calibre – men who would be very welcome among the Count's army.

And there was Adela, of course, now so easily included as one of the 'men'. I watched her and Sweyn riding together, both bright-eyed and eager for the battle to come. There seemed to be no obvious way to resolve their respective dilemmas – patience seemed to be the only answer. Perhaps time and future circumstances would heal their wounds or offer a solution.

14. Battle of Mazara

By the time we reached the Bay of Mazara, Count Roger's army had already launched its attack on the Byzantines. It was a chaotic scene. Although it was late September, it was still hot and dry and great clouds of dust billowed in the wake of horses, men and supply carts moving rapidly across the battlefield.

Not even the air out to sea was clear. The Byzantine triremes were belching volley after volley of burning cauldrons. Only later did I hear that it was called 'Greek fire' – a lethal weapon, the ingredients of which were a closely guarded secret, known only to the Emperor and his senior commanders.

Thick smoke made the whole sky above the ships as black as Hades. Where the cauldrons landed, infernos of flaming pitch raged. Men and horses were hurled into the air or knocked down like skittles, covered in burning pitch, destined to meet a grisly fate consumed by fire.

Ibn Hamed directed us to the centre of the action.

'Quickly, more and more are coming ashore. There are Thracian and Macedonian themes and, over there, Greeks – this is the elite of the Byzantine army.'

We soon reached Count Roger at his command post on a promontory just back from the bay. He lost no time in delivering his battle strategy.

'It is good to see you and your men. We have a few

problems; if we let too many more get ashore, we'll be overrun. My archers are trying to stop any more ships from coming in, and my cavalry are driving a wedge into their beachhead, but they must have five hundred men ashore already. I need you to support the cavalry, try to split their force in two, and then aim to cut off their retreat to the sea.'

We rode down into the fray and were soon in the midst of vicious hand-to-hand fighting. The sheer weight of numbers and the mass of bodies, both living and dead, made progress slow. I looked over to check on my comrades – all were flailing and hacking in a sea of carnage, benefitting from their hours of training. With her helmet down, Adela looked no different to anybody else and was holding her own. Edwin and Sweyn were close to her, each watching her flank, while Sweyn was easily distinguished by the speed of his blade and agility in the saddle.

Ibn Hamed called him over.

'Look, to the left, the two ships making for shore – the Varangian Guard, the Emperor's personal guard – there must be two hundred of them. Ride to the Count, tell him to direct his archers at them; they mustn't be allowed to come ashore.'

With Adela and Edwin in his wake, Sweyn rode like the wind to deliver his message, while Ibn Hamed and I protected our position. I was shocked by what I saw as the ships carrying the Varangian Guard drew closer.

'They look like Englishmen! They're carrying shields and axes like housecarls!'

'Many of them are. Norse, Danes, Balts, English; they are highly paid mercenaries, the best infantry you'll ever see. The one at the prow of the first ship, giving orders in the scarlet cloak, that's the Captain of the Guard, the finest soldier in your world and mine.'

He looked English too. I could see long blond hair trailing beneath his helmet, and the distinctive decorated circular shield of a housecarl. Then he fell backwards, struck by an arrow which pierced his hauberk at the top of his shoulder, and then by another which hit him in the chest.

'That is a piece of very good fortune. The Captain of the Varangians leads the army unless the Emperor is present. We have just killed their general.'

Ibn Hamed was smiling broadly. Arrows were now falling on the Varangians like hailstones and the order was issued for sails to be unfurled and for the oarsmen to row the Byzantine ships away. As soon as the men on the beaches saw their fleet turn seawards, there was panic and a mass retreat towards the ships. Roger immediately ordered his own cavalry squadrons and all his reserves to attack.

The Norman destriers flowed into the bay like a tidal bore. It was a mass slaughter. The Byzantines had no defence and a stark choice: stand and fight in a hopeless final redoubt, or discard their weapons and armour and try to swim to the ships.

Most chose the latter option. Many were drowned, and the rest were killed by the arrows and quarrels from the unremitting onslaught unleashed by the Norman archers and bowmen.

Those who chose to stand their ground fared little better. Initially, the separate themes formed their own redoubts, the Macedonians distinctive with their black-plumed helmets, the Thracians in their blue tunics and the Greeks wielding small, highly decorated shields. But soon, as numbers diminished rapidly, the three redoubts became one.

After about an hour, with Byzantine numbers reduced to under a hundred, Count Roger ordered his men to cease the attack. He then stood high in his stirrups and spoke to his foes in fluent Greek.

'I offer you quarter. Lay down your weapons, and you will not be harmed or enslaved. You are brave men, the most noble of a great army; you are free to find passage to your homes or to stay here in Sicily and make new lives. All are welcome here: Muslims, Christians, Jews. Our taxes are fair and our people are happy. You are even free to join my own army – we will gladly have you, if you will swear your allegiance to Sicily. It is your choice.'

In the many battles these men had fought, such generous terms were rare – especially the offer to continue their lives as professional soldiers. There was a little muttering in the Byzantine ranks, but it did not take long for swords and shields to be thrown on to the ground to the sound of widespread cheering from Count Roger's forces.

The Count ordered that the Byzantines be fed and quartered and rode among them to greet as many as he could. The effect he had on them was charismatic, and many rushed forward to kneel before him and kiss his ring. I reflected that we had been very fortunate so far in Sicily; we had met two remarkable men and found a haven of just and benign rule.

The Count soon made his way over to us.

'Ibn Hamed, I owe you a great debt. Your eagle eye in

spotting the Varangians and alerting me turned the battle.'

'My Lord Count, it is your archers you should thank. Hitting their Captain, probably killing the most important warrior in the empire, won the day for you. Their accuracy and speed of shot is a credit to your training and discipline.'

'Thank you, it is good to have the Emir of Calatafimi at my side; long may it last. Tonight we will celebrate our victory and toast our future together. I will tap a butt of the finest Sicilian wine and, for you, I will prepare a deliciously sweet punch made from my own orchards in Palermo. But first, I want to meet the English knights who carried the vital message. Prince Edgar, will you oblige?'

'I will be delighted. Edwin of Glastonbury you have already met, one of England's most senior knights. This is Sweyn of Bourne and his wife, who is also a knight in her own right, Adela of Bourne.'

'Edwin told me a good deal about you as we rode to Ibn Hamed's camp together, but I want to hear much more – especially about Hereward Great Axe, as he was known to me.'

Adela responded to the Count's invitation.

'Then we can exchange stories, my Lord. We are keen to learn about Hereward's time with you in Melfi and your early campaigns here in Sicily.'

Roger looked at Adela, almost in awe.

'Agreed – and you can also tell me more about you and Sweyn. You have my greatest respect to have become a Knight of Islam. Perhaps, one day, the Christian orders of knighthood will accept women into their ranks.'

'Only if we deserve it, my Lord; we do not crave charity.'

'Nor should you, Adela. I believe all people should make progress by merit. It has been the story of my family; my father was the modest lord of a small estate in Normandy, now we rule the whole of Italy south of the Tiber.'

Sweyn then spoke to the Count. 'My Lord, Hereward taught us that if a man or woman has suitable merit, there should be no limit to what they can achieve. That is why Adela and I follow the Mos Militum, a code that stresses talent above privilege and honour beyond self-interest.'

'I like the new code; I encourage it among my knights and follow it myself. Chivalry is the measure of a man. When we celebrate our victory, we will sing the songs of the troubadours about the love between a knight and his lady . . . in your case, of course, between a knight and a fellow knight.'

Little did the Count know that his well-meaning attempt at gentle humour was so wide of the mark as to be hurtful. I looked at Adela and Sweyn, who gave no hint of any discomfort. They had become very practised at disguising the true nature of their relationship.

There was a long and raucous celebration in Mazara that night, and several more over the following days in Palermo.

Count Roger invited all the lords of the various cities of Sicily, as well as its major landholders, merchants and knights, to a series of feasts to celebrate the submission of Ibn Hamed, the last Saracen to resist in the north and west of the island.

Desperate to spread the word about the beneficence of

the new Sicily, the feasts and attendant performances were as lavish as anything I had ever seen.

There was an endless supply of the finest food and drink, numerous tumblers, jugglers and clowns, and songs – the highlight of every evening – composed by William, Duke of Aquitaine, the finest troubadour of the day. Adela, Sweyn and Edwin knew the songs well because their home at St Cirq Lapopie, near Cahors, was at the heart of the lyrical tradition of the troubadour.

During the ensuing winter and spring we filled our time helping Count Roger build and train his army and oversee the building of new fortifications and defences. By the summer of 1085, much of Calatafimi had been rebuilt and the Emir reciprocated the Count's frequent hospitality by hosting a celebration of the progress.

Ibn Hamed strove to emulate the feasts of Palermo and even included in the fare wild pig and the best Sicilian wine for his guests – although, in the case of the pork, he had to ask some of his Christian Armenians to prepare and roast the meat.

One of the principal guests was Themistius, a strategoi of the Thracian theme of the army of Byzantium, the most senior man captured at the Battle of Mazara the previous year. He had chosen to settle close to Calatafimi, and Ibn Hamed had given him land in exchange for service as the leader of his knights, a vacancy that had been created when Sweyn put an end to Hassan Taleb's swaggering ways.

Themistius typified the Count's vision for Sicily. His family had been killed in the Byzantine wars against Alp

Arslan, Sultan of the Seljuk Turks, in the 1070s. The mighty empire of Byzantium, the surviving link back to the glory of Ancient Rome, was in chaos, and Norman Sicily offered a new beginning in a land of peace and plenty.

Men like Themistius were arriving from all over Europe, the Levant and North Africa to find a new beginning, and the island's prosperity thrived. We became part of that and often thought about making it our permanent home.

After the main feast was over, Count Roger, the Emir and a few senior guests sat on the terrace of the Emir's new palace, a fine stone fortress overlooking the valley, enjoying the cool evening air. Roger was slightly drunk, but sobered up quickly when Themistius began to speak about the dark days he saw looming for all of us.

'Although Byzantium is in chaos, the new Emperor, Alexius Comnenus, is making the army strong again. When we were humiliated at Manzikert by Alp Arslan, I thought Constantinople would fall, but we survived – just. Alexius wants to keep the Muslims to the south at bay. He sees his natural allies in Rome and the countries of northern Europe – a Christian alliance, as in Spain, to fight the Muslim Saracens. This could be very dangerous – a war about God.'

Count Roger was by now listening intently.

'You exaggerate, Themistius. Men fight for land and money, not for their gods.'

Ibn Hamed was concerned.

'There is much talk in the Muslim world about the one true faith and what should be done with those who don't follow the ways of Islam. Some are tolerant and see Christians as followers of the same God, but a different prophet; others see them as dangerous infidels, who should be put to the sword.'

I offered my own view.

'It is the same in the Christian world; we have many who think it a stain on God's name that Jerusalem is ruled by the Saracens.'

Roger had heard enough and was keen to return to the less vexing subject of the merits of Sicily's fine wines.

'Gentleman, we have peace and prosperity here. Constantinople and Jerusalem are a long way away; let us enjoy what we have. A toast, to my good friend Ibn Hamed and his people in their new home here at Calatafimi.'

Although the subject was not raised again, I thought about Themistius's warning many times and, on each occasion, the prospect seemed more and more disturbing.

As time passed, I began to wonder whether this threat of war between Christian and Muslim would be the test that destiny had prepared for me and my friends – just as the arrival of the Normans had been the anvil on which the lives of Hereward and his followers had been forged.

15. Mahnoor

Shortly after we returned to Palermo, Sweyn came to see me with Edwin. He was ill at ease.

'I have to leave Sicily.'

'I thought you and Adela were happy here.'

'She is – and, in a way, so am I. But I am the one who has to leave, not Adela. It is a terrible dilemma. The four of us have been together so long and I love Adela very much, but our relationship will never be what I want it to be.'

I looked at Edwin; he shook his head.

'I have met someone here, and she has helped break the spell of Adela. She is very beautiful, the daughter of a Muslim trader here in Palermo – you know him, Suleiman of Alexandria.'

'And I know his daughter, the very beautiful Mahnoor.'

'Yes, it means "light of the moon".'

'Have you told Adela?'

'Yes, she's very happy for me. We talked many times about me finding a woman who would return my love.'

Edwin got to his feet and started to pace up and down.

'I don't suppose you can take her as a mistress? You are, after all, already married.'

'Not in the eyes of God, or of any sane person. My marriage to Adela has never been consummated; it is not a true marriage.'

'What have you said to Mahnoor?'

'I told her about my situation as soon as I realized I had feelings for her – to do anything else would have been wrong. She understands and will stand by me.'

'What about her father? He might not be so understanding.'

'He doesn't know.'

Edwin started to pace a little faster, and I began to realize how difficult this situation could become.

'How did you meet? Her father hardly ever lets her leave the house. And when she does, she is closely guarded.'

'I saw her at one of the Count's banquets. I couldn't take my eyes off her . . . and, eventually, she smiled at me. Shortly afterwards, a pigeon was delivered to me by one of her servants. It was a homing bird with a message in a small capsule tied to its leg. We communicated like that for days. Now we meet when she goes to the markets. Her guardians don't go inside the shops, and I wait in the garden of the silk merchant. He's very discreet.'

'Muslim fathers don't take too kindly to young knights seducing their daughters – especially if they are already married.'

'I have not seduced Mahnoor; I wouldn't touch her until we are married.'

I was now as anxious as Edwin – there were, to say the least, a few issues to resolve.

'So, how do you propose to proceed?'

'I have agonized over it and talked it through with Adela, but I need you and Edwin to help me also – even if it means we are no longer brothers-in-arms. I think I have only two options; both are selfish, but I must take this opportunity to spend my life with the girl I love. I could either elope with Mahnoor and return to St Cirq Lapopie and raise a family, or brazen it out here and ask Count Roger to intercede with the Bishop to ask him to annul my marriage.'

'Both options bring great shame to Adela. In both cases, she will become the poor, abandoned spinster.'

'I know – and she knows it too. Her response was typical of her; she said she had endured far worse in life, and may yet again.'

'Will Mahnoor risk an elopement? Her father is very rich, she would lose her inheritance and have to face what I imagine would be a fearful wrath.'

'She said she would come with me, and her father would never find us in the forests of Aquitaine. We will live well, I'm not without funds; I have a share in St Cirq Lapopie and, at the last count, I'm not exactly a pauper.'

'What of your ambition to lead the life of a warrior?'

'That is my preferred option – to stay here, keep our Brotherhood together and seek more adventures.'

'I think we need to speak to Adela.'

'She is outside.'

'Tell her to come in.'

Adela also looked uncomfortable. 'I am sorry to continue to be a burden to you all.'

'Nonsense, you are no such thing. What has happened has happened, and now we must deal with it in whichever way is best for our Brotherhood. What do you think we should do?'

'I am delighted for Sweyn. I hoped it would happen a

long time ago. What he did for me in Durham was a wonderful esture, but the situation couldn't continue – especially when I discovered his true feelings for me. For him, it turned our marriage into a Purgatory, but now it's over. Mahnoor is very sweet and a perfect match for him. When Sweyn told her about the true nature of our marriage, she asked to meet me at the silk merchant's. She was in tears and said how relieved she was, because her feelings for Sweyn had made her feel so guilt-ridden. As for me, she could not have been more understanding. I told her my own story, and she just hugged me.'

'Sweyn has suggested two options. What do you think?'

'I'd be surprised if he could find happiness for long at St Cirq Lapopie. There is too much of a warrior in him. But, if that's his choice, my share of the estate is my wedding present to him. On the other hand, if he wants to stay here, then let's get on with making our plans.'

Adela was, as usual, blunt, keen to resolve issues quickly and move on. I felt we needed another opinion; I did not want our Brotherhood to be broken up, and I was desperate to find a way for Sweyn to stay in Sicily and yet still enjoy the happiness he had found.

'Sweyn, do you mind if we bring Mahnoor into this? I'd like to hear what she thinks.'

'Of course. She will soon be part of the family. I will send word to her – it may take a while, as her father watches over her like a hawk.'

Those last words of Sweyn's were the ones that concerned me most. After Sweyn and Adela had left, I asked Edwin for his thoughts.

'Mahnoor is a very valuable commodity – very rich and

very beautiful. Half of Sicily's rich young tups, and several of the older ones, strut at her door all the time. Her father has several guards watching over her all the time.'

Edwin knew her father well.

'Suleiman is not a pleasant man. I wouldn't trust him as far as I could spit. All sorts of dubious consignments arrive for him at Palermo harbour all the time. It is said he is supplying the Muslim rebels in the south with weapons from the Moors in Spain. He trades on the edge of the law and will do anything to avoid paying his duties and taxes. I think the Count has the measure of him but has not yet been able to pin him down.'

Sweyn had been right. It took a whole week for Mahnoor to appear.

If Sweyn and Adela had been apprehensive about the matter in hand, Mahnoor was visibly shaking.

'My Lord Prince, please forgive me, I bring you a big problem.'

'Dearest Mahnoor, my name is Edgar. We are a family of brothers and sisters and I hear you are soon to become one of us, so you must call me Edgar.'

'Thank you.'

She pulled away her veil to reveal a stunning, dark-skinned face of exceptional symmetry and flawless complexion. Her hair was jet-black and her eyes the colour of burned almonds, while her distinctive Arabic nose lent a hawk-like acuity to an otherwise tender image. She cannot have been more than sixteen but had an enticing sensual aura about her that was quite intoxicating.

'Does your father suspect anything?'

'Not about Sweyn, but he knows something is different.'

'Do you know your father's plans for you?'

'Yes, he wants me to marry another Muslim, of course, a man of some stature, an emir or a general.'

'How will he find such a man here?'

'He's going to send me to Alexandria at the end of the year. My uncle is there and is very well connected to everyone in the Caliphate.'

'What do you think of Sweyn's plans?'

'I am very frightened. My father will kill me if he finds out.'

'I'm sure he will be very angry.'

'No, I mean what I say. He will kill me.'

The poor girl was clearly not exaggerating.

'If I elope, he will find me and kill me. For him, it's a matter of honour. If I stay, he will not permit a marriage to a Christian, regardless of Sweyn's marriage to Adela. That doesn't matter – the important thing is, he's a Christian.'

Sweyn moved closer to her.

'What if I convert to Islam?'

'Do you know what that involves?'

'I'm not sure I'd make a good Muslim, because I'm not much of a Christian, but I'm happy to try.'

'You would have to learn Arabic and recite the Quran from cover to cover.'

'I can speak a few languages already; one more can't be that difficult. As for the Holy Book, I'll learn it by rote – you can teach me.'

Mahnoor embraced Sweyn and started to sob.

'Would you do that for me?'

'Of course I would! I would suffer any ordeal for you.'

I looked at Adela, who also had tears in her eyes. But I still had my doubts.

'Would your father accept Sweyn as a Muslim?'

'I don't know; he is a difficult man.'

I decided it was time for reflection.

'Mahnoor, when can we meet again?'

'In a few days my father is travelling to Messina and will be away for several weeks. I can come again during his absence.'

'Let's meet again then, when we can make our plans.'

The next day, I sought a private audience with the Count to seek his advice.

He could not have been clearer in his view of Mahnoor's father.

'Suleiman is a villain; he's part of the old Sicily, where Palermo was a crossroads for most of the thieves and cut-throats of the Mediterranean. I know he is smuggling weapons from Spain, but he is the most important Muslim merchant in Palermo and I don't want to move against him until things are more settled. But rest assured, when the time is right, he will rot in my dungeon.'

I explained Sweyn's infatuation with Mahnoor, the nature of his marriage to Adela and the options that Sweyn wanted to pursue.

'You English weave some complicated webs! I would never have guessed; Adela is an accomplished soldier, I just assumed they had grown up together and that marriage was a natural consequence.'

'All that is true – the difference being Adela's state of mind following her trauma at Bourne. She will never get over it. I would appreciate your help; the four of us are very close and I would like us to stay together and to add Mahnoor to our family, if at all possible. If not, then Sweyn must go his own way.'

'Well, I am happy to plead their case with the Bishop of Messina, but I think it's a lost cause. He will do as he's told, but Suleiman will not hear of it. He knows what a catch his daughter is and wants her married to someone of high birth in the Egyptian Caliphate. She has more than enough charm, and he has more than enough money to attract an emir of some standing – probably some old dog, tired of an ageing wife. He certainly won't let a junior knight with only modest means, who is both a Christian and already married, stand in the way of his scheme to live the life of a potentate in Egypt.'

Ibn Hamed reiterated Count Roger's view when Edwin and I rode out to Calatafimi to get his advice. He was perhaps even more vehement: any kind of legitimate bond between the two of them was out of the question.

And so, when Mahnoor arrived to see us for the second time, I had already warned Sweyn and Adela what my advice would be. Mahnoor seemed a lot brighter than before, but they were forearmed and much older and wiser than a sixteen-year-old girl who had rarely been far from her father's sight.

I dreaded what I needed to say to Mahnoor, and was distraught at the prospect of what it meant for the future of our Brotherhood.

'It seems highly unlikely that an annulment, a conversion

and a Muslim marriage is going to work. Quite apart from his renowned intransigence, your father's plan for you is so clear and determined that marriage to Sweyn is out of the question.'

'I suspected as much, but I just hoped that there might be a way. Thank you for trying.'

Sweyn put his arm around Mahnoor and looked her in the eyes.

'This is the closest we're going to get to a marriage ceremony, and here are our witnesses. Dearest Mahnoor, will you come with me to find a new life together in Aquitaine?'

'I will, without a second's hesitation.'

Adela embraced them both. Edwin shook hands with Sweyn and rather tentatively kissed Mahnoor on the cheek. I felt compelled to play Devil's advocate – partly because it was the right thing to do, but also because I was desperate not to lose Sweyn and the beautiful young Moor.

'Are you both sure? Sweyn, you go to a simple life tending your estate; no more gallant adventures as a knight.'

'I know the price, but it is one worth paying for the woman I love.'

'Mahnoor, you will lose your inheritance, never see your family again and live in a Christian world so very different from here.'

'My life so far has been like that of a bird in a cage, and my only future is to be slobbered over by a fat emir and then discarded to embroider in a harem with the other unwanted women. I am exchanging that for true love – is there really a choice to be made?'

Mahnoor's frank and succinct answer made me smile inwardly. There was no doubting her sincerity or her commitment to Sweyn. As for him, we all had our doubts, but he was so obviously smitten with his Princess of Araby that there was no choice but to let events take their course.

Arrangements were made the next day for passage to Narbonne on one of the Count's ships. Under cover of the dead of the night, the two young elopers were secreted in a cargo of silk and wine and given an escort of our sergeant-at-arms as well as his man and six of the Count's men, who would travel with them as far as Toulouse.

There was great sadness at the parting. Adela, Edwin and I stood on Palermo's deserted quayside as the wind of the turning tide caught the ship's sail and tugged it out to sea. I could not see them – they were out of sight deep amidst the cargo – but I held them in my mind's eye, huddled together, anxious but excited, like children on a daring adventure.

The ship was soon no more than a distant silhouette against the moonlit sky, the sound of its creaking timbers and straining sail gone; all we could hear was the lapping of the waves against the dock. Adela was the first to turn away, scurrying back into the city to hide her tears.

Our small quartet of brothers-in-arms was now a tiny trio: Edwin was losing a son, if a surrogate one; Adela a husband, if in name only; and I was losing a good friend I had grown to admire enormously.

It was October 1085, a time of year that always reminded me of the autumn days around Senlac Ridge. I was only a boy at the time, but my memories are so clear. I was at Westminster when I heard the news of the catastrophic defeat and of King Harold's death. I knew the Witan would want to proclaim me King – a terrifying thought, because I knew they would abandon me as soon as William got close to London.

Nineteen years had passed since those tempestuous days, but it seemed like many more.

Mahnoor was about the same age as I had been then. I was excited for her; she had made a brave choice to find her own way in life – something circumstances had compelled me to do – but I was concerned for her too; she was so young and naive, with a cruel and vengeful father to hide from.

16. Vengeance

Throughout the winter of 1085 and well into the spring of the following year, there was little of consequence to reflect on in Count Roger's Sicily. Two more Muslim enclaves embraced Roger's offer to join his enlightened domain and negotiations, rather than military campaigns, began with Noto and Enna, the last two emirates to resist.

The only incident of note occurred when Suleiman returned from Messina to find his daughter gone. His rage knew no bounds and both Mahnoor's bodyguards disappeared – consigned, it was said, to a watery grave in Palermo Bay.

Fortunately, by the time the notorious merchant came to see me about two weeks later, accompanied by three unsavoury characters armed to the teeth, he had regained sufficient composure to be civil – at least, to start with.

'What do you know about the disappearance of my daughter?'

'Very little, I'm afraid.'

'She has been kidnapped by one of your knights. I expect a ransom demand any day now.'

Edwin stepped forward, with Adela close behind.

'May I remind you that you are addressing a prince of the royal blood?'

'You may, but it makes no difference to me – let's put all pretence to one side. One of my daughter's servant girls finally confessed that she had been talking to an English knight. It didn't take me long to find out how they had been meeting, and the silk merchant told me what I wanted to know very quickly – I own his premises. So, I require an explanation.'

'Then you will have it. Sweyn – a Knight of Islam, dubbed by Ibn Hamed, Emir of Calatafimi, and a Knight of Christendom, dubbed by Roger, Count of Normandy – and your daughter Mahnoor are very much in love and have left Sicily to find a life for themselves.'

'You lie! She would never leave willingly. He must have persuaded her to see him alone, then taken her against her will. Where is she?'

Edwin went for his sword, as did Adela. Suleiman's three henchmen responded in kind. I raised my hand, signalling Edwin to desist, and tried to keep my poise.

'What I've told you is all I know. The same facts are known to the Count and the Emir. They left with the blessing of both of them.'

'I know, I have asked them. You lied to them too. You are protecting him. Where has he taken Mahnoor?'

'I don't know – and even if I did, I wouldn't tell you. If Mahnoor wanted you to know, she would have told you.'

'I will find her, with or without your help. I hold you responsible, and when I have found them and dealt with them, I will return here and deal with you.'

Edwin drew his sword in an instant and held it under the chin of the nearest of Suleiman's minders. This allowed Adela to grasp the Saracen merchant around the neck and press her seax to his throat just below his left jawbone.

'There is no bone between here and your brain. At the

right angle, and with almost no pressure, I can make the entire length of this blade disappear into your head. You'll be dead before you can utter a sound.'

Suleiman was a large man bedecked in gold and precious gems and wearing a fine pale-blue, silk-lined kaftan, tied at the waist with a black sash. His beard was oiled and combed into tight curls. On his head he wore a matching embroidered blue Imamah turban, wound over a skull cap, with its tail hanging under his chin and over his shoulder to finish halfway down his back. He began to sweat but stayed calm.

'You should be on my side. Isn't this kidnapper your husband?'

'Our marriage was over a long time ago, and he goes with my blessing too. He has my loyalty and respect, as does your daughter, and I don't like you threatening them, or Prince Edgar.'

'I've met your type before, neither man nor woman; they have them as a novelty in the whorehouses in Alexandria. It must be interesting to be able to give pleasure like a man and take it like a woman.'

Adela pressed the tip of her blade hard against Suleiman's throat, which began to bleed. She then flexed her muscles, as if about to strike, and hissed into his ear.

'Don't tempt me, you fat pig. I have also met your type before, and nothing would give me more pleasure than killing you here and now.'

The intensity of Adela's threat made me shudder and, I am sure, convinced Suleiman that she meant it. She pulled away, drew her sword and joined Edwin in standing sentinel in front of Suleiman's men.

The Saracen took a couple of deep breaths and got to his feet.

'This is not over. I will be back.'

Another year passed in the service of the Count, during which – for a while, at least – our habits were in stark contrast: Adela continued her relentless regime to achieve martial perfection, whereas Edwin and I both spent too much time cavorting with dusky young maidens who kept us amused during the balmy Sicilian nights.

To counter the ills of too much good wine and food, we sometimes joined Adela in her exacting routines. When it became clear that her skills, strength and health were improving, and ours were in rapid decline, we decided to be more temperate in our approach to life's pleasures and more diligent in our devotion to duty. Life was still good and we enjoyed ourselves, but we were more disciplined and used Adela's impressive regime as an inspiration.

However, in the autumn of 1086 matters in Normandy and England loomed prominently in our lives once more. It was October and I had – as always, when the leaves began swirling to the ground – been thinking of Senlac Ridge. It was now a full twenty years since the battle, but it was no distant memory. Like every Englishman, I thought about it constantly; every day brought fresh reminders of how irrevocably things had changed and how so many of our kin were unable to witness them because they lay rotting in the ground.

It was on typically Sicilian autumn day, warm and sunny with a fresh breeze off the sea, that a messenger from Count Robert in Normandy arrived in Palermo. He brought news of dramatic developments to the north. King William was still not at peace with his neighbours, or with himself. He was still tireless in pursuit of his enemies and in his determination to establish a unique legacy in history.

The King held sway over a huge domain that extended from the heartland of France in the south to his lordship of Malcolm Canmore's Scotland in the far north. I had been wondering whether, like his predecessor on the English throne, Cnut the Great – King of England and most of Scandinavia, who had hankered after the title 'Emperor of the North' – a similar accolade should be applied to William. Even now that he was approaching sixty, his warrior spirit still burned as brightly as it had done when, as a boy-duke half a century ago, he first wielded a sword.

The Danes were being particularly restless and threatening a huge invasion, while William was still fighting to retain control of Maine. To meet the challenge of the Danes, he had, we were told, undertaken a great audit of England to find every piece of land, each property of substance and all potential taxpayers, English or Norman, in order to fund an army the scale of which had never been seen before. The inventory was likened to the imperial levies of Rome – so exacting and methodical that every person, beast and acre in the land was counted.

Norman bureaucrats in their hundreds were sent to every burgh and village in the realm to undertake the census: no chore was left unaccounted for, no piece of thatch (even as small as the width of a man's arm) left unmeasured, and no crop, creature or artefact omitted from the national reckoning.

The result of the great stocktaking, the like of which was beyond contemporary comparison, made William far richer than he had imagined – so rich, in fact, that it emboldened his avarice. Not only was he prepared to fund an immense standing army in England, of over 11,000 men, to meet the Danish threat, but he was also willing to commit 8,000 men to the defence of Maine.

The messenger also carried a private parchment from Robert, sealed and addressed to me. It was a request for us to return to Normandy. His father's belligerence had led him to plan an attack for the following summer in the Vexin, to Normandy's south, where Philip of France had installed provosts in Mantes and Pontoise. William intended to root them out and had asked Robert to prepare the army and lead the attack.

It was a typically cunning move by the King; not only was it yet another test of his son's generalship, it was also a further test of his son's loyalty in the face of his friend and former ally, Philip of France.

I assumed this last point accounted for Robert's request for me to return. I anticipated that, as I had with Malcolm Canmore, I would now play the role of mediator between Robert and Philip.

It was another daunting task – but one, on reflection, that reinvigorated me. Life in Sicily had become too comfortable, and I was in danger of losing my sense of purpose. Not only that: Robert was a good friend, and I greatly admired Philip, so anything I could do to prevent war, and all that such a conflict would bring, represented a mission I was keen to accept.

*

Adela, Edwin and I completed our tasks for Count Roger by the end of the year and departed for mainland Europe in mid-January. We decided to take the same route as Sweyn and Mahnoor so that we could visit them at St Cirq Lapopie in Aquitaine. I had heard so much about the remote idyll in the Lot, a place so precious to Hereward and his family, and now I was keen to see it for myself. I also suspected that Sweyn may well have rediscovered his passion for adventure. Given that we were soon likely to be involved in more Norman military campaigns, I was hoping to persuade him to resume his place by my side.

St Cirq Lapopie was everything I had imagined. It was like an eagle's nest, standing high above the gorge of the river on a rocky limestone promontory. It had had the same effect on Edwin when he first saw it, all those years ago, when he sailed up the Lot as Edith Swan-Neck's emissary. I heard Adela whisper the word 'home' as she stared at the one place where she had found peace in her troubled life.

As we disembarked from the Lot barge and made our way up the steep path to the house, the greeting was not the one we had expected. No Sweyn. No Mahnoor. Only Ingigerd and Maria, in obvious and immense distress, with a trail of locals in their wake. They rushed to embrace Edwin and Adela, but their tears were not tears of joy at the return of two members of their family. I looked around and noticed that one of the barns had recently burned to the ground, but otherwise all seemed well.

Both women were in their early fifties, but looked fit and well. They had lived eventful lives and had, as the wives of the famous warriors Martin and Einar, often witnessed harrowing things. But the story they told us on our arrival was horrifying to the point of disbelief.

Sweyn had been away hunting with the estate steward and most of the men of the community, a week earlier, when the attack took place. It had begun in the middle of the night when a large gang of hooded men appeared, broke into the house and ransacked the cottages of every-one on the estate. Some of the estate men who had not gone with the hunting party resisted, but any who did were mercilessly cut down. The rest were rounded up, bound hand and foot, gagged and dragged away. The women and children were all herded into the barn, except Mahnoor.

No one could see exactly what happened next, but her suffering continued for some time. Her agonizing screams eventually turned into despairing whimpers before dwindling away to a merciful silence.

For at least another hour, everyone in the barn trembled in silence before the sound of horses signalled the attackers' departure – but not before they had thrown torches on to the thatched roof. Only the nimbleness of one of the older boys, who had managed to climb up to the eaves and kick a hole in the straw before clambering down the outside wall to unbar the door, saved the occupants from being burned alive.

Mahnoor was nowhere to be found and everyone assumed she had been taken by her assailants. But the men were found, dashed on the rocks below, eleven good men of Aquitaine, husbands, sons and brothers, all inno-cent victims of a vicious assault.

The most grisly discovery was made at dawn when the

son of the pigman went to check on his herd. Mahnoor's head had been impaled on a lance and stuck in the ground in one of the sties. Her luxuriant jet-black hair now fell in blood-soaked threads down her face, her jaw hung open hideously and trails of dried blood ran from her mouth, nose, ears and eye sockets. Her once captivating eyes had been gouged from her. What was left of her body was strewn around among the pigs, parts of which were still being consumed.

Of course, being fed to swine, the creature most reviled by Muslims, was a horrifying fate to one of her faith, as was the insult daubed in her own blood on the wall of the sty – 'infidel'.

The most wretched part of it all was the fact that Mahnoor had just discovered she was pregnant. Sweyn's hunting trip had been intended to put fresh meat and game on the table of a grand feast to celebrate the news.

The hunting party returned the next day, by which time, mercifully for Sweyn, all trace of the barbarism had been removed and Mahnoor's remains buried. He hid his immediate reaction from everyone by turning his back when Maria and Ingigerd told him what had happened and walking away to the forest, a place he always returned to in times of stress. It was, after all, the place where he had found refuge after the massacre at Bourne.

He asked just one rhetorical question as he left, which was to say that he presumed the band of assassins had spoken Arabic? When Maria confirmed that they had, he hesitated for a moment before continuing his desolate trudge into the wilderness.

It is impossible to imagine what thoughts went through

his head in those dark minutes and hours that followed but, just before dusk, he returned and asked to spend time alone at the side of Mahnoor's grave.

Maria and Ingigerd took him food and a cloak later in the evening, and a fire was built nearby to warm him against the chill of winter. He politely resisted all attempts to comfort him and spent the night huddled next to the grave of his beloved wife, the mother of his unborn child.

The women took it in turns to check on him during the night, but on each occasion he was still in the same position, numb to all entreaties and to everything around him. Just before dawn it started to snow and, within minutes, he was covered in a shroud of snow, but still he did not move. They took him a bowl of game soup and a beaker of mulled wine at sunrise, which he consumed without seeming to taste or savour it.

Then he smiled a mournful, weak smile; for the first time, there were tears in his eyes.

'I have to go. I know who did this terrible thing. I will avenge my wife and make him pay for what he did here.'

He said nothing more, other than to ask that one of the enclave of Arab merchants in Toulouse be paid to come and read from the Quran over Mahnoor's grave. By the middle of the day he had loaded a small boat and was rowing himself down the Lot to Cahors.

When Ingigerd and Maria had finished their dreadful account, we immediately began to make a plan. We knew precisely where Sweyn was going and exactly who the culprit was whom he intended to slay. We assumed he would not go to Count Roger, but would want to exact his own revenge, and thus would need all the help we could offer him. Unfortunately, he had a four-day start on us. Ironically, we had almost certainly passed him somewhere on our journey, but on the busy road from Cahors to Toulouse it was easy to pass people unnoticed.

Adela was understandably impatient.

'We must leave immediately! If we ride like the wind, we can catch him. He will want to get to Sicily as quickly as possible, but not as quickly as we want to catch up with him.'

Adela was probably wrong; a four-day head start for a man with only a single objective in his mind was a lot to make up, but it was worth a try. And she certainly tried.

We bought a string of horses in Cahors and rode them as hard as was humane. She did not want to stop and so, when the horses could do no more, we walked. It was the hardest task I had ever undertaken and my admiration for her grew by the minute. She never seemed to tire.

She was counting the miles and checking them off against the formula she had worked out to measure our progress against his. By the time we got to Narbonne, she had calculated that we were only a day behind him. She was right; we reached the quayside late in the afternoon and were told that an English knight had boarded a Cypriot dhow bound for Palermo that morning. We immediately commissioned a ship of our own at an exorbitant price and just caught the evening tide. We were then only twelve hours adrift.

Our vessel, a modified Norse knaar, rigged for speed – for whatever dubious cargo, we decided it was wise not to enquire – was owned by a Maltese merchant. Adela spent most of the crossing standing at its tall curved prow, peering expectantly out into the Mediterranean, hoping, at any moment, to see Sweyn's ship.

We reached our destination only two hours after Sweyn, but by then he had disappeared into the warren of markets and narrow thoroughfares of a bustling Palermo morning. We immediately went to Count Roger's palace to alert him. He sent out patrols on to the streets to search for Sweyn, while we went to secrete ourselves close to Suleiman's wharf – in the hope of intercepting Sweyn before he could come to harm.

We had no intention of preventing Suleiman from meeting his fate; we just wanted to be sure that Sweyn did not throw his life away in a futile gesture.

However, we had underestimated him.

When we reached the pier where Suleiman traded, there was a major commotion. A large crowd of people had gathered, many of whom were clamouring to peer inside one of Suleiman's many warehouses. A detachment of the Count's guard was trying to restore order and, at my command, cleared the way for us.

What we saw was a gruesome spectacle. Sweyn had his back to us, his head bowed. He was standing with his legs apart, his sword held limply in his hand with its tip resting gently on the ground. On the floor around him were three dead men, Suleiman's henchmen, blood seeping from several wounds to their bodies. A little further away, bound by the wrists, ankles and chest to an ornately carved chair, was the corpulent frame of Sweyn's main prey.

Suleiman's body sat bolt upright, but shorn of its head.

His kaftan was crimson, no longer pale blue, and blood flowed copiously into the dust of the warehouse floor. The head, smeared in blood, lay in the grime some feet away, where it had rolled against a bale of silk. Sweyn would never give the details of what had transpired in that warehouse, but the fact that his victim's turban sat neatly on a nearby sack suggested that it had been a cold and calculated execution. Whatever had taken place only moments ago, it was done very quickly and carried out without mercy. So should it have been.

Adela added the final touch. She picked up the fat Saracen's head, carried it through a rapidly retreating crowd with its blood splattering the dockside, and threw it as far as she could into the sea.

'Let the fish gnaw at your bones, you filthy bastard!'

She then hurried back to Sweyn, who was still standing in his mesmerized pose, and tried to pull him away. Edwin and I helped, but Sweyn was transfixed and the three of us struggled to get him to move. Eventually, he breathed more easily, let his blade fall to the floor and sank to his knees in convulsions of grief.

The Captain of Count Roger's guard then appeared. He arrested Sweyn, placed him into our custody and required us to deliver him to the palace early the next morning.

'As you know, I insist on justice being administered according to the law in my domain.'

Sweyn was standing before Count Roger, looking as morose as he had done the night before. He had spent the night in a foetal embrace in the arms of Adela; neither of them appeared to have had much sleep. He did not respond to Count Roger, so I tried to defend what he had done.

'Roger, the crime committed in Aquitaine was truly bestial and there is no doubt that Suleiman ordered Mahnoor's murder. The other men Sweyn killed were almost certainly part of the group who carried out the attack.'

'I agree, but now we will never know.'

Adela spoke up softly.

'My Lord, the important thing is that Suleiman is dead and that Sweyn was his executioner. That's what the man deserved.'

'Yes, but if we had put him on trial we could have discovered the rest of the perpetrators and perhaps found a punishment for him that would have been much more painful and long-lasting.'

Finally, Sweyn spoke.

'Sire, I am sorry that my act of vengeance happened in your realm, but I had no choice. The others are of no consequence; Suleiman was the devil responsible for Mahnoor's death, and I had to be the one to kill him. No other outcome would have brought this to an end. Now it is over; do with me what you must.'

Roger had given the whole ghastly affair a great deal of thought. He too was a warrior, and he had a warrior's instincts. He stood and put his hand on Sweyn's shoulder.

'I think, in similar circumstances, I would feel the same way and would have acted as you did. As you say, it is now at an end. You have my deepest sympathies for your loss. I wish you God's speed to wherever you go.'

Adela and Edwin led Sweyn away as Roger took me by the arm.

'Strictly speaking, by the rules I insist on here, he should stand trial, so get him off the island as quickly as possible. I will make sure Suleiman's crime is well known – not even the most fanatical anti-Christians will have any sympathy for him. Everyone knows what he was like. Travel well, Edgar, and look after your little band of brothers.'

'Thank you. And God keep you till we meet again.'

Count Roger of Sicily was a fine and noble man. I had learned a lot from him; his wise governance treated all the people of his island as equals before the law, a law he administered with a benign firmness. As with all powerful men, it was prudent not to cross him, but for those who accepted his demands for a peaceful and flourishing realm in the interests of all, he was the ideal lord. I really hoped that we would meet him again one day.

We left Sicily with mixed feelings. It had been a privilege to serve Roger and fascinating to meet Ibn Hamed and to enjoy an insight into the world of the noble Muslim. On the other hand, Themistius's warning about a forthcoming religious war troubled me, a feeling exacerbated by our encounter with the loathsome Suleiman and his hateful prejudices.

I knew only too well what can happen when hatred fills men's hearts.

It had occurred to me several times during those final days in Sicily that my brothers-in-arms and I had a simple choice. A comfortable, perhaps long and peaceful life was available to us in that idyllic place. Alternatively, a more precarious, probably shorter, but potentially more rewarding future awaited us by returning to the maelstrom of politics in England and Normandy.

I knew that Sweyn and Adela would not hesitate in choosing the life of risk and reward, and that Edwin would always follow them. For me, there were still moments of doubt.

Would I be courageous enough to meet the challenges that lay ahead?

Would I be strong enough to overcome them?

Although I was not certain what the answer to those questions would be, I knew I had to find out.

PART FOUR

Brothers at War

17. An Ignominious Death

Our journey back across the Mediterranean and through Aquitaine was a much less frenetic one than the journey that had brought us back to Sicily. Sweyn wanted to return to Mahnoor's grave and carried some of Sicily's rich volcanic soil to scatter on her resting place.

Although the mood at St Cirq Lapopie remained sombre, we relaxed and gave Sweyn time to come to terms with the awful tragedy that had befallen him. There was some talk of selling the estate and moving away from Aquitaine – Count Roger's Sicily was discussed, as was a new start in England. Eventually, Ingigerd and Maria decided they were too old to start a new life elsewhere. They concluded that St Cirq Lapopie was the one constant factor in the lives of several diverse people and that they would keep it as an anchor point for everyone for as long as possible. For Sweyn, St Cirq Lapopie now offered only terrible memories of Mahnoor's death; it was time for him to resume his life as a warrior.

I had sent word to Count Robert, explaining our delay but, after a few weeks, with a strong hint of spring in the air, we bade farewell to Ingigerd and Maria once more and travelled down the Lot to Cahors. This time we headed north at the old city and began the long trek to Normandy.

Sweyn was still quiet, not brooding, but he seemed hollow, the flame of life flickering only faintly. Adela and Edwin stayed very close to him; he was lucky to have them.

For my part, stoicism seemed to sit well with me and I thought it wise to represent that for Sweyn.

The stay at St Cirq Lapopie had been yet another link to Hereward that made me feel even closer to him and his extended family. The thought did cross my mind that it might be my resting place one day.

The journey through Aquitaine, into the Limousin and on to the Paris of Philip of France, reminded me of the immense scale of Europe. It was a confusing place with boundaries that were difficult to defend, its many counts and dukes fighting over every village and town and fortified position.

In the North, the two great powers – France and Normandy – were at one another's throats again, where, ironically, in a land so large, the heartland of each was right on top of the other.

Under the circumstances, I thought it wise to make a courtesy call on Philip, during which I could gauge his current view of Robert. As always, the King was charming and reiterated that the real fly in his Frankish ointment was William, not his son, for whom he still had a high regard. Armed with this, we headed for Caen, where Robert was assembling his army.

It was good to see my old friend again. He had survived another three years of his father's boorishness and bad temper and was as relaxed as I had ever known him. Typically, when he heard of our service to Roger of Sicily – a fellow Norman whom he greatly admired – and of Sweyn's bereavement, he immediately granted Adela and Sweyn a small estate near Bosham in Sussex, the ancestral home of King Harold. He knew that Roger would appreciate the gesture, a reward for the two young knights who had served him so well, and that its location would be very special to both of them.

By the end of June 1087, the Norman host was on the march: 4,000 infantry, 2,000 crossbowmen and archers and 2,000 heavy cavalry. It was led by nearly 200 knights and the same senior commanders who had been with Robert since his rebellion against his father: Ives and Aubrey of Grandmesnil, Ralph of Mortemer, Hugh of Percy, Robert of Bellême, Hugh of Châteauneuf-en-Thymerais, William of Breteuil and Roger of Tonbridge and Clare.

When we reached the Vexin at Gisors, we were met by William and 1,000 more cavalry, including his elite Matilda Conroi mounted on their huge black destriers. They were an impressive sight, but he was less so. He had become fat to the point of ridicule. His face was mottled and swollen, and his breathing was laboured. However, despite his appearance, he had lost none of his swagger and fortitude.

His greeting to me was perfunctory; for Robert, there was no gratitude or even recognition for his efforts in assembling a mightily impressive body of men, just an order, barked in that unmistakable voice.

'We leave at first light.'

We turned south-east at Gisors and followed the south bank of the River Epte until it met the Seine. We then made camp next to the great river in the lea of the Bois du Chênay. The Fortress of Mantes was in sight through the trees, less than four miles away. Since we had entered the lands of Guy of Poissy – the French Castellan installed in Mantes by King Philip – William had adopted his usual scorched-earth campaign tactic, burning everything we passed.

His assault on Mantes began early the next morning. The fortress and church stood on slightly higher ground on the opposite side of the river. The modest buildings of its surrounding community huddled around the fortress walls and ran down to the water's edge, where there was a small wooden bridge and quayside.

The Mantes Bridge had been torched during the night by the defenders, but William's cavalry had forded the Seine downstream, at Bonnières, and were ready to attack from the north-west. He was using the north-east bank of the river as a shooting position for his archers, while his infantry and supporting crossbowmen were following the cavalry and marching to their rear, preparing to cross the bridge at Bonnières.

The weather had been extremely hot for several days and this morning was no exception. Already large clouds of dust were making for poor visibility, which only added to the discomfort of men and horses in searing heat in full battle armour.

The Norman force outnumbered the French garrison at Mantes by a huge proportion and, as is usually the case when a vastly superior force threatens an attack, the defenders would have readily surrendered had terms been offered. They were not forthcoming. William intended to teach the Castellan – and, in particular, his lord, Philip of France – a lesson.

Robert looked concerned.

'Father, there are many civilians in Mantes and an order

of clerics. They are just simple folk of the Vexin and care nothing for Normandy or France.'

'They will in the morning.'

I tried to support Robert in persuading the King to show restraint.

'Sire, you will lose men in the assault and gain many enemies. However, magnanimity will cost you nothing and will win many friends.'

'You are clever with words, Prince Edgar. My son likes you and I have come to respect your counsel, but you know nothing of war and how to win. Leave that to me.'

He stared at me with a look that suggested I had reached a line of tolerance with him, but that I should be careful not to cross it. I took the hint. William was a brute and always would be. Age had tempered him a little, and he had learned that pragmatism sometimes demanded judicious restraint, but he was a force of nature, a warrior with instincts as old as time.

William turned away. He ordered his archers to shoot their first volley into the fortress and signalled for his cavalry to charge. After three volleys of arrows, a volley of incendiary arrows was loosed. It created mayhem among defenders and civilians alike. The whole place was soon alight and the fortress's small garrison rapidly emptied itself down the streets to try to reach safety.

It was a pitiable sight. The houses were so close together that the fire swiftly spread from roof to roof, turning the narrow streets into infernos of smoke and flame. The few, both civilians and soldiers, who did escape were met with the brutality of the Norman cavalry, who cut them down without mercy.

We sat on our mounts on the opposite side of the river in total silence. Sweyn, Adela, Edwin and I looked at one another. This was a very different Norman approach to their enemies from the one we had witnessed in Sicily. This was the old Norman way – total war.

The archers, their work done for the day, stood and stared without a flicker of emotion. The whole of the Norman high command sat impassively. They had seen it all before. It was William's way; it had always been so. Only Robert and his personal retinue of knights looked ill at ease.

We could hear the roar of flames and the screams of the dying and every time the wind created a gap in the veil of smoke we could see people staggering around, their clothes alight, trying to reach the river, or rolling on the ground to try to extinguish the flames.

'After them!'

William suddenly bellowed and pointed to the southeast. Guy of Poissy was making a run for it towards Paris with a small group of knights from the rear of the fortress.

'Some hunting at last!'

Despite the intense heat, with his Matilda Conroi trailing in his wake, he was off at a gallop like a young huntsman in pursuit of his quarry, shouting orders as he went.

'Occupy the city! Offer no quarter! Spare no one!'

Then William's age and bulk finally got the better of him. The dust was swirling around so prodigiously that it was difficult to see exactly what happened, but the mighty warrior had made his last charge. He had gone no more than 100 yards when he appeared to slump forward in his saddle. His mount stumbled and he plummeted over his horse's shoulder and hit the ground heavily.

Robert rode off to help his father immediately. By the time he arrived, a large group of the King's squadron was trying to get him to his feet.

'Leave him be!'

Robert knew there may well be broken bones or internal injuries and ordered that a space be cleared so that his father could be laid flat and get some air. William was barely conscious and badly shaken. He complained of severe dizziness and started to retch. This gave him great pain in his groin, which he seemed to have ruptured on the pommel of his horse.

'Send for the physicians, quickly!'

After several minutes of examination by his doctors, they concluded that William had had a seizure, which had caused the fall, and that his stomach had indeed been ruptured when his massive frame struck the pommel of his saddle. Taking Robert to one side, his senior physician, the learned Gilbert of Maminot, a former chaplain who William had made Bishop of Lisieux, explained that the seizure was not the first, but was a particularly severe one. Paralysis was a distinct possibility – at least, in some parts of the King's body. The physician was also very concerned about the rupture. It seemed to be a deep one, and there was certain to be internal bleeding.

He added that, in normal circumstances, the King should not be moved, but given that he was lying on a battleground beyond Normandy's borders, he recommended that William be taken to Rouen as quickly as possible.

*

Although a wagon was made as comfortable as possible for him, the journey to Rouen, a distance of over forty miles, was agonizing for William. When he was conscious, he was constantly sick and complained that the world was spinning around him. The pain in his groin and stomach was so great that he was unable to move, and his chest and jowls were so large that it was impossible to get a bowl under his chin, so new vomit replaced the old before his servants could remove it.

He was eventually taken to St Gervais, a priory on a hill to the west of Rouen, clear of the noise of the city and the heat of the lower reaches of the Seine Valley.

The great warlord, William, King of England and Duke of Normandy, the most fearsome figure of his age, languished in his bed, drifting in and out of consciousness for many weeks. He was in great pain from slow internal bleeding, which became more and more acute as time passed. There were surely many who thought a slow and painful death was what he deserved, given the suffering he had inflicted on others.

As he lay dying, the manoeuvring and scheming at court intensified. There were many scores to settle and debts to pay.

Robert was at the centre of it all and tried, as firstborn and regal Count of Normandy, to act as honest broker, but the ambitions were too great, the greed too excessive and the rewards too tempting to assuage – especially between Robert and his brothers, Rufus and Henry. Robert was now thirty-five. Rufus was twenty-nine and still a great trial to Robert, while Henry, aged nineteen, was old enough to be a real nuisance.

I gathered up Edwin, Sweyn and Adela and went to Robert to offer our support.

His mood was sombre.

'There will be war. Even if I can keep the peace between myself and my brothers, there are too many powerful earls to keep in check. Odo is still in my father's dungeon, but he is just one of many looking for an opportunity. My father has surrounded himself with the biggest gang of bullies in Europe, and now I am going to have to try to control them.'

As I had several times over the years, I felt truly sorry for my friend.

'Has the King given any hint about his succession?'

'None – it is driving Rufus insane. He wants everything and has hinted to Henry that if he gets England and Normandy, he will install him as Count of Normandy, with the authority I currently exercise under my father.'

'What of the earls and bishops?'

'The English earls will support whoever is made King of England; they are my father's men. The Norman bishops and counts will support William's choice as Duke of Normandy; they are loyal Normans and, mostly, less ambitious than those who went to England.'

'And what about your support? Who can you count on?'

'My friends only – no political allies – but they are a powerful bunch; most of them are the sons of my father's biggest supporters.'

Robert had revealed his naivety. In saying he counted on his friends, not on political allies, he had exposed his lack of tactical cunning – not a sin for any man but, in the position he was in, it was innocent at best, gullible at worst.

*

In early September 1087, William's demise appeared imminent. His pain had not subsided, and his bouts of consciousness were shorter and less frequent. He summoned his entire family and senior acolytes to his bedchamber and proceeded to announce his Verba Novissima.

To his relief, Robert was granted the Duchy of Normandy. But, to his horror, the Kingdom of England was bestowed on William Rufus. His father did not give reasons – he did not have to. He had left his legacy, and that was the end of it. Henry Beauclerc, the youngest of the three siblings, was granted no titles but the sum of 5,000 pounds of silver, enough money to make him one of the richest men in Europe and thus very dangerous.

William Rufus grabbed the parchments attesting his kingship of England and struck north for the Channel within an hour of his father stamping his seal on them. He was at Canterbury within three days, ready to have his sovereignty confirmed by Lanfranc, the Archbishop of all England.

Henry summoned his father's chancellor immediately, so that preparations could begin for the extraction of the 5,000 pounds of sterling for his windfall. So vast was Henry's inheritance that the carts lined up outside the treasuries at Rouen and Caen resembled the caravan of wagons used to carry the legendary dowries of Babylonian princesses.

Robert immediately travelled to see King Philip at Melun. Now that he was to be confirmed as Duke of Normandy, he was keen to heal whatever rift had been created by his father's brutal behaviour at Mantes.

The result of the rapid departure of the three sons was

to prove disastrous. The old King died suddenly, early on the morning of the 9th of September 1087. Before his death, he ordered that all his political prisoners be released and begged forgiveness for his many excesses. He apparently hesitated about the release of his half-brother, Odo, but then relented. Morcar, the former Earl of Northumbria and survivor of Ely, was released – but, sadly, Rufus immediately ordered his re-arrest. William's regalia was sent to his parish church and his cloak to the foundation he had established at Senlac Ridge.

Chaos soon reigned in Rouen; rumours spread that the three sons had gone to raise armies and that Normandy was about to descend into civil war. All the nobles and bishops at William's deathbed dispersed to their homes to secure them against the expected mayhem, leaving the King alone. His chamber and body were plundered by servants and outsiders, and his corpse abandoned on the floor.

It was left to a minor local landowner from St Gervais to rescue the body and prepare it. A barge was ordered and the royal remains were floated down the Seine for burial in Caen, where more ignominy befell the greatest ruler of his era.

There were many clergy present for the funeral, but only Henry of the immediate family; neither Robert nor Rufus made the journey. Very few of his magnates were in attendance; they were too busy plotting how to maximize their position under the new regime. Would they support Rufus, be Robert's men, or back neither and ally themselves with one of William's many enemies?

I was given a formal invitation as a prince of the household and was able to secure positions close to the altar for the four of us.

The senior member of the family who was present, William's aged first cousin, Abbot Nicolas of St-Ouen, son of Duke Richard III, presided over the funeral in Caen Abbey. As the Bishop of Évreux rose to give the address, a local man, Ascelin, son of Arthur of Caen, stepped forward and demanded that William not be interred in the abbey because the land it stood on had been stolen from him by the Duke many years earlier. Most of the local congregation agreed with the heckler and pandemonium ensued. Calm was restored only when Count Henry agreed to pay compensation out of the funds his father had just left him.

The incident reflected all that was true about William's tenure. The sense of dread he embodied, which had guaranteed subservience, was only superficial — now that his presence was no more than a haunch of flesh, the aura had been dissolved. Those once cowed were emboldened to speak their mind.

Greater indignity was to follow. When the casket was brought forward for the body to be lowered into it, it was too small. With everyone turning away in embarrassment, the funeral attendants tried to force the issue by attempting to prise the King's quart-sized frame into a pint-pot of a coffin. At this point, the bungling of the embalmers proved to have been as monumentally inept as that of the coffin-makers.

Still rotting on the inside, the bloated corpse burst open like the putrid carcass of an animal, splattering those nearby with its rancid contents. The smell was so unbearable that the abbey emptied within minutes. The only saving grace for those lowly clerics left to clear up the mess was that the suddenly deflated corpse could now be squeezed into its resting place, allowing the task to be hurriedly completed and the coffin sealed.

The era of William, Duke of Normandy, conqueror of England, was over.

Like so many others, I was not sorry to see him go. His ambitions had brought death to tens of thousands and pain and suffering to many more. He had killed the noble Harold and destroyed the mighty English army at Senlac Ridge; he had cut down the Brotherhood of St Etheldreda – the bravest of the brave – at the Siege of Ely and taken Hereward from us. In doing all of that, he had denied me the throne that would, one day, have been mine. I no longer resented that, but I did feel bitter about all the other things he had done.

Adela spoke for the others over dinner that night, a meal that was much more like a celebration than a wake.

'A lot of people will rest easier in their beds now that he's gone. Good riddance to the bastard!'

While I shared her sentiments about his passing, I feared that her prediction about people sleeping more comfortably in the future would prove to be wrong. William had changed all our lives for ever. I pondered how profoundly our lives would yet be changed in the lengthening shadow of his legacy.

18. The Anointing

William Rufus became William II of England in a grand ceremony in Westminster Abbey on the 26th of September 1087. He had required my attendance to kiss his ring at the appointed time, thus adding authority to his succession, and Robert was happy to give his blessing for me to travel to England with my small band of brothers-in-arms.

The saintly King Edward's most celebrated building was crowded with the great nobles of the realm, dressed in their heraldic finery, their ladies in fine silks and jewels. Horns saluted, drums beat the rhythm of the procession and the monks chanted in homage as Rufus became King of England.

Perversely, there were not many Englishmen there; I guessed that not more than one in ten was a native of our island. I performed my role and knelt before our new lord and kissed his ring, thus anointing him on behalf of my kith and kin. It was a strange sensation, not helped by the contemptuous smirk which met my eyes as I looked up at him. I had a lingering sense of betrayal, a sin I could have redeemed there and then by plunging my seax deep into his chest. But it would have been merely a gesture, and a futile one at that; there were legions of Normans to take his place.

After his crowning, Rufus dutifully carried out his father's wishes and distributed money to all the churches of England. He freed Bishop Odo, but had Earl Morcar re-arrested. However, he was moderately well treated in a manner befitting an earl of the realm. The people of England appeared to grudgingly accept Rufus as the legitimate heir to the throne, although resentment at the Norman lordship still ran deep.

The plots that had been hatching within the Norman hierarchy regarding the successions – both in England and in Normandy – soon began to unfold.

Odo was at the centre of it all and had recruited the powerful Robert of Mortain to the cause. By Christmas, they had been joined by Geoffrey, Bishop of Coutances, and his nephew, the Earl of Northumbria, as well as by Roger, Earl of Shrewsbury, and Count Eustace of Boulogne. By March 1088, they were strong enough to make their move.

We had returned to Rouen earlier in the year, where a messenger arrived just after Easter summoning me to Rochester to meet Odo and his co-conspirators. I told Duke Robert about the summons.

He agreed that I should go, but warned me to be extremely careful.

'Odo is ruthless and ambitious and will do anything to further his own cause. He is not my father's half-brother for nothing.'

'I presume he thinks that by usurping Rufus and offering you the throne, he can become your regent in England.'

'Exactly! He still wants the throne of Rome – and de facto rule of England from Westminster would go a long way to securing that. He would have the money and the influence to buy himself the papacy. But don't worry, Edgar, you are just the messenger.'

'Thank you for that reassuring crumb of comfort. I suppose I have done worse things in life.'

I decided it was wise to travel with Edwin and Adela and leave Sweyn behind, given that he had already crossed swords with Odo six years earlier when he arrested him at Rochester. We arrived at our clandestine rendezvous in Upchurch, a small settlement near the Medway, one of Odo's many manors in Kent. With guards all around and the local peasants dismissed to their fields, we met in a small barn, hardly big enough and certainly not grand enough for the elite of the Norman aristocracy.

The Bishop was in his pomp, clearly overjoyed at playing the role of kingmaker. His entourage – big, burly men who could easily have been mistaken for housecarls had they not been wearing their fine armour and gleaming weapons – stood around him in a brooding arc that made the three of us seem like a tiny morsel about to be snapped up in the jaws of a huge beast.

Odo wasted no time in telling us of his intent.

'Your loyalty to Duke Robert is well known. Carry this message to him. We will raise a rebellion here in England to install him as King. The only condition is that during his reign he rules from Rouen, where he will continue as Duke of Normandy. He will come here for only four crown-wearings every year – at York, Winchester, Gloucester and Westminster.'

'My Lord Bishop, do you expect him to accept that?'

'I expect you to carry my message.'

With that I was dismissed like a pageboy.

Our journey to England had been uneventful – not so the return to Rouen.

It was May and the weather had been mild but, in mid-Channel, our ship suddenly hit a wall of heavy mist. Our captain, one of Robert's most experienced sailors, tried to stay calm, but I could see that he was concerned. From the helmsman's position it was only just possible to see the curve of the prow; beyond it was a void.

The captain ordered our sail to be lowered, a torch lit and our horn sounded, but it was too late. We heard the wash of the other ship before we saw it, only seconds before it hit us. I saw the serpent prow first, high above my head. Seconds later, it rammed us amidships. A large Norman merchantman, fully laden, low in the water in full sail, she split us almost in half.

We were all in the water in an instant. Thankfully, spring had warmed the sea sufficiently so that our lives were not under imminent threat, but it was vital that we look for something to cling to and then try to retrieve our armour and weapons.

We were carrying little cargo so, although badly holed, we did not sink immediately. Two of the captain's crew were killed in the impact and Edwin seemed badly dazed. With our captain's help Adela and I managed to pull him on to the merchantman, which, apart from some sprung timbers along her prow, seemed seaworthy.

Adela then jumped into the water again and swam back to our ship, now sitting very low in the water. The captain of the merchantman steered his ship alongside our stricken vessel and Adela started to throw our armour, weapons and anything else she could find on to its deck. But I soon became alarmed as our ship began to list to port and rapidly take on water.

'Adela, get off the ship! She's going down – you must swim for it!'

'Not without my seax!'

She dived beneath the waves just as the ship slipped quietly beneath the surface. I immediately dived in after her, knowing that she could easily become entangled in the rigging or be enveloped by the sail. The sea was calm but I was not a strong swimmer and, still wearing my leather jerkin and heavy boots, I soon began to flounder.

I swallowed water and was fighting for air when I saw Adela's shiny seax within inches of my face. Its blade was catching the light of a torch that had been lit to help search for us. Adela had found her weapon at the last moment and was now holding it in her teeth as she pulled me towards the safety of the merchantman.

Once aboard, she turned to me. 'You can't swim, can you?'

Somewhat embarrassed, I had to confess that it had been many years since I had tried to swim – and that was only in a shallow pond in Hungary.

'Then you are very brave. Thank you for trying to help me. You nearly drowned!'

'It should be me thanking you. I would have drowned had you not appeared from the depths!'

Adela smiled at me before marching purposefully towards the captain of the merchantman. When she arrived within a foot of him, despite the fact that he towered over her, she threw a prodigious punch with her right hand, catching the captain square on his jaw. The leather glove of her hand was still sopping wet with seawater, so the impact of the punch produced a plume of spray that followed the captain's descent to the deck of the ship, splashing over him moments after he landed.

He lay there, dazed for a moment, before rousing himself and reaching for his battle-axe. As he did so, he felt that Adela already had the point of her seax under his chin. The angry face of our own captain was glaring down at him.

'I should let this knight kill you – I know she'd like to. It's what you deserve! How can you have been in full sail in these conditions? You had no beacon and sounded no horn.'

Realizing that he was in no position to argue, the prostrate man relented.

'I am sorry, the mist comes and goes. I thought we would soon be clear.'

I then intervened, partly to make our progress to Normandy as swift as possible and partly to save the beleaguered captain from being filleted alive by Adela's blade.

'We are on Duke Robert's business. This ship is requisitioned until we reach the coast. After that, I will leave it to you and our captain to decide how you settle your differences.'

We made our way to Rouen as quickly as we could and told Sweyn of our adventure in the Channel before reporting back to Robert. He seemed happy and comfortable in his new ducal guise. He had placated Philip of France and made recompense to as many of those with a grievance against his father as he could find, including the people of Mantes.

In the burning of the town, two revered anchorites who had chosen Mantes for their devout seclusion had been burned alive. To salve his conscience, William had granted a large sum to the church and Robert had generously added to it in order to pay for the building of a new cathedral to replace the chapel that had been burned to the ground in the sacking of the town.

'Do you like my new regalia?'

'It's very impressive.'

'It's all new and very expensive. I've got rid of that ridiculous baculus my father used to carry around and locked it away in the treasury; the damn thing used to terrify me.'

I told Robert about Odo's plan and its conditions.

'That's typical of him. Rufus should never have freed him. He thinks I'm more pliant than Rufus and that, if I rule from here, I'll be King in name only and he'll be able to do as he pleases.'

'His ambition is the papacy, so he'll want Canterbury first, then your support for a bid to be Pope.'

'He's very cunning. By appearing to promote me as King, he also hopes to gain favour with Philip, who would be vital to his papal campaign.'

'So, what will you do?'

'What do you think his chances are of unseating Rufus?'

'He's got the backing of most of the old guard, but the younger men don't like him and neither do the English. He can raise a strong force from the elite Norman garrisons but, strange as it may seem, most of the younger nobles have Englishmen in their service and they will fight for Rufus, who they accept as their King, rather than Odo, who they remember as William's senior henchman during the Conquest. It will be a close call. Odo's not a soldier — he's a bishop, albeit an ambitious one. He may overplay his hand.'

'That's good advice. I don't want to raise an army and secure victory for Odo so that he can make me a puppet king. I think I'll stay in Rouen. If I go to England, I'll become a co-conspirator. That will be unforgivable in Rufus's eyes. Normandy is enough of a realm for me at the moment. Let's see how Odo's rebellion unfolds.'

'Fine, but what exactly should I tell him?'

'You'll think of something, my friend. You're good at that.'

'Then may I make a suggestion?'

'You may — any clever ideas are welcome.'

'It is important that you appear to be lending support without actually committing yourself in person. If I report back that you wish Odo every success and that you will be sending some men to join the cause, Edwin, Adela and Sweyn could bring them on later, making sure that their progress was appropriately unhurried.'

'A cunning plan, Edgar. And who would lead this squadron?'

'Well, discretion is vital under the circumstances, so I would suggest that Edwin leads it, and Sweyn and Adela act as his aides-de-camp.'

Robert seemed amused.

'I suppose that means a promotion and extra pay for the three of them into the bargain?'

'Yes.'

'Agreed. But make sure they deserve it!'

I was sure they would be pleased — especially Sweyn,

who had not used his prodigious skills in combat since Mahnoor's death.

'I will return to England tonight. I will need some messengers – so that I can send word to Edwin about the timing of the arrival of your men.'

'Very well, I will send eight conroi, half my personal squadron; they will be ready in two days. I will also send some Flemish infantry – they're always keen to fight if the price is right – and four companies of archers. Edwin will be Squadron Commander; Sweyn and Adela will be your aides, with a troop of my own knights led by Hugh Percy and Ralph of Mortemer. I can't have the entire force led by the English!'

I returned to Rochester to give Odo Duke Robert's answer.

Again, Odo's ominous circle of supporters stood around him like bodyguards. This time, the setting was his great hall, high in the keep of Rochester's imposing motte and bailey, not a tiny barn in the countryside. The setting made the gathering much more imposing. It was obvious that these men meant business.

Odo's planned rebellion was not just an idle conspiracy; he meant to seize the throne.

As soon as I told him of Robert's support, Odo ordered his forces to launch the attack, but he was not pleased that the Duke had decided to stay in Normandy and that he was only prepared to commit a small force.

'I suppose he's trying to be a clever bugger and having it both ways, leaving it to me to present him with a kingdom.'

'It is nearly 1,000 men, including the finest from his personal squadron.'

'Don't try to deceive me; I know exactly what his game is.'

'I think you both understand one another's tactics. The field is yours; Duke Robert lends his support.'

'I was told you were clever with words. I know the field is mine. But as you know only too well, kingdoms are won by men who are prepared to fight for them, not by sitting back and waiting to see how the tide is turning.'

'My Lord Bishop, Robert will throw himself into the fray when the time is right. If he came here with a large army and took the throne, he would, understandably, want to rule both England and Normandy from here, something I think you would prefer not to happen. You were very clear that you hoped Robert would spend most of his time in Normandy.'

I had countered Odo's initial gambit, and he knew it. He did not want Robert in England, interfering with his plans to be England's sub-regulus and to use it as his stepping stone to the papacy.

'I know my nephew is not cunning enough to have thought all this through, so it must be you. You should have been a cardinal. They're all like you – very clever and very devious.'

Odo meant his comment as a compliment, one that I was happy to accept.

I took my leave, musing on Odo's bold words. I was sorely tempted to comment that he was about to make his bed and was going to have to lie in it.

19. Revolt at Rochester

The main centres of the uprising were in Northumbria, the south-west and in Kent and Sussex. Instigated by the rebels, raiding parties from the Welsh tribes also crossed into the Marches to loot and plunder, and Malcolm of Scotland seized the opportunity to attack in the north-west.

It was the middle of a particularly warm spring, and the country appeared prosperous and serene. The burghs were flourishing and the farmers busy in their fields. The uprising caught Rufus completely by surprise. He was hunting in the New Forest when news of the rebellion reached him, and he returned to Winchester immediately.

He summoned his council and ordered half his treasury in Winchester and a quarter of his London bullion to be made available to pay for a counter-attack.

England was soon in chaos. The Norman hierarchy was split almost down the middle; in many places, earls and bishops who supported Rufus were neighbours of those who supported Odo. Sometimes the fighting was a small local skirmish, but there were also large pitched battles involving hundreds of men.

There were many Englishmen in the service of their Norman masters and many minor English landowners whose land had not been lost to Normans; all were caught up in the fighting. The bloodshed was wholesale and affected almost every corner of the land. Families were divided; brother fought brother, and lifelong friends became mortal enemies.

My assessment of Odo as a wily and ambitious bishop, but a less competent general, proved to be accurate. Instead of using both the element of surprise and his superior numbers to press home his advantage, he dithered. The rebellion was well supported but concentrated around the strongholds of the rebels. Rather than riding out to coordinate the separate groups and take the fight to Rufus, he sat in Rochester waiting for the King to come to him. Robert of Mortain did the same in Pevensey.

This was disastrous for the rebellion. It gave Rufus time to gather his forces and to persuade many isolated rebels in small pockets around the country to abandon the cause. By the generous use of the vast wealth of his Exchequer, he assembled a large army of loyal Norman lords and knights and, enticed by bulging purses of coin, a significant number of English infantry.

Gilbert of Clare was the first rebel to surrender at Tonbridge. He had been wounded in the initial assault and capitulated within two days of the arrival of the King's army. Rufus then moved towards Rochester to cut off the head of the rebellion – Odo of Bayeux himself. But the Bishop was not there. He had panicked when he heard about Tonbridge and learned that Arundel had fallen to the King, and fled in the middle of the night to Pevensey to seek the protection of his ally and brother, Robert Mortain.

Even though he travelled with only a handful of men, he was seen by the King's scouts and, within hours, Rufus was aware of the Bishop's mad dash. He immediately turned south to Pevensey, where both leading conspirators were now holed up together.

I decided to intercede with King Rufus to prevent further bloodshed and sent word to Edwin to set sail from Normandy and make landfall at Rochester, where further instructions would be waiting.

By the time I reached the King, he was already camped outside the great walls of Pevensey and had begun to throw a cordon around the defenders. He had chosen to lay siege and the likelihood was that it would be a protracted affair. Robert of Mortain was one of the richest men in England and had spent the years since the Conquest reinforcing the high Roman walls so that the castle was one of the most formidable in the realm, second only to the great tower at London.

Rufus was not pleased to see me, nor was he civil.

'Tell me why I shouldn't have you arrested as a traitor?'

'Because, sire, I am loyal to you and so is your brother.'

'Well, you both have a strange way of showing it. An insurrection in my first year on the throne, hundreds dead – where is the loyalty in that?'

'Robert did not instigate it; it is Odo's work and that of his supporters.'

'So, why has a fleet of over sixty ships just sailed from Dives?'

I decided to play a mischievous feint I had been thinking about for a few days in the light of the poor showing of the rebellion.

'Your brother is loyal, my Lord King. He sent me to Bishop Odo to persuade him to call off the rebellion, but Odo would not hear of it. The fleet sailed a few days ago on my orders. They are meant to intervene on your behalf, should Odo refuse to stop the rebellion.'

'Do you expect me to believe that?'

'It is true, my Liege.'

Rufus had changed. His mannerisms were far more effeminate than I remembered, his clothes more flamboyant and he had a plethora of boyish-looking young men around him who were neither knights nor pages. His father would not have tolerated this while he was alive.

The King's rudeness towards me continued.

'I don't like you and I don't trust you – an English prince who spends his life courting favour with his Norman masters. Have you no shame, man?'

'Sire, I do have some regrets, but I try to live a good life and behave honourably. Will you let me talk to Odo and persuade him to abandon his cause?'

'No, I will not. I plan to deal with him myself.'

In the face of the King's intransigence, I took my leave.

But Rufus was right. I did live a strange life, where shame had been a frequent companion, and my deceit in suggesting to Rufus that Edwin's force was intended to support him rather than Odo was perhaps less than honourable. However, my shame was a thing of the past. I knew now that I had the skills and bravura to step into the lion's den – and not only on the battlefield. I had become adept at winning wars of words, turning verbal battles into dramatic victories by the use of my wits and my guile.

I quickly returned to Rochester to meet the fleet and explain my strategic volte-face to Edwin before he committed his force to the wrong side.

I reached Rochester just as the ships were unloading their men and horses. There was much celebrating in Odo's beleaguered garrison. Having been abandoned by the Bishop, they now thought that Robert had sent an army to rescue them. Little did they know that our intentions were 'flexible' at best and that Odo's cause was all but lost.

After explaining the situation to Edwin and the others, it was agreed that we should quickly send word to Duke Robert to explain the current circumstances and my decision to switch the allegiance of our men. As it was a matter of some delicacy, I despatched Sweyn and Adela with a small company of cavalry to carry the message. Scouts were sent to Pevensey to report on the progress of the siege.

Meanwhile, we sat and waited. Several weeks passed in the midst of another hot summer until, in the middle of July, Sweyn and Adela returned with a sealed parchment for Rufus from Duke Robert. We left Edwin in Rochester and set off for Pevensey within the hour.

The rebellion was over in the rest of the country. Rufus had acted swiftly and decisively and his supporters had followed his lead. One of the most dramatic stories came from the far west. The rebel earl, Geoffrey of Coutances, had recruited hundreds of troublesome Welsh tribesmen to swell the numbers of his own retinue and those of his landowners. They had laid waste to vast parts of the Marches and slaughtered livestock, burned villages and torched acres of tinder-dry crops. It was reported that for days on end the whole of Shropshire, Worcestershire and Herefordshire had been covered in a pall of acrid smoke.

This wanton destruction united non-rebellious Normans and non-aligned Englishmen in fierce indignation and common cause. Wulfstan, Bishop of Worcester, became the voice of incensed protest, issuing a solemn curse on the rebels. Over eighty years of age, a patron of music and learning and the only surviving Englishman from pre-Conquest days to hold the rank of bishop in the realm, he then led a citizen army to challenge the Norman rebels in battle.

Driven on by his oratory, a motley crew numbered in thousands, composed of English clerics, townsfolk and yeoman farmers, lined up behind Norman lords loyal to King Rufus and hurled themselves on to the rebel army. In a battle of astonishing savagery, joined just four miles east of Hereford at the confluence of the Wye and the Lugg in the tranquil water meadows of Mordiford, Wulfstan's zealots cut the insurgent Normans to pieces.

After the melee, Wulfstan stepped into the morass of bodies and, from the middle of the battlefield, said Mass for the dead and dying. He then proceeded to preach to the dead about their wrongdoing in threatening the peace and security of England before condemning them to the fires of Hell for eternity. He ordered a mass grave to be dug, insisting that every participant in the battle, whether earl or villein, wielded a pick or shovel until the task had been completed. The number of dead was so great that the grisly chore was still underway a week later.

As we made our way to the forces of King Rufus besieging Pevensey, Sweyn, Adela and I reflected on Wulfstan's deeds and what had become of our homeland. Bishop Wulfstan was the oldest and most senior Englishman of stature in the land. He had lived through the reigns of the Danish kings and the long tenure of King Edward. His loyalty to Harold was absolute throughout 1066 and the revolts which followed, but now, regardless of what had happened in the past, like us, he found himself fighting for a regime which had subjugated his own people.

'Does it really matter to be English or Norman?'

Sweyn would never have asked such a question before, but his love for Mahnoor, a girl of a different faith from a distant land, had led him to question many of his assumptions previously cast in stone.

'I'm not sure. I often ask myself the same question. We're all God's children. Perhaps that's all that matters?'

Adela also had her misgivings about a blind devotion to the English cause.

'If you think about what Hereward and the Brotherhood fought for at Ely, it wasn't simply justice for the English; it was justice for all men and women. There were Normans within the Brotherhood, as well as men from Spain and Wales, and many Anglo-Danes from the north.'

Sweyn warmed to the point.

'We have spent a large part of our lives in Aquitaine and recently in Sicily where Count Roger is creating a domain based on fair and equal treatment of all men.'

Adela quickly added a rejoinder.

'And women! Where the Mos Militum is a code of honour accepted by knights and where I, as a woman normally denied independent status, can rise to the level of a knight of Islam.'

We could smell death two hours before we reached Pevensey. The defenders had finally capitulated and those who had survived the six weeks of the siege were being led away – at least, those who could walk. Farm carts carried those too weak to go on foot, and more carts brought out the dead, which was by far the greater number.

Odo and Mortain, together with their knights and their elite guards, looked reasonably well fed and watered, but the rest of the garrison – over 400 people – were in a dreadful condition. Water had been severely rationed from the outset and food supplies started to dwindle after a couple of weeks. In the end, rats were being caught and eaten and the final supplies of flour limited to a handful per person per day. Order had been maintained only under pain of death until the majority were either dead or too weak to protest.

In the reckoning that followed, supervised by King Rufus himself, Robert Mortain was treated remarkably well. He was banished from England and required to live in Normandy, but his English estates were left intact. The same generosity was shown to the rest of his fellow conspirators. Only Odo was treated harshly by Norman standards. In the eyes of the English, who had been on the receiving end of his cruelty many times during and after the Conquest, he was lucky to escape with his life. Rufus considered execution, but decided that the killing of a bishop, even with legal endorsement, who was so close to the ecclesiastical hierarchy of the whole of Europe, was unwise at the beginning of his kingship.

The punishment began with Odo being paraded out of Pevensey's keep through a cordon of the local community, accompanied by the deafening echoes of the King's victory horns. He was then stripped of all his regalia as Earl of Kent and Bishop of Bayeux, his rings and seal and fine clothes, and left standing in front of the crowd dressed only in his woollen pants.

I was near the King, no more than ten yards from the great Norman lord who had once sat at the top of both the secular and ecclesiastical hierarchies of England and Normandy. He shivered in the cold air and, no matter how hard he tried to appear noble and dignified, looked like a peasant standing trial for stealing game from a king's forest.

He had soiled his pants, his face was unshaven and he looked pale and dirty. The crowed bayed and jeered and hurled insults at him in English and French, the mildest of which referred to his girth and dishevelled appearance, while the worst included every vile taunt imaginable.

Odo caught my eye and that of Sweyn, who he must have remembered from their previous bloody encounter. He looked at us with a withering stare that would condemn us to Hell if it had its way. I felt sorry for him – he had reaped his own whirlwind but, even so, it was always sad to see a man humiliated, especially one previously so high and mighty.

Rufus then passed judgement.

'Odo of Bayeux, for the crimes you have committed against your sovereign lord and the people of England, you are banished from this land. You will be escorted to the coast at Dover through all the burghs of Kent and put on a humble merchant ship bound for Normandy, where the Duke will determine your fate. You are never to set foot in England again.'

He was then bound at the wrists and led away on foot, tethered by rope to a mounted escort. Making him walk across his earldom tied to a horse was a significant humiliation for a man who had often ruled England as sub-regulus when Rufus's father was in Normandy. Rufus no doubt also hoped that many local people would find various forms of verbal and physical insult to direct at him during his long journey.

Odo's vast estates were confiscated by Rufus and taken into his household, thus swelling his coffers significantly. He had handled the crisis and its denouement well. Not only had he acted swiftly to meet the armed threat, but by pardoning Odo's co-conspirators he had guaranteed stability within the Norman hierarchy for the time being. On the other hand, his degradation of Odo showed that he could be resolute when he needed to be, even with the second most powerful man in the land.

Before the King left for Westminster later that day, he summoned me.

When he spoke, it was almost like an aside.

'Get that little army of Robert's back on its boats and take them back where they belong. Tell my devoted brother that the King of England is grateful for the Duke of Normandy's support but, as you can see, it isn't really necessary.'

They were clever words and did not require an answer, but I could not resist a sentence or two in similar vein.

'Sire, I am sure the Duke of Normandy is mightily relieved that you have dealt with the minor local difficulty that the King of England has had with one of his clerics. Rest assured, when your uncle reaches Normandy, Duke Robert will ensure that he is treated in a manner that you would find appropriate.'

With that, I bowed and left. There was nothing more to be said.

20. Battle of Alnwick

Events over the next few years unfolded in a series of complicated and confusing political manoeuvres by Rufus in numerous attempts to commandeer his brother's dukedom in Normandy.

He used England's vast wealth to win the support of magnates in the north of Normandy and to recruit mercenaries to threaten Robert with force. Eventually, he had a sufficiently strong power base on the coast to spend most of his time there and become de facto joint lord of the dukedom. Robert had no choice but to accept this and was forced to attend Rufus's courts and crown-wearings, to his increasing humiliation.

The King also extended the authority of England into Wales and the North, building castles deep into Wales, in the remote Pennines and into Cumbria as far as Carlisle.

There was also a new ingredient in the regal mix. Henry Beauclerc, by now in his early twenties, was not without talent or ambition and had established a stronghold at Domfront, a towering fortress above the Varenne, in Normandy's north-west. So, by 1093 a pair of quarrelling sons had become a trio and the dukedom was governed by one anointed duke and two pseudo-dukes.

We continued in the service of Duke Robert, a task that became more and more onerous as the plots and intrigues became more and more convoluted. Robert bore it all with good grace and continued to be thoughtful and generous.

Although Edwin remained steadfast and content, Sweyn and Adela had become restless. They no longer shared a chamber, but did share a tent on campaigns and were as close as they had always been. Their ambitions remained unfulfilled – they often said that the skirmishes and squabbles of spoiled dukes and kings should not be the preoccupation of chivalrous knights.

A familiar set of circumstances alleviated our tedium in the middle of 1093. Malcolm, King of the Scots, had taken advantage of the civil strife between the Normans at regular intervals to fill his treasury with barrels of English coins and cartloads of clerical plate. In 1091, I had been an intermediary and negotiated yet another settlement between him and the Normans when King Rufus sent a huge army and navy north of the border to threaten his realm.

Since then, the significant reinforcement of English fortresses at Carlisle, Durham, Newcastle and Bamburgh had led Malcolm to feel threatened and he now asked to see Rufus in Gloucester.

Once again, the King asked if I would play honest broker. As usual, Robert was generous to his brother and agreed that I could go. By the time we arrived in Gloucester, Malcolm had been escorted from the border with all the courtesies appropriate to a visiting monarch and had been welcomed to the Royal Burgh of Gloucester with due ceremony on King Rufus's behalf by Alan the Red, Earl of Richmond.

Then the good manners ceased.

Rufus refused to see Malcolm in person, insisting that he negotiate with Alan of Richmond and Hugh, Earl of

Chester. Malcolm was incandescent when I tried to persuade him to meet with the two earls.

'Who does he think he is, the little sodomite!'

'Malcolm, he knows exactly who he is – he's the King of England. It would be wise to negotiate. Although Normandy is divided and the three sons fight all the time, they will unite against you if you give them enough cause – and they're getting richer and stronger all the time.'

'Where is Rufus? I hear he's gone hunting.'

'He may have done.'

'You know damn well he's gone hunting! Where are his hounds? They were here when I arrived.'

I had no plausible answer to give Malcolm.

'Well, you can tell him that as he likes it up the arse, he knows what he can do with the negotiation!'

Malcolm did not wait for an escort. He summoned his retinue and was riding north for Scotland within the hour.

When I reported the outcome to Rufus – without, of course, Malcolm's colourful invective – he smiled mischievously. His refusal to see Malcolm was a deliberate provocation, and it had worked perfectly. Instead of meeting the Scottish king, he had returned to Gloucester with his courtiers, their carts full of venison and boar, and had begun his regular regime of feasting and frolicking after a successful hunt.

Rufus had built a sumptuous new Great Hall in Gloucester and liked to go there as often as possible to enjoy the plentiful game in the nearby forests. The walls were covered in vast tapestries embroidered in Flanders and were lit by huge torches which, even on the darkest nights, bathed it so brightly that it was like daylight.

His hunting dogs took pride of place. The King's high table was at the western end of the hall, with a huge hearth behind it. The eastern end was a mirror image, with its own massive fireplace, some thirty paces from its twin, except that it was the exclusive domain of his dogs. When all his guests were assembled and the entire court sat down after grace was said, Rufus demanded that his dogs be fed first, while his noble lords and ladies waited patiently for the regal dogs to finish. Only when the dogs had had their fill, and were lying farting and snorting by their fire, was the court allowed to begin its feast.

Rufus's effeminate appearance had become impossible to ignore. He had grown his thinning red-blond hair, which he now parted down the middle, and wore even more outlandish jewellery and yet more ostentatious clothes. He was surrounded by his coterie of young men who fawned all over him, each trying to catch his eye.

Concerned for my sister in Dunfermline, with Malcolm almost certain to do something rash, I approached him and asked for his leave to travel north.

'Sire, as you know, Margaret, King Malcolm's wife, is my sister. I would like your permission to follow Malcolm to Scotland. He is very impetuous, but I'm usually able to placate him.'

'Are you playing another astute game with me, Prince Edgar, as is your wont?'

'No, sire. I am genuinely trying to protect my sister and to prevent Malcolm from overreacting to the provocation you have inflicted on him.'

'You are impudent to suggest such a thing!'

'Sire, please. Malcolm may not be able to discern your

tactics, but I see them clearly. You could achieve what you want in Scotland without bloodshed. Let me go and try; I've done it before.'

Rufus smiled. Despite his foppish appearance he had become a clever and ruthless politician.

'Very well, but don't placate him too much. I've got him just where I want him.'

We made haste to Scotland and, travelling lighter and faster than Malcolm, managed to get ahead of him before Preston so that I could speak to Margaret in Dunfermline before he arrived.

The sturdy walls of Malcolm's fortress were always a welcome sight, and Margaret looked as serene as ever.

After a long embrace, I introduced my friends.

'Edwin of Glastonbury, Knight of England, Sweyn of Bourne, Knight of Normandy and Islam, and Adela of Bourne, Knight of Islam.'

Adela chose not to curtsy, so all three bowed deeply.

'A lady knight, how interesting; I didn't know women were allowed to be knights in the world of Islam.'

'Ma'am, we are not usually, but I earned the right.'

Margaret smiled benignly, then took Adela's hand to lead her away.

'I'm sure you did. Come, tell me about it.'

Margaret was a wonderful host and made us all very welcome. She made a particular fuss of Adela, insisting that she sit next to her at dinner later that day.

Adela reciprocated my sister's warmth by wearing a dress, one given to her by the Queen. It was only the second time I had seen her concede to female convention, the other time being her wedding day, and she looked as fetching now as she did then. Sweyn and Edwin beamed when they saw her – proud of her as a fellow knight, but also as a handsome woman.

Over dinner, I could not help but hear how well Margaret and Adela got on with one another. Margaret was a marvellous listener and conversationalist and made everyone feel at ease. Adela was charmed by her. Inevitably, they talked about me and I was gratified that they were full of praise for my kindness and wisdom. The only negative part of the eavesdropping concerned their misgivings about the lack of appropriate women in my life. I overheard that my greying hair and increasingly gaunt appearance should be telling me that I needed to settle down and raise a family!

Malcolm returned the next morning and, although calmer than when he had left Gloucester, was still in no mood to listen to reason.

'I suppose you've come to tell me to calm down?'

'Yes.'

'Well, your fop of a King has set me up for a fall, but I'm going to teach him a lesson. He's not half the man his father was. I respected William and his army, but this boy is no match for me.'

'He may not be William the Bastard, but he's cunning, immensely rich and can call on the same Norman army his father built.'

'I have always listened to your advice and followed it. I'm going to do it again. I'll avoid a direct confrontation, but I'm going south to plunder and burn until he comes north again to settle with me, then I'll retire once more to count the windfall for my treasury. But if he insists on a fight, then so be it: this time I'll fight.'

'I think this time you should reconsider; he's up to something. What he did in Gloucester was far too deliberate. I smell a rat.'

'Nonsense, he's just an arrogant little upstart.'

No amount of cajoling could persuade Malcolm to be cautious. So, while we stayed with Margaret in Dunfermline, he launched a series of raids deep into England, returning with more to plunder each time. When he returned to his fortress in early November, I tried once more to persuade him not to go south again. My suspicions had grown as he reported only token resistance from the Normans in the west as far south as Lancaster.

'His tactic is to make you complacent. Winter is coming; lie low until the spring.'

'My scouts tell me his army is on the move through Mercia. When he gets to Durham, I'll pull in my horns and parlay with him on my terms. There's time for one more raid. I have my eye on Alnwick.'

Neither Margaret nor I could make him listen. Two days later, he was heading south yet again.

Margaret was very anxious.

'Would you go with him and try to make him come home as soon as possible? He's taken Edward with him – he wants to toughen him up, but he's only a boy.'

I knew how important young Edward was to Margaret. She had already lost her stepson, Duncan, who was still confined in the Norman court at Rouen. But Duncan was the offspring of Malcolm's Norwegian first wife, Ingebjorg, whereas Edward was Margaret's firstborn and thus very precious to her.

'Of course. I'll try, but Malcolm is very stubborn – I can't make him listen to me.'

'Do what you can and bring them home safely.'

The King did not care one way or the other whether we accompanied him or not; his only condition was a blunt instruction to stay out of his way. So, to comply with his demand and to avoid compromising our relationship with the Normans, we kept a safe distance from his raiding party, but followed close behind. At regular intervals Sweyn and Adela would go on scouting missions to look for signs of a Norman ambush.

Malcolm had only 250 men when we left Scotland, but after each successful plunder he used a company of men as escorts for the cartloads of spoils on their journey back to Dunfermline, thus progressively depleting his force. He travelled in a wide arc from west to east, sacking Carlisle, Brampton, Gateshead and the new Norman castle on the Tyne. He then turned north through Morpeth and Ashington. By the time he approached Alnwick, his force numbered fewer than eighty men.

I sent Adela and Sweyn to make a reconnaissance of Alnwick and check for surprises in its hinterland. Sweyn returned with a report about the garrison and explained that Adela had gone to watch the road from Bamburgh, where we knew there was a significant Norman presence. It was the end of a cold late-autumn day during which a bitterly cold wind had blown in off the North Sea to the east. The chilling shiver of an approaching winter made me feel even more uneasy and compelled me to go to Malcolm to plead with him yet again.

We arrived to find him making camp for the night. He had secreted his men on high ground in the forest to the west of Alnwick. The wind dropped at dusk and the first flurries of winter's snow swirled around us as the King's steward offered us some warm mead.

I took Malcolm to one side.

'Alnwick is a formidable fortress. The garrison is at least thirty strong, and half of them are Norman professionals. You don't have enough men.'

'I've been looting England since I was a boy. Don't tell me my business! My men are more than a match for thirty Normans.'

Malcolm had hardly finished his sentence when Adela came into view, at full gallop.

'To your horses! Norman destriers, two hundred yards behind me!'

Malcolm's men, although battle-hardened and ferocious, had taken off their mail and picketed their horses; fires had been lit and food was being prepared. The sentries, although posted, were of little value, as the Normans were coming on so quickly. Sweyn and a few others managed to get to their horses, but most were caught on the ground with only their swords and shields for protection.

In the encroaching gloom, the Normans, at least two hundred of them, came through the trees like a wave breaking on the shore and cut through Malcolm's men ruthlessly. Masked by the trees, it was hard to see them until they were right on top of us.

Edwin was speared in the back of his shoulder by a lance, which pierced his mail hauberk and knocked him to the ground. Sweyn's horse was killed under him when it was impaled in the neck by the sword of a Norman knight. He managed to get to his feet as the horse fell, but was slashed by several swords as he was surrounded by a circle of destriers. I saw him fall to the ground and his helmet roll off to reveal a deep wound across his forehead. The number of attackers between us meant it was impossible for me to get close to him, so I looked for Adela.

She had positioned herself next to Malcolm and his son Edward and was in the middle of ferocious fighting. After sounding the alarm, she had brought Malcolm and his hearthtroop a string of horses from the picket lines, and they had managed to get mounted to fight on more equal terms. But they were heavily outnumbered. I tried to reach them, but my path was blocked by a mass of men and horses.

Then I suffered a terrible blow to the back of my head and my memory of Alnwick came to an abrupt end.

Consciousness only returned two days later, when I became aware of hazy shapes floating above me and a distorted voice echoing in my ears. Slowly, I was able to focus better and hear more, but with greater clarity came another sensation – an almost unbearable throbbing head. The only respite to be found was in the comfort of bouts of sleep. Only after several days did the pain diminish, and I eventually began to see and hear clearly.

By then, I knew the fate of my friends. Edwin was not badly hurt; the lance had made a deep gouge in his shoulder but had only hit muscle. With the aid of a sling, his arm was healing well.

Sweyn had fared much worse. The gash to his forehead ran from his left temple across his forehead and over his right cheekbone. The nose guard of his helmet had saved his life, but his handsome young face had suddenly become the battle-scarred mien of a thirty-year-old warrior. He had also suffered several deep cuts to his arms, back and shoulders and had lost a lot of blood.

Only through a stroke of immense good fortune had his life been saved. A Norman knight who had trained with him in Rouen had recognized him, even though he was lying on the ground and his face was covered in blood. The knight's quick reactions in stemming the flow of blood from his many wounds had prevented Sweyn from bleeding to death.

Adela had also been badly injured. Standing between Malcolm and several Norman attackers, her shield arm had finally succumbed to a rain of blows that left her body exposed. She was then struck by a sword on the left shoulder that had been so badly damaged in Sicily, and her chest was smashed by a mace, a weapon much loved by Norman knights.

Her collarbone was now shattered into even smaller pieces than before and she had broken several ribs down the same side. She was in great pain, breathing was a constant agony, and movement of any kind was impossible. There was also the likelihood of internal bleeding – something which, it was presumed, would soon kill her.

Sadly, an even worse fate had befallen Malcolm and Edward. The hearthtroop defending them soon dwindled to nothing as the Normans closed in. Eventually, they were the last men standing and, although Malcolm pleaded for his young son to be spared, they were hacked to pieces like cornered animals by a throng of Norman knights. At the vanguard was Robert of Mowbray – a tenacious warrior and Lord of Bamburgh, who had been asked by Rufus to lay and spring the trap to snare Malcolm – and Arkil Morael, Steward of Bamburgh, a huge man with a bloody reputation for wielding his battle-axe to murderous effect.

Robert of Mowbray was intensely loyal to King Rufus, having been generously pardoned by the King for his part in the rebellion of 1088. As we suspected, Mowbray had been tracking Malcolm's progress and had waited until his force was small enough to be vulnerable. He had picked a moment when Malcolm was at his most complacent – when the Scottish King thought he had his quarry holed up in Alnwick and he was the hunter but, in fact, he was the prey.

Yves de Vescy, Lord of Alnwick, had been told to retreat behind the walls of his fortress, to offer no resistance, but to post look-outs on all routes to the settlement. As soon as Malcolm's force was spotted, the look-out was to ride to Bamburgh to alert Lord Mowbray. Mowbray had his men ready to ride at an hour's notice so, when he heard of Malcolm's approach, they were able to cover the fifteen miles from Bamburgh to Alnwick in under three hours.

Malcolm did not stand a chance.

Worse news arrived from Dunfermline within a few days. On hearing of the deaths of her husband and son,

Margaret had taken to her bed and, within three days, was dead herself. How she died immediately became the subject of rumour. Cynics suggested she took her own life, while romantics believed she died of a broken heart. Either way, my beloved Margaret was dead and Scotland had lost one of its most revered queens. I had suffered some dark moments in my life but, lying motionless in great pain, with my friends badly injured, and knowing the sister with whom I had shared so much during our traumatic childhood was dead, was almost too much to bear.

I thought back to our earliest years together in the royal house of Hungary, in a strange land and among people with an even stranger language. My father, the Atheling Edward, son of Edmund Ironside, had been exiled as a boy with his twin brother, Edmund, in the time of Danish rule in England. After a long and complicated journey via the courts of Scandinavia and Russia with Emma, King Cnut's wife, constantly plotting to have them killed, they had arrived in Budapest to find a peaceful refuge under the benign protection of Andrew, King of Hungary.

Sadly, my uncle Edmund died shortly afterwards, but my father prospered and married my mother, Agatha, a first cousin of Henry IV, King of Germany and Emperor of the Holy Roman Empire. Unfortunately, although their union gave us the distinction of a lineage stretching back to both Alfred the Great and Charlemagne, that was the extent of their contribution to the lives of their children.

Margaret, the firstborn, was seven years older than me, and the shy and awkward Christina was my senior by five years. While my parents enjoyed life at court, my father hunting and my mother embroiled in the romances and intrigues of the nobility, we were left to the care of wet nurses, nannies and governesses, none of whom spoke English.

Margaret was our saviour, constantly telling us stories about an England she had never seen, describing it as an idyllic kingdom where, since the Cerdician King Edward had replaced the Danish kings in 1041 and remained childless, I would one day rule. She taught us the basics of English and insisted that when we were alone we only spoke English together. As a result, when we returned to England in 1057, I quickly became fluent.

The return to England was traumatic for all of us. My mother was taken ill – or so she said – and never left Budapest, and my father died in mysterious circumstances within days of us arriving in Kent. It was said he had been poisoned, and there were many potential culprits, including King Edward himself, for whom my father was a rival claimant to the throne, and Harold Godwinson, Earl of Wessex, who had travelled to Budapest to bring us home. But I always doubted that it could have been Harold and remain convinced that it was Edward's doing.

In fact, it was Harold Godwinson who arranged for our immediate flight to Scotland and the protection of King Malcolm, an act of kindness that no doubt saved our lives. Although Malcolm Canmore was not the kindly host that Andrew of Hungary had been, at least we were out of the reach of those plotting to kill us.

At length, I realized that my reminiscing was only making my depression worse. I decided to break the spell of my melancholy by concentrating on the future and on the well-being of my friends.

It was not easy, but with an improvement in my physical condition came a revival of my spirits.

We were being cared for by the monks of Tynemouth Priory, a recent foundation in a bleak but beautiful position facing the sea at the mouth of the Tyne. Malcolm and Edward had been buried in the grounds on the order of Roger Mowbray, who wanted to insult their memory by insisting that they be buried on English soil. Malcolm's men suffered even greater indignities. The bodies of the dead were thrown into the sea at Alnmouth, a few miles from the ambush, and the survivors were mutilated in various ways before being sent back to Scotland in carts.

Few made it back alive.

As soon as I was reasonably coherent, Roger of Mowbray came to see me with Arkil, his large and brooding steward. Although civil, he came directly to the point.

'The King requires an explanation. Why were you with the King of the Scots when we attacked?'

'Please tell the King that I was doing what I said I would do when I sought his permission in Gloucester to come to Scotland. I was trying to persuade King Malcolm to return home and cease his raids.'

'So, why did you and your knights raise your swords in the attack?'

'I would have thought the answer to that was obvious! We were trying to defend ourselves. Your ambush was executed in the murk of dusk, and you were on us like a bolt of lightning. In the mayhem, it was every man for himself.'

Roger looked at me intently and paused for a moment before answering.

'Very well, I and the King have our suspicions and, as I'm sure you know, he has little regard for you. Nevertheless, he is prepared to give you the benefit of the doubt and has instructed me to give you an escort to Westminster for yourself and your party. You are to travel as soon as you are well enough. He will see you there.'

'Thank you, Lord Mowbray. That is appreciated — as are your care and hospitality at Tynemouth Priory.'

I went to see Adela every day, but her improvement was slow. To our great relief, any internal bleeding had stopped and had not been life-threatening. Even so, her bones took a long time to heal and, after several weeks in bed, she was still very weak. Edwin and Sweyn were soon fit and well, although Sweyn's scars were very prominent, as they would be for the rest of his life.

21. Vision of Beauty

It was the middle of February 1094 before we were able to begin our journey southwards. My request to travel to Scotland to pay my respects at Margaret's grave was denied, but I was allowed to pay homage at Malcolm and Edward's resting place. They had been interred close to the edge of the steep cliffs above the sea – a dramatic place that I felt sure Malcolm and Margaret would have approved of, had it been in Scotland.

We stayed at Durham on our journey, where much work was in progress. William of Calais, who had been appointed Prince Bishop by old King William in 1080, had just begun work on a cathedral to match the great churches of Normandy. Huge timber scaffolding was being erected to give the masons platforms from which to build the mighty walls. At ground level the stonework was already as tall as a man at the eastern end. The crypt had been dug out and the great stones of its columns were being dropped into place by fascinating mechanical devices made from pulleys and ropes, powered by the muscle of men and oxen.

The work had brought many people to the burgh, including craftsmen from Normandy and beyond. Although still a small island of modest civilization in a sea of death and desolation, it was beginning to resemble the burghs of the south.

Early the next day, as we were preparing to leave, Adela suddenly stopped herself in the middle of mounting her horse and spoke to Sweyn.

'Do you recognize that woman – the one on horseback, in a nun's habit?'

'My God, she looks just like Torfida.'

'She does.'

'How old was Estrith when we last saw her at Ely?'

'Thirteen, I think.'

'So, how old would she be now?'

'In her mid-thirties.'

'Well, could it be her?'

Sweyn began to smile as he realized that Adela may be right.

'It just might be.'

The two of them ran off towards her, with Edwin and myself in their wake. Sweyn got the question out first.

'Madam, may we ask you your name? We think we may know you . . .'

'I am Adeliza, a sister of Whalley Abbey. And you, sir?'

'I am Sweyn of Bourne . . . I am sorry . . . we thought we recognized you.'

'Who did you think I was?'

Still convinced she was right, Adela interrupted with a mix of excitement and impatience in her voice.

'We thought you were Estrith of Melfi, the daughter of Hereward of Bourne.'

The nun looked around nervously to be sure no one was listening.

'Come, let us go somewhere where we can talk quietly.'

The nun ushered us away behind the huts where the

masons lived, where she was sure no one could see or hear her.

'I'm sorry, I have to be so careful . . . It's Adela, isn't it?'

Both in a deluge of tears, the two women fell into each other's arms.

'I recognized you and Edwin; Sweyn I didn't recognize, he was so young when I saw him last. And you, sir, should I recognize you?'

'I am Edgar – we have met before, but it was a long time ago.'

Edwin helped the nun with more details as Adela added Sweyn to their embrace.

'This is Edgar, Prince of this realm.'

'My apologies, my Lord, I intended no disrespect.'

'Don't apologize. I am just Edgar. These are my good friends – like your father was and, I hope, you will be too.'

'Thank you. Yes, I am Hereward's daughter, Estrith of Melfi, not Adeliza of Whalley. I travel incognito; the Normans have forgotten who I am, but I don't want anything to remind them.'

Adela launched into all sorts of reminiscences. Realizing that there was a lot to talk about, I suggested we ride out into the woods beyond the River Wear so that we could relax and exchange our stories at leisure, well away from the din of the masons' labours. Our escort came with us but respectfully kept its distance.

Adela soon resumed the eager questioning.

'We went to Launceston and heard the terrible news about Gunnhild. It must be hard for you not to have your sister with you.'

'It is, but her suffering was so great, her passing was a

mercy. I have tried to make my own way ever since. Our guardian, Robert of Mortain, was a good man, a typical Norman – uncompromising and strong-willed – but he was kind to us and we grew to like him. When Gunnhild died, he let me leave, which I appreciated greatly.'

Adela explained that, although we had pleaded with him, he refused to tell us where she was.

'I'm not surprised. That was his way; he'd made me a promise and that was the end of it. He's dead now; I heard he was banished to Normandy after his support for Odo's rebellion in 1088 and died there a couple of years ago.'

'We searched high and low for you, but could never find you.'

'I would have been in Normandy at that time. I did take Holy Orders and I am an ordained nun, but my skill is masonry.'

Although we were all intrigued to know how a nun became a mason, Sweyn was the first to voice the other question we all wanted to ask.

'Forgive me for asking you something that may be painful for you to answer, but we all think about him every day. What can you tell us about what happened to your father?'

'Don't be afraid to ask, he was like a father to you as well. Sadly, I can't give you an answer. I wish I could. What happened in St Etheldreda's Chapel will haunt me to my dying day, as it did Gunnhild, even in the agony of her death throes.'

We had found a place to sit in a beautiful glade. Even though it was late February, the bright sun of a crisp, clear day had dried the grass. Estrith got up and started to pace around, probably so that she could turn away from us should she want to hide the anguish on her face.

'At the end of the siege and the awful carnage, William had my father flayed close to death. We were dragged into the Chapel, where a terrible confrontation began. William demanded that our father renounce the Oath of the Brotherhood of St Etheldreda, the solemn vow that all the defenders of Ely had taken. When he refused, the King was on the verge of striking him down with our father's own weapon, the Great Axe of Göteborg, when there was a blinding burst of sunlight. The King was transfixed for a moment, then he staggered from the Chapel and suddenly collapsed, clutching his chest. He was carried away and we were locked in, alone with our father, who was on the brink of death. It was pitiful . . . he was in such pain and we were just girls with no idea what to do . . . but he survived . . . he was so strong. We nursed him as best we could, until he regained some strength . . .'

She turned away for a while, fighting back the tears. The glade fell still, with only the faint babble of the distant Wear breaking the silence.

'The King didn't return for several days. When he did, he brought Robert of Mortain with him. He dragged us out of the Chapel, slamming the door behind us, leaving the two of them alone. What happened then is known only to the King and my father, and anyone they chose to confide in. Earl Robert put us in a cart and we were heading to Cornwall within minutes. Ely was soon lost in the distance, but the air was still ringing with our howls and screams.'

Estrith resumed her seat next to us, more composed

now that she had recounted the worst part of her story.

'Although there are all sorts of stories and rumours, most people think William had my father executed and buried in secret, just like King Harold. He must have assumed that if his martyrdom could never be verified, nor his grave identified, it would make his memory less potent for the English. Earl Robert would never confirm or deny anything – except to say that the King had made one concession, which is that Gunnhild and I would be spared and placed under his care.'

Sweyn then made clear his unshakeable belief about Hereward's fate.

'He is alive, and one day we'll find him.'

Estrith looked at him with a kindly, almost motherly expression.

'He would be almost sixty years old by now. It is hard to imagine he's still alive, given all that he suffered in his life. But I admire your faith, Sweyn. If he is to be found, then I'm sure you're the man to do it.'

She started to sob and Adela put her arms around her. After a while, she continued her tale.

'At first, life in Cornwall was a living hell. We hated all Normans, especially William and his henchmen such as Earl Robert, and refused to speak to him or anybody in his household. He lost patience with us and locked us in a cell, feeding us through a hole in the door. After several months and a harsh winter, Gunnhild became delirious with fever and I decided to compromise. I don't think she ever fully recovered from that ordeal and feel certain it hastened her untimely death. We were released from the cell, given a guarded chamber, and life slowly became more tolerable. As we conceded more, Robert gradually allowed us more comforts until eventually we became part of his household. Strange as it may seem, we grew to respect him; we could have had a much worse jailer.'

I looked at Adela, sitting side by side with Estrith. They were two remarkably strong women who, by sheer will-power, had succeeded against huge odds – one terribly traumatized who became a knight in all but name, the other similarly damaged, who, behind the facade of a learned nun, became a churchwright. Both had embraced professions that I thought were the exclusive preserve of men. I could not resist the obvious question, at the same time changing the subject to a less emotional one.

'How did you learn the skills of masonry?'

'Well, I'm not exactly a mason. I don't have the skills – I'm not very good with my hands – but I help the master masons with their calculations. My mother was fascinated by architecture and mathematics, and I have inherited her passion. She and Hereward travelled all over the world and she saw all the great buildings of Byzantium, Greece and Italy and learned their secrets – except, they're not secrets. They are strict formulae which determine how buildings are constructed.'

Adela was hanging on her every word.

'And the masons accept you?'

'A little. All the churchwrights are men, so I have to be careful not to claim to be one. I go by reputation and rec-ommendation, which is why I started in Normandy, where all the great churches are being built. Some of the old masons there remembered my mother, which helped me at first. Because of my nun's habit they see me as a well-educated sister of the Church who has a gift for calculating, rather than as a churchwright. But, without thinking about it, they do let me help with the design.'

'So, why are you here?'

'This new church is going to be very special. William of Calais wants it to be the finest building in England. When I heard about it, I came to help.'

'And you were welcomed?'

'Yes, I was lucky to be recommended by Walkelin, Bishop of Winchester; his church has just been completed, and I did a lot of work on the vaulting for the roof. I specialize in the calculations to make the roof strong. Although I work with the master mason, I spend most of my time with the carpenters, because they make the timber frames that support the roof. Winchester has a big roof, and the beautiful stone vaulting above the nave is only decorative; the real work is done by less attractive but very sturdy oak beams above the stonework, which carry the weight of the outer roof. The design is very elegant and precise.'

I sat and watched Estrith holding court, her audience rapt. I had heard that Torfida could enthral people in the same way and that Estrith looked just like her. She was certainly a handsome woman. She had unblemished skin, the colour of rich cream, dark eyes and black hair, now greying a little at the temples, and her face had a serenity that was disarming. She possessed a slim figure, but her feminine curves were still apparent despite her heavy nun's soutane.

Most charming of all was her intellect and aura of mystique. A woman of mature years, she had been raised by a mother with remarkable gifts, who had passed on to her as many of them as possible, and an equally extraordinary father. They must have been an amazing inspiration through astonishing and traumatic times.

Since childhood, she had continued to learn. She had devoted her life to acquiring knowledge and ideas, enjoying nothing more than sharing her wisdom with others.

I watched her with growing wonder – a vision of beauty and someone I hoped would become a permanent fixture in our lives.

22. The Twenty-third Psalm

After much discussion and soul-searching, Estrith decided to relinquish her opportunity to help bring to life William of Calais's dream for Durham Cathedral and instead travel to London with us. From there, assuming that King Rufus did not have an unpleasant surprise in store for us, we would go to Normandy to resume our service with Duke Robert.

Our somewhat unusual quartet of brothers-in-arms had become a yet more peculiar quintet that now included two women, one of whom was a churchwright disguised as a nun. Nevertheless, I was delighted that Estrith had joined us. She was an intimate link to Hereward and Torfida, the only blood relative still alive. She carried their wisdom – and, indeed, their mystique.

For our meeting with King Rufus, I persuaded Estrith to change her allegiance from sister of Whalley Abbey to a Scottish foundation, where there were unlikely to be any Norman links. She decided that St Andrews in Fife had a reputation worthy of her, and thus she became a holy sister of St Andrews, Scotland.

When we arrived in Westminster, the head of our escort went to the King's palace to announce our arrival, only to be told that he was too busy with affairs of state to see us and that we were free to return to Normandy at our leisure. Relieved not to be cross-examined by an irate

King, we continued on to Normandy as quickly as we could.

Once in Normandy, we agreed we would make a plan for the future. We were getting older. I was over forty, Edwin three years older; neither of us had wives or children, and the shallow pleasures of casual sex had become less and less appealing. Adela was in her fortieth year and still searching for some kind of fulfilment. Only Sweyn was in his prime, but since the death of Mahnoor he lacked the energy he had shown before and hardly ever glanced at a woman.

When we reached Rouen, we realized why Rufus had been too busy to see us. Yet again, he was fomenting trouble with Duke Robert, but this time without any real success. Robert's patient tolerance of his brother's aggression had won him many admirers, while his astute governance and restrained rule of the dukedom had brought it growing prosperity. Once again, he let his brother's bravado wash over him and calmly carried on being Duke. A very frustrated King Rufus eventually returned his attention to England, where he continued to fester and plot new acts of devilment.

When we introduced Estrith to Duke Robert, he was intrigued by her and fascinated to hear the detailed account of his father's famous encounter with Hereward at Ely. The siege was still a popular subject with the storytellers, both Norman and English, even though almost fifteen years had passed.

There was an ever-growing number of different versions of what had happened in the denouement of the siege, some highly fanciful. The Norman accounts tended to take the view that William had meted out due justice to a troublesome outlaw by killing Hereward with his own hand, while the English liked to think that somehow or other the great English hero had escaped and was still living an idyllic existence with his family deep in England's Bruneswald.

Duke Robert was ignorant of the true events that had unfolded.

'I had heard that my father had collapsed at Ely, but he would never talk about it, or mention what happened to your father.'

'My Lord Duke, I have thought about those moments in St Etheldreda's Chapel every day of my life and I still can't decide what happened. Was the blinding light an act of God, created by Him through St Etheldreda on behalf of the worthy cause of the Brotherhood? Was it the power of the Talisman of Truth, the ancient pagan amulet my father always wore? Or was it simply a coincidence, when the sun suddenly appeared from behind a cloud? My soul tells me it was an act of God, my heart says it was the Talisman, and my head says it was a coincidence. My mother spent her life wrestling with conundrums such as these.'

'Whatever it was, it affected my father very much and brought on a spasm of pain that put him on his back for over a week. I don't suppose we'll ever know what happened when he finally returned to the Chapel – but, whatever it was, it made Hereward into England's hero and confirmed my father's reputation as the most ruthless man in Europe.'

I had always thought that Robert secretly admired Here-ward – as he would anyone brave enough to challenge his father.

Then, quite suddenly, Estrith walked up to the Duke and touched his hand, something that protocol did not allow, even for a sister of the Church.

'Sire, please understand, I don't have any ill will towards you or any other Norman. King William is dead, my father is almost certainly dead, the past is the past – it is over.'

Robert was not offended, nor did he pull away. He placed his hand over hers, and the son of England's conqueror and the daughter of his nemesis embraced. It was as if they were playing out the final act in the drama that was Ely. Tears ran down Estrith's cheeks and Adela put her hand to her face to hold back her sobs; all of us had tears in our eyes and lumps in our throats.

Robert took a deep breath and, with a fidget of mild embarrassment, changed the subject.

'What are your plans?'

'Estrith would like to go south to St Cirq Lapopie. She hasn't seen her surrogate aunts, Ingigerd and Maria, in over twenty years.'

'Do you think I could come with you?'

Robert's response was like a bolt from the blue, leaving all of us shocked – not unpleasantly so, but certainly surprised that a sovereign duke would want to travel with a small and insignificant band such as ours.

'But what about your dukedom and your quarrelsome brothers?'

'Normandy more or less runs itself these days, and I've got the powerful barons nicely balanced in a kind of harmony, which they accept through gritted teeth. Most of them dislike Odo so much, they are mainly preoccupied with keeping him at bay. As for my brothers, Rufus needs Henry if he's to be strong enough to unseat me in Rouen, but Henry is content building his strength in the Cotentin. He may ultimately have eyes for Normandy, but he'll want England first, so Rufus is the one in his way, not me – at least, not yet.'

We all looked at one another and nodded our approval and, as head of the St Cirq Lapopie household, Edwin made the formal response.

'My Lord, it would be our honour to receive you at our humble home on the Lot. But, sire, it is only a modest farmhouse.'

'That is of no consequence, I will bring only a small retinue and we will make camp in your fields. Perhaps I'll go and see that firebrand Raymond of Toulouse, who has been causing turmoil among the knights of Europe with his campaign to free the Holy Land from Islam.'

While Duke Robert made his plans to join us on our journey, we brooded on the news about Raymond of Toulouse's cause.

We all thought back to the words of Themistius, the Thracian strategoi we had listened to in Sicily, when he talked about a looming holy war between Christians and Muslims. It was a worrying prospect for all of us and particularly unedifying for Sweyn, who had fallen in love with a Muslim girl only for her to be slaughtered by a fanatical father. The fact that we were about to depart for St Cirq Lapopie, the site of her grave, only added to his dismay.

That night, over dinner, he made his feelings clear.

'I would like to visit the Holy Land, but I don't want to fight the Muslims; some of them are brother knights and began our code of chivalry, the Mos Militum.'

Adela was also troubled.

'As far as I know, the Muslim lords of the Holy Land allow pilgrims to visit the sacred sites freely and permit freedom of worship for Christians and Jews. Why would we want to fight them?'

Edwin, as always, was happy to do what Sweyn and Adela wanted to do, and his view was measured and wise.

'I have no quarrel with the Muslims. We were well treated by Ibn Hamed and his knights, and I have great respect for their culture and learning. To provoke a holy war, just because the lords of the Holy Places are Muslims, is dangerous talk. Isn't the Holy Land sacred to Muslims too?'

I was also concerned, but tried to allay their fears.

'Let's make the journey to St Cirq Lapopie – and, if Duke Robert wants to go and see the Count of Toulouse, then we'll hear from the horse's mouth what his campaign is trying to achieve.'

The journey south was as enjoyable as ever. It was the height of spring and nature was at her most fecund. We travelled well; Duke Robert was not only good company, he brought a small retinue of soldiers and a vast corps of cooks, stewards and butlers with enough provisions to feed a glut of dukes. We progressed like the grand entourage of a Byzantine emperor with all the trappings of a papal convoy.

The huntsmen went out every day to kill fresh meat, and the stewards bought local vegetables along the way. The butts of wine never seemed to empty, no matter how hard we tried to drain them, and the minstrels sang us to sleep every night.

It was on one such typically blissful evening that we discovered that Estrith had the most stunning singing voice. Duke Robert was spellbound.

'Where did you learn to sing?'

'My father's oldest companion was Martin Lightfoot, a man from the land of the Welsh princes. He had a fine voice and would sing to us all the time. He taught me the songs of his homeland and how to sing lullabies. During my novitiate, I learned plainchant and the music of the mass.'

'You have a beautiful voice.'

'Thank you, my Lord.'

Every night thereafter, at Robert's insistence, Estrith became the highlight of the post-prandial entertainment; she always sang unaccompanied and brought a heavenly calm to the entire camp. Even the cooks and stewards stopped what they were doing and sat on the ground to listen. Her songs about the delights of young love and the chivalrous deeds of heroes brought moments of dewy-eyed reflection to even the most redoubtable of Robert's soldiers. Only the sentries on watch kept their backs to her, but they smiled to themselves as they stood sentinel.

My thoughts during those precious moments were always of Hereward and Torfida. Their lives were the perfect inspiration for a songwriter, and I felt sure that in the villages of England, far away from Norman ears, songs were being sung that very night about the noble deeds of

Hereward of Bourne and his beguiling bride, Torfida of the Wildwood.

Robert's fascination for Estrith was all too obvious to everyone – but, like most besotted men, he was sure his feelings had gone unnoticed. At the end of one of her most charming performances, he confided in me.

'Edgar, I want to tell you something in confidence.'

'Of course, I shall be the soul of discretion.'

'I am very fond of Estrith.'

'We all are; she is wonderful.'

'No, I mean, I'm very fond of her! I have been ever since you introduced her to me in Rouen.'

I decided to stop teasing him.

'Yes, I know.'

'How do you know?'

'Well, the clues are well hidden, of course, but there are some small hints: hanging on her every word; staring at her like a lovesick boy; beaming at her with your head tilted to one side like an imbecile whenever she appears; and generally following her around like an unweaned pup would follow its mother . . . And these are just some of the less noticeable ones!'

'Oh . . . is it that bad?'

'Yes, I'm afraid it is.'

'I make no excuses; I can't get her out of my mind.'

'Robert, she's a nun.'

'I know, but will you speak to her for me?'

'No, I will not, she's a nun and that's all there is to it.'

'But she only became a nun so that she could be accepted by the masons.'

'I'm sure there's more to it than that.'

'Please speak to her for me. If she's a committed bride of Christ, then so be it, but I have a feeling she isn't . . . I can hear it in her voice.'

'The answer is still no.'

'I can't sleep at night!'

'Robert, you're the Duke of Normandy and she's a nun. You could be excommunicated!'

Robert was in no mood to listen to my objections, and continued to press his cause.

'Just ask her about her feelings for me! That's what friends are for.'

I tried to think of a way to distract him from his feelings for Estrith,

'Look, when we get to Cahors, we'll spend a few days whoring. They've got dusky beauties from the south there, and big, blonde, Germans – you can fill several beds with a selection of them.'

'I don't want an assortment of whores, I want Estrith.'

As one of the most powerful men in Europe, Robert was used to getting what he wanted. Despite his easy-going manner, it was obvious that he would not be denied.

I decided to capitulate.

'Very well, I'll speak to her.'

'Tonight?'

'No, it's late, and she's asleep.'

'Tomorrow?'

'I'll try.'

'Good, it's agreed. Tomorrow it is.'

Robert, Duke of Normandy and lord of all he surveyed, walked off with a spring in his step like a love-struck adolescent.

I smiled as he went. I also felt like a boy again, charged to be a go-between for a pair of novice lovers.

The next day, during one of our stops to rest the horses, I took Estrith to one side.

'I have to broach a somewhat delicate subject with you.'

'That means it's about sex.'

'That's an unusually frank response for a nun.'

'Do I shock you?'

'No . . . well, yes.'

Estrith's candour was a revelation. She had never given the slightest hint of being anything other than a pious nun. I pressed on, searching for the right words.

'Actually, the "delicate subject" does not concern me.'

'What a disappointment, I've never bedded a prince . . .'

Estrith sensed that her bold statement had discomfited me. She paused before continuing.

'The habit is real and I have taken the vows, but they are a means to an end. My passion is building churches, not praying in them. As for my womanly passions, I have them like anybody else – perhaps a little more than most.'

I understood her plight. To make her way in the world as a woman, she had only two choices: to marry a man of substance or status, which in itself would mean her husband would almost certainly constrain her options, or take Holy Orders and devote her life to Christ and worthy causes, a choice that meant she would adhere to the demands of chastity and charitable servitude. She had chosen the latter, but only to further her real objective, which was to express her talents and fulfil her destiny.

'Your honesty has made it easier for me. My mission doesn't involve a prince; it is a duke who desires you.'

'I feared so. He's not very good at disguising his feelings.'

'No, indeed not . . . but there it is.'

'I'm sorry that you have had to act as ambassador. I confess, it's not the first time an intermediary has approached me on someone else's behalf – though not usually a royal prince. I don't regret my denial of my vows, but they're not real – I took them so that I could do what I want to do. It may not be very virtuous, but I ask you – in my place, what would you do?'

'So, what shall I tell my impatient duke?'

'Although I'm flattered to be pursued by the Duke of Normandy, the answer will have to be no. It's perhaps best that you suggest that it's more to do with my devotion to God than my preference for handsome young masons over rather diminutive and somewhat rotund dukes.'

Passing on Estrith's rejection to Robert was not easy, but her suggestion of a somewhat ambiguous phrasing made her response more palatable for the Duke.

'Robert, I'm sorry to tell you that her calling to follow Christ is sincere. It was not an easy conversation to have with a woman who has taken Holy Orders; she was flattered that you desire her, but she has asked that you respect her calling.'

'Damn! I was certain she was a woman of the world. What am I going to do now? I won't be able to look her in the eye.'

Robert's concern was one that I privately shared.

Despite my worries, it was Estrith who found a way to restore the ease and mutual respect of their friendship. She handled the next encounter with Robert very well.

The following evening, when it was her turn to sing, she walked up to him, curtsied and, with a charming smile, asked him to choose what he would like her to sing for him. The warmth of the gesture took away any embarrassment Robert might have felt, and the evening passed as pleasantly as any other.

However, it took me several days to get over the forthright honesty of Estrith's response to Robert's request. I now saw her very differently; my feelings for her had been transformed from admiration to fascination.

There had been little rain and, three days later, we sweltered beneath a searing sun as we crossed the Dordogne at the ancient bridge at Souillac. The lush green of the countryside became a little less verdant and the dust of the road a lot more tiresome. Our tranquil journey was becoming less so, and it was a comfort to know that the cool breezes of the Lot would soon bring some respite from the heat.

The last two days of the journey became a cause for concern. Suddenly, the trickle of travellers passing us going north ceased – a sure sign of problems ahead. Robert sent men down the road to find out what was wrong. They returned the next morning with the bad news.

'Sire, the road is deserted all the way to Cahors, where the city gates are closed and men are patrolling the walls.

Trade on the Lot is prohibited. It's putrid fever, my Lord. No one may enter or leave the city.'

Robert looked at me quizzically. I had not heard of putrid fever either, but Estrith had.

'The Greeks call it typhus. It's a plague.'

She immediately rode off.

I called after her. 'Where are you going?'

'To help! Putrid fever is a killer.'

Adela then called to her.

'If you have the skills to help, we must ride to St Cirq Lapopie. It's only twenty miles from Cahors; they may need your help there.'

Estrith stopped and swung her mount round.

'I'm sorry, Adela, I wasn't thinking straight. You're right.'

Robert beckoned to us to go, saying that he would follow on with his retinue as quickly as he could.

Within minutes, we were off at a gallop with Adela in the vanguard.

Our anxiety grew as we travelled upstream. Every small settlement along the banks of the river was deserted, and we met no one on the road.

Adela kicked on even harder.

When we reached St Cirq Lapopie, we were met by an appalling sight. The farmhouse and barns of the main house and all the small cottages of the surrounding community were no more than charred shells. There was no sign of life, human or animal, only the buzz of flies and the hum of crickets.

We all cried out for Maria and Ingigerd, and Adela and

Sweyn jumped off their horses. They started to kick at the scorched timbers, hoping to find a clue as to what had happened.

I looked around and noticed that Edwin was nowhere to be seen, while Estrith was peering towards the edge of the fields to the south, next to the forest.

'I think I can see graves over there, just below the big oak. I think there are lots of small crosses.'

She was right. I could see them too. I was about to point them out to Sweyn and Adela when Edwin appeared from the trees to the east. Behind him, limping slightly and looking very frail, was an old man. He looked like a hermit – his grey hair and beard were long and knotted and his clothes, no better than rags, were hanging loosely on his wizened body.

'This is Old Simon. He lives in the woods, and has done so since before we came here thirty years ago. He was old then; I can't imagine how old he is now.'

All he could say in English was, 'Sorry, Master Edwin, sorry,' which he kept repeating.

Estrith went to give him some water, but he backed away and would not come closer to us than a few yards.

Adela began to talk to him. He spoke a language from the Pyrenees Mountains to the south, which was very different from the language of Aquitaine, and only Adela understood it.

The fever had spread from Cahors, where hundreds died. When it came to St Cirq Lapopie, Ingigerd and Maria made sure that the people did not get too close to one another and families were told to eat in their own homes. But it made no difference. Within a month, the whole community had gone – more than eighty people. Maria died in the first week, but Ingigerd was almost the last to succumb, even though she was almost sixty years old and quite frail.

Lime pits were dug and used to bury the bodies, but the last few went unburied and Old Simon was too scared to go near the houses to lay them to rest.

'That accounts for the human remains over there.' Sweyn pointed to the main house. 'That was Ingigerd's chamber. What's left of her is lying in the corner.'

It was about a week later that the human scavengers came. Wild men from the Central Massif, who had heard about the putrid fever, came and looted everything and then burned every building to the ground.

Old Simon had stayed in the forest and kept his distance. But just before she died, Ingigerd had sent the last fit person, a little boy no more than five years old, to him with a scroll, asking him to keep it until any of the family returned.

He now laid the scroll on the ground and walked away, repeating to himself, 'Sorry, Mistress Adela, sorry.'

Sweyn went to retrieve the scroll and read it to us. It was written in Norse, Ingigerd's native tongue, a language nobody in the Lot would understand, but one of several languages that Torfida had always insisted was spoken within their household.

I hope this message reaches one of you, one day. I told Old Simon to keep it under the stone where he hoards those boars' tusks he likes to collect. I knew you would look there, if you found him dead.

A terrible plague has descended on us, here and all around us.
Maria has already died and my time is not far off. This fever
shows no mercy. We have heard that Emma and Edgiva and
their families have been taken from us and, worst of all, our
beautiful daughters, Gwyneth and Wulfhild, and all our grand-
children. What has happened to us is too much to bear. My only
comfort is that with my death will come the end of my despair.

Sweyn had to stop. He sank to his knees in anguish, and
Adela wailed and cursed God for taking her entire family
away.

Edwin went to Sweyn and helped him to his feet while
Estrith tried to comfort Adela. I quickly did some dis-
tressing arithmetic. Of Hereward and Torfida's original
extended family of eighteen, these four were now the
only survivors – and each was childless. After all the years
of peril they had lived through, six had died in a month,
along with all their children. Who would now pass on the
family's heritage?

Sweyn regained his composure and finished Ingigerd's
message.

I pray that you all find what you so bravely search for and that there
are many more adventures to add to the ones we shared together.
The deeds to St Cirq Lapopie and our chest of silver are buried in
the forest. Old Simon knows where, but in case he is also dead, its
location is ten yards to the north, directly between the two oaks we
planted in memory of Hereward and Torfida.

    With all my love,
    Inga

Nothing much was said for the rest of that day. We all found places to be quiet and reflect on all that had happened. Sweyn went to sit by Mahnoor's grave, Edwin and Adela walked among the crosses in the meadow by the trees, and Estrith sat on the rocks high above the river to watch the sun go down.

After a while, I joined her. She had tears in her eyes.

'I am such a pale shadow of my parents. One was the most remarkable woman I have ever known; the other was England's greatest hero. I loved them very much and I cherish their memories, but they left me with a terrible burden. I want to be like them, but I can't be. I have neither my mother's intellect nor my father's courage.'

'You do yourself a disservice. How many people, men or women, could do what you do as a churchwright – maybe a handful in Europe? As for courage, when you heard about Cahors, you didn't hesitate to rush off to help and accept what was almost certainly a sentence of death.'

'I just feel unfulfilled. Hereward and Torfida knew what their destiny was and never wavered. I have no idea what mine is, or where to find it.'

'The same applies to each of us. You have joined a group, all with the same dilemma. We try to help one another. I am a lost soul too. At best, I'm a curiosity – the ageing prince who should have been a boy king of the greatest prize in Christendom.

'I try to take comfort in one of the things my father always said, which was that, if we strive to do what is right and live our lives as nobly as we can, our destiny will unfold of its own accord. But as for me, I don't always do what is right and often my actions are not particularly noble.'

She seemed so miserable, tears rolling down her face, and I realized how lonely she must have been, trying to make her way in a man's world while having to hide her real identity.

'I'm sure that Hereward and Torfida had their doubts and also made mistakes. And remember, their destiny, although noble, ended in tragedy.'

'I know, but I wouldn't mind a tragic end to my life if I had lived it well and had achieved what they achieved.'

The silence settled between us for a few moments. Then she turned to face me, wiped the tears from her face and managed a faint smile.

'When you came to me with Duke Robert's proposition, did you think less of me because I answered so openly?'

'No, not at all . . . although it was a surprise, because you looked and acted like a nun.'

'I have broken my vows with men, but I hope you don't see me as an immoral creature.'

'I look at you very differently now – as a woman, not as a nun.'

She put her hand out and gently placed it on my face.

'You are a very kind man, Edgar, and a good listener. Adela has told me how helpful you have been to her and Sweyn. Although what has happened here is so tragic, I have found my family again and I feel better than at any time since Gunnhild died. I don't want to spoil that.'

I found the new Estrith very attractive and was disappointed that our relationship could never be more intimate than the one we already shared, as close confidants within our family, no matter how much I might wish for it to be otherwise.

She turned away to watch the last moments of the setting sun, which lit her lovely profile with a soft amber glow. She seemed so serene now, a look which confirmed that a platonic friendship was surely the best basis for our relationship.

I couldn't help voicing the question that was uppermost in my mind.

'Why did you never marry?'

'Earl William kept to his word and let Gunnhild and I decide whether we wanted to be married. He dealt with all the suitors as we asked, which always meant sending them away. We both realized when we reached marriageable age that acquiring a husband would almost certainly mean the end of our useful lives, so we vowed never to marry.

'Gunnhild died a virgin, and I was also chaste when I left Launceston. She was much stronger willed than me; without her influence, I soon succumbed to temptation. There weren't many men – always young and single – and I made sure that no one would be harmed by the liaison. I am not ashamed of what I am; I'm not so very different from most women – or men, for that matter.'

She smiled again. It was a kind, gentle smile. She knew I desired her, and her smile seemed to acknowledge that, had our circumstances been different, we might have been lovers.

Perhaps it was wishful thinking, but I took comfort in believing that it was true.

At first light the next morning, we began the gruesome task of burying the dead.

Estrith conducted a short service and recited the Twenty-third Psalm:

> 'The Lord is my shepherd; I shall not want.
> He makes me lie down in green pastures,
> He leads me beside still waters,
> He restores my soul.
> He guides me in paths of righteousness for his name's sake . . .'

She ended with the comforting lines:

> 'Surely goodness and mercy will follow me
> All the days of my life,
> And I will dwell in the house of the Lord for ever.'

She then added a few words of her own.

'Dearest Ingigerd and Maria, may you rest in peace. Those of us who remain will continue to live our lives as we always have, in the noble tradition of Hereward and Torfida and all their brave companions.'

After an hour or so of quiet reflection, we then went into the forest to retrieve the family chest and the deeds to the land. It was where Ingigerd had said it would be, two feet below the ground in the middle of a pretty glade which, in years to come, would be shaded by the two fine oaks planted in memory of Hereward and Torfida.

Edwin opened the heavy chest and took out the deeds. Beneath them was a surprisingly deep layer of silver coin. There were Frankish sous and deniers, German marks, English and Norman shillings, a few pieces struck with Muslim inscriptions and even some with images of Byzantine emperors – all in all, it must have added up to several pounds of silver.

'Edwin, that's a lot of silver.'

'Ingigerd and Maria were very frugal, and the estate made a good profit. But there's also money in there from Hereward and Torfida's day. They hardly ever spent anything on themselves. A quarter part of it now belongs to you, Estrith.'

'Nuns are not allowed to have any money.'

In response to Estrith's words, Adela initiated a general discussion about our future.

'What are we going to do with St Cirq Lapopie? There is no one left to work the land, and everything else has gone.'

Sweyn offered a solution.

'Let's sell the land to the merchants of Toulouse; they are always looking for sound investments. It is still productive and, with a few families to work it, could soon be a thriving community again. We could make it a stipulation of the sale that we retain the small plot where Mahnoor and the others are buried. We could then add the money from the sale, extract what we need to live on for a while, and deposit the balance with one of the Jewish or Lombardian moneylenders.'

The others nodded their approval, and I threw in my lot with them.

'I have a few pounds of silver. I will add my coin to the deposit and we will all be partners in the investment. Edwin can be our chancellor and hold our purse; he is very careful with money. Agreed?'

Everyone agreed in a chorus, and there were embraces all round before we mounted our horses to leave St Cirq Lapopie for what we assumed was the last time.

Edwin, ever watchful of disciplines and routines, reminded us that even accounting for Duke Robert's slower progress, he was likely to be close to St Cirq Lapopie. We looked forward to his company on our journey back down the Lot to Cahors, although none of us relished imparting our grim news.

Adela took a short detour via Old Simon's shelter to leave a small purse of silver for him. I doubted that he had ever had the need for money, but it was a kind thought all the same.

Although I had spent only a day and a night in the home that Hereward's family had made their own, I felt I belonged to it – as if it was now part of my heritage and my legacy.

23. Soldiers of Christ

We met Duke Robert and his retinue downstream only about an hour after our departure. When we told him what we had found at St Cirq Lapopie, he reported back to us on the discoveries his scouts had made regarding how widespread the epidemic was. People were stricken all the way to Bordeaux in the west, where thousands had died, and the fever had reached Angoulême in the north. But it had not spread as far as Toulouse in the east, which Robert ordered should be our next destination.

Everyone's mood was sombre. Robert had issued strict commands that no contact be made with any of the local people; there was to be no hunting, no food was to be purchased and no water to be taken from wells. A combination of the meagre diet and the fear of a slow and painful death cast a pall over everybody.

When we reached the River Tarn at Montauban, we found that the Count of Toulouse had been able to contain the epidemic by closing all the bridges across the river. He had issued the same order for the Garonne beyond Moissac, using the two wide waterways to create a physical barrier all the way from the Central Massif to the sea. Crossing over either river was on pain of instant execution. It was an astute public ordinance, but presented us with the inconvenience that we were also denied entry to the County of Toulouse.

When we tried to cross the ancient wooden bridge, the Count's men, to their credit, remained steadfast in denying us, even though they were commanded to let us pass by a sovereign duke. Sadly, a brief skirmish was the only way to get them to relent, during which several of the Count's men were killed, as well as two of Robert's hearthtroop.

Sweyn played a significant role in the skirmish by using his prowess as a horseman to gallop across the bridge and leap the makeshift barricade on the southerly side. It was a dangerous manoeuvre; he was an easy target for the several archers who unleashed their arrows at him, two of which struck his shield while one glanced off the lamellar mail protecting his horse's chest. He then turned and used his lance to stunning effect, impaling one of the sentries and creating a major diversion which allowed more of Robert's men to storm the barricade. With Edwin at her side, Adela was in the thick of the supporting assault, hacking her way over the barrier in harmony with the best of Robert's knights.

When we reached Toulouse, Count Raymond rode out to intercept us, less than pleased that we had breached his cordon sanitaire against the putrid fever. He was at the head of a body of men at least 500 strong.

When our two parties had approached within ten yards of one another, he halted his advance and bellowed a warning.

'I am Raymond St Gilles, Count of Toulouse, Duke of Narbonne and Margrave of Provence. You are not welcome here. Our land is under dire threat from an epidemic of a deadly fever. I order you to turn round and go back north of the Tarn at Montauban.'

Robert shifted slightly in his saddle, clearly annoyed at such an inhospitable reception, but he chose not to respond in kind – and, specifically, not to recite his many lordly titles.

'My Lord Count, I am Robert of Normandy. I am here with Prince Edgar of the royal house of Wessex and England. I am afraid we had no choice but to breach your cordon at Montauban. Your men did you great service, but we had to force the issue.'

'I know who you are. In all other circumstances my welcome would be fulsome and my table yours, but you have travelled through the heart of the plague and I cannot permit you to enter Toulouse.'

Robert, resigned to the impasse, sat back in his saddle. In his way stood a large body of men with a leader who, by the look of him, was not often bested.

'Very well, I understand your concerns. No one in our camp is ill; nevertheless, we will retreat into the forest and forage there for two weeks. If, at the end of that time, we remain clear of the fever, I will petition you once more to enter your city.'

Raymond of Toulouse was disarmed by Robert's diplomatic compromise.

'I will take you at your word, Robert of Normandy. I will return on the morning of the day after the full moon, and we will discuss this again.'

The Count posted sentries to ensure that we kept our bargain, and rode back to his city.

Once again, Robert's growing acumen had defused a potentially fractious situation.

*

Two weeks later, precisely when he had said he would, Count Raymond approached our camp and sent in his physicians to monitor our well-being. Everyone had to be examined – in particular, removing their shirts so that they could be scrutinized for the telltale rash of the fever on the chest. When it came to the turn of Adela and Estrith, they had no hesitation in exposing themselves, although they did turn their backs to the rest of us.

In Estrith's case, she had abandoned her nun's habit and chosen to wear the plain male attire of a minor noble-man – plain leggings and shirt, covered by a long, flowing surcoat, but minus the armour and weapons. After confir-mation that our entire retinue continued to enjoy robust health, we were allowed to accompany Raymond through the gates of Toulouse.

A fine city, much more like the affluent cities of south-ern Europe than those of the north, Toulouse reminded us of Sicily. Moorish influence from Spain was obvious in the architecture of the buildings, all of which had the pink hue of the clay building bricks inherited from Roman times.

The most impressive of all Toulouse's fine buildings was the Cathedral of St Sernin, which was in an advanced stage of construction. It was one of the largest buildings we had ever seen, built over an ancient crypt which, we were told, was 600 years old and contained precious relics given by the Emperor Charlemagne as well as the remains of many saints, including St Sernin himself.

Count Raymond hosted a banquet in his citadel in hon-our of his guests that evening. It was a grand affair which was marred by a long litany of prayer, led by the Count both before and after the food, and the discreet counsel of the stewards, who told us that he disapproved of drunkenness.

The Count, although he had the frame and demeanour of a battle-hardened warrior, was clearly a religious zealot. Well into his fifties, he sat with his son, Bertrand, a man of about thirty, who was the image of his father and who, given the way he modestly sipped at his goblet of wine, seemed to be similarly devout. Robert and I agreed that our stay would not be a raucous one. I was abstemious, but Robert proceeded to ignore the advice of the stewards and imbibed the deep-red wine of the region liberally.

Estrith was asked to sing and charmed our new host as completely as she had delighted Duke Robert. Although she was a few years older than Bertrand, he took a particular interest in her. After her performance, he leaned over to speak to me.

'Why does she dress as a knight?'

'Well, partly because Adela does and partly out of convenience. We are a group of brothers-in-arms.'

'But two of you are women.'

'It is Adela's calling. She chooses the way of the warrior. Estrith is not a knight – in fact, she is an ordained sister of the Church and a renowned churchwright.'

'How interesting. I would like to talk to her about our new cathedral. She and I have a lot in common. I have considered becoming ordained, and I take a particular interest in the building of St Sernin.'

I felt a distinct twinge of jealousy at Bertrand's thinly disguised fascination for Estrith, especially as his amorous glances towards her seemed to be reciprocated in equal measure. Perhaps his religious purity applied only to drink and excluded the intoxicating effect of women – or perhaps he was simply a charlatan.

My thoughts were interrupted by Bertrand's question.

'And what of Adela; surely you don't permit her to wield arms?'

'Indeed I do. She is a very accomplished knight.'

'I have never heard of such a thing! Women are not allowed to enter an order of knights.'

'That is true in Christendom – although I would allow it – but she was made a knight of Islam in Sicily, as was Sweyn, by a fine man called Ibn Hamed, Emir of Calatafimi.'

The look of horror on Bertrand's face confirmed my sudden realization that I had made a serious error in mentioning our Muslim affiliations to this Christian dogmatist. Our conversation did not last much longer, and my companion was soon engaging in animated whispers with his father.

After the feast, Count Raymond led us all to the crypt of St Sernin, where he began to lecture us about the sins of Islam and the righteousness of Christianity.

'Nearly four hundred years ago, the Moors of Spain, those heretics who worship a false god, came within a hair's breadth of taking this city. We were besieged for three months, a stranglehold only broken when my noble ancestor Odo, Duke of Aquitaine, appeared with his army and defeated the Arabs outside the city walls. Ten years later, the Arab general, Abd al-Rahman, brought an army over the Pyrenees to the west and conquered

Bordeaux. Again, Odo ended their marauding at Poitiers and killed al-Rahman on the battlefield, saving Europe from the infidels –'

Robert, now somewhat inebriated and weary of Raymond's hectoring, interrupted.

'So, Raymond, does your history lesson have a point, or may we return to more entertaining matters?'

Visibly irritated by Robert's sharp question, the Count's voice rose in annoyance.

'My point is very simple. The Moors are still in Spain – and, more importantly, their Muslim brothers are lords of the Holy Land. It is an abomination. They should be cleansed like vermin in a granary!'

Such invective was too much for Sweyn, who rounded on the Count, despite the fact that he had no business addressing his superior unless spoken to.

'My Lord, why is it a problem that Jerusalem is ruled by Arabs? Their prophet, Muhammad, is no different from Christ; we all worship the same God Almighty.'

For Count Raymond, there were at least two heresies in Sweyn's terse comment. His temper rose and his voice ascended to a yet higher pitch.

'Prince Edgar, I hear that you let your knights dally with infidels; they would be better off learning manners.'

'Forgive my young friend, my Lord Count, he was married to a beautiful Muslim girl, who was killed in tragic circumstances.'

'Pity it was not by my hand; there are no beautiful Muslim girls, only faithless bitches.'

Edwin had grabbed Sweyn before he could make any move towards the Count, and he and Adela started to drag him up the spiral stairs of the crypt. I tried to bring Raymond's homily to an end.

'We all need rest . . . to our beds, Count Raymond –'

But before I could finish, the Count bellowed.

'That young knight is not welcome in my city, neither is the she-male who cavorts with Arabs.'

Robert and I helped get Sweyn away before he could do any more damage. We hurried to our camp just outside the city.

At that point, I realized that Estrith and Bertrand had not joined us in the crypt, preferring to seek another form of entertainment rather than suffer Count Raymond's oration on Christianity.

Duke Robert went to see Count Raymond early the next morning. He made our excuses and we were on the move in an easterly direction by early afternoon. Edwin stayed behind to finalize the sale of St Cirq Lapopie, a task he concluded with little difficulty. We had decided to avoid any further risk of infection with the putrid fever by following the Tarn as far as Florac, traversing the Massif and then heading north along the Valley of the Rhône at Montélimar.

As soon as we had settled into a comfortable pace, I took the opportunity to make a sensitive but necessary enquiry about Estrith's nocturnal adventure the night before.

I took it as a mark of our friendship that Estrith was able to speak frankly to me.

'It came as a bit of a shock to hear the Count denouncing the English from his bedchamber; we were in the next chamber, and Bertrand was terrified of him. He had to smuggle me out before his father discovered us. I heard all the details from Adela this morning. He's a dangerous man.'

'So, now you've bedded a Count; the social standing of your conquests is improving.'

'As I feared, you don't approve. You know I can't resist a sturdily constructed roof – and Bertrand's a well-put-together structure with strong timbers and a king-post that bears a good load under stress.'

Estrith's frank architectural analogy made me smile, but I was concerned about her.

'Estrith, be serious . . . it's not that I don't approve, but I don't want you to come to any harm. You've only just met Bertrand – he could be as dangerous as his father, who's not only mad, he's also delusional.'

'I'm sorry, Edgar, we've always been honest with one another. You're right. It was a bit foolish, but he's a handsome young brute and . . . we had had too much wine. In my heart, I cannot believe what we did was wrong. But thank you, I will be more careful.'

I was still concerned about Estrith's evident fondness for Bertrand; the father's behaviour made me very wary of the son. Besides which, deep down, I was a little jealous of the young man.

By the time we returned to Normandy, the winter of 1094 beckoned and we decided to stay in Rouen until early the next year. It was a frustrating time for all of us. Although we were privileged to be under the benign eye of Duke Robert, none of us was any nearer to discovering our destiny.

Edwin became older and wiser, Sweyn and Adela honed their fighting skills relentlessly, to the point where it did not seem possible for them to get any better, and I continued to admire Estrith from afar.

Sweyn's latest accolade was to become the victor ludorum in Rouen's annual test of knightly skills and be all but unbeatable in the joust, while Adela persuaded more and more men to adopt the Mos Militum – so much so that it started to be called 'Adela's Code'.

Meanwhile, I was fascinated by Estrith's new project. She had been sketching it for days and her outline was immediately recognizable, even to a layman, as the timber frame for the roof of a large building. She showed it to me with the glee of a child with a new toy.

'It's a cat's cradle in wood in three ascending layers, closing at the apex, with the whole structure supported by the twenty-four "feet" made of timber. At each of the two tiers above the bottom level there are also twenty-four smaller feet, each one throwing the structure further into the void.'

Estrith explained that not only was the geometry of the roof vital, the precise construction of the joints was also essential to the strength of the structure.

'It is not just a matter of mortising and tenoning them, it is a matter of the angle at which you cut them! The twenty-four supports, twelve on each side, act like the head of a mason's hammer, pulling the weight downwards through the wall rather than outwards against it. They are the key to a more elegant roof and much higher walls. I've decided to call them "hammer beams", each of which will sit on a stone corbel projecting from the top of the wall of the building. The roof won't need any other support.'

I could see the main point: the twelve feet on either side of the structure did not have cross-beams connecting them to the twelve feet on the other side – a feature of all rectangular roofs I had ever seen. As far as I knew, only domed roofs could be constructed without connecting beams, so I remained sceptical.

'How can it work? How will it take the weight of the laths for the thatch, and the thatch itself?'

'Oh no, this is not for a thatched roof – it is for a lead or tiled roof, or even a stone one.'

'Surely not, it will collapse under the weight.'

'It will not!'

Estrith was furious that I should doubt her.

'I have been careful in my calculations; it is simply a matter of arithmetic. I now need someone to build one. To prove it to you!'

After much debate through the spring of 1095, we had decided to return to Sicily. Count Roger had asked Robert for help to launch a campaign to add Malta to his fiefdom, and we all relished the thought of returning to the Mediterranean and renewing our friendship with him.

However, events elsewhere were destined to take us in another direction.

For months, much of the idle talk among knights had been dominated by Raymond of Toulouse's calls for an end to Muslim rule in the Holy Land. Then, in March of 1095, Pope Urban II, a clever and ambitious pontiff, was holding an ecclesiastical council in Piacenza in northern Italy when a lightning bolt struck from out of the blue.

The Emperor of Byzantium, Alexius I, sent an emissary to the Pope asking for help in his fight against the Turks, his troublesome neighbours in Anatolia. Although the Turks were far from being the lords of Jerusalem, they were Muslims; Raymond of Toulouse and many others used this to promote a wave of anti-Islamic sentiment. The Pope replied with a call to arms, asking Christians everywhere to promise, by taking an oath, 'to aid the Emperor most faithfully against the pagans'.

What started as a typical request for military support to overcome an opponent, issued by the leader of one version of Christianity to another, escalated like wildfire. Oaths were taken everywhere, and thousands enlisted to become 'Soldiers of Christ' – young and old, men and women, clerics and laypeople, soldiers and civilians.

With Raymond and Bertrand urging him on, the Pope, having unleashed the beast, tried to harness its power, but it was already too potent for any one man to control. Many men of violence convinced themselves that they could be redeemed by more acts of violence, but this time perpetrated against those who defiled God. Even poor people thought that salvation would follow from joining the cause to cleanse the Sacred Places.

We kept our counsel, not wanting to commit to a campaign that seemed dubious at best, while realizing that a major test for all of us was unfolding.

In November 1095, we travelled to Clermont in the Auvergne to hear the Pope address the great and good of Normandy, France and Aquitaine. His speech added fuel to the bellicose mood of an audience that already had the fire of vengeance in its belly.

'Your brethren who live in the East are in urgent need of your help, and you must hasten to give them the aid which has often been promised them. For, as most of you have heard, the Turks and Arabs have attacked them. They have occupied more and more of the lands belonging to those Christians; they have killed and captured many, and have destroyed their churches and devastated their empire. On this account I, in the name of the Lord, beseech you as Christ's heralds to publish this everywhere and to persuade all people of whatever rank – foot soldiers and knights, poor and rich – to carry aid promptly to those Christians and to destroy that vile race from the lands of our friends.'

He went on to describe in appalling detail the atrocities committed by the Turks and Arabs against Christians – rape, murder, torture, mutilations – such that by the time he had finished even noble archbishops were baying for blood. The Pope called for an 'armed pilgrimage' a 'crusade' to 'free Christians from the brutal oppression of heathens'.

The holy war that Themistius had predicted had begun.

By the time we returned to Rouen, the five of us had made a decision about our future.

Duke Robert asked to see us; he was anxious.

'Do you believe all these stories about the terrible crimes committed by the Muslims?'

I thought this was an ideal opportunity for Sweyn to give his opinion.

'Robert, would you let Sweyn speak? As you know, he loved a Muslim woman very much and, had a vengeful father not interfered, she would have borne him a child.'

'Of course, Sweyn, speak your mind.'

'My Lord, Mahnoor's father was a vile and cruel man, but so are many in Christendom. On the other hand, she was the most gentle, beautiful creature who ever walked this earth. All of us became very fond of the Muslims of Sicily and their code of conduct; we live by it to this day. I have no doubt that the Pope's words are chosen in order to rouse his audience, and that Count Raymond is at the back of it.'

Adela then asked for permission to speak.

'Sire, it is said among the knights that the Pope wants to unite all Christians under his own sovereignty. He was born into a noble French family and his lofty ambitions are no secret. This is the campaign of a pope who wants to be pontiff in Constantinople as well as in Rome, and behind him stands a man we all know to be driven by an insane hatred.'

The Duke thought for a while before asking me for my view.

'Edgar, I am being asked to go on this Crusade and lead the Norman contingent. Sovereign lords from all over Europe are being asked to contribute to a huge army. The Pope wants 40,000 men, fully armed and provisioned for a campaign lasting several years. What do you think?'

'If this comes to pass, it is clear that the world will never be the same again. Everyone must make a personal decision. We have been having our own discussions and have come to a view about how to proceed. We are happy to share it with you.'

'I would like that.'

'Estrith will explain on our behalf; she thought of most of the detail.'

Estrith took a deep breath before describing our idea.

'My Lord, as you know, my father and his followers took a pledge at Ely – the Oath of the Brotherhood of St Etheldreda. Edwin, Sweyn, Adela and I all took the oath; Edgar lent his support from his exile in Scotland. Although it was taken in the context of our resistance to your father, the vow was a cry for liberty and justice for all men everywhere. Its words were fashioned by my father and were very clear and precise: "On the holy remains of the martyr, St Etheldreda, and in the sight of God, I swear to assert the rights of all Englishmen to live in peace and justice. By wearing this amulet of the ancients, I attest to my belief in truth and wisdom. By this salute, I enter the Brotherhood of St Etheldreda and do solemnly commit my life to it and its noble cause. So help me God."

'In the light of what is happening throughout Europe, and the threat of wanton killing on a scale never seen before, we have decided to form a new brotherhood and to take a new oath.'

'Is it an oath for knights and princes? Or may a duke bow his head to a principle?'

Not deterred by Robert's sarcasm, Estrith responded pithily. 'Everyone who takes an oath in the eyes of God takes it as an equal.'

'Well said, Estrith. Tell me the words of the oath, so that I might practise.'

'Sire, do you mean you would like to join our brotherhood?'

'Indeed! I am sure it is a very worthy cause.'

'We want to go back to Ely to swear the oath on the tomb of its patron saint, St Etheldreda, where the original oath was sworn. We have chosen a name. My father's amulet, the Talisman of Truth, disappeared after Ely. It could have been lost in the mayhem, or it could still be around his neck – either a living neck, or one at peace in his grave. The Talisman is claimed by many people to have mystical powers; some say it's a pagan charm, others say it's a Christian relic which symbolizes Christ delivering us from evil. It contains an image of the Devil and his familiars, trapped by a splash of the blood of Christ.'

'I have heard many stories about the amulet; I would like to see it one day.'

'Perhaps you will. Sweyn and Adela are certain my father is still alive and still carries the Talisman with him.'

'How old would he be now?'

'He would be in his sixtieth year, my Lord.'

'Then it is possible.'

'Sire, because this Crusade is in Christ's name, we will call ourselves the Brethren of the Blood of the Talisman, but our name, our oath and our bond as brethren will be known only to us.'

'And the words of the oath?'

'Sire, ours is a brotherhood of equals and the words are our secret.'

'So, am I permitted to enter your brotherhood, or not?'

I intervened to help make our position clear.

'What Estrith means is that, as members of the Brethren

of the Blood, we carry no titles and all are equal. We will be honoured to count you among our number, but we will no longer be in your service and we will not owe you fealty as our lord.'

Estrith then recited the words she had devised for the oath:

'In the presence of God and his disciple, the blessed martyr, St Etheldreda, I swear to uphold the vows of the Brotherhood of St Etheldreda at Ely and give unwavering service to the Brethren of the Blood of the Talisman.

I will adhere to the moral code of the Mos Militum and fight for justice and freedom wherever they are denied.

I will give service to the cause of righteousness in the image of those who went before: Hereward and Torfida, Martin, Einar and Alphonso, and all the members of the Brotherhood who gave their lives in pursuit of liberty.'

We were all moved by the simplicity and power of the words.

I reminded Robert of the seriousness of our undertaking. 'Our covenant and identities will be known only to us, and no one will be admitted to the Brethren without the unanimous approval of all members.'

'So, what does this mean for the Pope's Crusade?'

Sweyn gave our answer.

'For several reasons, we have decided to join the Crusade. First, we can find out the truth behind the stories being woven for the Christians of Europe. More importantly, we want to try to prevent bloodshed by appealing to reason and the tenets of the Mos Militum, a code shared by Muslim and Christian knights alike. Finally, we are all aware that, should the Crusade happen in the way it is being planned, it will be the most important event in our lives since Senlac Ridge and your father's conquest of England. And we all want to be part of it.'

Robert was clearly inspired by all he had heard.

'Good, then let's begin. I will get myself organized to leave for Ely immediately, so that I can join you in swearing the oath. I will travel in secret; I don't want Rufus to know our plans. Then, when we return to Normandy, we will start to build an army to travel to Constantinople.'

I was heartened by Robert's enthusiasm, but I knew that it was a very long way to the Holy Land. It was going to cost him several Danegelds to get his army there and – God willing – back again.

24. Brethren of the Blood

Disguised as Benedictine monks and nuns, we arrived in Ely in early December 1095. It was an emotional experience for all of us. So much had happened in all our lives as a consequence of the events at Ely in that momentous autumn of 1071.

Estrith was particularly distraught to discover that St Etheldreda's Chapel had been torn down, along with the abbey and its cloisters, so that there was no trace of any of the buildings that were so prominent in her memory. In their place, twelve years of toil by an army of masons, carpenters and blacksmiths had produced the substantial beginnings of yet another towering tribute to Norman audacity. Begun by Abbot Simeon in 1083 under the direct instructions of Robert's father, the walls were already high enough to be seen across the Fens for miles around, making the new cathedral resemble a ship floating across the watery landscape.

The King had been true to his word and ordered that the keystone of the central arch of the crypt be positioned exactly where St Etheldreda's tomb had stood. He had been tempted to destroy the tomb, but relented on advice from Simeon and his clerics. To Estrith's great relief, the tomb had been moved down into the crypt when it was finished a year ago.

Abbot Simeon had died and King Rufus had not

appointed a replacement, so we sought the help of Gyrth, acting Abbot, who happened to be English, to gain access to the crypt. We swore him to secrecy about our visit, and he agreed to grant us access to the crypt at the end of the working day.

He met us after evening prayers, and gave me the sad news that Wolnatius, the survivor of Ely whom I had met on my previous visit, had died a few years ago. As far as Gyrth knew, he had been the last survivor of the siege still alive.

As the monks of Ely made their way back to their cells after prayers, we lit torches and made our way to the crypt. Striding across the huge flagstones of the nave, I was amused to think about the price the quarry in Northamptonshire had received in payment for the stone: 8,000 barrels of Ely's finest produce – eels!

As we descended to the crypt, we all felt apprehensive. What we were about to do would forge an unbreakable covenant between us – one which we knew, in due course, would almost certainly reveal our true destinies. Not only that, but we were going to take the vow in a place that held so much meaning and symbolism.

The din of the hordes of workmen had stopped and the gentle plainchant of the monks had drifted away, but the silence was only fleeting as a raw easterly wind began to whistle through the fragmentary skeleton of the cathedral and our footfalls boomed around the vast space. Our breath turned to mist in the cold night air and the echoes made us whisper to one another.

Sweyn led the way. He was the first to lift his lantern to reveal the low, vaulted ceiling of the crypt and the colossal round columns that supported their counterparts in the nave. The space was bare, except for St Etheldreda's tomb, standing proudly in the middle. Estrith recognized it immediately, and we all stood back to allow her to reflect on those chilling moments when her life and that of her sister had been spared by the intervention of a mysterious burst of sunlight.

Estrith went over to the tomb. It was just as it had been described to me. The plain stone sarcophagus was topped by a finely dressed slab, unadorned save for the outline of the saint's form chased into it and, carved in relief, standing proud of it, her hands in prayer. We stood in silence, deep beneath the nave, the echoes gone, the wind now barely audible.

It is strange how something as plain as a block of stone can strike fear into the hearts of even the most resolute of men. Cold and unyielding, and piled high with others of its kind, it creates an eerie presence that seems to possess a life of its own. The stones of the crypt reverberated, as if they could speak, and gave birth to dark corners and gloomy shadows which concealed secrets and mysteries.

Estrith ended the unnerving silence by pulling a rosary from a small purse on her belt.

'Nobody noticed me take this when we were dragged from the chapel all those years ago. I have kept it ever since. As we don't have the Talisman to wear, I thought we should each wear this rosary as we take the oath.'

Made of striking pearls and rubies, the beads culminated in a delicate silver cross on which was chased the figure of the crucified Christ. Estrith placed it around our necks in turn. We then each placed our left hand on St

Etheldreda's hands and clasped our right hand to our chest in the Roman salute of the Brotherhood of Ely, taking it in turns to recite the words which would become the guiding light of the rest of our days.

Robert was the last to take the oath. He had remembered the words perfectly and recited them with meaning, reaffirming a vow that had been intended to persuade his father to be a fair and just king. Had he been a better king, after Ely? Some say he did become a more sympathetic ruler; others say his tyranny never abated. Regardless of that, his firstborn and successor as Duke of Normandy had taken a new oath, affirming everything that the Brotherhood had fought for. Their suffering and death had not been in vain.

We placed our weapons on the tomb, formed ourselves into a circle around it and held hands as Estrith prayed for us.

'Blessed martyr, protect this small band of sinners and help us to be courageous in everything we do. We will strive to bring honour to your name and live up to the example of those who showed us the way. In the name of God Almighty. Amen.'

And so, our small group of brothers-in-arms had become a true brotherhood. Not only that, we had sanctified our bond in the exact place where Hereward's brotherhood had been formed. We all felt elated to be able to inherit the legacy of all that had been hoped for at Ely, but we were also daunted that with swearing the oath came so much responsibility – both as brethren and as individuals.

*

We made haste to Normandy, where Robert had to finance, recruit and prepare a new army for an expedition the like of which had not been attempted since the days of the legions of Rome.

Robert garnered his resources over the first few months of 1096 in concert with many others from as far afield as Germany, Christian Spain and southern Italy to put together the host of avenging Christians that the Pope had called for. We heard the news of each new contingent and listened to the ever more hateful rhetoric with growing anxiety.

Besides Robert of Normandy and Raymond of Toulouse, the men who provided the majority of the Crusade's money and manpower were some of the richest men in Europe: Godfrey of Bouillon, the second son of Count Eustace of Boulogne, who mortgaged all his estates to pay for his adventure; Count Robert of Flanders who, like Raymond of Toulouse, was driven by religious fanaticism; Stephen, Count of Blois, who was bullied into going by his domineering wife to atone for his many sins; and Baldwin of Boulogne, Godfrey's brother, who was motivated by simple greed and had every intention of staying in the Holy Land to create his own Christian fiefdom.

The formidable Bohemond of Taranto, the eldest son of Robert Guiscard, also 'took the cross' to the Holy Land, as it came to be known – through the practice adopted by the Crusaders of sewing a cross on to their surcoats, or painting it on to their shields. A man who stood a head taller than any of his contemporaries, he was as fierce as he was tall and had spent his life fighting Byzantines and Muslims in southern Italy and the Adriatic.

Bohemond also brought a large group of Norman knights from Calabria, Apulia and Sicily, battle-hardened men used to fighting Arab armies. Among them was another giant, Tancred of Hauteville – only twenty years old and fluent in Arabic, he had already made a reputation for himself as a ferocious warrior.

There was one other leader of the Crusade, whose army of peasants, thieves and vagabonds left Europe long before the knights and professional soldiers. Peter the Hermit, a short, skinny ascetic with long, unkempt hair, was not fond of washing himself or his meagre clothes, walked barefoot, drank only wine and ate only fish. Despite his repulsive appearance and odd habits, he was a remarkable orator who inspired large crowds, which followed him around as if he were a messiah. By May of 1096, his multitude, over 20,000 strong, was on its way to Constantinople. The horde had almost no money, few weapons and little idea where the Holy Land was, but they had a blind faith compelling them to go – men and women, young and old, from all over Europe.

When Peter the Hermit's followers reached Germany, their anti-Muslim hatred found another, much easier target – the other 'infidels', the placid and inconspicuous Jews who had lived at peace in Europe for centuries. Like a contagion, as the Crusaders passed through the towns and cities of central Europe, their fanaticism spread to the local population, inciting them to slaughter their Jewish neighbours and fellow citizens in their thousands.

What we feared would happen had begun, but long before we had expected it. The Jews just happened to get in the way.

*

Robert's biggest dilemma in preparing his army was how to pay for it. The sum required was so huge, it would have impoverished his duchy for years.

He called the Brethren together to discuss it.

'I estimate I need four times my annual income to pay for the thousands of people who want to make the journey. Several of my ancestors made pilgrimages to Jerusalem; most never came back. I've been checking the accounts. Do you realize that, as well as knights and infantry, I need to take a complete duplicate of my administration and every skill and trade in the realm, from grooms to blacksmiths, whores to falconers? My steward has calculated that we will need four hundred carts and double the number of oxen to pull them! I think we can find enough whores, but where will I find eight hundred oxen?'

Imperturbable as always, Edwin came up with the obvious solution.

'Can't you take fewer people?'

'If only that were possible; every priest in the realm is preaching salvation to those who take up the cross. They are swearing oaths to God to free the Sacred Places. Once they've done that, I can't deny them passage. That would be tantamount to heresy – and would lead to me being accused of the same crime as the Muslims.'

I had anticipated Robert's dilemma and had been thinking about it for a while.

'Robert, I have a suggestion for you.'

'Please! I need a very large pot of gold.'

'Well, I think I know where there is one. Rufus covets Normandy like a parched man craves water. Why don't you pledge him a controlling share of the wealth of the dukedom? I have spoken to your Chancellor, and he estimates its value at around 10,000 German marks. According to the great ledger of taxes and tithes drawn up in your father's reign, if the King were to impose a geld of four shillings per hide throughout the entire kingdom, he could raise the money. He wouldn't be very popular, but I don't think that would bother Rufus.'

'Edgar, you're a cunning old fox; that might work!'

A few weeks later, Rufus, King of England, made a personal delivery of the huge geld.

He entered Rouen in grand style with enough coin to acquire two-thirds of the duchy: 67 barrels, each containing 100 pounds of silver. In exchange he took possession of his homeland and united England and Normandy. His long-term ambition had been achieved – sovereignty over a land that stretched from the wildernesses of Wales and Scotland to the gates of Paris.

Robert, although saddened by the loss, was at long last freed from the burden of his inheritance and possessed of sufficient resources to begin a dramatic new adventure in a distant land.

PART FIVE

For God's Sake

25. The Purple

We had to reach the Alps before winter, and in September of 1096 all was ready for the long journey across Europe. The various contingents took different routes, partly out of preference, but also to help spread the impact of the vast horde on local supplies of fresh food.

Robert's Norman army included many Norman knights based in England and a few dozen native Englishmen who could afford the costs of horses, grooms and men-at-arms. I was given the honour of leading the English with my own staff and retinue. Edwin became my standard-bearer and Sweyn my aide-de-camp. He was granted a full knight's title by Robert – Sir Sweyn of Bourne – which allowed Adela to revert to her role as Sweyn's wife and take the title Lady Adela of Bourne, thus granting her sufficient status to mix with other high-born Crusaders. Robert also found a title of esteem for Estrith, appointing her as Abbess of Fécamp, a dormant appellation within his gift for a foundation that had been closed during his father's reign.

Several other lords and knights brought their wives – some even brought their children – so Adela and Estrith had far more female company than they had been used to.

Our route took us via Lyon and Geneva and we crossed the Alps well before the first snows, refreshing ourselves with an extended stay outside the gates of Turin. We were fêted everywhere we went with wild cheering and gifts of food, wine and religious relics. Masses were said for us, and many of our knights were blessed with more amorous gifts by women along the route.

In some places, a few particularly ardent souls took the spontaneous decision to join the Crusade, closed up their houses, gathered their belongings and weapons and found a place in the convoy.

I often looked back to admire the remarkable sight that we presented – an immensely long band of colour weaving its way through the lush autumn countryside. The usual martial array of heraldic pennons, gonfalons and war banners in every hue imaginable had been superseded by the blood red of Christ's cross. It also seemed to be painted on every shield and embroidered on every surcoat and cloak, creating a striking statement of common cause.

Songs and prayers often broke the monotonous trundle of the carts and the clatter of hooves, and there were always the laughter and animated conversation of excited people, enthused by their mission.

Robert was a well-organized leader. The daily march was carefully shepherded and the route meticulously plotted; only the dust of southern Italy created some minor inconvenience. We all had mixed feelings. The cause seemed worthy enough – to replace oppressive Muslim rule with a benign Christian realm like the one Count Roger had created in Sicily, a sovereignty now welcomed by Muslims.

But what if the stories were exaggerated, or not even true?

When we arrived at Bari, we met with the two larger convoys, the armies of Robert of Flanders and Stephen of

Blois. A huge armada of Pisan, Genoese and Venetian ships was waiting for us, but the captains advised us that the autumn gales of the Adriatic were too great a risk and suggested we sit and wait for the spring. That was easier said than done but, with his typical calm efficiency, Robert made a detailed plan which the other two leaders were happy to accept.

To prevent us swamping the local population and resources, we retreated far into the woods of the hilly hinterland to make camp, and only quartermasters and stewards were allowed to Bari to buy provisions in the markets. Most of our food we would find for ourselves in the forests and rivers, and we would make our own entertainment.

After an uneventful but surprisingly cold winter gorging ourselves on fish and game, we finally crossed the Adriatic and landed in Durazzo in late February 1097. There we met two more huge caravans of Crusaders: the knights of Bohemond of Taranto, who had sailed from Brindisi; and the biggest army of all, the formidable collection of zealots and soldiers of fortune under the command of Raymond of Toulouse and his son, Bertrand, who had chosen to cross the plains of northern Italy and follow the Adriatic coast from Trieste.

We used the old Roman road from Durazzo to Constantinople and made good progress despite the now gargantuan scale of our army, a host of over 60,000. Despite our best efforts, Count Raymond was impetuous and cared little for the peasant communities we were passing. We descended on them like a plague of locusts, leaving in our wake fields, barns and markets bare of anything edible or useful.

Discipline began to decline and soon money was no

longer left in exchange for goods; they were simply stolen. Whores weren't rewarded for their services, and eventually were discarded altogether in favour of the rape of local women.

Alexius, the Emperor of Byzantium, had sent emissaries and small units of the Imperial Guard to greet us in Durazzo, no doubt to keep an eye on us. Understandably, these men tried to prevent the looting and, inevitably, violent clashes followed, among the worst of which took place in the Ancient Greek city of Thessaloniki, one of Byzantium's most important centres of trade and learning.

Although we insisted that the army camp outside the city, many of the young knights were restless and knew that, like any other thriving port, Thessaloniki's waterfront would have available all the diversions a saddle-weary soldier would require. By mid-evening on the first night, the noise of mayhem was already drifting up the hillsides of the city. Most of our leadership was indifferent to the problem, but Robert asked me to mount my contingent and bring order to the city. He gave me two of his conrois to add his authority to our presence.

What we found when we arrived in the narrow streets of the docks area was akin to a battleground. The Emperor's men had scattered to the hills, intimidated by the huge number of ill-disciplined Christians. Shops and warehouses were ablaze, carts were piled high with anything of value, and bodies were strewn everywhere. The brothels were empty – the girls had presumably recognized the danger signs and left – but women were screaming from every direction as our valiant Christian Crusaders marauded through the streets, kicking down doors and looking for women and girls.

I organized small squads of a dozen men, with a senior knight leading each one, and sent them on street-by-street missions to stop the looting and rape. Their task was unpleasant, but not difficult, as most of the miscreants were so drunk they were unable to put up much of a fight. Adela was a particularly effective admonisher, kicking and punching the men until they did her bidding but dealing gently with the women she found, making sure that someone was on hand to take care of them.

We organized carts to transport the men back to camp in disgrace, and we helped the locals to identify their belongings and then returned what was left of them. Sadly, as in the examples from central Europe, it was Thessaloniki's Jewish community which bore the brunt of the crimes. The docks area was a Jewish enclave and, once again, they had been in the wrong place at the wrong time.

As we got close to Constantinople, the final groups of Crusaders joined us – Germans, north Europeans and Lotharingians, led by Duke Godfrey of Bouillon – making us into an army over 80,000 strong.

Both Duke Godfrey and Count Raymond had had difficult journeys, beset by indiscipline, poor morale and clashes with local communities. Robert called several Councils of War to try to restore discipline, but each ended in chaos as the rival lords argued every point. I tried hard to use common sense in the debates and argued vociferously for unity. I think my words won me some admirers, but they made little difference to the outcome. Obduracy ruled – egos were too big to listen to reason.

*

When we reached Byzantium's fabled capital, we found its gates barred against us and an envoy from Emperor Alexius waiting to escort us to an audience with the man who wore the Purple of Rome – a ruler whose empire was over 1,200 years old and who still thought of himself as Roman.

Just as we called the Byzantines 'Greeks' because of their language and affiliation to the Eastern Church, they called western Europeans 'Latins' because of our use of the Latin language for all our formal documents and because of our adherence to the Church of Rome. Although it had been only forty years since the Great Schism between the two Churches, it looked like it was going to be a permanent rupture in the faith.

All the senior command staffs of the Crusader armies were summoned, and Robert managed to obtain places for Adela and Estrith in the entourage as interpreters. The cream of European aristocracy – over 200 dukes, counts and knights, and some of their wives and daughters – were escorted through the gates of the world's most magnificent city and seated in royal carriages to be given a ceremonial entrance.

Horns and trumpets signalled the beginning of the procession as a company of the Emperor's personal bodyguard, the legendary Varangian Guard, led the procession. The entire route was lined with soldiers from the many themes of the Byzantine army: Macedonians, Thracians, Thessalonians and men recruited from as far away as Cyprus, Mesopotamia and Crete.

We 'Latin Princes' were people used to the best that money could buy, but none of us had seen anything on such a scale or possessed of such opulence and grandeur.

Shaped like a triangle pointing at the sea, the city was surrounded by water on two sides. On the landward side, it was defended by not one but two mighty walls – each five miles long, sixteen feet thick and over seventy feet high – with huge open spaces in between. It was impossible to imagine them ever being breached.

We were told that more than half a million people lived in the city, ten times the number of inhabitants in the biggest cities in the West. We had seen Rome, and the superb basilica of St Peter's, but most of the population lived in modest wooden homes amidst the crumbling remains of the city's former imperial glory. But Constantinople was awash with magnificent palaces, churches and public buildings; its homes were full of the finest furnishings, marbles and mosaics; its people were dressed in the finest cottons and silks and adorned in gold and precious gems.

Constantine himself watched over the city, represented as Apollo in a huge bronze statue atop a column 170 feet high. The Emperor Justinian, captured on horseback in marble three times lifesize, presided over the Hippodrome, an arena with a capacity for 100,000 people. The most impressive sight of all was the Basilica of St Sophia, a building of great antiquity, but far bigger than any Christian church in the West, even the ones newly constructed. The top of its dome was as high as the statue to Constantine and over a hundred feet across.

Estrith stared at it, open-mouthed.

'My mother told me about it. Isn't it magnificent? The calculations are outstanding! They were done by the architect Isidorus of Miletus and the mathematician Arthamius of Tralles. No need for my hammer beams; the key is the circular dome. The weight is distributed evenly to the massive walls, buttressed by the even bigger corner columns. But the strength comes from the apex, which holds the roof like the locking ring at the top of a tripod; the pressure from any one direction is held by an equal force fighting against it.'

She made it sound simple; I was sure it wasn't.

The Emperor's palace, the Blachernae, stood proudly on a hilltop in the north-west corner of the city with views of the sea and the surrounding countryside. Without wishing to be too disparaging about the abodes of my noble comrades, it made their ducal palaces look like peasants' hovels. Emperor Alexius had granted us a rare privilege in greeting us at the Blachernae, his private palace, rather than at the Great Palace, usually used for ceremonial occasions. The Great Palace had been built by the Emperor Constantine hundreds of years ago but had, like Byzantium itself, fallen on hard times. An important part of Alexius's rebuilding of his city and empire had been the commissioning of a new palace to match those of the great Caesars of the past.

Alexius had been one of Byzantium's highest nobility, and was a highly renowned general, when he became Emperor in a palace coup over fifteen years earlier. The empire was on its knees: the army was demoralized after a crushing defeat at the infamous Battle of Manzikert; the treasury was bare; and a succession of weak or despotic emperors had sapped the energy of the people.

In truth, the empire had been in a constant state of struggle for hundreds of years against fierce warrior-tribes from the North and the messianic valour of Islam from the south. By the time of Alexius's accession, the chalice of the Purple could well have been a poisoned one and the empire in its death throes. However, slowly and shrewdly, with a combination of diplomacy and aggression, generosity and ruthlessness, Alexius had managed to rebuild the army, refill his treasury and restore the vigour of the people.

When several significant Muslim leaders died in quick succession and internal squabbling between the Shia believers of the Fatimid Caliphate of Cairo and the Sunnis of the Abbasid of Baghdad weakened it, Alexius chose the moment to make his move. His masterstroke was to appeal to his Christian brothers in the West to do his fighting for him. Perhaps, like Pope Urban, who yearned to unite the two Christian Churches under his governance in Rome, Alexius dreamed of uniting East and West under his sovereignty in Constantinople and recreating the glorious empire of Ancient Rome.

Now, as we arrived at what we assumed was the Emperor's Great Hall, we were amazed to discover that it was only an anteroom for guests to await an audience with him. Even more remarkably, there were two more grand halls after the first, for guests or delegations of increasing importance. Each one was covered from floor to ceiling in intricately woven tapestries – at least three times the size of any I had seen before – the finest marbles, laid in complex symmetrical patterns aglow with vibrant colours, and astonishing mosaics, the quality of which was breathtaking. They depicted hunting, harvests, banquets, bathing and Byzantium's great military victories in such detail and realism that it looked as if the people and animals were alive beneath one's feet.

When we finally arrived at his reception hall, it was so large that all 200 of us seemed swallowed by it, even though the Emperor's court, entourage and bodyguards were already there in significant numbers.

As we took our positions, standing in neat rows beneath the imperial dais, lords in the front rows, lesser mortals in order of precedence towards the back, the Emperor sat in silence, acknowledging only the most senior men with a slight nod of his head and the hint of a smile.

Alexius Comnenus was in his early forties, well set with a neatly cropped beard, heavily flecked with grey. His demeanour was that of a man of stern resolve, but his physique was unremarkable in appearance, apart from piercing steel-grey eyes. However, his clothes and armour were far from ordinary.

On top of his imperial purple surcoat he wore a lamellar-armour jacket made from plates of solid gold, and gold wristlets and armbands. His sea-blue silk cloak was held across his chest by a deep-purple ruby the size of a quail's egg, and his finely tooled gold crown was studded with pearls, some of which were strung and cascaded down either side of his face like wringlets of hair. All his weapons, most held by his pages behind him, were studded with precious gems. His sword hung from his belt, the scabbard of which was made from gold inset with more rubies than it was possible to count.

Strangely, of all his splendours, I was drawn mostly to his boots. It is often said that you can judge a man by his footwear – well, make of Alexius's boots what you will. They had the look of riding boots, but were made from the most luxurious soft leather, which the fullers had managed to dye a rich purple to match the rest of his regalia. Then, to finish them off, an elaborate design had been sown into the boots using the same pearls as those of the Emperor's crown.

The overall effect was awe-inspiring and led me to think that this is what it must have been like to stand before a Hadrian or Augustus.

To the Emperor's left were his wife, Irene, modestly clothed in white silk but weighed down with gems and gold jewellery, and his eldest children, Anna, a striking girl in her mid-teens with a very inquisitive eye, and John, a small, unattractive boy of about ten.

With only the slightest movement of his index finger, the Emperor summoned one of his entourage, who addressed us in Greek. Estrith was brought forward to stand beside me and translate.

'His Imperial Majesty welcomes you to Constantinople, city of the Caesars, and to Byzantium, an empire without equal in the world. His Majesty has asked me to thank you for responding to his offer to join with him in opposing the enemies of Christianity who occupy the Sacred Places and who have been plaguing the gates of Europe for centuries. He has also asked me to inform you of the unfortunate circumstances surrounding the followers of Peter the Hermit, who arrived here some months ago at the head of a large group of pilgrims who had also answered His Majesty's offer of brotherhood as soldiers of Christ.'

As the Emperor sat and scrutinized us, his herald described the wretched state of the ragtag army of Peter the Hermit's 'People's Crusade', as it had come to be called, when it arrived at the gates of Constantinople. Many had been killed in skirmishes with locals or had died of disease along the route. Even so, the Emperor was astonished by the number who had answered his call and horrified by their looting and violence.

The Emperor kept them provisioned and tried to persuade their leaders to wait until the arrival of the professional armies of the Latin Princes before crossing the Bosphorus into Asia Minor. They would not wait, and chaos ensued until Alexius organized hundreds of ships to take them across to the Byzantine-controlled coastal strip on the other side. Unfortunately, they had no appreciation of the power of the army of the Muslim Turks, stationed only two days' ride away at the stronghold of Nicaea.

The Christian rabble soon began raiding into Muslim territory. The scenes were reported with disgust in Constantinople: children and babies hacked to pieces; girls and old women raped and tortured in unspeakable ways; everything of any value taken; all who resisted put to death.

The Turks soon retaliated. In one incident, a large group of Germans and Italians became trapped in the fortress of Xerigordos, where they held out for eight days. By the end, the defenders were drinking the blood of their horses and lowering rags into the sewers in order to drink the liquid squeezed from the extracted contents. When the Turks eventually broke in, they put everyone to the sword.

The rump of the People's Crusade was camped at Civetot on the coast. When they heard about the massacre at Xerigordos, they immediately set out to attack the formidable Turkish fortress at Nicaea. With little military acumen, they were slaughtered in their thousands long before they reached the fortress, as Estrith graphically reported to us.

'There was a bloodbath that was to leave a pile of bodies as high as a mountain. The Turks then fell upon Civetot to commit another massacre, killing all those too old, young or ill to fight, and taking as slaves young girls and women, and young boys whose face and form pleased them.'

Peter the Hermit had been in Constantinople, negotiating with the Emperor, and thus had survived, along with only a handful of others rescued by a contingent of the Varangian Guard.

Alexius then got to his feet and spoke for the first time.

'My noble Lords of Europe, we are grateful for your presence here but, as you have heard, our enemy is formidable. You must not commit your armies in a land you know little about without my guidance. I have been fighting fierce barbarians to the north and cunning infidels to the south all my life. Do not underestimate the Muslim as a man or as a soldier. He is our equal, of that there is no doubt, but he follows a faith that denies the true God, and for that we must pray for his soul. Perversely, he thinks that we are the lost souls, denied everlasting peace – that is the simple truth of it. This is a fight to decide the true path to Heaven, not a campaign against ignorant barbarians.

'Let me now make some things clear concerning your expedition into the Levant. I will be the watchful angel for your adventure and provide you with transportation across the Bosphorus and adequate provisions for your journey. In return, you will undertake to liberate the Holy Places in the name of Christianity and under my sovereignty. If you wish to create your own fiefdoms in these lands, you will become sovereign lords under my protection and owe fealty to me. To these ends, with God Almighty as your witness, you will now be required to take an oath to affirm your agreement.'

Alexius had played his trump card and, with its impact reverberating around the hall in agitated whispers and gasps, he sat down to be cooled by a pair of tall, bare-breasted, jet-black girls armed with fans of ostrich feathers.

Raymond of Toulouse strode forward, a pace beyond the others.

'Your Majesty, I am Raymond, Count of Toulouse. Does that mean that your army will not be joining our march on Jerusalem?'

'My Lord Count, my job is to use my army to guard your rear and help with the evacuation of the sick and wounded. I will man a heavily armed supply line for the entire length of your journey and duration of your stay; a force consisting of many thousands of men.'

Raymond of Toulouse, clearly disconcerted, was about to challenge the Emperor when Stephen of Blois sank to his knees, eager to take the oath. Others quickly followed, leaving Raymond isolated. He eventually agreed to the Emperor's terms, except for the clause about the sovereignty of Christian fiefdoms. Realizing that it could be dealt with at another time, Alexius nodded his agreement and the oath-taking began for all of us.

During the protracted ceremony, I noticed Estrith smiling at young Bertrand and, once again, I felt the pangs of jealousy.

A little later, Estrith suddenly tugged my arm and whispered in my ear. 'Look, hanging from the Emperor's belt. Is it possible?'

Alexius had leaned over to talk to his wife, exposing

something attached to his belt and hanging just below his golden jacket. I also recognized it immediately. It was Hereward's now legendary amulet, the Talisman of Truth.

'Not now!'

Estrith wanted me to approach the Emperor there and then, and I had to repeat myself three times before she relented.

'The Emperor has just pulled off an amazing political coup; it's the work of a genius. We must let the dust settle.'

At the end of the oath-taking, an army of stewards emerged carrying outrageous gifts for everyone. There were caskets of gold and silver coin, bales of silk, jewellery, carved ivory, jade, carpets – the favours just went on appearing, as if conjured by a magician.

For several days afterwards, yet more presents were delivered to the camps of the Crusaders as each contingent's leadership was invited to the palace in turn to meet Alexius in person. The Emperor briefed them about the general strategy and subtle tactics of the war against the Muslims, as well as the details of his plan for the taking of Jerusalem.

Robert's exalted status among the Latin Princes meant we were quite near the top of the Emperor's list and only had a few days to wait for our appointment. Even so, it was difficult to get Sweyn and Adela to agree to wait until the audience before pursuing the tantalizing subject of the object we had seen hanging from the imperial belt.

Meanwhile, my envy for Bertrand's good fortune in being the man lucky enough to send a tremor through Estrith's elegant timbers again got the better of me when she and I were next alone together.

'I assume the presence of the young ascetic with the morals of a stud bull means your abbess's veil has slipped again?'

Estrith's response was typically forthright.

'Edgar, are you protecting me now? Or lecturing me?'

'I'm sorry, that wasn't fair.'

My apology appeared to take the sting out of my earlier taunt, and Estrith continued with more restraint and some hesitation.

'We have spent a couple of nights together, but . . . if you must know . . . there will be no more trysts with Bertrand.'

'Why?'

'Apart from the fact that you're right – he's an empty-headed hypocrite – his passions extend a little too far for my tastes. He wanted . . . well . . . let's just say, I'm not feeling very wholesome at the moment.'

'I understand. It will not be mentioned again.'

I felt so sorry for Estrith; she had so many gifts and was so generous of spirit. All she wanted was to express herself, but the strange world we lived in made that so difficult for her.

Once again, I thought for a moment about how things might have been different between us. I convinced myself that, were I to become her husband, I would let her spread her wings and fly.

But as soon as those thoughts came into my head, I dismissed them.

That time had passed.

26. Talisman of Truth

The thought of meeting the Emperor of Byzantium in person was nerve-racking at the best of times, but with the added anticipation of what the discovery of the Talisman might mean, we approached the imperial dais feeling somewhat tense.

The great gilt throne, topped by the empire's fabled double-headed eagle, was empty when we arrived, but the sudden snap of the guards coming to attention signalled the entrance of the man whose lineage allowed him to wear the imperial purple of Rome. We all knelt; Robert and I were allowed to kiss his ring, a cameo of exquisite delicacy bearing the same imperial eagle.

Robert made the introductions. The Emperor was understandably intrigued by a female knight and a sister of the Church – all the other women he had met had been the kin of Crusader lords. He was particularly concerned about Estrith's status.

'Madam, Muslims are very honourable men, especially towards noblewomen, but they may be less than worthy in their treatment of women who choose to travel alone. You may be more vulnerable than you realize.'

'Your Majesty, you are generous in thinking of my safety, but we are bound to one another as brethren; where one goes, we all go.'

'Very well, but I beseech you to take care, and your menfolk to look out for these two ladies.'

I could sense Adela stiffen next to me and I nudged her knee with mine to encourage her to hold her tongue, but it did not have the desired effect.

She clasped the hilt of her sword and straightened herself.

'Majesty, we will all take care of Estrith.'

The Emperor looked annoyed at first – few people as lowly as a knight, particularly the oddity of a knight in female form, would have spoken directly to him before – but he soon smiled.

'How fascinating; I would like to learn more, but I have matters to discuss.'

He then went through the details of the campaign as he saw it, outlining the specifics of the logistical support he planned and giving us the benefit of his vast combat experience against the Muslim armies. Worryingly, it soon became clear that he was already frustrated at the attitude of several of the more forthright Crusaders.

When he had finished, we thanked him profusely for his guidance and wisdom.

Robert then broached the subject we had waited so patiently to raise.

'Your Majesty, Prince Edgar begs your indulgence; he has a question for you.'

'Of course.'

'Majesty, you wear an amulet on your belt. We think it is something we recognize, an object of great importance to us.'

'I think you must be mistaken; it is a charm I bought

many years ago from a trader in oriental treasures. It is from the lands far to the east.'

Once again, Adela had the temerity to speak up. I made to stop her, but the Emperor gestured for her to continue.

'Your Majesty, the stone contains the image of the Devil and his familiars, entombed by a splash of the blood of Christ. It is called the Talisman of Truth. The last time I saw it, it was being worn by Estrith's father, Hereward of Bourne. He and his wife, Torfida of the Wildwood, were the Talisman's guardians.'

'I'm sorry to disappoint you; this is a very different amulet, nothing like the one you describe. It is amber, but has no images in it, just a few trapped insects.'

The Emperor then stood and we were abruptly dismissed.

The journey back to our camp became a long discussion about whether the Emperor was telling the truth. All of us thought him perturbed by our questions, but could not understand why he would want to hide something from us.

Estrith was certain that what he carried was the Talisman.

'He knows something. It is definitely the Talisman, and the infuriating thing is that whoever gave it to him probably knows what became of my father.'

Edwin was more pragmatic.

'You were a few feet away; you could have been mistaken. As for the Emperor's reaction, he probably thought it discourteous of us to ask.'

Although I had not seen the Talisman as many times as

Estrith, I was also sure it was the amulet Hereward had worn. But I thought it unlikely to be still linked to Hereward after all these years.

'Even if it is the Talisman, it could have gone through many hands before arriving here – anyone could have picked it up at Ely. But, I agree, it is an amazing coincidence that we should find it hanging from the gilded belt of the Emperor of Byzantium.'

The others had been too far away to see what Estrith and I had seen, but Sweyn was adamant.

'The Emperor is hiding something. All he needed to do was show it to us and that would have been an end to it. It's the amulet all right. And when we've finished our business in the Holy Land, we'll get to the bottom of it. Then it will lead us to Hereward.'

Robert pointed out that that might be easier said than done.

'Sweyn, emperors are not usually in the habit of bending to the will of anybody – let alone a lowly duke and an even lowlier knight.'

'On the contrary, chivalry demands that he return it to Estrith. It is a sacred relic, entrusted to the care of Hereward and Torfida by her father, the Old Man of the Wildwood, and before him by Emma, Queen of England, and a long line of forebears stretching back to the emperors of Rome. Estrith is Hereward and Torfida's only surviving relative, thus she is now the guardian of the Talisman. It belongs to her and her alone.'

Robert did not respond. Like the rest of us, he was impressed by the clarity of Sweyn's answer and the forthright way in which he delivered it.

Edwin brought the discussion to an end by reminding us of the practicalities we faced in the expedition we were about to undertake.

'We have three weeks to get ready for the crossing. There is much to do. Let's deal with the dilemma of the Talisman when we return.'

Ships arrived from every port in the Mediterranean for the crossing. The distance was not great – only about half a mile in places – but the number of Crusaders was huge and the volume of supplies immense. The Emperor rode down to the quays every morning to check on progress and each time was hailed as the great leader of Christendom and cheered wherever he went.

Alexius had brokered a flimsy compromise with the Latin Princes about the campaign's leadership, strategy and objectives, but the details were vague and few of us expected the agreement to last for long.

First of all, Raymond of Toulouse was to act as primate of a Crusade Council of War, a body consisting of all the leaders of the various contingents. It would be his job to ensure a consensus on routes and battle planning.

Secondly, all inhabitants of liberated cities and territories were to be treated humanely, and freedom of worship would be permitted.

Finally, the Princes were at liberty to create their own fiefdoms in the freed cities, but subject to the above conditions and their original oath to the Emperor – to bow to his sovereignty over all land and people restored to Christian rule.

I was by far the most junior member of the Council of

War, leading the smallest contingent, and was surrounded by powerful individuals who made little attempt to hide their personal ambitions. I feared men like Bohemond of Taranto and Tancred of Hauteville were going to do just as they pleased, regardless of what the Council said – or the Emperor, for that matter.

The day before our departure, we were summoned to see Alexius. A feverish sense of anticipation began to course through our veins. None of the other contingents' leaderships had been asked to go to the Palace, so we hoped and prayed that the call had something to do with the Talisman.

When we arrived in the inner sanctum of the Blachernae, we were ushered into a much smaller but no less ornate room than before. It was deserted; there was no furniture, just a bare room of tapestries and mosaic. Then a wide door to our right was opened and two Varangians appeared and stood guard as the Emperor walked in.

We all bowed.

The Emperor addressed us directly.

'The man who gave me the Talisman is waiting next door to see you. There is a reason why I denied that the amulet was what you said it was – but he will explain that. He would like to see Estrith alone first, then the rest of you. Forgive me; there is much to do before tomorrow.'

The Emperor then turned and left. As he did so, a steward appeared and beckoned Estrith towards an identical door on the opposite side. Sweyn was not happy for Estrith to go alone, but she was halfway to the door before he had time to raise an objection.

The wait seemed like an eternity. It was probably only a few minutes, but it felt like an hour.

Suddenly, the door was thrown open to reveal Estrith all but dragging a large and unmistakable figure behind her. She was crying and laughing at the same time, almost hysterical with emotion. Adela immediately started to weep as well, as she joined Estrith in embracing the man none of us had seen in over twenty-five years.

The men stood back, but Sweyn had tears in his eyes and his chest heaved in spasms.

I quickly calculated that the man before us must have been sixty-one or so years of age, but he looked ten years younger. His girth was more substantial than I remembered, and his hair was full of grey streaks amidst the flowing golden-blond locks, but there he stood, Hereward of Bourne, England's great hero, a man of legend.

Sweyn and Adela had been right: he was alive still.

It was a miracle.

Then Hereward spoke, and I was transported back to 1069 and the measured but powerful voice of his rousing oratory during the rebellion. I was the Prince Atheling, the heir to the throne of England, high born, with a royal pedigree centuries old, and he was a minor thegn from a tiny village in the shires; yet he was the giant, I was the sprat. He was all that I wanted to be: a leader of men in reality, not one whose only claim to leadership was his conception twixt royal bed-sheets. He had become the towering presence in my life; now, when it did not seem possible that he could still be alive, he had appeared again.

I knew that, as before, he would be an inspiration to me and our Brethren.

'Emperor Alexius has given us a room where we can sit and talk, and has had food prepared for us.'

We all embraced and I introduced Hereward to Robert.

'My Lord Duke, I didn't think I would ever see my family and friends again. That I should do so in the presence of the son of King William is, to say the least, somewhat of a surprise. However, Estrith tells me that you are sworn together as brethren, so I am honoured to meet you.'

'The honour is mine, Hereward of Bourne; I have heard so much about you. I look forward to hearing more.'

Beneath a heavy ruby-red cloak fastened by an intricate bronze clasp, Hereward wore the blood-red tunic, trimmed with gold embroidery, of a Captain of the Varangian Guard. Over one shoulder, held by a finely tooled leather strap, he carried a large circular shield adorned with the motif of the winged lion of the Guard. Slung over the other shoulder was a heavy battle sword with a fine gilt handle and delicately worked sheath. Along his belt were leather pouches for two shorter stabbing swords, a small close-quarters axe and a jewelled dagger.

But there was something missing, the most fearsome weapon I had ever seen – the Great Axe of Göteborg.

'Where is your axe?'

'It's over there, in the corner; I'm getting a bit old to carry it around all day.'

He beckoned to one of the Varangians to get it for him. Even though the soldier was a large man himself, he struggled to carry it, holding it with reverence, as if it had magical powers. When he handed it to Hereward, he grasped it easily in one hand and lifted it at arm's length. It seemed even bigger than I remembered; the shaft was the diameter of a man's wrist and its head stood almost at shoulder height. The two huge, crescent-shaped blades still shone as brightly as when they had first been made.

'Do you remember this?'

Sweyn went up to him and asked to hold the Great Axe.

'I remember it well . . .'

He did not continue his sentence; dealing with the weight of the weapon took all his concentration and breath.

Several hours of fascinating conversation followed, as we told our stories and Hereward told his. Although he had obviously told Estrith a more intimate version during their private meeting together, he did share with us a brief account of what happened between him and the King in St Etheldreda's Chapel at Ely.

Estrith held him around his waist and rested her head on his shoulder as he described the bitter-sweet paradox of William finally acknowledging the courage and worthiness of the cause of the Brotherhood, and deciding to spare Gunnhild and Estrith, but demanding that a dreadful price be paid. The King insisted that Hereward was never to see his daughters again, who would be put in the care of Robert of Mortain. He must agree to leave England in secret, never to return.

The King had devised an infernal pact between them, a perfect example of William's fiendish cunning. Hereward had no choice but to agree – it did represent an acknowledgement of sorts that the sacrifices of the Brotherhood had not been in vain – so the pact with the Devil was done.

He created a new identity for himself – Godwin of Ely,

soldier of fortune – cut off his distinctive blond locks and, after a few years' service in the bodyguard of a German prince, slowly made his way to Constantinople. He enlisted in the imperial army of Byzantium, which already included several of King Harold's housecarls who had survived Senlac Ridge. A handful of them recognized him, but never revealed his identity, following the strict code of honour practised by the Emperor's soldiers.

When Alexius became Emperor in 1081, Hereward joined the elite Varangian Guard. He soon rose rapidly through the ranks and won universal acclaim as its most formidable warrior. The new Emperor, a 24-year-old seasoned soldier himself who had first gone to war as a boy of fourteen, soon picked out Hereward to be the man around whom to rebuild Byzantium's shattered army and appointed him Captain of the Varangians.

He became close to Alexius, for whom he had immense respect, both as a man and a soldier. He revealed to him his real identity and the truth about his life before his arrival Constantinople.

Hereward led the Guard in the great victory against the Pechenegs at Levunium in 1091, after which he was paraded, garlanded, through the streets of Constantinople. He was fifty-five years old by then and his many injuries, scars and broken bones were getting the better of his ageing body. His eyesight was not as keen as it once was, and his reactions were slowing. He decided to retire and entrust Alexius with the Talisman in recognition of his great achievement in neutralizing an enemy of the Empire that had been plaguing its northern border for years.

Alexius wanted to award Hereward a huge pension and vast estates in gratitude for his faithful service. Hereward refused the offer, content with a modest casket of silver and a small plot of land in the western Peloponnese. It was one of the most remote places in the empire, and the grant of land was entirely virgin territory – almost all of it comprised Mount Foloi, a heavily wooded, rugged mountain with commanding views to the west and out to sea. Hereward had seen it many years earlier and decided it would be the ideal place to retire to.

He built his own shelter above the oaks and pines, just beneath the top of the mountain, where the chill and the winds of winter would remind him of England. He hunted, foraged and farmed just as he had done as a young man in England's wildwood after he had been banished by King Edward at Winchester.

He said he never got lonely; he had so much to reflect on. And so many memories to keep him company, he added poignantly, with a tear in his eye and a kiss for Estrith.

'And I had Torfida for company. She said she would always be with me. She has kept her promise and she still is.'

I suddenly remembered the giant blond Varangian on the prow of the Byzantine ship at the Battle of Mazara, whom Ibn Hamed had said was the Captain of the Guard.

Adela had remembered too and got the question out before me.

'Surely it cannot have been you leading the attack on Mazara in Sicily? It was in the autumn of the year 1084, I think . . . but we believed the Captain had been killed?'

'Were you there?'

'Yes, we were in the service of Roger of Sicily.'

Hereward looked at Estrith. 'And you?'

'No, I was building churches in Normandy at the time.'

'Like mother, like daughter. Well, fate would have dealt me a strange blow if it had been me at Mazara – killed in battle against my old friend, Count Roger, with my own family serving in his army. Fortunately for me, the Emperor did not send me on the campaigns against the Normans in Italy and the Balkans because of my previous service with the Guiscards and my close bond with Roger. The man who was killed that day was my deputy, another Englishman, John of Worcester, a fine man and a great soldier. He took an arrow which pierced his armour, broke his ribs and ruptured his heart. He was dead in moments.'

Sweyn then continued the reminiscing.

'There are so many stories about you and Ely! You must have been tempted to come back to England, especially after you retired from the army and William died.'

'I was very tempted – but William kept his side of the bargain, and I kept mine. I paid a high price, but not as high as the one paid by the rest of the Brotherhood.'

Adela then spoke.

'So, you have become like the Old Man of the Wildwood?'

'I certainly live like him, but without his knowledge and wisdom. I am no seer, just an ancient soldier.'

'Did you never find a woman to spend your retirement with?'

'No woman would be mad enough to spend her days with an old man in a thatched lean-to at the top of a mountain.'

Then Hereward got to his feet. Suddenly, it was as if we were back in 1069; he had that fiery look in his eye.

'I go the coast three or four times a year and enjoy the hospitality of the local governor at Messene. I've been following the Emperor's plans with great interest. With the northern border secure, his dilemma now is the world of Islam, especially the Seljuk Turks, who pose an even more formidable threat than the Pechenegs.'

Sweyn was spurred on by Hereward's enthusiasm.

'I always knew you were alive. And I often thought about the Varangians, because I knew that many of King Harold's housecarls came here to enlist.'

'All those Englishmen are gone now, either perished in battle or retired to live out their days in peace. When Alexius called for help from the Latin Princes, I thought it might lead to one last adventure in my life – during which there was even the vague possibility of hearing a little of what became of all of you.'

Adela sprang to her feet.

'Does that mean you are coming with us?'

'Of course, let me repeat what the Emperor's messenger read out when he appeared with his escort through the mist of my mountain home early one morning: "A brethren of Latins, led by a Norman duke named Robert and an English prince named Edgar, is at the court of His Majesty, the Emperor Alexius. One of the brethren, the Abbess of Fécamp, is called Estrith of Melfi. They have asked about an amulet called the Talisman of Truth." He then looked at me and said that the Emperor thought I would like to return to Constantinople immediately and that they would escort me to a ship waiting in the harbour at Messene. As you might imagine, I was gathering my things before the messenger had finished speaking. It was the longest journey of my life, but now I'm here.'

Estrith brought us all together in a circle, while Hereward took the oath of the Brethren of the Blood. She then spoke for all of us.

'Now we are seven and united as a family at last. Let us pray for those no longer with us: Torfida, who met her end in the wildwood from whence she came; Martin, Einar and Alphonso in the heroic struggle at Ely; Gunnhild in the terrible pain she bore so bravely; and, in the tragedy of the putrid fever, our beloved sisters, Emma and Edgiva, Gwyneth and Wulfhild, Maria and Ingigerd. Let us also pray that Cristina is alive and well in Oviedo and enjoying a long retirement.'

Hereward said 'Amen' with the rest of us before adding his own reflections.

'It is strange to think that those we remember so clearly as young and strong are now lying in the ground or are old and frail. My darling Torfida and our daughter Gunnhild, and so many loyal friends who became our family. Dearest Cristina was the oldest of all of us; she would be almost seventy now. I will send a messenger to Oviedo with our greetings and news. It will make an old lady happy to know we're all together again.'

Hereward then turned to me. I saw his mischievous grin before he spoke again.

'My Lord Prince, Hereward of Bourne at your service. May I accompany you tomorrow on your expedition to Jerusalem?'

I grabbed him and embraced his mighty frame.

'As long as you don't start ordering me around!'

'Perhaps I would have done once, but you were a boy then. Now you are our leader and I will be proud to serve you. You have kept my family together for me and brought them to Constantinople. More than that, your Brethren have kept alive what the Brotherhood fought for at Ely. For all those things, I will always be grateful.'

I was moved by the great man's words.

They made me feel humble, but very proud.

27. Battle of Dorylaeum

The vast army of Pope Urban's Holy Crusade began to march east only a few days after it had been ferried across the Bosphorus. It was already mid-May and as hot as Hell. I had experienced the heat of Sicily, but few of the Crusaders had been that far south. What was even more disconcerting was to be told that beyond Anatolia, where we would turn south to Palestine, the heat of the day would be unbearable from spring until autumn. God help our men and horses.

Nevertheless, we were a fine sight – a rich tapestry woven from the many shades of bay, black and grey of our horses, the shimmering silver of our armour and the vivid crimson of our emblem, Christ's crucifix. The seamstresses would be put to work to record scenes like these as soon as the Princes returned to Europe. At the front of the column, the crest of every hill provided an opportunity to look back and admire the spectacle.

In the far distance a rising veil of dust threatened to obscure the sun. The air around us was filled with sounds – from the piercing clamour of armour and weapons and the soft hum of more than two dozen languages, to the deep rumble of carts and the relentless thunder of horses. Mingled together it was sufficient to make the ground shake and the birds flee.

At no vantage point was it possible to see the back of

the mass of soldiers and all the paraphernalia of war that accompanied them. There were few cities that came close in number to even a third of the size of our massed ranks, yet we were on the move.

Every time I saw our long tail of humanity stretching into the distance, I revised my calculations, until, at over 75,000, I gave up and decided our multitude was too big to be counted. There can have been no force of its size to have left Europe since the days of Rome's legions. We were a holy behemoth, woken from its long slumber and now making the world tremble.

The fortress at Nicaea was not far from the narrow strip of Byzantine territory on the Anatolian side of the Bosphorus, but it was a formidable obstacle. Its lord, Qilich Arslan, the Seljuk Sultan of Rum, was taken by surprise at the appearance of another Christian army so soon after the destruction of the army of Peter the Hermit. He was away with his army, far to the east, settling a small local dispute. A brave and resourceful leader, he had made a grave error of judgement, letting our vast army surround his city unopposed.

Scaling ladders, platforms, mangonels and springalds were prepared for the assault and, true to his word, the Emperor supervised the supply route from a base at Pelekanum on the coast. He also committed 2,000 of his elite soldiers under the command of Tacitius, one of the most renowned leaders of his army.

The first major encounter of the Holy War initially went well. The Council of War functioned as intended; the siege of Nicaea was well planned and the attacks efficiently coordinated. Both traditional siege tactics were employed simultaneously: a complete encirclement of the city to enforce a slow strangulation of all life's necessities and to break the will of the defenders; and an all-out, frontal attack by siege engines, battering rams and manned assaults of the walls to bludgeon the beleaguered inhabitants into submission. But the Seljuks did not lack mettle, and the siege continued for several weeks.

Then, just when we thought we were unassailable, the tenacity and organization of the Christian army were put to the test. A lone spy was discovered in the Christian camp – a wily Seljuk soldier, speaking Greek and passing himself off as one of Tacitius's men. Under some painful interrogation and the threat of yet more hideous torture, he revealed that Qilich Arslan had just returned from the east with a huge army and was poised to strike. He was camped only a few miles away, and final preparations had begun.

The Council of War met that night to plan the response. Under orders to prepare in total silence, the army began to get into position from 2 a.m. By first light that morning, we were in position to ambush our ambusher.

The contingents of Raymond of Toulouse and Baldwin of Boulogne were to hold their ground in the north, at what was anticipated would be the centre of the Seljuk attack, while Bohemond of Taranto and Godfrey of Bouillon were to lay in wait to the east, ready to spring the trap. Robert's contingent was to keep up the pressure on the city, while my small group was assigned the role of battlefield reconnaissance, reporting directly to Bohemond of Taranto.

The Seljuks appeared within an hour of the time we had calculated, swarming down from the hills like marauding ants. Their strategy was awe-inspiring, but predictable. Surge upon surge of closely grouped mounted archers cascaded down the slopes, loosing rapid volleys at speed from their small, highly manoeuvrable Steppes horses. Normally an onslaught that proved deadly to its opponents, it was a futile assault against a force of our magnitude with the resolve of its Norman and Frankish backbone.

Raymond and Baldwin's position held firm. As soon as the entirety of the Seljuks' attack had floundered against the Christian bulwark, Bohemond and Godfrey launched their heavy cavalry against the now static Seljuk army. Mayhem ensued and, realizing that his position was hopeless and his elite regiments were being carved into disparate and increasingly vulnerable groups, Qilich Arslan ordered an immediate withdrawal, prudently saving his army from complete annihilation.

Sweyn and Adela were riding to Robert's position with news that the battle had turned in our favour when a large column of Seljuks wheeled round towards them in a desperate search for an escape route from the battlefield. A group of about ten saw the two isolated Christian knights and bore down on them. Sweyn and Adela turned and rode back towards us at a gallop, but their attackers had too much momentum and would soon overhaul them. I immediately ordered our force to go to their aid, but knew we had little chance of reaching them before they were overwhelmed.

Sweyn's horse fell under a hail of arrows, one of which struck it in the neck, throwing Sweyn to the ground with a sickening thump. By the time he got to his feet he was still stunned and the Seljuks were almost on top of him, but Adela had ridden back to get him and offered him her hand to help him on to her horse. With no chance of escape, she turned her mount towards the Turks and managed to get one arrow away. It was an outstanding shot that took the leading cavalryman right out of his saddle. Adela's mount then started to panic and reared up as it saw the Turkish horses only yards away, tipping Sweyn off its back and unseating Adela.

Sweyn hurt his shoulder in the fall and could not get up, so Adela stood over him with her sword drawn. She managed to deal with the first Seljuk to reach her by crippling his horse. After swaying away at the last moment to avoid the cavalryman's lance, she crouched low to slice his mount's fetlocks with her blade, bringing horse and rider crashing to the ground. By then, two more were about to strike. She managed to avoid the first lance by deflecting it with her sword, but the second one caught her on the top of her helmet.

She stumbled away before collapsing, blood streaming down her face, just as Sweyn, now getting to his feet, managed to use his shield to defend himself against the next attacker before he was caught across the back of the shoulder by a blade swung by a Turk who had come up behind him. He cried out in pain and fell forwards in a heap.

Adela, unable to see through the stream of blood running from a deep gash to her head, threw off her helmet and wiped the blood away with her sleeve. She then ran back to protect Sweyn, screaming obscenities as she went. The Seljuk, who had appeared behind her and was about to strike with his sabre, hesitated when he realized the Christian knight beneath him was a woman.

Adela turned and the two foes looked one another in the eye momentarily. Adela, covered in blood and with the fierce look of a determined warrior, set herself to defend the blow. But the Turk put up his hand to his comrades, returned his sabre to its scabbard and blessed himself before taking off his helmet and acknowledging Adela with a long and deliberate nod of his head. A handsome, swarthy man with a thick, curly black beard, he sported the red silk pennons of an officer tied to his conical helmet. Even though Adela was badly shaken, she nodded her head in reply and the Turk replaced his helmet. We were now only yards away ourselves; the Seljuks galloped off to seek their own escape.

Neither Adela nor Sweyn had suffered life-threatening wounds. Sweyn's mail hauberk had absorbed most of the impact, but the bruising to his back was severe and there was the possibility of a broken shoulder blade.

Adela's injury looked much worse, because of the amount of blood. She had a deep gash above her hairline, which would have left her hideously scarred had it been much lower. After the bleeding had stopped and she had been cleaned up, the damage did not appear too severe – other than to her helmet, which was in great need of the care and attention of the armourer.

Hereward was very impressed with the resolve they had shown and their martial skills.

'You have been well trained and showed great courage. Adela, you saved your husband's life; he should be very proud of you.'

'I am, Hereward. And fear not, Adela will remind me of it every day!'

'I feel honoured to be part of your Brethren. I would have had you both in the Varangian Guard in the blink of an eye.'

Adela did not complain of either dizziness or nausea, so it appeared her skull had not been damaged, but we knew from many battlefield injuries to the head that the full impact could well reveal itself later. As a precaution, she and Sweyn were sent back to the battlefield infirmary at the supply base established by the Emperor at Pelekanum.

When the Seljuk defenders at Nicaea saw what had happened to Qilich Arslan's relieving army, they soon sued for peace. At this point, the first fissure occurred in the delicate relationship between Alexius and the leadership of the Crusaders. Led by Count Raymond, all the Latin Princes, except Robert and I, wanted to sack the city and exact revenge for the massacre of Peter the Hermit's followers. When we tried to point out that it was the Christians who had initiated the brutal killing, our pleas fell on deaf ears. The Latins wanted blood and plunder – Muslim blood and Muslim treasure.

In a remarkable example of fortitude, the Emperor's man, Tacitius, faced them down. Following strict orders from Alexius, he announced that the Christians were not to enter the city, that he would take the surrender on behalf of the Emperor, there would be no looting, and Qilich Arslan's wife and family would be given safe escort to the east. He posted Byzantine guards at the doors of the Seljuk treasury, and the city gates were barred.

The Latin Princes fumed with anger. But, once again,

Alexius played his hand well. Within hours, a huge convoy of carts appeared, laden with chests of gold and silver coin for the lords and knights, gifts of silk, jewellery and perfume for the women, and purses of bronze coin for the foot soldiers and non-combatants.

The stick of Tacitius had come close to creating a mutiny, but the gilded carrot had saved the day.

Wisely, the Emperor waited for two days to let the victorious Latins drink themselves into a stupor and then recover before summoning the Princes to Pelekanum to plan the next phase of the campaign. Again, the Council of War worked efficiently. Its main decision was to split the army in two for the long journey through Anatolia. The supply line would be getting longer, and so local foraging would be more important, putting huge pressure on local stocks of food and water. Two smaller armies on different routes would be less demanding. It was agreed that the two forces would join again at an old Byzantine fortress at Dorylaeum, just over a hundred miles to the south.

Qilich Arslan was still licking his wounds, but had not been idle. He had recruited his allies – Hassan of Cappadocia, several Persian princes and the Caucasian Albanians. He had swallowed his pride and appealed to his long-term enemies, the Danishmendid Turks, from the east, led by Prince Ghazi ibn Danishmend, promising them half the Crusader booty if they would help him achieve victory. Knowing that the Crusaders were carrying not only their own treasuries, but also the vast wealth that Alexius had bestowed on them, the offer was too good to turn down.

When Sultan Arslan learned that the Christians had split

their army, he knew they had given him a chance for revenge.

Accompanied by Tacitius and his cohort of Byzantines, Duke Robert and Bohemond of Taranto headed the vanguard of the first half of the Crusader army on the march to the south at the end of June. Robert again asked us to act as a mobile corps, to do reconnaissance and act as liaison between the two armies. Other than the appalling heat, which was causing many casualties among the old and sick, the first two days were uneventful.

Sweyn had recovered well, as had Adela, although where the surgeons had had to shave her hair in order to stitch the gash on her head she now had a large bald patch. The ugly scar and three-inch-wide causeway from her forehead to the top of her head did little for her allure, but she cared not and covered it only when the midday sun became unbearable.

Then, early in the morning of the 1st of July 1097, a date I will remember all my days, Qilich Arslan and the massed ranks of the combined armies of all the Turks of Anatolia struck.

There had been no reports from our scouts, and our patrols had seen nothing untoward. We were in the centre of a wide, open plain with hills all around, not far from Dorylaeum, when we first became aware of an attack. The first hint was like a distant roll of thunder, but one that was continuous and quickly became much more ominous as the ground beneath us began to shudder.

'Cavalry!' shouted Hereward. 'Thousands of them!'

With the formidable Bohemond acting as his mouthpiece, bellowing orders up and down the column, Robert coolly and calmly took control. Our entire force was corralled into a tight circle, with the baggage train, women, children and clerics in the middle, surrounded by a solid ring of knights and foot soldiers.

'Like an English shield wall!' cried Bohemond.

The order was repeated like an echo by every captain and sergeant.

Hereward rode up to Sweyn.

'I hear you were the best horseman in Duke Robert's service. Ride to Count Raymond's army. Tell them to hurry.'

With that, Hereward slapped the flank of Sweyn's horse to send him away at a gallop. Adela saw him go and was in his wake in seconds.

Hereward then signalled to me and Edwin. We rode over to Robert, who was still calmly marshalling his forces.

Hereward spoke first.

'Robert, I have sent Sweyn and Adela off to alert Count Raymond.'

'I have already sent riders.'

'I'm sure you have, but I wanted at least two of my rapidly diminishing family to see out the day. What's about to come over those hills is a horde the like of which would make God quake.'

Hereward then addressed the three of us.

'You have troops to command. With your permission, I'd like to stay with Estrith, who is with the civilians, trying to calm them. I abandoned her and her sister once before on the cusp of a battle. I don't want to do it again.'

Robert turned to me as we watched the great man ride away. 'Was he as fearsome as the storytellers would have us believe?'

'No, much more so. And, I suspect, he still is.'

Hereward was right about the impending onslaught. The sun was still low in the east, so what crested the ridge and poured over the hills beneath appeared like a wall of water in silhouette. Like the flow of hot pitch, it filled the gullies and valleys first, then spread out over the flatter ground until the whole perspective of our eastern quadrant was made black with men and horses. Even the green of their Islamic war banners became menacing dark shadows against the glare.

The sound became deafening as the chilling war cries of the Turks added a piercing shrill to the ever-deepening thunder of thousands of galloping horses. I had never seen anything like it and estimated we were facing an army at least twice the size of ours, perhaps as many as 60,000, not counting the ones who had yet to come into view.

In an extraordinary illustration of Norman military discipline, Robert and Bohemond and all their senior knights rode around the defensive ring, appealing for courage and calm. Robert issued a command to help morale, which was repeated by every Crusader present: 'Stand fast together, trusting in Christ and the victory of the Holy Cross!'

There was sheer terror in the centre, where the monks and nuns said prayers and heard the confessions of the non-combatants. Volley after volley of arrows, like showers of heavy rain, fell from the clear-blue sky, killing hundreds, especially the civilians without armour. Javelins and spears flew through the air, hurled from horseback by the Turks with great force and deadly accuracy, killing anyone in their path, with or without armour. But they were only the pin-pricks of the battle; the real pain was inflicted by a whirlwind of slashing sabres as the Turkish cavalry tried to hack its way through our defensive ring.

As one wave of attackers exhausted itself, Sultan Arslan withdrew it to regroup and sent in fresh replacements. There was no such respite for our defensive wall, which, with the sun rising ever higher in the sky, had to endure the onslaught without rest. Squads were organized to clear the dead and wounded, and young boys hurried forward with pails and ladles to allow the men to slake their thirst.

As our numbers dwindled, Edwin and I had been filling gaps in our defences for some time, until eventually Robert, Bohemond and Tacitius were also in the thick of the fray. The time for issuing orders had passed; even the most senior of us had to fight for our lives.

We had held our ground for over five hours. Old men, boys and the injured began to pick up weapons and join the defensive wall, while Estrith and Hereward led the women to clear the bodies and help the wounded. I looked along our lines; we were at breaking point. I wanted our Brethren to be together at the end and was trying to decide when would be the best time to send Edwin to bring Estrith and Hereward to stand with us in a final redoubt, when I saw a cloud of dust to the north.

Moments later, thousands of crimson Christian crosses painted the distant horizon the colour of the setting sun. As soon as the Turks realized that the advancing phalanx was the balance of the Christian army, they fled as rapidly as they had appeared.

Ten thousand bodies lay on the ground, both Christian and Muslim. Robert ordered that all be buried with dignity and that imams be brought from Nicaea to read over the graves of the Turks. Some among Bohemond's contingent objected, preferring that they be left to rot like wild beasts where they had fallen, but such had been the quality of Robert's leadership in the battle that he got his way.

For the Christian dead, eternal salvation beckoned. Prompted by the speeches of zealots such as Count Raymond, the notion that death on the Crusade would bring God's forgiveness for all sins and a place at his side in Heaven had become accepted as gospel by the Crusaders.

Hereward went over to Robert and Bohemond to congratulate them on the way they had held the army together and inspired their men.

'My Lord Duke, Count Bohemond, my congratulations on an outstanding example of leadership under the most demanding of circumstances.'

Bohemond responded with only a perfunctory nod and a very pointed question.

'Captain, I hear that you served as a housecarl for King Harold of England and fought at Senlac Ridge.'

'That is correct, my Lord.'

'Did you ever know a man called Hereward of Bourne? He also fought at Senlac Ridge and before that was in service with my father, Robert Guiscard, and my uncle, Roger.'

'All Englishmen have heard of Hereward of Bourne, sire.'

'In his service to my family he was called Sir Hereward Great Axe. He carried a double-headed axe like yours – so formidable, I was told, that no other man could wield it. I was a very small boy when he and his companions left Apulia for Normandy, but the stories about him lingered and are still told to this day. My hazy memory is of a man who bore a strong resemblance to you; indeed, you would be about the same age.'

It was obvious that Bohemond strongly suspected that Hereward and Alexius's retired Captain of the Varangians, Godwin of Ely, were one and the same.

Nevertheless, Hereward kept up the pretence.

'My Lord, I am flattered to be likened to one as noble as Hereward of Bourne. But that's all it is – a likeness.'

'May I try your axe? It intrigues me.'

'Of course, sire.'

Bohemond stood almost six inches taller than Hereward – both dwarfing me, and especially the diminutive Robert – and had the same substantial frame, but he lacked the strength that Hereward had in his tree-like limbs and he struggled to keep swinging the axe freely.

Hereward grasped the axe from the Norman's faltering grip.

'It has killed many foes, some even as big as you.'

He took the Great Axe of Göteborg and, with an easy, single-handed swing, rested the haft of the axe over his shoulder, then walked away. As he did so, he winked at Robert and me.

How many times in his life had the gargantuan Bohemond, a colossal figure from a legendary family, been made to look feeble?

28. Wastes of Anatolia

Invigorated by our victory, we set a course south-east, across the arid plains of central Anatolia. For those of us who had survived so far, there was much envy of our dead comrades who basked in Heaven, for we endured a living Hell.

All the locals we passed, cowering in their dark hovels and cool caves, looked at us in amazement as we staggered and stumbled in the scorching heat. They thought us mad, and so we were. Qilich Arslan had destroyed every village, killed every beast and poisoned every well on our route and for miles around. We had gone beyond the reach of the Emperor's supply lines. We were on our own.

Our progress became slower by the day, the death toll escalated, and hunger and thirst killed many, especially the old and young. Disease spread, and many turned around in a vain attempt to find their way back to Constantinople, their will broken. Some just walked off to find the shade of a tree, where they curled up to await the comfort of death.

The huge destriers, the Normans' legendary war horses so critical in battle, were unable to cope with the conditions; most died, leaving many of our knights to walk like infantry. Our beasts of burden died too, and everything that we could not carry ourselves had to be discarded. Basic campaign discipline started to be ignored. Animals and people were not kept apart, latrines were not dug, and disease and infection spread. What had once been a mighty, well-disciplined army now resembled a ragged stream of hapless humanity.

The Princes tried hard to keep up morale, but they too were wilting.

Sweyn seemed to find strength when it had deserted everyone else. With Adela always at his side, he rode up and down the long meandering lines of Crusaders, encouraging them to keep their discipline and commitment. He won many admirers, including Hereward.

'When we found him in the forest at Bourne, he was all but dead. Now he is an example to us all, with such determination – he reminds me of my old friend Martin Lightfoot, built like a hunting dog and with the stamina to match. He and Adela make a fascinating couple, more like brother and sister than man and wife. Why have they never had children?'

As Hereward was a fellow member of our Brethren, I was tempted to reveal the true nature of Sweyn and Adela's marriage, but thought it better that they should tell him in the course of time if they wanted him to know.

'I'm not sure, but I suspect they're both much more interested in living the life of a warrior – and emulating a certain Hereward of Bourne – than in having children.'

Robert asked the Brethren to gather in his tent one night after supper – which consisted of a few pieces of dried goat's meat and one swig of wine that the heat had turned to vinegar – in order to discuss the dilemma. He had been doing some arithmetic.

'We are dying in droves. By the time we cross Anatolia our numbers will have halved, our horses will be all but gone, and there will be no pack animals left to pull our baggage train.'

Hereward offered the wisdom of his years of service in conditions such as the ones we were now facing.

'Qilich Arslan is your biggest enemy, not this god-forsaken place. He is making you pay for Nicaea and Dorylaeum by laying waste to everything in your path. But he could also be your salvation. He must still be close by, waiting until you are weak enough for him to strike again.'

'You make our prospects sound worse, not better.'

Sweyn suddenly got to his feet.

'But he's got what we need.'

Hereward looked elated; Sweyn had understood his intention.

Robert was still unsure.

'And?'

'We take it from him.'

'How?'

'A small force attacks as a diversion.'

Adela was quick to see the possibilities.

'An even smaller force spirits away his baggage train, horses, goats and whatever else we can plunder.'

'Exactly.'

There were smiles all round as spirits lifted for the first time in several weeks.

Robert then threw in some words of caution.

'Everyone is in a bad way. We have to be careful; if the others hear that food and water and horses are just over the next hill, there will be a mass exodus within the hour. The Crusade will be over.'

Hereward suggested a plan.

'For obvious reasons, Robert must stay with the army to continue his duties. Estrith will stay with the sick and wounded. The attacking feint should be undertaken by the English contingent, led by Edgar and Edwin. I will pick a hundred or so of Tacitius's Byzantines – he can be trusted, and I know his men – and Sweyn and Adela will lead them to capture Sultan Arslan's baggage train from under his nose.'

'And what will you do?' asked Adela.

'I'll be right behind you two, keeping an eye on you. But first, we have to find Arslan. At first light tomorrow, Adela, Sweyn and I will slip out of camp with a dozen or so Byzantines who know this land and go in search of a Seljuk sultan.'

Three days later, the hunting party returned.

At what I suspected was Hereward's prompting, Sweyn gave the news and repeated the detail of the feint.

'Arslan is about thirty miles away to the north-east. It looks like he's poised to strike. Men are arriving from the east all the time. Edgar, when can you be ready to leave?'

'This evening, under cover of darkness; we don't want to alert too many curious eyes. I'll tell Robert. Estrith, will you carry on with your duties with the sick?'

'No, where my family goes, I go. Besides, I don't want to have to answer all the questions in the morning about where the English have gone!'

Robert gave us as many of the skinny Arabic horses

and surviving pack animals as he could spare to carry away our ill-gotten gains. He also granted us extra rations of food and water and provender for the animals.

By dawn the next morning, our small band had made excellent progress.

We found some shade and rested during the day, before travelling again at night. Nobody slept much in the heat of the day, but it was a time for reflection. Sweyn did most of the talking, usually in the form of questions and always aimed at Hereward.

'How long did it take you to overcome the fear of battle?'

'I never did, it is always there. Anyone who tells you otherwise is either a liar or a fool.'

'But it must get easier to deal with?'

'In a way, but the fear doesn't go away, you just learn how to turn it to your advantage. Do you fear what we are about to do?'

'Yes, I do, but I would only confess it to the Brethren.'

'It's a wise man who admits to his fears and anxieties – and also a strong one. Your fear will keep you alert and, when the time comes, you will turn it into the strength you need to do what you have to do.'

Edwin and I sat and watched as the great man bestowed his wisdom. Estrith was coiled around him in a loving embrace, while Sweyn and Adela sat at his feet, hanging on every word.

It brought back some fond memories from England, as well as many sad ones.

We launched our attack on Qilich Arslan's camp in the dead of night.

After locating the baggage train and leaving Sweyn and Adela's team in position, we attacked from the opposite side; fortunately, it was the dark of the moon. A group of junior knights found a hidden position in a dry river bed. They acted as a platoon of archers and loosed a storm of fire arrows into the black night. There was soon chaos as the fires took hold and thick smoke swirled around. We then rode through the Seljuk camp, making the kind of commotion worthy of several thousand horsemen rather than several dozen.

All in all, we made three sorties through the camp before the Turks got themselves organized sufficiently to inflict on us increasing numbers of casualties. We then withdrew and took up positions that would enable us to cover the escape of our bounty hunters.

Sweyn and Adela's party worked by stealth; their mode was the way of the silent assassin. Sentries were attacked from behind, their throats cut by an English seax or the life strangled out of them by a Byzantine garrotte, picket lines were cut, corralled animals let loose, and our strings of horses loaded with as much food and water as they could carry.

Then, on Adela's signal – a single fire-arrow shot horizontally into the air – Sweyn led his band away into the night, first at a trot, in the hope of not giving away their direction of escape, then at a canter, and finally at full gallop. I split my English group into three; we each let off several volleys of covering arrows before riding off as loudly as we could in different directions to confuse the Seljuks as much as possible.

Our agreed rendezvous point was the site of our last

camp. We reached it as dawn was breaking and, with it, the warm light of day brought a wonderful sight. There were dozens of swift Steppes ponies laden with all sorts of provisions – not enough to feed an army for long, but sufficient to gladden the hearts of our demoralized companions for many days.

We knew Qilich Arslan's cavalry would be fanning out all around us, so we did a head count and moved off at speed. We had lost more than a dozen noble Englishmen, who had sacrificed their lives for their fellow Crusaders. It was yet another paradox to ponder: the vast majority of the Crusaders were Normans or Franks – the very same people who had conquered their English homeland and ruled it so ruthlessly – but such was the Crusader ideal, they had given of themselves willingly.

One of them was Algar, a righteous 31-year-old son of a thegn who had fought and died at Senlac Ridge, who slumbered in his mother's womb at the time. Another was Storolf of Nottingham, a daunting man in his fifties, who had been with the Mercians who ambushed the Normans at the Malfosse on the night of the Battle of Senlac Ridge. He then joined King Harold's exiled sons in Ireland but was disillusioned by their capricious behaviour and became a soldier for hire, wherever he could get paid. When he heard of the English contingent to the Holy Land, he joined in the hope that it would cleanse him of the sins of a lifetime of killing by day and debauchery by night.

We estimated that we were about three hours away from the Crusader column when a large group of Seljuks, perhaps 200 of them, crested the hill behind us.

Sweyn immediately swung his mount round and bellowed an order to the captain of Tacitius's Byzantines.

'Captain, take half the men and take our bounty on to the column. Everyone else, dismount.'

I looked at Hereward, who was already dismounting; he nodded his approval, so I issued my own order.

'Edwin, take the horses on. I'll stay.'

Sweyn had assumed command.

'We must make a stand here to save the supplies. Form up as a phalanx of archers; keep the reins of your horses secure. Adela, give us the range. We shoot on her signal.'

I looked at Hereward again; he nodded, this time with a smile.

'Now!' was Adela's shrill signal as we launched our first volley at a range of 300 yards.

We got two more away before the Turks were on top of us. Now we had to suffer their incoming volleys as they surrounded us.

'Mount! Fight your way out! Follow Hereward's lead!'

Sweyn beckoned to Hereward to clear a path for us. For the first time in many years, we saw the Great Axe of Göteborg wielded to murderous effect, cutting a swathe through the Turkish cavalry and leading the English contingent away. Sweyn was almost the last to mount, courageously ensuring that everyone got to their horse. It was then that Estrith was struck, taking a Seljuk arrow to her upper back. She was wearing mail, but the arrow cut through it. She squealed in pain, lost control of her mount and fell to the ground.

Adela used her eastern close-quarters bow with venom, wounding two Seljuks with successive arrows and giving

Sweyn time to leap from his horse, pull the stricken Estrith from the ground and lift her over his shoulder. She let out another shriek of pain. Adela then grabbed the reins of Sweyn's horse and wheeled it round so that he could throw Estrith across its shoulders, remount and make his escape.

With his horse pirouetting in panic amidst the confusion of the moment and with the weight of two people on its back, Sweyn kicked his mount towards the northeast, the wrong direction, galloping back from whence we had come. Several Turks were between Adela and the route Sweyn had taken, leaving her isolated.

Thinking she was behind him, Sweyn continued his rapid exit.

Adela, realizing that several of the Seljuks were about to ride off in pursuit of Sweyn and Estrith, stood high in her stirrups, threw back her helmet to reveal feminine features and yelled at the Turks in Arabic, 'It is I, Adela of Bourne, Knight of Islam!', and charged at them, swinging her sword in wide arcs.

She was immediately surrounded by a circle of Seljuks. Some hesitated and blessed themselves, but the majority did not falter.

Hereward swung our horses round. We were over 500 yards away as a dozen or so Turks closed in on Adela, dragging her from her horse.

I looked to the horizon and could see Sweyn about to disappear into the safety of higher ground, oblivious to Adela's predicament. More and more Seljuks were cresting the horizon all the time. Hereward looked at me and then turned to our comrades.

We all signalled our approval as Hereward hoisted the Great Axe above his head and issued the order.

'Charge!'

The Turks saw us coming at about 100 yards and began to form a defensive wall of horsemen. They loosed a hail of arrows towards us but our momentum was prodigious, and Hereward's awesome presence – his Great Axe glinting in the sun, his crimson cloak as a Captain of the Varangians flowing behind him – put them to flight.

Adela was safe, but had suffered a trauma all too reminiscent of the horror of her adolescence. Her armour had been pulled off her back, her shirt torn from her; she was rigid with terror, naked from the waist up. Hereward leant from his horse to offer her his arm. At that moment, he and Sweyn were the only men in the world for whom she would have moved. Without looking up, she stretched out her hand and Hereward swept her up behind him on to his horse's flanks, covering her in his cloak.

Even then, she cared nothing for herself and kept repeating the same anguished questions: 'Where's Sweyn? Is Estrith safe?'

Our escape was a close call; only the speed of our horses saved us as we took flight through clusters of arrows launched high into the air, aimed to fall on to our path to safety.

As we neared the Crusader column, the Turks gave up the chase, but not before loosing one last cascade of arrows.

The projectile that killed Edwin was one of the last to land. It came out of the sky, almost at a right angle to the ground, and caught him close to his spine at the nape of the neck. He rode on for a while, not uttering a sound, with a fixed stare on his face, but pain and failing consciousness soon combined to loosen his grip on his reins. He fell to the ground with a sickening crash, tumbling randomly like someone already dead. After coming to a stop, he did not move again. I was certain his wound was fatal; regardless, we could not stop to help him, but I made a mental note of his position in the hope of being able to retrieve his body later.

It was then that I saw Adela had also taken an arrow. Hereward told me later that he felt the impact, but that Adela had not let out a sound; she just winced and gripped him even harder around his waist.

The Seljuk threat had receded, so we slowed our gallop and I rode over to ask Adela about her injury.

'It hurts a little . . . But what of Edwin? Did I see him fall?'

'He's gone, Adela. He took an arrow through the back of the neck.'

She sank her head into Hereward's broad back and closed her eyes in a grimace – not for her pain, but for Edwin. She must have been in great agony; the arrow had gone through the fleshy part of her buttock and impaled itself in the saddle of Hereward's mount, pinning her to the leather in the process.

Every lurch of the horse's gait must have sent a jolt of torture through her entire body.

The journey back to the Crusader column seemed interminable. Adela was losing a lot of blood, but we thought it better to keep moving; attempting to move her and extract the arrow without the help of the physicians would almost certainly have made her injury worse.

When we finally reached the column, joyous celebrations had already begun to greet the arrival of the Turkish provisions. We were hailed as heroes, as if we had returned with the keys to the gates of Jerusalem. Suddenly the English contingent, previously only an insignificant appendage to the great Norman-Frankish-Germanic host, had saved the day, even for their Norman masters.

Robert's physicians were summoned to help Adela, but in her forthright way she made it clear what she wanted done.

'Please lift me and the saddle off the horse as one and put me on a saddle stand. I would also like a shirt to cover me, please.'

She was placed on a tack stand, as requested, and one of the English knights gave her a shirt.

'It's a bit big.'

She tried to raise a smile, but she looked very pale and her voice started to quiver.

'Let us help you.'

'Thank you, Edgar, but there is only one way to do this.'

She and the saddle were soaked in blood, the colour matching Hereward's cloak, which she now threw off, nonchalantly exposing herself, then put on the shirt. She asked Hereward to help her: 'Would you break off the arrow?'

Hereward's large hands made it look puny, and he snapped it with ease. It had entered Adela's buttock, making a deep wound, but only appeared to be pinning soft tissue.

'Edgar, would you now help Hereward lower me down. I need the saddle to be raised off the ground so that I can use my legs to lever myself off this cursed thing.'

She seemed very weak by now, and I was not certain her plan would work.

'Are you sure? If the barb is still in your flesh, it may not be as easy as all that.'

'Don't fuss; I think the arrowhead is in the saddle. Besides, I can't think of another way to do this – other than letting an army of physicians loose on me with my arse in the air and a saddle sticking out of it.'

Hereward nodded and so did the physicians; she was right, as usual. A pile of saddle blankets was used as a support about a foot off the ground and we carefully lowered Hereward's saddle and Adela on to it. She then put her heels underneath herself in a squatting position and took a deep breath.

'Gentlemen, I may curse a little in a moment!'

She placed one hand on the saddle's pommel and the other on its cantle and gave a mighty heave, as if giving birth. She did not curse, but did let forth a deep, guttural rumble, which turned from a growl of agony to a cry of relief as she freed herself.

Blood started to flow more copiously, and she fell into Hereward's arms. She was very pale and her voice thin.

'Now it's time for the physicians to stitch me. Would you and Edgar hold me? I need a piece of leather to bite on.'

The physicians moved towards her. Although barely conscious, she did issue one final command.

'Only one of them – the old one. I don't want some young tup thinking about what else he might stick in me as he brandishes his cordwainer's needle.'

Just as she had in Sicily, Adela bore the pain stoically. The arrow's entry and exit holes, each the size of an English shilling, were about two inches apart.

She would not be going anywhere near a saddle for some time.

The Latin Princes, relieved that the decline of their army – almost to the point of oblivion – had been averted, convened their Council of War. The discussion was brief and the conclusion unanimous: the army would avoid terrain like the inhospitable ground we had just crossed and instead turn north-east at Heraclea to find more fertile land. It would take us on a long, meandering detour via Caesarea, Coxon and Marash, costing us many weeks, but would ensure that many more of us were likely to reach our destination.

Three days later, with the army rested, fed and watered and provisioned sufficiently for some time, we moved off. Adela, now fêted as a heroine rather than shunned as an oddity, rode in a cart like a queen of Egypt, with people coming up to her to thank her and give her presents.

There had been no sign of Sweyn and Estrith, and we began to fear that they had not made a safe escape after all, or had been cornered subsequently. Hereward went out several times to try to track them, but found nothing.

It was ten days later when they finally appeared, early one morning, silhouetted against the far horizon – two blurred figures, with a third mount strung behind them – almost like a mirage in the rising heat of the desert.

*

They were moving painfully slowly, their horses stumbling beneath them. Riders were sent to bring them in. Huge cheers echoed up and down the column when the Crusaders realized that Sweyn, the young English knight who had acquitted himself so well against the Seljuks, and Estrith, who had become known as the English angel for her care of the sick and aged, had survived their ordeal.

When we saw them close up, they were a pitiful sight.

Estrith had lost consciousness and was barely alive; Sweyn was only able to mutter a few incoherent words. They had clearly not eaten or drunk anything for days. The dust of the desert, baked to their skin and clothes, made them look like they were already desiccated by death. Even more abject was the baggage on the third horse – Edwin's rapidly decomposing body, which we assumed they had discovered along their route, thus explaining why our recovery missions had been unable to find it.

After a few gulps of water, Sweyn managed to explain that they wanted to bring Edwin back to us so that we could all be present at his interment. And so, Robert picked out a small retinue and stayed behind with us as the Crusader column moved on.

We found a peaceful spot next to a small, bushy hillock, where we planned to put Edwin to rest. Then we made camp, waiting for Estrith and Sweyn to recover sufficiently so that we could conduct a ceremony together to mark his passing.

It took several days, but eventually we gathered at the side of Edwin's grave and Estrith said a few words.

'Here lies Edwin of Glastonbury, a noble knight of the royal blood of Wessex, Knight of Normandy, Knight of Islam and a Brother of the Blood of the Talisman. Always loyal, ever honest, never self-serving; he was a true knight. May he rest in peace. Amen.'

Then we each placed one of our belongings into an oak casket given by Robert.

Adela offered a bronze brooch which Edwin had always admired, Estrith a small silver crucifix which blazed in the early morning sun, Sweyn a Saxon seax with a finely tooled leather scabbard, and Hereward a lance with a pennon of crimson, gold and black, the colours under which they had fought in 1069.

My tribute was chosen easily. Edwin was a cousin to King Harold, of the Cerdician blood of Wessex, so I wrapped the casket in my war banner, the Wyvern of Wessex, and we dug it deep into the ground next to him.

That night, we celebrated his life with a feast of dried-mutton stew, while Estrith and Sweyn told us the story of their isolation in the desert.

'Estrith's wound was deep and the barbs of the arrow had torn a lot of flesh. I feared it may have shattered bone, so we decided to lay low in the hills for a while. It took me two days to find water. I had to dig deep; it only filled my water sack once a day, and most of that went to the horses.'

Estrith smiled at him and placed her hand affectionately on his. 'He hardly took any for himself – what he didn't give to the horses, he gave to me.'

Sweyn continued.

'It was obvious that we had to try to catch the column,

which we knew would be moving ever further away from us. We travelled only at night, but we had no food and very little water. We saw Edwin's body only because his horse whickered as we passed. It had stood over him until it sunk to its knees, exhausted and dying of thirst. We managed to revive it with the last of our water and used it to carry his body. We had no idea he had been killed; we had assumed you had all got away from the skirmish . . .'

Sweyn's evident sorrow threatened to overwhelm him. It was Estrith who took up the story, turning to Adela.

'Adela, you saved our lives, we will always be in your debt. We are sorry those thugs molested you.'

'Don't mention it. You would have done the same for me.'

Our Brethren now numbered five again – and three of those were lucky to be alive.

Although I was still convinced that we were right to pursue our destiny in Palestine, it was proving to be a severe test for all of us – far worse than I could ever have imagined.

We had lost Edwin, a rock we all relied on, just at the point when we needed him most. I feared our trials and tribulations were going to get worse before they got better.

29. Siege of Antioch

We caught up with the column to discover that, in the absence of Robert's calming influence, discord had broken out among the Princes. Tancred of Hauteville had decided that the circuitous north-easterly route was too slow and had turned south again to go through the dangerous Cilician Gates and take the direct route to Antioch via Tarsus and the Belen Pass.

At least Tancred still expressed his intention to keep his oath to the Emperor and liberate Jerusalem. Baldwin of Boulogne, on the other hand, had revealed his true ambitions. He had heard of rich pickings to be had in the ancient cities of the Valley of the Euphrates and, without warning or discussion, had disappeared in the dead of night with a force of 200 knights to go in search of plunder and the creation of his own fiefdom in the fabled lands of Babylon.

We first saw the walls of Antioch towering in the distance in late September 1097. It was one of the mightiest cities of the Muslim world and the gateway to Jerusalem. Ruled by Seljuk Turks, its inhabitants were among the most diverse in the world. Jews, Christians and Muslims lived together in a population of dozens of nationalities and languages. Founded in the time of Alexander the Great and named after one of his generals, it had huge walls and tall towers with no fewer than six massive gates.

So large was the perimeter of the walls it was impossible for the Crusaders to fully encircle them, thus giving the defenders access and egress to break any siege.

Antioch was not going to be taken easily.

We started to make semi-permanent camps in a ring around the city. It seemed certain that a long and frustrating winter beckoned.

Sweyn was full of vim and vigour, and Estrith was now fully recovered from the arrow to her shoulder. Adela was not so lucky. Her wound had soon become infected and, although every known technique, from voracious maggots to a hot iron, had been used to clean the wound, it had not fully healed. She was still unable to ride and was in much pain. More worryingly, the inactivity was weakening her and making it hard for her to fight the infection.

Hereward was concerned too, and we decided to talk to Adela. Hereward came directly to the point.

'You're not getting better. We need to get you up and about and build your strength.'

'I know, but I feel so weak – in spirit as well as in body.'

'That's not like you.'

Tears began to fill her eyes as Hereward put his arms around her. 'May I take a look?'

'Of course. You're the only man in the world I'd happily show my arse to!'

Hereward examined the wound and then spoke to Adela reassuringly, but disingenuously.

'It's looking better, but it might be wise to cauterize you again, just to be on the safe side.'

'Don't tell me lies, Hereward of Bourne. I know it's

getting worse. Tell them to strike deep this time to kill whatever is eating away at me.'

'Get some rest; we'll do it in the morning.'

Hereward looked anxious as we walked away.

'It's her last chance. Could you smell it?'

'What?'

'Gangrene – the rotting of the flesh.'

The cauterizing of the wound the next day was vicious, even by the standards of a procedure that is at the best of times brutal. But Adela survived and the physicians gave her a strong potion to make her sleep.

As she slept, Hereward again seemed troubled.

'Have you noticed that Sweyn and Adela do not share the same tent any more?'

I had not, but thought it now wise to share with him the true nature of their marriage, and the story of Mahnoor of Palermo and her tragic death.

'How sad for both of them. When Adela has rested, I'll talk to her. I think there are some things I can help her with –'

Hereward's words were interrupted by the arrival of Estrith, another of our Brethren who seemed anxious as she walked away to talk with her father in private.

They soon came back and sat on the ground outside my tent. Hereward's face showed no emotion.

Estrith took my arm. 'Please, sit with us; I have something to tell you. I have been very foolish.'

I feared another Bertrand of Toulouse transgression had occurred, but the revelation was of a different order.

'I have sullied my vocation again.'

I looked at Hereward, but his expression had not changed.

'With Sweyn.'

I was struck dumb.

'It happened when we were alone in the desert. I was so scared and he was so kind to me and so courageous; he got us through an ordeal we should never have survived. He had to check my wound every few hours. I was always naked from the waist up when he did it . . . well, I'll spare you the details.'

'What are his feelings?'

'He's a young man, I'm an older woman, I think he's proud of his conquest and keeps coming back for more, but it's just an infatuation.'

'And you?'

'The same; it will pass.'

'Then, let it do so.'

'It's not as easy as that.'

She paused and looked at her father, who put his arm around her.

'I'm pregnant.'

'You can't be!'

'I know, I know. I'm nearly thirty-nine years old; I never dreamed I could fall pregnant, but I have. God works in mysterious ways.'

'He certainly does.'

I needed time to think. This was a dilemma which could affect us all, and Estrith faced the prospect of a pregnancy and birth in the most challenging of circumstances. But it did not take me long to realize that it was a problem for the

Brethren as a whole and one we had to discuss together.

'Our Brethren makes us equals; each is responsible for and to each other. You have told your father and me; now Sweyn needs to tell Adela, and then we must come together to discuss what needs to be done. It affects us all. You are the Abbess of Fécamp, a gift from Robert. Zealots like Raymond of Toulouse will take the moral high ground; this is supposed to be a Christian Crusade against an alien and immoral faith.'

'Yes, but it's a Crusade that slaughters Muslims like animals.'

'I'm not condoning it, but people like Count Raymond think our enemies *are* animals.'

'But only because of what we do, which makes them retaliate against us like animals. It is madness!'

Hereward then offered some wise advice.

'Let's discuss the virtues of the Crusade another time. For now, it's important that Sweyn speaks to Adela; then we must bring Robert into our confidence and decide as Brethren what we are going to do.'

Two days later, with a blood-red sun sinking below the horizon beyond the Orontes River, we sat in Robert's tent within sight of the mighty Dog Gate of Antioch. The setting sun brought a rush of cooler air from Mounts Staurin and Silpius behind the city, a welcome breeze at the end of a warm autumn day.

Adela had been carried in like a babe in arms and sat impassively. Sweyn and Estrith looked uncomfortable. Robert took the lead in the discussion.

'Adela, how are you?'

'Sore, just as you would be if someone kept searing your arse with a hot iron.'

'Sweyn has spoken to you?'

'He has.'

'And what are your thoughts?'

'I am concerned for our Brethren. Estrith and Sweyn know their own minds and are free to make their own choices, but it might have been wiser had relationships within our Brethren remained platonic. And the child makes that even more difficult.'

Adela looked at me, and I looked at Estrith, remembering the time when I had made my own clumsy proposition to her, and thinking of how events might have unfolded if we had let our relationship become a sexual one.

Estrith stood and paced around nervously.

'Sweyn and I were in extremis – the odds were we would not survive. What happened, happened. We shouldn't have let it continue when we got back to the camp, but forbidden fruit can be very tempting. It was a mistake; we're sorry.'

Sweyn then spoke.

'I make no apologies for what happened. They might have been our last hours on earth; our moments together were tender and loving, and I have no regrets. When we came back to camp, I couldn't just end it. I hope Estrith feels the same way.'

She did not respond, so Robert asked the most important question of all.

'So, now that we have a new member of the Brethren of the Blood of the Talisman, how shall we ordain his or her arrival? Once we have decided, let us celebrate!'

Robert was being typically considerate, but he knew it was not as simple as he implied.

It was left to me to play Devil's advocate.

'As one of the senior Latin Princes of this righteous Crusade, what will be the reaction among your peers and within the rank and file? After all, Sweyn is a senior knight, now lauded for his leadership against the Seljuks, as is Adela; Estrith is the Abbess of Fécamp and the "angel" of the camp among the sick and wounded. If Sweyn's fathering of the child is concealed, we still have to find an alternative sire, which might make matters worse.'

Sweyn now got to his feet. 'There will be no denial of my role as the child's father. It is our child and I will be a loving father to it.'

Robert pondered the situation for a while.

'Well, it might be difficult at first, but it will blow over.'

'Robert, you know as well as I do that it won't "blow over"; at the very least, Estrith will have to leave the Crusade. Adhemar Le Puy, the Papal Legate, is an ambitious and devious man and he knows that the zealots won't tolerate a pregnant abbess in their ranks. Worse still, Raymond of Toulouse still holds a grudge against us after the argument Sweyn had with him in the crypt of St Sernin's in Toulouse; he could call for Estrith's excommunication, or worse.'

Hereward spoke for the first time. 'Estrith, do you want this child?'

'Do you mean, will I get rid of it? The answer is emphatically no.'

'That's not what I meant. Will you nourish it and nurture it and devote your life to it?'

'Father, it is my child and I will do everything in my power to care for it as it should be cared for.'

Hereward stared at his daughter for a long time before making a suggestion.

'I would like some time to talk to Estrith alone and also to have some time with Adela and Sweyn. May we reconvene at the same time tomorrow?'

We all thought this a good idea and agreed to his plan.

There was no setting sun the next day. The long hours of sunshine were becoming fewer, reminding us all that winter would soon be upon us, and that even in the eastern Mediterranean the days could be cold and miserable.

It was my turn to lead the meeting; Hereward asked for permission to speak.

I often wondered what words had been said by the three of them in the hours between the two gatherings, but they had been spoken by a very select group within our Brethren: two sons of Bourne, a daughter of Bourne and one of its granddaughters; and they concerned yet another generation from that small but far from inconsequential Fenland village.

'I have a suggestion which I believe will resolve the dilemma we face and, more importantly, is in the best interests of the child. This siege is going to take many months. Antioch must fall if Jerusalem is to be taken, so the army will be camped here for some time. Adela should not be here in her condition throughout the winter; she needs warmth and the care of the best physicians. Estrith hardly shows, so we are the only ones who know she is pregnant . . .'

Hereward paused to gather his thoughts before continuing.

'Estrith and Sweyn have agreed to the following; it is important that it is endorsed here, so that our Brethren can continue in its bond of loyalty. What will be agreed here will be known only to us, until such time as Estrith, Sweyn and Adela decide to tell the child about our decision. If that hasn't happened at the time of the death of the last of us, it falls to the last surviving member of the Brethren to care for the child and tell it the truth about its birth. In due course, the child will be admitted to the Brethren in its own right.'

He put his right arm around Estrith's shoulders and sat her down next to Adela. Then he asked Sweyn to sit on her other side.

'We four are now the only survivors of our home in Bourne. Until recently, it looked like its lineage would die with us, but now, miraculously, my grandchild will continue not only that ancestry, but also Torfida's and mine. Estrith and Adela have agreed to travel to the coast at St Symeon, where the Emperor is establishing a supply base for the siege here at Antioch. They will then sail to Constantinople, where Estrith will enjoy her confinement under the protection of the Emperor and where Adela will be able to recover away from public view in the Blachernae. I have spoken to Tacitius; he will provide an escort, make the arrangements with the Emperor and tell him about our deception and need for the utmost discretion. If, by the time the child is born and weaned, it is safe for it to return to the Holy Land, they will join us, hopefully in a liberated Jerusalem.'

There were smiles all round from the four children of the Fens, but Hereward had saved the crucial part of the plan until last.

'After the birth and weaning, the three of them will emerge from the Blachernae and Adela will be presented as the mother of the child. No one will know otherwise, except us. Estrith will, of course, stay close to the child, but it will be raised as the natural child of the marriage of Adela and Sweyn. In truth, we Brethren will all be its family and guardians, as we are for one another. We will tell the Princes and those whom Estrith has been caring for that she is returning to Constantinople to care for Adela's wound and to help her with what would be a very difficult pregnancy.'

Adela laughed out loud. 'A difficult pregnancy – it's the conception that would have been the difficult part, with me in this condition!'

There was laughter all round and the four of them embraced warmly. Robert and I looked at one another. We both smiled. It was a remarkably simple solution, but one that could only work through an exceptional rapport between Estrith and Adela.

I had to ask the question.

'Can the two of you deal with this – especially you, Estrith?'

'As my father said, it is in the best interests of the child and of the Brethren, so we will make it work. I know that the bond between mother and child is very strong, but I'm not giving my child up. We will still be a family, and I will see the child all the time.'

'That could make things worse, not better.'

'Perhaps, but I think I can cope with being Aunt Estrith rather than Mamma. Adela will be better at that.'

Adela seemed relaxed; her demeanour was certainly very different from the day before.

'I'm not sure I will make a better mother – it's the last thing I ever thought would happen. But the only things that matter are the six of us and our new member – the little beast. And mark my words, girl or boy, it will be a little monster; I will make sure of that!'

Everyone laughed at a typical Adela comment, but I had one more question.

'All you have ever wanted to be is a warrior. You have achieved that and won the admiration of your fellow knights and thousands of Crusaders. Are you prepared to give that up to raise a child, one that isn't even yours?'

'Well, it certainly helps that I have achieved what I've achieved. The welcome we received when we returned from the raid on the Seljuks was everything I had been looking for. But I'm now forty-three years old, I don't have many warrior days left – especially with the disadvantages I have as a woman barely five and half feet tall. Hereward and I talked for a long time last night. He explained some things which helped me realize that perhaps I have finally buried the past. He also told me some home truths about what is eating my backside. I may not survive at all. And if I do, I may not be able to walk properly, let alone ride a horse. But this child offers me a new challenge – one that I'll meet head on – the first part of which is to survive for at least nine months so that our plan can succeed.'

Robert nodded and smiled at me; perhaps it might work, after all.

By midday next day, Estrith and Adela had left for the coast and we threw ourselves into the complex business of laying siege to the mightiest fortress in the eastern Mediterranean.

Hereward proved to be right about the length of the siege of Antioch. The Crusaders faced interminable difficulties, unable to encircle the vast walls completely. Yaghi-Siyan, the wily governor of the city – a former slave from Turcoman, far to the east – was able to bring in provisions from time to time and had an army formidable enough to sally forth occasionally from the walls and attack us, causing mayhem, much loss of life and a significant lowering of morale.

The winter threw itself into the conflict and became a key part of the city's defence. Rain, mud, and even snow, made life miserable for the besiegers in their tents, while those under siege enjoyed the comforts of their firesides, kitchens and beds. Although some supplies were getting through from the Emperor's base at St Symeon, Yaghi-Siyan's allies – Ridwan, Sultan of Aleppo, and his brother, Duqaq, Emir of Damascus – made constant attacks on the supply lines and even engaged the Christian army in full-scale battle.

It was a long and debilitating winter, which seemed to go for ever.

We had to build defensive towers of our own to protect our supply lines from the coast. By May of 1098, six months into the siege, our army was demoralized and, through the ravages of war, famine and disease, had been reduced to fewer than 25,000 men, with no more than 1,000 war horses, none of which were heavy Norman destriers.

Inevitably, the Princes began to argue about tactics and strategy and more blatant self-interest emerged, especially when news reached us that Baldwin of Boulogne's audacious adventure into Mesopotamia had become an outrageous success. With a force of barely 200 knights, he had managed to conquer the ancient and wealthy city of Edessa and create a Christian county, installing himself as its potentate.

Bohemond of Taranto now revealed that he wished to be made Prince of Antioch after the city had been taken and that he would not continue with the Crusade unless his demand was met. The Council of War was convened but it broke up in deadlock, with the Princes screaming at one another.

Then a new threat united us once more. Reports began to arrive that Kerbogha, Atabeg of Mosul, was approaching with a huge army, said to be over 50,000 strong, to relieve the city. With our reduced numbers, we were in a very vulnerable position and could easily end up trapped like rats in a barrel between the towering walls of the city we were besieging and a formidable advancing army.

At this point, we suffered more desertions. Stephen of Blois, one of the staunchest supporters of the Crusade, had had enough. His will was broken and news of an approaching horde of Seljuk Turks was the final straw. He and his large contingent took flight in the middle of the night and made for the coast at Alexandretta.

Tacitius then announced that he was taking his Byzantine contingent back to Constantinople. He kept his real reasons to himself, saying only that he had been ordered to return. Panic and anger spread throughout the army – panic because of the encroaching Turks, and anger because the besieged seemed to be faring better than the besiegers. Another Council of War was called; this one was much more amiable and focused.

Raymond of Toulouse summarized the situation.

'My Lords, our siege is now in its seventh month. We are slowly strangling the city, but it has a thick neck and our grip is not as strong as it once was. We have fought off Ridwan and Duqaq, but now Kerbogha approaches with many allies and mercenaries. We have a ready-made fortress from which to defend ourselves; it stands behind us. Unfortunately, we are not welcome inside! What are we to do?'

The Count's droll introduction made everyone smile and lessened the tension in the gathering.

Robert got up to speak.

'My Lords, Count Raymond, may I offer the floor to Godwin of Ely, an Englishman who served as Captain of Emperor Alexius's Varangian Guard for many years? He is a good friend of the Norman contingent and of Prince Edgar's English knights.'

The Count looked at the other Princes, who all gave their approval.

'Thank you, Duke Robert. My noble Lords, Count Raymond, over the past few days one of our knights has spent several hours inside the walls of Antioch.'

There were gasps of admiration around the room and

some incredulity. Although our encirclement of the city was greater than it had been, it was still possible for the defenders to get in and out in small numbers under cover of darkness.

'A young knight in the service of Prince Edgar, Sir Sweyn of Bourne – who, you will remember, is the knight who led the daring attack on Qilich Arslan's baggage train – disguised himself as an Arab and mingled with a group of scavengers returning to the city. He is fortunate to be dark-skinned and can speak some Arabic.'

I looked at Robert, who shook his head. Hereward's announcement was as much of a surprise to him as it was to me.

'My Lords, would you allow Sweyn of Bourne to give you his report?'

There were enthusiastic approvals all round. Sweyn looked confident and poised as he started to speak.

'My Lords, I have made contact with a man called Firuz. He was born an Armenian Christian, but converted to Islam some years ago. He is an armourer by trade, but in the siege he defends one of the isolated towers on the south-eastern side of the city. He is not disillusioned with his faith, but he is greedy. His terms are simple: he wants safe passage for himself and his family within an hour of the deed being done, a large estate in Sicily, one hundred pounds of silver and a knighthood conferred by Count Roger of Sicily. In return, on a night of the dark of the moon, he will leave a section of wall unguarded next to his tower, so that a small assault party can scale the walls. He will then lead us to the Gate of St George so that we can overwhelm the guards, open it and let in our army.'

Bohemond of Taranto asked the most important question: 'Can we trust him?'

'He's prepared to offer his son as a hostage, my Lord.'

There was a stunned silence for a few moments as the Princes came to terms with the audacity and simplicity of Sweyn's solution to their dilemma. Count Raymond got to his feet.

'Sweyn of Bourne, you and I had a serious disagreement in Toulouse, after which I vowed that, when the time was right, I would teach you a lesson about how a knight should behave. Well, boy, if you pull this off, that incident will be forgotten and you will receive a significant reward of your own.'

Bohemond of Taranto then spoke. 'I will pay the geld of silver and, as Roger of Sicily is my uncle, the lands and the title will not be a problem. When is the dark of the moon?'

'Three days, my Lord.'

'Then we'll be ready. By the way, how did you find this man, Firuz?'

'It's not difficult to find greedy men, my Lord. There isn't much food in the city and many are hungry. I went to the brothels, where people are usually discreet, and said that I had a bag of silver to buy a leg of mutton for a family feast and asked where I might find one. I was eventually sent to Firuz. Hidden beneath his forge, he had food and wine sufficient to feed a prince's court for a month. I knew I had found the right man.'

Bohemond slapped Sweyn on the back with his huge hand and hurried off to begin preparing for the assault on the city. Robert and I rushed over to congratulate Sweyn on his remarkable coup.

'It was Hereward's idea.'

'I couldn't pass as an Arab, so Sweyn had to take all the risks. We weren't hiding anything from you; I just wanted Sweyn to have his moment and for it to be as big a surprise for you as it was for everybody else.'

Just as Hereward finished speaking, Bohemond reappeared. Hereward stood up to greet him.

'My Lord?'

Bohemond did not reply, but stared at Hereward intently.

'I know who you are, Hereward of Bourne. It is too much of a coincidence that Sweyn is a son of Bourne and that he came to the Holy Land with Prince Edgar.'

Hereward did not respond. His expression impassive, he just stared back at the giant Norman. Bohemond's craggy face then creased into a smile.

'Do not worry, Godwin of Ely, your true identity is safe with me, especially after the service given to us today by Sir Sweyn.'

Bohemond then offered his hand and Hereward shook it firmly.

Sweyn was given the honour of leading the scaling party.

The plan worked perfectly; within twenty minutes of the grappling hooks landing on the battlements, St George's Gate was open and a great tide of Crusaders rushed in. Antioch, the last major obstacle on the road to Jerusalem, was at the mercy of the Christians.

From that moment onwards, events did not unfold as Sweyn had hoped.

Robert had persuaded the Council of War to agree that

civilians would not be harmed, but it was an empty promise. The Christian army showed no mercy.

Eight months of privation and the bloodlust of the Crusaders combined to create a frenzy of killing that lasted all night. By dawn, the streets flowed with rivers of blood and piles of bodies made them impassable.

Blinded by their indiscriminate savagery and the blackness of a moonless night, the marauding Crusaders put to the sword Syrian Orthodox Christians, Armenians, Jews and Greeks, who all perished with their Muslim neighbours.

In what should have been a moment of great elation for Sweyn, he stood on the battlements of the city and, instead of hailing the victory, let out an anguished cry.

'*Why?*'

30. Besiegers Besieged

Sweyn's achievement had saved the Crusade, but only just in time. Kerbogha's vast army appeared on the horizon in the middle of the afternoon. The entire Crusader army and all its civilian entourage hurried into Antioch and the gates were closed behind them.

We took stock of our position. It was grim; we had the city's strong walls around us, but it had been under siege for nearly nine months and its granaries and storerooms were empty. Our supply line to the coast was gone and Kerbogha's army was big enough to completely enclose us and gradually tighten the noose. Worst of all, the city was full of bodies and we faced a fight against time to burn them before they contaminated the wells.

Having spent nine months in Purgatory outside the walls, we now faced a living Hell within them.

The Muslim army was so huge it seemed to occupy every foot of ground around the entire city. Their war drums boomed incessantly and their cries for vengeance filled the air day and night. There were soon many desertions from our ranks, including the previously faithful Ives and Aubrey of Grandmesnil, who lowered themselves down ropes and made a cowardly dash for the ships at St Symeon.

We were already feeble and demoralized, but conditions for our army soon got worse. The only foodstuff we had found in any quantity was a store of spices. Ingenious, if hardly appetizing, methods were devised to put it to use. One of them was to make a soup of spices from leaves plus a few thin slices of animal hide and enliven it with blood bled from our precious horses. It did little for the well-being of our horses, and probably did us more harm than good.

Kerbogha's army attacked constantly, using a seemingly inexhaustible reserve of men. They always attacked more than one wall at a time, wearing us down in an ever downward spiral of despair. Often the Turks attacked in such great numbers that they reached the top of the battlements, where the hand-to-hand fighting was ferocious. Bohemond created small groups of his best men to act as elite squads and close any breaches in our defences.

Sleep was all but impossible, except in brief respites of no more than two hours twice a day. We were fortunate that the men still standing were the elite survivors of countless battles, deprivations and diseases and thus made of the sternest stuff. Bohemond was the strongest of all and relied more and more on Hereward's experience and military acumen. They became very close, with Sweyn acting as their main aide-de-camp, delivering orders to the other princes and senior commanders.

Raymond of Toulouse became ill and was unable to lead the Council of War, so Robert took on the role. Hereward and Sweyn had devised an astonishingly daring plan, which they had shared with Bohemond, Robert and me. Bohemond was so impressed that he wanted to present it to the Council himself – and, of course, in doing so, take all the credit.

The Council, shocked at first, soon realized the merits of the plan and readily agreed. In fact, we had little choice;

another week of the onslaught we were facing would have seen our resistance collapse.

On the 28th of June 1098, the great Battle of Antioch began.

Sweyn and Hereward's strategy was based on careful observation of the way in which the Seljuks attacked, combined with simple battlefield psychology. Kerbogha kept the greater part of his army out of harm's way at his main camp about five miles from the city, from where small units were despatched in waves to attack the walls, before retreating for rest and rearming.

We formed ourselves into four distinct groups within the walls: Godfrey of Bouillon led the Lotharingians and Germans; the Papal Legate, Adhemar Le Puy, took charge of Raymond of Toulouse's southern Franks; Bohemond headed his Italian Normans; and Robert, together with Robert of Flanders, commanded the northern Franks as well as the Normans and my English contingent.

We poured from different gates of the city in the hottest part of the day, taking our attackers completely by surprise, and fanned out in a wide arc. The dual keys to the manoeuvre were speed and ferocity. Our momentum would force the Turks to retreat and try to make a stand – which we had to prevent them finding the ground to make – and our reputation as awesome warriors would strike fear into the hearts of our retreating enemies.

Few of us had steeds of any sort – some knights even took to going into battle on donkeys and mules – but we had to mount a classic infantry charge in full armour in the middle of the Syrian summer. Not a very tempting prospect, but one about which we had no choice.

The plan worked perfectly and the Turks began to fall back towards their main camp in droves. Then simple battlefield psychology played its part. As soon as he saw our attack, Kerbogha should have committed his main force, which would easily have halted our momentum and, caught in open ground, on foot and vastly outnumbered, we would have been annihilated. But he hesitated and prepared his army to hold its ground and defend our attack, rather than come out and meet it head on.

It was a crucial mistake.

Our much smaller army was made up of the most fearsome warriors in Europe, fighting for their survival; his much larger force was full of mercenaries, allies of dubious commitment and men whose homes and families were far away and far from peril.

As Kerbogha's main force took up its positions, all they could see were hundreds of their colleagues streaming past them and all they could hear were their cries of terror and the sound of mayhem in their wake. Realizing that his army's will to fight was beginning to desert it, Kerbogha compounded his original mistake in hesitating by ordering a belated attack.

It was the worst possible decision: some of his men followed orders and advanced with intent, others advanced, but reluctantly, while the remainder just turned and joined their fleeing colleagues.

It became a rout as Kerbogha's massive army disintegrated and scattered, leaving the Atabeg to return to Mosul with his tail between his legs. The Crusader army achieved many remarkable feats on the battlefield; this was undoubtedly its finest moment.

The Atabeg's tents were captured intact, full of gold and other treasures, including huge stockpiles of arms and strings of horses and, most important of all, food, the like of which we had not seen for months. We looked on in wonder, not at the chests of coin, the gold goblets, fine carpets and tapestries, but at the pens of sheep, the butts of wine and the sacks of corn and flour.

We were in the Garden of Eden, and Jerusalem beckoned.

However, Bohemond got his way and took control of the city. He was in no mood to strike out immediately for the prize we had come for. In truth, few were – enough was enough, and it was time to take stock.

Alexius failed to join us, as had been promised, and so there was no pressure on us to move on. The Emperor had set out from Constantinople, but had met Stephen of Blois halfway across Anatolia at Philomelium. Stephen told him that the Crusaders' cause was finished and that most were already dead, and so Alexius returned home.

The rest of 1098 became a bizarre mix of blissful recuperation, interspersed with frequent bouts of squabbling between the Princes about who should be in control of the many cities that now fell within their sphere of interest.

Now that all the local sultans, emirs and atabegs had been neutralized, all the cities of Anatolia, Syria and Mesopotamia were at the Crusaders' mercy, and they took full advantage.

The inhabitants of each city that fell were put to the sword without mercy, only adding to the already murderous reputation of the Crusaders. Sweyn used his ever growing influence to try to persuade the young knights of the values of chivalry and the importance of the Mos Militum. Many sympathized with his basic philosophy, but few were prepared to extend to their Muslim enemies the status of an equal and to treat them as fellow warriors worthy of respect. The hardships of the Crusade had been too great, the hatred of the enemy too ingrained. The preaching of zealots such as Raymond of Toulouse, which cast Muslims as inferior and heretics, was too powerful for most to resist.

Sweyn talked openly about leading a revolt against the zealots by the younger, more enlightened knights, but Hereward, Robert and I managed to persuade him to keep his arrows in his quiver for the time being – certainly until we reached Jerusalem.

In October of 1098, the few remaining Princes in Antioch who still determined to go on to Jerusalem – Raymond of Toulouse, Tancred of Hauteville, Robert and I – decided that we would prepare to march on the Sacred Places in mid-January, as soon as the worst of the winter rains had stopped.

Shortly afterwards, the most special moment of the year occurred: a bodyguard of Alexius's imperial troops, accompanied by a platoon of Varangians, appeared through the Bridge Gate of the city. They were leading an elaborate covered carriage from the Emperor's personal caravan. It was strange to see a body of men dressed, armed and behaving like highly disciplined soldiers; it had been such a long time since we had had the same bearing.

As soon as it came to a halt, Estrith rushed to greet us, shortly followed by Adela, who moved more slowly thanks to a severe limp and the hindrance of the care she had to show the bundle in her arms, a child they had not yet formally named. The three-month-old baby was a boy, who went by the title 'Herry' for the time being.

He was dark like his father, bright-eyed and lively, and everyone wanted to assign his looks and character to various of his parents and grandparents. Sweyn was the first to pick up his son, soon followed by Hereward, proud to hold his grandson.

A feast was hastily organized and we sat and listened to one another's stories. The birth had been straightforward; the Emperor Alexius had treated Estrith and Adela like his daughters; life in the Blachernae was a little like being a bird in a gilded cage, but splendid all the same.

Adela had eventually recovered, but only just. The Emperor's physicians immediately stopped the use of the hot iron, saying that too much tissue had already been lost. They used instead the maggots of the blowfly, bred especially for the purpose and much more effective than the maggots used by the Crusader physicians. The treatment was uncomfortable at best and involved her lying on her stomach most of the time, but it worked. She had been left with a large hollow where her right buttock should have been, a mass of ugly scarring and a pronounced limp.

Adela, as ever, put it in her own inimitable way.

'I'm still not a bad offering for a quick tryst, as long as I stay in the maiden's position.'

The only sad story they brought was that the Emperor's emissary had returned from Oviedo with the news that Cristina had died a few years earlier, but had lived out her days happily in the care of Doña Viraca, the Countess of Oviedo, who was Doña Jimena's formidable mother.

The emissary also brought news from Spain that Doña Jimena was alive and well in Valencia with the Cid, who was still Lord of the Taifa, but that he was not faring so well. His age and many battle scars were catching up with him and his body groaned and moaned at him all the time.

We were all sad to hear about Cristina, and Hereward in particular was unhappy to know that the Cid was losing the great strength and vigour for which he was famous.

He made himself a promise. 'When this campaign is over, I will travel to Valencia to see my good friend the Cid. We can reminisce together before time has its way with us both.'

Estrith suddenly looked heartbroken.

'I thought you would come back to England with us?'

'If only I could, my darling Estrith! I would love to see England's forests, heaths and fens once more. But many years ago, I gave a king my word, a vow I will never break. I will be content to end my days on my mountain, watching the sun going down to the west, until the sun sets for me also.'

He did not need to elaborate, and quickly changed the subject to a happier theme.

'So, what shall we call the boy? He can't live his life with a name like "Herry"!'

Estrith put her disappointment to one side. 'Adela and I thought you would all have some good ideas about names and that we would name him here.'

Sweyn then spoke up, as a boy's father should, firmly and clearly.

'It is obvious what his name should be – Harold. Harold of Hereford.'

Robert looked perplexed.

'I think I understand the reason for Harold – your noble King before my father put his large Norman boot in it – but why Hereford?'

Hereward was delighted.

'It is where Torfida and I met and this long saga began. A good choice, Sweyn; it gets my vote.'

Everyone concurred and toasts were made to the boy's health and prosperity. Sweyn picked up the child and handed him to Hereward.

'Hereward, I would be honoured if you would proclaim his name. I want him to be told about this moment when he is old enough, so that he can remember it all his life and pass the story on to his children.'

Hereward held the boy in the cup of his mighty palm and raised him high above us. The baby thought about crying for a moment, then realized that the occasion was too significant for such trivialities and instead gurgled to himself contentedly.

'In the presence of the Brethren of the Blood of the Talisman – Hereward of Bourne; Estrith of Melfi, Abbess of Fécamp; Adela of Bourne, Knight of Islam; Sweyn of Bourne, Knight of Normandy; Edgar the Atheling, Prince of England; and Robert, Sovereign Duke of Normandy – I name this child Harold of Hereford.

'May his life be a long and honourable one, lived by the traditions and oaths of our Brethren. We welcome him to our midst.'

31. Jerusalem

The Crusader army, refreshed, replenished and reinvigorated, marched out of Antioch on the morning of the 13th of January 1099. But it was not the mighty host that had left Europe two and a half years earlier. No more than 1,000 knights and 6,000 infantry were under the command of the Latin Princes, now a handful of men, the only survivors of the cream of the aristocracy of Christian Europe.

Bohemond bade us farewell; he was too preoccupied with securing his hold on Antioch and its satellite cities to join us. But before he did so, he had offered Sweyn an extremely enticing inducement to join his contingent of Italian Normans – the lordship of Harim, a fortress city thirty miles to the east of Antioch.

'You have a family now. It is time to settle down; there can be no better place than here in this new Christian world. Help me make it secure for our children and grandchildren.'

'My Lord, your offer is extremely generous, but I must continue to Jerusalem and complete our mission.'

'Are you implying that I am not completing mine?'

'No, sire, I just want to see Jerusalem.'

'I hear that you have been at the heart of much debate among the knights about the ethics of war.'

'I and many others, including many Muslim knights,

414

follow the Mos Militum, a code of chivalry that encourages us to behave with honour and discipline.'

'I have heard of it. It is dangerous. There is only one code to follow in war: kill or be killed.'

'I don't think my prowess in battle has ever been questioned. But what concerns me is fair treatment for our vanquished opponents, and the protection of civilians.'

'Do you mean Muslims?'

'Yes, my Lord.'

'That is dangerous talk, Sir Sweyn. There are many on this Crusade who would call that heresy.'

'I know, my Lord, but they are misguided.'

'Count Raymond tells me that you once eloped with a Muslim girl while still married to the brave Adela. Is she the one who seduced you with the sinister ways of the infidel?'

Sweyn bristled. Hereward put his heavy, battle-scared gauntlet on the young knight's forearm, while Robert intervened.

'Prince Bohemond, we have much to do; Jerusalem beckons.'

Bohemond, clearly angered that Sweyn had turned him down, sneered at us all and rode away.

Hereward reassured Sweyn. 'You handled that well. Bohemond is not a man to pick a fight with, even when he provokes you. Come, let's move off. I want to see Jerusalem.'

It took us five months of steady progress to reach Jerusalem. With Robert in a position of much greater influence, our progress was marked by shows of force and negotiation with the local emirs rather than naked brutality. Tripoli,

Tyre, Beirut, Haifa and Caesarea all fell under our control.

But Jerusalem would be a different matter.

The Fatimids from the Caliphate of Cairo – Shia Muslims of a very different persuasion from their Sunni brothers, the Seljuk Turks – were in control of the Holy City, and its governor, Iftikar ad-Daulah, was a shrewd and resourceful leader. Much smaller than Antioch, less than half a square mile in area, the city had towering walls and a resolute garrison stiffened by 400 elite cavalrymen dispatched from Cairo.

Despite its formidable fortifications, it was nevertheless a thing of wonder. We climbed to the top of the Mount of Olives to see the holiest place in the world for the three religions of Abraham. There before us, beyond its lofty walls, were the Dome of the Rock, the Temple of Solomon, the al-Aksa Mosque, and the Holy Sepulchre – the most revered buildings in the world. They glowed in the sun, their walls bleached white, their domes, minarets and crosses gleaming symbols of man's devotion to his maker.

Estrith was moved to tears. 'Why would men fight over such a place?'

Sweyn was moved to anger. 'Let's try to make sure that they don't.'

Iftikar ad-Daulah had prepared his ground well. Every stick of timber for miles around had either been taken inside the city or burned, all the wells had been poisoned, livestock taken, granaries emptied, and he had a strong supply base on the coast at Ascalon, fifty miles to the west.

To avoid a repeat of the disaster of Antioch, an immediate attempt to scale the walls was made, with disastrous consequences. The lack of timber meant we had far too few scaling ladders and no siege towers, so the attack was called off before any more casualties were inflicted.

At the end of June, finally abandoning their greedy marauding across Syria and Palestine, more Crusaders arrived from the north. They swelled our numbers to 1,000 knights and 12,000 infantry, but also brought their bigotry and avarice.

Robert found it hard to keep control in the camp. Raymond of Toulouse had lost all sense and reason and, with the newly arrived Peter the Hermit and other zealots, had taken to walking barefoot around the walls of the city in prayer.

Despite his overbearing manner, Bohemond would have been useful to us, but, alas, his own cupidity had got the better of him.

One group of new arrivals became a godsend. William Embriaco, a gifted builder, boat builder and siege engineer, appeared from the coast with a large contingent of Genoese sailors. They had dismantled their boats at Jaffa and hauled the massive timbers, ropes and shipwright's tools overland. We immediately got them together with Gaston of Brean, a genius in the science of siege engineering, and together they built battering rams, mangonels, scaling ladders and towers of amazing scale and power.

The towers were over fifty feet tall – mounted on wheels and built on three levels, they were designed to sit hard against the city walls. The assault troops were protected by thatch, covered with several layers of hide.

Then Tancred of Hauteville began his particular brand of intimidation.

First, a captured Muslim knight was paraded in front of the walls before being beheaded by one of Tancred's henchmen. Then Tancred began to catapult bodies into the city, some already dead, some not so fortunate, who met their deaths dashed against its ramparts and buildings. To his credit, the governor did not retaliate in kind, but did expel all the Orthodox Christians from the city – a reasonable response that seemed only to anger the Crusaders even more.

One of the many zealots and visionaries with the army was a priest, Peter Desiderous, who claimed to have had a visitation from the much respected Adhemar Le Puy, Pope Urban's Apostolic Legate, who had only recently died. Le Puy had commanded him to remind the Crusaders that they were pilgrims and that they should form a procession around the city, praying for strength from God for their attack on the walls.

Although it may have seemed a trifle too devout for the more worldly of the Crusaders, it had a dramatic impact. Not only did many of them work themselves up into a religious frenzy, but the arrows, stones, excrement and hot oil that were hurled at them by the inhabitants of the city only added to their fury.

The assault began on the morning of the 14th of July 1099, with the Crusaders attacking the city on two fronts at once. The sky was immediately filled with missiles flung from both sides. There were stones, firebrands and a whole range of improvised projectiles, flammable, sharp or heavy.

The fighting lasted for two days until Gaston of Brean's

towers made a breakthrough. With Godfrey of Bouillon himself on the highest level, one of the towers reached the top of the wall. The defenders had one defensive weapon left, which they had held in reserve, a form of Greek fire that was thought to be impossible to extinguish. They poured vats of it on to the tower, but the banished Christians from the city had revealed the secret of how to kill the deadly blaze: vinegar, which the Crusaders had stored on the inside of the tower in skin sacks and used liberally to douse the fire.

As soon as the flames were out, Godfrey let down the hide-covered protective wooden lattice at the front of the tower and used it as a bridge to stride on to the wall, leading a mass of knights behind him. As soon as this bridgehead was established, dozens of scaling ladders were thrown against the wall and the Crusaders poured into the city.

What followed brought shame on us all.

After three years of struggling against overwhelming odds, on a tortuous journey replete with astonishing acts of bravery, for what most thought was the noblest of causes, the Crusaders once more behaved like wild animals. All sense of decency deserted them; their humanity was forgotten in order to slake their bloodlust.

There had been other atrocities and much cruel barbarity, but what happened in Jerusalem over the course of the night of the 15th of July was on an unprecedented scale. Almost the entire population of the city was raped, tortured and butchered; Muslims and Jews, none was spared, save a few of the elite Egyptian cavalry and the Governor, Iftikar ad-Daulah, who hid in the Tower of David and negotiated surrender.

It is difficult to estimate how many died, but it must have been in the tens of thousands.

Robert led our Brethren as we struggled in vain to prevent the carnage. He ordered his contingent to stand down, but only a few did. We were joined by some who were loyal to the Mos Militum and we managed to get a few poor souls into a safe house and keep it guarded while we went in search of more to rescue.

Harrowingly, when we returned, the guards had been overwhelmed and their charges massacred. In all, we managed to get two dozen out of the city and sent them with an escort towards the coast.

Word spread that, before they were killed, many of the richer citizens had swallowed their gold bezants and jewellery to prevent the Crusaders stealing them. Thus there followed horror upon horror, as crazed Crusaders sliced open the bellies of the dead in a grisly hunt for coins and gems.

Every place of worship, every public building, every home was looted until the carts could carry no more. Nothing of any value remained; the city was cleansed of everything with the blood of its people.

Within minutes of the end of the carnage, the Crusaders flocked to the Holy Sepulchre to give thanks for their deliverance. Heaving from their exertions, dripping in their sweat and the still-warm blood of their victims, they knelt in prayer.

We turned away; whichever God they were praying to, it was not our God.

*

There was one final battle to be fought in the Crusade.

News arrived within a few hours of the slaughter at Jerusalem that Malik al-Afdal, the Vizier of the Caliphate of Cairo, was approaching with a Fatimid army 30,000 strong, landing his force at the port of Ascalon. It had elite Egyptian cavalry at its core and troops from all over the Caliphate: Berbers, Bedouin, Ethiopians and squadrons from the personal bodyguards of all the emirs of the Fatimid cities along the North African coast. It was at least as powerful as any army we had faced in the entire Crusade.

The Princes, emboldened and briefly united by their achievements, decided on yet another unpredictably daring response. They would not sit behind the walls of Jerusalem and wait for the attack; they would ride out and meet it head on. Although their newly purchased horses were less sturdy than their European mounts, the knights could fight on horseback once more and relished the prospect.

We had no stomach for any more fighting of the sort that had come to be the hallmark of Crusader behaviour. Sweyn, Hereward, Adela and Estrith took Harold and headed north to Jaffa with Hugh Percy and an escort of Robert's men to organize a fleet for our departure from the Holy Land.

Robert and I took advice from the Brethren and wrestled with the dilemma for many hours before deciding that it would be wrong to desert the cause at the moment when its objective had been achieved, no matter how much unnecessary blood had been spilled in doing so.

We reached the vicinity of Ascalon on the evening of

the 11th of August. It soon became clear from the reports of our scouts that we had been fortunate and that the audacity of the Princes had worked in our favour once more. Malik al-Afdal had spent the day preparing his army to march on Jerusalem the next morning and then bedded it down for the night. Feeling certain that his quarry would hole up in Jerusalem, he had posted few sentries and made no provision to defend his camp against a surprise attack.

Godfrey of Bouillon led a Council of War, where the decision was quickly taken to rest for only a few hours and then to form up as close to the Fatimid army as possible during the darkest hours of the night, waiting for the first hint of dawn. When there was just enough light to illuminate our path, we would charge, en masse, straight into the Fatimid camp.

When the moment came, Raymond of Toulouse took the right flank, Godfrey of Bouillon the left, with Robert of Flanders, Tancred of Hauteville, Robert and myself in the centre. The first rays of the sun caught the crimson of our flags and war banners before bathing us all in its early morning gleam. With the light radiating behind us in an iridescent glow, and the thunder of our horses booming ever louder, we must have presented a terrifying vision as we fell upon the enemy camp out of the night.

We were outnumbered by at least three to one, but our group of men was the elite residue of an army which itself was the best Europe had to offer when it set out three years earlier. It had survived battle, deprivation and disease and had been forged in incredibly challenging circumstances.

Many were also inspired by mystical relics unearthed by

the Crusaders and brought to the battlefield. Raymond of Toulouse carried the Holy Lance, found in Antioch, which was said to be the spear that had been plunged into Christ's side on the cross. Arnulf of Chocques, the new Patriarch of Jerusalem, held aloft the True Cross, believed to be a piece of Christ's crucifix, discovered hidden in a silver case in a dingy corner of the Holy Sepulchre in Jerusalem.

Most of the foot soldiers had walked from Jerusalem barefoot, like true pilgrims, and dozens of knights had worn sackcloth on the journey to purge themselves in preparation for the battle. Mixed in equal measures with a voracious greed and a lust for violence, religious zeal had driven these men throughout the Crusade; it was a frightening brew.

Only on the eve of battle did they wear their garments of war – which, to them, represented another form of reverential clothing, because killing infidels was another kind of devotion to God.

The Battle of Ascalon was hardly that; it was more like an ambush that led to a stampede of terrified men. The Fatimid cavalry had no time to find their horses, let alone mount them; thousands were cut down in their camp as we charged straight through their neat rows of tents. Of those who managed to retreat, some made for the shore in a vain attempt to reach their boats, while others rushed to get through the gates of Ascalon before they were barred against them.

Our losses were minimal, theirs so great that it was easier to count the survivors than the dead. Al-Afdal managed to get into the city and set sail for Cairo, leaving the remnants of his army to fend for themselves. The victory neutralized the Fatimid threat from the south, just as Dorylaeum had nullified the Seljuks in the north.

The new Christian realms in the Holy Land were secure for the foreseeable future.

Our obligations to the Crusade now met, we prepared to return to Jerusalem immediately.

Robert gave his men twenty-four hours to take their share of plunder from the Fatimids' weapons and belongings, and our portion of the spoils of Ascalon's treasury was shared out equally. But we refused to let our men enter the city, and we issued strict orders against rape or killing.

Within the week, we were on the road to Jaffa. Robert had lost almost three-quarters of his knights and an even higher proportion of his infantry and civilians. All his destriers had perished, the finest body of cavalry flesh in the world, and almost all the money he had raised from the sale of his dukedom had gone. He took very little from the spoils of Jerusalem – just enough to get us home.

My English contingent had suffered similar losses. At the roll-call at Jaffa we counted 63 able-bodied men, 11 crippled or dying, and only 7 civilians, all of them monks.

Estrith and Adela were the only female survivors, and young Harold of Hereford the only child.

32. The Parting

Our arrival in Constantinople brought a few weeks of comfort as we enjoyed the delights of the Blachernae, but it was also tinged with bitterness. Hereward insisted that he would return to his mountain home in the Peloponnese – no matter how hard Estrith, in particular, tried to persuade him to change his mind.

In September, he found a trader bound for Iberia and prepared to leave for Valencia to visit the Cid before the autumn gales became too severe. But he was forced to abort his trip when the captain brought him news, from a ship newly arrived, that his old friend had died peacefully in his bed in the middle of July. Doña Jimena, grief-stricken, had gone into mourning and refused to see anyone.

The Emperor summoned us for an audience.

Hereward had arrived before us; he had discarded his imperial garb and reverted to being the Old Man of the Mountain. He embraced all of us in turn.

'Adela, let me kiss my grandson. Take care of him for me.'

Estrith burst into tears.

'Please, Father, don't go!'

Hereward had turned to leave, but he now stopped and thought for a while before addressing his daughter.

'I once left you and Gunnhild to fight a battle. It was the most difficult thing I ever had to do. This time there are no more battles to fight; there is no reason why I should leave you again. But I can't go to England.'

'Then let me come with you.'

'Estrith, I live in a lean-to at the top of a mountain in the middle of a wilderness, and winter approaches.'

'It will do me good. Besides, it's how my mother and grandfather lived in the wildwood. I can work on designs for my roof of hammer beams —' her eyes widened in anticipation '— I will stay until the spring and then go north to join the others in Rouen.'

'What about Harold?'

She looked at Sweyn and Adela, who smiled and nodded their approval.

'It will do him good too. He needs toughening up, if he is to follow in the footsteps of his father and grandfather.'

Hereward's face softened.

'I'm not the most engaging company.'

'Neither am I, but I have a child to care for and a complicated roof design to perfect, I don't need much company.'

He looked at Alexius.

'Sire, she will need an escort in the spring to take her to Normandy.'

Alexius signalled his approval.

'It will be at Messene on the third new moon of next year.'

Estrith rushed at Hereward and threw her arms around him.

Alexius called to his steward, 'Some wine, I have a toast to make!'

The stewards handed round silver goblets and poured generous amounts of Byzantium's finest black wine.

'To Harold of Hereford, a noble knight in the making.'

The toast was repeated, and Alexius got up from his throne to thank each of us in turn. He then turned to Sweyn.

'I have a son, John Comnenus, twelve years old; he is away with his companion, John Azoukh – a Seljuk Turkish slave given to me as a gift, who I have adopted. He is good for John Comnenus, because my son has everything and John Azoukh nothing. Don't spoil your son; make him strong like you and your father. When he is older, bring him back to Constantinople, I would like to meet him and you can introduce him to my two sons.'

'It would be an honour, Your Majesty.'

'And now, let us talk about the Talisman of Truth; it is obviously still working its magic, because it brought us all together. In due course, I will give it to John Comnenus when it is time for him to wear the Purple, but I think John should be the recipient of the Talisman only for the beginning of his reign, when he will need it most. After that, its guardianship should become the responsibility of your Brethren, who may be able to put it to better use elsewhere. I will tell Prince John this, so that when the time is right you can come and collect it.'

'Majesty, I will tell Harold this also. Thank you.'

'I also have a gift for the boy. Keep it safe for when he is older.'

The Emperor handed Sweyn a small casket containing ten gold Byzantine bezants, a small fortune by anybody's standards.

Sweyn fell to his knees and kissed Alexius's ring.

*

That evening, as Hereward made ready to leave, I sought him out so that we could reflect on the past and, more importantly, look to the future.

'It must be very gratifying to know that Estrith and your grandson will go with you to your mountain home.'

'It is something I'm looking forward to, although I'm a little concerned that Estrith will find it somewhat primitive.'

'I'm sure she will adapt perfectly; it sounds like a paradise.'

'It's strange how life seems to exist in big arcs of destiny. Torfida, Estrith's grandmother, was raised in England's wildwood by her father, the Old Man of the Wildwood. Now young Harry will spend his early days with an old man of the mountain.'

'Perhaps that's the Talisman at work. You must be pleased that the Emperor has chosen Harry to be its guardian one day.'

'I am, but it's also a heavy burden to place on the boy's shoulders.'

'Well, he's got a fine pedigree. I'm sure he'll be worthy.'

'My Prince, you must help him and Estrith as long as you can.'

'I will, of course. But why do you address me as "Prince" all of a sudden?'

'Out of respect; you were born a prince, but had that title taken from you. Now, in my eyes, you've regained that title and are a prince by deed, not by birthright.'

I was stunned by Hereward's words and moved to embrace him, but he backed away, clasped the hilt of his sword and bowed deeply before turning away towards his chamber.

'Look after my daughter and grandson, Edgar, Prince of Wessex and England.'

I knew this was the last time I would ever see the great man. Once again, he had changed my life and, as he disappeared from view, I felt the tears welling in the corners of my eyes.

Within the week, our flotilla of ships was bound for Brindisi with sails full and a strong wind astern. Hereward, Estrith and baby Harold had already sailed for Messene.

Our journey was uneventful until we reached southern Italy, where a strange and wonderful thing happened: Robert fell in love. While his father, King William, was alive, he would not let Robert marry, for fear of a royal marriage compromising the delicate balance of politics in northern Europe. Only once did a marriage of alliance make sense, when he was betrothed to Margaret of Maine, but her untimely death put an end to that scheme. After the King's death Robert seemed content with a host of pretty concubines and conquests, all of little consequence.

That changed when we arrived in Conversano in Puglia, as guests of Count Geoffrey, its Norman lord and nephew of Robert Guiscard. He was a charming old man, but his daughter, Sybilla, equally charming, was far from old; she was a girl just turned sixteen, buxom and vivacious. Robert, all but fifty years old, was smitten.

It was a good match. He was Duke of Normandy – the land of Geoffrey's birth, and one of the mightiest realms in Europe – and his exploits in the Holy Land meant that he was one of the few Latin Princes whose reputation had been enhanced by the Crusade. He was hailed everywhere as not only a hero but also a true soldier of Christ, a man to be revered. She, for her part, brought a significant dowry from one of the richest counties in Italy, sufficient to pay back the share of Normandy that Robert had mortgaged to King Rufus.

Sweyn and I took to her readily; she was very easy on the eye, made excellent conversation, had a sharp mind, ready humour and knew how to charm men. She also won over Adela, whose limp was becoming more and more noticeable as her injuries made her increasingly frail. Sybilla brought her a treat of some sort every day and helped her to walk in the hills around Conversano, to try to keep her mobile.

If the new fashion of Courtly Love was what I assumed it to be, then Robert became the embodiment of it. He was like a new man and confessed that, in the bedchamber, Sybilla was all that one would hope for in a delectable young woman: initial innocence, but with a growing appetite to learn. He often joked that his only complaint was ever increasing exhaustion, but of the most delightful kind.

In a grand ceremony, Robert and Sybilla were married in February 1100 by Eustachio, Bishop of Brindisi. While Robert enjoyed his honeymoon with his bride in her father's seaside fortress at Monopoli, Hugh Percy and I led our contingents back to Normandy.

Our progress was remarkable. We were fêted everywhere, our path was strewn with garlands and gifts, Masses were said in our honour, and bishops anointed us. The welcome in Rouen was even more remarkable. The Crusaders had brought great honour to Normandy and the news that Duke Robert would be returning with a new bride, who would produce not only an heir but also swell the ducal coffers, only added to the excitement.

Thousands lined the narrow streets approaching the great cathedral, the massive bronze bells of which rang and rang in a never-ending chime of rejoicing. People cheered and rushed forward to bury their faces in our crimson and white capes; some even kissed our feet. Our weapons gleamed, our clothes were freshly washed, and we had trimmed our hair and beards. Pennons and gonfalons fluttered in the breeze as our crimson and white banners flew proudly above our heads.

Some of the more excitable and, indeed, naive assumed that, as we had been to the Holy Land, we must have met Christ himself, and therefore were insistent that we bless them! We were the all-conquering soldiers of Christ and thoroughly enjoyed the adulation.

The crowds knew nothing of the horrors that had been committed in the name of Christendom. In the eyes of the good people of Rouen, the day was one of celebration, where they could salute those who had helped a Christian God return to the Holy City where he belonged. Little did they know that, in truth, he had never left it – and in the light of what had been done there, he had probably now disowned it.

Awaiting us on the steps of the cathedral was the formidable William Bonne-Âme, the Archbishop of Rouen and Normandy, flanked by the entire senior ecclesiastical hierarchy of Normandy. An open-air Mass was held – which went on far too long, leading some of the men to suggest that the two-hour service was a greater trial than all the privations they had suffered in Palestine.

Rufus had ruled Normandy in Robert's absence, in accordance with their agreement. He was in England when we arrived, but it was reported to us that he was none too pleased at the news of our ecstatic welcome by the citizens of Rouen, having been certain that Robert, like so many other Crusaders, would never return.

Sweyn, Adela and I agreed that we should move on to England as soon as possible, not only to get our brave contingent back home, but also to see if we could gain an audience with King Rufus to report on Robert's achievements in Palestine before anybody else could pour poison into his ear.

The day before we were due to leave, Sweyn summoned me to Adela's chamber.

She had been a source of growing concern to us on the journey back from the Holy Land. Her discomfort seemed to be increasing by the day, not just from her shattered shoulder and damaged backside, but throughout her body. She was losing weight and looking drained and aged. She was prostrate when I arrived, and was clearly in great pain.

'Edgar, I am done for.'

'I have seen you in pain before; it will pass, like before.'

'Not this time.'

'We'll call for Robert's physicians; they looked after us well in the Holy Land.'

'They're butchers and idiots! But regardless of that, what ails me is deep inside; it's in my bones, I can feel it.'

Sweyn leant down, pulled Adela to him and hugged her.

She started to cry. 'I'm scared. I've only been really frightened once before, and you know when that was. I made a promise afterwards that I would never let myself be frightened again, but I am now.'

I joined Sweyn in holding her.

'We'll stay here with you until you are well.'

'You will not! I don't need a pair of nursemaids, and you have things to do in England.'

'They can wait.'

'No, you must leave, as we agreed. You will be fêted when you arrive; even Rufus will have to welcome you. To those who matter, especially the young knights, you can tell the truth about what happened in Palestine and spread the gospel of the Mos Militum. Do that for me.'

As I held her, I realized how thin she had become. A woman with a small frame in any case, she must have lost a stone or more in the last few months. I felt desperately sorry for her, and totally inadequate in being unable to help.

'There is nothing more we can do for you here, dearest Adela. Let us take you to the nuns of Rouen so that you can get the care you need.'

After making us promise that we would not leave her side, Adela eventually agreed to make the short journey, with our help. As we got her ready, there were tears in my eyes and in Sweyn's when we realized how much pain she was in.

On the way to the priory, every movement of the cart saw her wince, but every time we looked at her, concerned for her welfare, she forced a smile in an attempt to reassure us. On our arrival, the Mother Superior and one of the nuns showed us the way to their infirmary.

Adela seemed to have steeled herself to her fate but, as she was carried away, she made two last requests.

'When you get to England, kiss its soil for me and make sure that you tell young Harry about me. I enjoyed looking after him; he's a sweet little boy.'

Sweyn did not want to leave her, and it took him many minutes to say his private goodbyes to her.

As we rode away from the convent, I thought about how courageous Adela was. Her life had left her with many scars, but she had fought her injuries and her demons with great courage. Now she faced another even greater challenge, and probably one that she would not be able to overcome.

I looked at Sweyn. His eyes were squeezed shut and tears streamed down his face.

We did not speak; there was nothing to say.

PART SIX

Legacy

33. Deadly Arrow

It was good to be in England again. It was summer and England's green meadows were a pleasant contrast to the parched earth of the Holy Land. The sun shone to greet our English contingent, proudly carrying their crimson Crusade pennons and banners. Maurice, Bishop of London, greeted us on the steps of St Paul's at Ludgate and said Mass in the open air to welcome home England's soldiers of Christ.

King Rufus was nowhere to be seen, not even when we arrived at Westminster. The official version, offered by William, Count of Mortain and Earl of Cornwall, who welcomed us on behalf of the King, was that he had many difficult issues to deal with in Winchester, but that he hoped we would travel there to be welcomed by him in person. The truth was not difficult to discover, as it was common knowledge at court. Rufus was hunting in the New Forest and too preoccupied indulging himself with his hunting companions to greet those who had fought so courageously in the heat and dust of Palestine for three years in England's name.

Sweyn and I said our farewells to our brave and loyal men – who dispersed with their memories, bitter and sweet, to every corner of the land – and we prepared to rush back to Adela. We had decided that, our duty done in returning our men to their homes, Adela would forgive us for waiting a while before spreading the gospel of the Mos Militum.

*

The next morning, news arrived that would change the destinies of us all.

The first hint was a scurry of courtiers and officials suddenly making a din in the quiet of the early morning. Then we heard the fateful words shouted across the courtyard by a young knight: '*The King is dead! The King is dead!*'

I turned to Sweyn.

'Where is Henry Beauclerc?'

He shook his head.

'Please find out. If only Robert was in Normandy! He could be King of England within the week.'

A flurry of activity followed, as England's Norman masters plotted and schemed about the succession. The activity was clandestine enough to begin with, but when it emerged that Rufus had been killed by a stray arrow during his hunt in the New Forest, the intrigues reached fever pitch.

Stories of a conspiracy spread like wildfire among the young knights at court. Sweyn, his ire about Norman morality reawakened with a vengeance, recounted these stories for me with relish.

'You will find this amazing, even by the standards of intrigue of the Norman aristocracy.'

'I hope you are not including Robert in that sweeping remark?'

'Of course not. Robert is one of us now.'

'You mean, English?'

'Sire, you know what I mean; let me get on with the story. Henry Beauclerc is hardly ever seen with the King. Rufus surrounds himself with his bumboys, which Henry finds disgusting. Henry very definitely prefers women to men and is said to have lost count of his illegitimate children. He spends most of his time on his lands in the Cotentin in Normandy. But, it seems he appeared in England only two weeks ago, a sudden arrival that everyone here found hard to believe was the result of an unexpected rush of brotherly love.'

'So where is Henry now?'

'Wait, I'll come to that. As soon as Henry heard that Robert had survived the Crusade and was on his way back from the Holy Land, he realized that his future was in jeopardy. It seems that he had an agreement with Rufus to rule Normandy as soon as it was confirmed that Robert was either dead or would not be returning from Palestine. Even if he did return, Rufus would call in his loan to Robert, who would not be able to pay. Henry would cover the debt and acquire the duchy through Robert's default.'

'Very cunning.'

'That's not the half of it. The fact that Robert had married Sybilla, complete with a dowry sufficient to buy back his inheritance, and with the likelihood that she was already carrying Robert's heir in her belly, didn't just threaten his future plans, it ruined them.'

'So, he came to do a deal with Rufus, before Robert returned?'

'That's what everybody assumed, but Henry's scheme is far more devilish than that.'

I began to realize the diabolical level to which Henry had sunk, even before Sweyn had finished his account.

'Henry was there when Rufus was killed. They were in a deep part of the New Forest, where Rufus had seen a stag he wanted as a trophy. There were several others with him, including Walter Tirel of Tonbridge and Lord of Poix, whose father fought at Senlac Ridge. He is married to Adelize, the daughter of Richard Fitz Gilbert, whose dislike for Rufus is well known. It is said that Tirel shot the arrow that killed Rufus, but that it was an accident. Tirel's arrow hit Rufus square in the chest and ruptured his heart. He died almost immediately. Realizing what he'd done, Tirel fled, apparently bound for Normandy.'

'Could it have been an accident?'

'It's possible, but few believe it. Tirel is apparently one of the finest shots in England. Those who know him say that he is too good a huntsman to loose an arrow accidentally and that if he shot Rufus through the heart, he meant to do it.'

'I suppose an accidental arrow would have found a less deliberate target than a man's heart. When did this happen?'

'Three days ago. Henry had Rufus buried in great haste and without ceremony in Winchester the next morning.'

'And where is Henry now?'

'Here, in London.'

'Already?'

'He didn't even attend his brother's interment. He left it to the monks of St Swithun's of Winchester and hurried to the King's treasury, where he bullied William of Breteuil into giving him possession. At first, Breteuil refused, but Henry drew his sword and threatened to cut him down. He then rode day and night to reach London, where he secured the King's other treasury at Westminster. He's been behind closed doors with his supporters ever since, all of whom, by another unlikely coincidence, happen to be in London.'

'And they are?'

'Henry and Robert of Beaumont, Walter Giffard, Robert Malet, Roger Bigot, Robert Fitz Haimo, Robert of Montfort and a couple of others whose names I can't remember.'

'A powerful bunch! Are there opponents?'

'Some, but Henry's moving too fast for them to get organized. Many would be loyal to Robert, especially after his leadership in the Holy Land, but they are scattered all over England.'

'Yes, but Henry's not King yet; there is the small matter of a coronation.'

'He's ahead of you, I'm afraid; he is to be crowned tomorrow. He brought the crown with him from Winchester.'

I had witnessed many shameful things and seen many examples of the dark side of human nature, but this was a tale of avarice that took the breath away.

'But tomorrow is the Sabbath, and Anselm of Canterbury is in exile in Normandy. Don't tell me that Thomas of York is already in London and prepared to crown a king on a Sunday?'

'No, Maurice, Bishop of London, is going to preside.'

'Can he do that?'

'It seems so.'

'I feel so sad for Robert. While he's been fighting in Palestine, his brothers have been living off the fat of the land in England and Normandy, and now Henry has killed his own brother to grab the English crown. He will surely want Normandy next.'

'Can't we intervene somehow?'

I felt the same as Sweyn; with Robert weeks, or even months, away from Normandy and England, there had to

441

be something we could do to further his cause or protect his duchy. But what? After sending a messenger to Hugh Percy in Normandy, telling him to get the news of Rufus's death to Robert with all speed, Sweyn and I opened a flask of mead and began plotting.

If we were to do anything, we had to make our move that very night.

By mid-evening, we had concocted a story that was at least as audacious as some of the battleplans we had employed in the Holy Land, and no less risky. It also meant taking a significant liberty in our friendship with Robert, but all the same, we thought the subterfuge was in a good cause – not only his, but also England's and what the Brotherhood had fought for at Ely. Although we were only two members of our Brethren, we decided to act in its name and do as we thought they would do.

So, with not a little trepidation, we approached the Great Hall of Westminster, where we assumed Henry would be, and asked the sentries to summon their captain.

'Captain, please tell your lord that Prince Edgar of England is here to see him.'

As he opened the great door to take in our request, we could hear the distinct sounds of feasting, with much raucous laughter, before the heavy oak planks slammed shut again, leaving us to stare at a magnificent building, on a par in scale and style with any in Europe and only recently completed by Rufus as a symbol of the power of his realm.

When the door reopened and we were invited in, the din of celebration had subsided. Henry was at the far end of the hall, a walk that seemed to take an eternity, being at least the length of a tilt field. As we approached, most of guests scattered, including the young women recruited to bring the celebrations to an ending appropriate to a gathering of England's most important men. Only a dozen or so men remained – the ones Sweyn had named – and all sat around Henry as if he were already King.

'Count Henry, my Lords, please don't let our sudden arrival drive your guests away.'

'Prince Edgar, welcome to my court. Don't worry about my guests, I can soon call them back. What brings you to Westminster?'

'I have returned with the English contingent from the Crusades, but Duke Robert had asked me to travel to see you at your fortress in Avranches and bring you his greetings and best wishes, and to do the same with King Rufus while I am here in London. Sadly, circumstances have now changed my itinerary. I also have some messages for you, which are private family matters. But first, my condolences on the tragic death of the King. It was a sad day for all of us.'

'Thank you. I just hope I can carry on his good work.'

'My Lord Count, I had no idea, you are to succeed your brother?'

'Indeed, I am to be crowned tomorrow. I would welcome your presence.'

He seemed far more confident than I had remembered. I hoped I appeared similarly poised.

'It will be an honour, my Lord. I think you will remember Sir Sweyn of Bourne; he distinguished himself in the Holy Land and has become very close to your brother, Duke Robert. He rode into battle at his side many times.'

Henry nodded an acknowledgement, and Sweyn returned the gesture by bowing his head and grasping the hilt of his sword.

'I have heard glowing accounts of the bravery of all of you. You do us a great honour.'

He was already talking like a king. Although, in truth, humility had never been one of his strong points.

'Duke Robert is with his new bride, the Duchess Sybilla, a most charming and beautiful addition to your family, if I may say so. He sends his greetings.'

Henry smiled, a thin, perfunctory smile, almost a sneer, while his henchmen stared at us with a contempt usually shown to bonded peasants. Even though I had led the Anglo-Saxon English contingent in Palestine, I had long since been denied the courtesy usually shown to a royal prince, where counts and earls and all below them would stand when I entered a room.

'Thank you, Prince Edgar. Where is my brother now?'

'He is on his way home from Apulia. Hugh Percy led about a third of his army; your brother is leading the rest, a force of many thousands. He drew men to his colours throughout the campaign: Norman knights from Italy and Sicily, Franks, Provençals, Germans. When men like Raymond of Toulouse, Bohemond and Baldwin of Boulogne decided to stay in the Levant, many of their men flocked to Robert's banner.'

The mood in the room suddenly changed. Henry's scornful demeanour softened and his henchmen began to look discomfited.

'The treasure he brings from Jerusalem will fill many a king's treasury, quite apart from the huge reward he was given by the Emperor Alexius. And there is the dowry he carries from Sybilla's father, who, as you know, is the richest man in southern Italy.'

'Prince Edgar, Sir Sweyn, do join us.'

Henry had taken the bait, even though I was stretching credibility to the limit. He clapped his hands and told the stewards to bring wine.

'Would you join our coronation eve celebration? I will call the girls back.'

It looked like a night of drunken revelry and wanton debauchery beckoned – but all in a good cause.

After about half an hour, Henry summoned me to a quiet corner of the hall. He dropped the faux act of king-ship and treated me like an equal.

'Edgar, you have some private messages from Robert? But before you tell me about them, let us talk about the harsh realities of life.'

'Of course, where I've been for the last three years has been all about the harsh realities of life.'

'Was it as awful as I have heard?'

'No words can describe it, other than Hell on earth.'

'You have my sympathy and respect.'

'Thank you.'

'Your courage and leadership in the Holy Land will earn you great respect here, from both Normans and English-men. I would welcome your support at my coronation tomorrow and during my reign.'

'That you will have.'

'I am very keen to consolidate the blending of Normans and English in my realm. The vast majority of the lords who will owe me fealty after tomorrow are Normans who were born here and speak English like a native. I intend to consolidate our position in Wales and Scotland and have a fancy to let our destriers enjoy the rich fodder of Ireland. I need to build a new army – an army of Englishmen, led by Normans. I am going to take an English wife. Will you help?'

'I will, of course. Do you have someone in mind?'

'Yes, she is ideal, the daughter of Malcolm Canmore and Queen Margaret – your niece, Edith.'

I tried not to let my shock be too obvious. But he was right, of course. She was ideal – the daughter of the royal house of Scotland and a direct descendant, through my sister, of the Cerdician kings of England. Their children would create an Anglo-Norman dynasty, which had to be in the long-term interests of the English, so I quickly warmed to the idea.

'I will do all I can.'

'It is delicate. Your sister sent her to the nuns at Romsey several years ago, where your other sister, Christina, is abbess. Some say she has taken Holy Orders and wears the veil. She says that she hasn't taken her vows – and only wore a veil because her mother told her to, in order to protect her from lustful Normans.'

'I'm not sure I can help much on ecclesiastical matters.'

'You don't have to – just deal with your niece. Rufus banished Anselm, the clever Burgundian Archbishop of Canterbury. I'm going to bring him back and tell him to proclaim that she's not a nun. People will believe him.'

I could not help thinking about the irony of Edith wearing a veil to protect her against 'lustful Normans' while she was likely to end up marrying the most lustful of them all.

'Now, about my brother. What do you understand to be his intentions with his mighty army and treasure of Solomon?'

The satirical tone of Henry's question made me wonder how far he'd seen through my pretence, but there was no turning back now, so I ploughed on.

'First of all, when Robert and I last spoke, he knew nothing about the tragic circumstances of Rufus's death; indeed, he is unlikely to know for some time yet. Even so, I don't think anything he asked me to convey to you is altered in any way by the King's death or your succession to the throne. You should know that Robert is much changed by events in the Holy Land, as we all are. The truth of it is, although our intentions may have been noble, we Christians behaved in a way that many of us, including Robert, found appalling. We were participants in some of it and we all carry regrets that will haunt us for the rest of our lives.'

'What sort of appalling things do you mean?'

'Well, in short, the wholesale slaughter of soldiers and civilians alike – women and children included – rape, torture, mutilation and the breaking of all God's commandments. Most of it was done without provocation or justification and all of it in Christ's name.'

'I see, but how does that affect me?'

'Robert will pay back to the English treasury his mortgage on his share of Normandy's wealth. Robert desires only to live out his days quietly in Normandy. He has no designs on the English crown at Westminster and will not use his powerful allies and army, or his significant wealth, to force a claim for the throne.

'That is a concession to Rufus, not to me.'

'But it applies to you now.'

Henry had seen the hole in the middle of our pretence, as Sweyn and I had thought he would, so I played the gambit that we had discussed.

'As testament to his sincere belief in harmony and his regard for you, Robert is prepared to share the Duchy of Normandy with you. You would have Lower Normandy – the dioceses of Avranches, Sées and Coutances – which you would rule from Caen. Robert would have Upper Normandy – the dioceses of Lisieux and Évreux – which he would rule from Rouen. He is also prepared to use his now considerable influence in Rome to have Pope Paschal declare both parts of Normandy as separate dukedoms.'

'That is generous indeed! I am happy to accept his offer.'

Sweyn and I had anticipated this predictable response as well. I smiled; it seemed right to treat his reply as lighthearted, even if he may well have meant it.

'Very amusing – of course, your succession here in England, and particularly your ambitions on our Celtic borders, means that it is impossible for you to rule Lower Normandy as well.'

I swallowed hard, realizing that I was in the middle of a fake game of chess, with two realms and the fate of thousands of people resting on the outcome.

Henry stared at me, as if trying to see behind my eyes.

I tried to hold my composure and forced another smile, this one more pronounced.

He smiled back; had the moment passed? Had the deception worked? If it had, it was time to haul the catch in.

'Robert would be happy to swear an oath recognizing your sovereignty here and guaranteeing his loyalty and his support for your attempts to strengthen our kingdom.'

'Edgar, you are a very shrewd emissary, you should have been an ambassador. Do your advice and Robert's loyalty come at a price, by any chance?'

'Only two small amounts. Robert would, of course, expect you to take an oath affirming his lordship of Normandy and your acceptance of mutual loyalty and cooperation.'

'And?'

'The second trifle would be of enormous benefit to your reign and go a long way to securing the loyalty of your magnates and the affection of your English subjects.'

'This sound like more than a trifle.'

'Not at all, it would be a simple affirmation of the laws of England and your respect for them. There would be nothing new; you would acknowledge the laws enacted by your father, King William, and those he respected from his predecessors, particularly those of King Edward and Cnut the Great. You would also reject the excesses of Rufus's reign and promise to correct the wrongs he did. You could call it your Coronation Charter and have it read in every burgh in the land. It would be a hugely popular beginning to your reign.'

Henry stared at me again, as if I were a strange creature he had never seen before.

'Edgar, Prince of the English, you are a clever man, and, I suspect, a cunning one. But I like the idea of a Coronation Charter being read all over England. It will begin my rule in England with an outcry of popular support – something my brother never had, and certainly not my father. Can you read Latin?'

'I can.'

'I will get my scribes out of bed. You can work on it with them tonight – all night, if you have to. I'll read it in the morning and, after my coronation at Westminster, I will ride to the old city to proclaim it from my father's chapel of St John the Evangelist in the Great Tower. I will call it Henry of England's Charter of Liberties.'

I nearly lost control at that point. For some unfathomable reason, he had proposed a title for the Charter that I would never have dreamed of suggesting, fearing it might seem too bold. I changed the subject immediately to help hide my elation.

'And what will I say to Robert?'

'Again, you are very astute. I wonder how much of what you told me are my brother's words – or are they yours? But it doesn't matter much; tell him I agree to the oaths. We will take them together, at a place of his choosing – as long as it's not the Holy Land, of course – when he's finished bedding his young bride. By the way, is she tall, average height . . .?'

'She's very petite.'

'That must be a relief for little Shortboots! I will leave you to your scripting; I have the two lovely daughters of a London goldsmith awaiting my pleasure. He has sent them to plead his case to become one of my assayers. He doesn't have very strong credentials, I'm afraid, so they are going to have to do a lot of pleading.'

34. Treaty of Alton

Sweyn and I rode out for Romsey the day after Henry's coronation to fulfil the undertaking I had given to the King to help with his plan to marry my niece.

Although I would never tell him so, it was not a difficult task. Edith knew her own mind and she had had enough of convent life. She had turned twenty years of age and, although she had attracted many suitors, this new one would make her Queen of England.

Archbishop Anselm was recalled from Normandy and he duly resolved the ecclesiastical issue of Edith's status as a nun. Taking the Norman name Matilda, she was married and crowned Queen later in the year.

Significantly for me, as the Queen's uncle, the marriage made me a part of England's royal household and rendered my status as a prince of the realm real again. I was entitled to an allowance from the King's purse, a small retinue of my own and a chamber at Westminster. I made Sweyn my steward, thus making him an official member of the King's court and free to come and go as he pleased.

There were only a handful of Englishmen in his position.

When we returned to Westminster from Romsey, we were met with the news that a guest had arrived to see us – a nun, Estrith, Abbess of Fécamp.

We were lodging in the King's palace at Westminster, a beautiful collection of buildings behind old King Edward's towering cathedral and very close to the River Thames. Estrith was waiting in the King's garden just upriver, next to the stairs which led down to the mooring for his royal barge. It was a bright, fresh morning and I could see, even at a distance, that Estrith looked as fetching as ever.

She rushed towards us and embraced us, while a young nun showed us the heavily swaddled two-year-old Harold of Hereford, who was smiling cheerfully. Sweyn beamed in delight at being reunited with Harry.

Estrith glowed with pride as we admired her young son. 'He's doing well. This is Mabel, who is helping me with him.'

Sweyn had a stream of questions – rate of growth, appetite, temperament – all the usual things that every father demands to know before deciding that, firstly, his son is just like him and, secondly, he has no peers in all the important gifts. Here was a boy who I felt sure was destined to live a life as remarkable as his parents and grandparents.

Mabel and I stood back after a while to let Sweyn and Estrith walk along the river, which was in full flow with the deep waters of a high tide, and enjoy a few private minutes with their son.

However, when they returned, Estrith's happy demeanour in greeting us was soon gone.

'We mustn't be too much longer, we don't have much time. Mabel, please take Harry for a while.'

Estrith took us across the great close between the cathedral and the palace and into the Benedictine infirmary behind the cathedral cloisters. Dozens of sick and dying filled every available space of the long, rectangular room as the nuns and monks did their best to cope with what seemed to be an overwhelming number of patients. We went into one of the private bedchambers at the end of the room, where two nuns were leaning over a bed, tending to a patient.

'It is Adela, she is dying.'

We rushed to her side, but the fragile figure of jaundiced skin and bone was unconscious and barely breathing.

'I shouldn't have done it, but when I returned to Rouen from the Peloponnese with Harold, I heard that Adela was with the nuns. When I went to see her, she bullied me into bringing her to England; you know what she's like. The nuns said she had been fighting death for weeks, hoping that you two would return soon. She wanted to die on English soil and be buried at Bourne. I have no idea how she survived the crossing; I had to pay the captain a fortune to take her because he was certain she would die at sea and bring his ship bad luck. When we were on board, she just stared over the side, desperate for the first sign of England. It was sheer willpower that kept her alive.'

I took one of Adela's hands and Sweyn the other. She was cold and her hands, almost without flesh on them, weighed no more than a goose feather.

Sweyn spoke to the sisters. 'When did she become unconscious?'

'Yesterday morning, sire. She is your wife?'

'Yes.'

'I'm sorry, sire, she is unlikely to see out the day.'

Sweyn let his head fall to his chest.

I spoke to Adela, hoping against hope that she could hear me.

'I have some wonderful news for you. Rufus is dead, killed in a hunting accident. King Henry I, the new King, has put his seal to a Charter of Liberties for all Englishmen. It guarantees respect for the law and the right of everyone to be dealt with fairly according to the law. What was fought for at Ely has not been forgotten. We're going to take you to the Fens to celebrate.'

She did not respond visibly, but both Sweyn and I were sure she squeezed our hands.

Adela of Bourne, Knight of Islam, died later that day without regaining consciousness.

We travelled to Bourne immediately with, to his immense credit, a royal escort provided by King Henry, where we intended burying her with as much ceremony as we could muster.

Bourne had sprung to life again, reborn after the dark days of the Conquest. The little Saxon church was being rebuilt and new houses were sprouting all over the village. Everyone knew of the tragic history of Bourne and welcomed the opportunity to meet Sweyn, one of their own, and Estrith, the daughter of the man whose deeds would make their village part of English folklore for ever.

At our request, Simon of Senlis, Earl of Huntingdon, sent four of his knights and a platoon of men to join the King's men in an honour guard. The Abbot of Ely, Richard Fitz Richard, sent two monks to pray for Adela and a choir of six more to sing plainchant during the interment.

We waited until dusk and lit the road into the village with beacons so that we could bring her body home like the returning heroine she had become. Estrith, Sweyn and I, with Harold in his father's arms, walked behind the cart that bore her body as it entered the village, and the entire community formed a cortège to accompany her to her grave.

As the amber glints of the processional torches lit our tear-stained faces, the honour guards raised their swords in respectful salute and the monks sang their simple melodies. Sweyn and I lifted Adela's body, wrapped in a simple linen shroud, and placed it in her grave. Her weapons and armour were laid on her body and we took it in turns to cover her with earth. Nothing was said; she did not want any words spoken or prayers read. She had asked Estrith for silence when the time came so that she could hear the sounds of the Fens drift over her on the evening air.

She had searched all her life for her destiny and had found it in many places (Normandy, Sicily and Palestine) and in many forms (as a Knight of Islam, as a leading proponent of the Mos Militum, as a founder of our Brethren and in the Charter of Liberties) and in love, generosity and devotion – the love she had shown to Sweyn during their phantom marriage, the generosity she had shown to Estrith in helping her to disguise her pregnancy, and the constant devotion she had always shown to all of us.

Now she had come home.

The journey back to Westminster was a time of sombre reflection for the three of us.

Adela's death, coinciding with the King's Coronation

Charter, seemed to bring to a close many of the paths we had each pursued. Estrith had turned forty, Sweyn was nearer forty than thirty and I would soon be in my fiftieth year. Yet, there were new challenges: Estrith and Sweyn had a two-year-old son to worry about and I, on a foundation of falsehoods, exaggerations and subterfuge, had built a concordat between the two most powerful men in northern Europe that one of them was totally unaware of.

We had much to think about.

Estrith had hardly spoken about her time with Hereward and Harold on his mountain. I wanted to know more.

'What was it like?'

'Just as he said it was: a lean-to at the top of a craggy mountain, bitterly cold in winter, hot as a blacksmith's forge in summer. But it was a very profound experience for me. My father has become a perfect reflection of my grandfather, the Old Man of the Wildwood. He is totally at ease with the world around him, able to listen and dispense his wisdom. He seems not to need a woman, or any companionship. Of course, I couldn't help living out the fantasy of being my mother, learning about the world at the feet of my grandfather.'

She turned away, paused for a moment, before continuing.

'I don't think he believes in God. I'm sure he thinks Christ was a great prophet, but I don't think he accepts that He is divine. He may not believe in any kind of God, as we understand it. He talked a lot about the old religion and the truths of the ancients, like the Wodewose of the Forest, the Green Man, the guiding spirit of Nature. He also mentioned the Talisman and how its messages had guided him and Torfida to their destinies. It gave us a lot to talk about.

'Amazingly, at no stage did he ever tell me what he thought, and he certainly never suggested what I should think. He just kept posing questions. He kept saying that life is a search for more questions, not a search for answers.'

'What will you do now?'

'I don't know . . . Sweyn and I have a decision to make about Harold. He thrived on his grandfather's mountain. He never got sick, ate like a horse and slept like a baby.'

'He is a baby!'

'Yes, that's what I meant. When he's older, I will be able to tell him in the smallest of detail and hour by hour about his time with his famous grandfather in his mountain eyrie. I'm so glad we had that time together.'

'It must have been difficult to leave?'

'Not really – we were both content, and my father had spent time with Harold. He took us to Messene and we said our farewells. There were tears, of course, but he is happy reflecting on his past and searching for more questions to pose from his mountain top. He is fit and strong; I think he will live for many years yet. As for me, seeing him again and spending that time with him was the fulfilment of an impossible dream. I am very fortunate; I feel blessed to have had my time with him and privileged to have known him as a father.'

By the time we reached Westminster, Sweyn and Estrith had had their conversation and a decision had been reached about young Harold.

While in Bourne, the monks from Ely had told Estrith about a new church, only four years into construction, in the Burgh of Norwich. She reminded us that, when we first met, she had been about to start work on Durham Cathedral. Norwich, she said, was a good place to resume her career as a churchwright, make her hammer-beam roof a reality, and a safe place to raise young Harold. Sweyn would visit whenever he could, but the facade of the child being Adela's would remain in that Sweyn would formally entrust the care of the child to Estrith.

We took steps to secure the boy's future. Sweyn's status at court meant that Harold would inherit his rank as a knight of the realm, subject to him passing the tests of knighthood at the appropriate age, and I bequeathed a few of my English holdings to him in a document that Estrith would hold until he reached adulthood.

She also took a casket, to be handed to him when he reached his majority. It contained a large purse of silver, ten gold Byzantine bezants, a vellum scroll with the Oath of the Brethren of the Blood written on it and the names of its founding members, and St Etheldreda's rosary that Estrith had carried with her since the fall of Ely.

So, after our own fond farewells in Westminster, Estrith headed back the way we had come to Norwich, while Sweyn and I sailed for Normandy with all the pan-oply of the progress of a royal prince, but also with the onerous task of telling Robert the detail of the pact I had agreed with Henry on his behalf.

When we reached Rouen, Robert and his entourage had just arrived. They had received news of Rufus's death while in the Rhône Valley but had not hurried back,

Robert preferring to show his bride the sites and introduce her to the lords and princes along the way. As I suspected and hoped, he had no real desire to claim the English throne.

Telling Robert about his agreement with Henry turned out to be no hardship at all. He laughed heartily at my cunning and thanked me for moving so adroitly. He was particularly pleased about the Charter of Liberties; as I had said to Henry, Robert was a changed man as a result of the Crusade and his single priority was now Sybilla.

'We are going to Mont St Michel to pray for our firstborn. Sybilla hasn't conceived yet; the sea air will do her good.'

Robert sailed to England in the summer of 1101 to formally ratify the pact with Henry. He took a large force with him, just in case his brother had had a change of heart, but when they met at Alton in Hampshire, there was an outpouring of what can only be described as brotherly love.

Robert renounced his claim to the English throne and each acknowledged the other as their legitimate heir until they produced a son. Henry renounced all claims on territory in Normandy and agreed to pay Robert the huge sum of 3,000 silver marks as an annual tribute, about one tenth of his royal budget. This particular clause brought a distinct smile to Robert's face. He told me later that, with part of the first instalment, he was going to buy Sybilla the biggest jewel in Christendom.

Finally, they pledged their loyalty to one another and promised to come to one another's aid. The agreement was signed and sealed at Winchester, and Sweyn and I breathed a huge sigh of relief.

Henry and Robert travelled to London together, and they stayed together until Christmas – hunting, visiting the great Norman magnates of the realm, viewing their mighty churches and fortresses and reinforcing the power of Norman hegemony.

The sea air of Mont St Michel had not enhanced Sybilla's fecundity, but England's temperate climes had, for shortly after we returned to Rouen, she announced that she was pregnant.

Sweyn and I took great satisfaction in knowing that the child had been conceived in our homeland.

Robert and Sybilla's child, William Clito, was born on the 25th of October 1102, in Rouen. It was an occasion of great joy throughout the duchy. The boy was a healthy young heir to continue Normandy's powerful dynasty.

But prodigious joy soon turned to unbounded sadness.

Sybilla never recovered from the birth and her condition slowly worsened. There were rumours of poison but, in truth, the birth had been difficult and she had become septic. She fought the ever-tightening grip of the infection in increasing pain until it killed her in March 1103. Robert was unable to cope with her death and, like his legacy from Palestine, was changed by it ever after.

He had a white marble slab made for her like the one for his mother's tomb, on which were carved the words:

No power of birth, nor beauty, wealth, nor fame
Can grant eternal life to mortal man
And so the Duchess Sybilla, noble, great and rich,
Lies buried here at rest, as ashes now.
Her largesse, prudence, virtue, all are gifts
Her country loses by her early death;
Normandy bewails her Duchess, Apulia mourns
her child –
In her death great glory is brought low.
The sun in the Golden Fleece destroyed her here,
May God now be her source of life.

My niece, Edith, now Queen Matilda of England, also produced an heir for her husband, in the autumn of 1103. He too was given the name William, and the suffix Adelin, a corruption of Atheling, in recognition of his English pedigree.

Whether the birth of the young prince was the catalyst, who thus supplanted Robert as heir to the English throne, or Robert's grieving over Sybilla, which left him paralysed as an effective leader, or Henry's latent Norman predilection for more and more power and glory, it was difficult to tell, but it soon became clear that Henry was going to break the Treaty of Alton and that he probably never had any intention of honouring it in the first place.

Henry started to turn the screw.

Firstly, he failed to forego his holdings in Normandy and found various excuses for not paying Robert his annual tribute. Then, in 1104, Henry moved against William, Count of Mortain and Earl of Cornwall, the man whose father had been at Ely and who had taken care of Estrith and Gunnhild so well. The Count was Robert's leading ally in England and a man widely respected by his peers. When Henry claimed some of his lands in the south-east of England, the Count took offence, which the King interpreted as treason, and used it as an excuse to seize all his holdings in Cornwall, forcing the Count to flee to Normandy.

Henry then added insult to injury. He travelled to Normandy unannounced in August of 1104, visited several lords and counts he hoped would become allies and entertained them lavishly from his fortress at Domfront. Finally, he made a move that at first seemed laughably naive, but in fact revealed the extent of his manoeuvring: he let it be known that he was considering convening a court of all the nobles of Normandy to debate the failures of his brother's rule of the duchy.

Robert, ever generous and still inconsolable following Sybilla's death, failed to respond. Sweyn and I tried to persuade him otherwise, but he always saw the good in people rather than the bad and, given that our warrior instincts were also diminished by our own recent experiences, we found it hard to disabuse him of such noble sentiments.

We were getting older, Robert's stalwarts in Normandy were getting older, while Henry and many of his supporters were in their prime.

The King had taken great pains, and spent a great deal of money, to cultivate the young Prince Louis, heir to the French throne, whose father, King Philip, once our great friend and powerful ally, was also ageing, becoming more and more corpulent and distracted from the affairs of state by countless nubile concubines at court.

On several occasions, we forced Robert to look at the noose that Henry was tightening around the neck of Normandy, but he chose not to react. Eventually, in exasperation, one night after dinner at his palace in Rouen, we confronted him. He had been in a better mood at table and I suspected he had been finding comfort with a strapping young maid at court, the daughter of a lord from Alsace. We used the comradeship of our Brethren to try to goad him, but Robert was dismissive of our concerns at first.

'It has nothing to do with our Brethren – this is a matter between Rufus and me, and the people of Normandy.'

'Robert, Sweyn and I are closer to you than anyone, please listen to us.'

'I am listening.'

'But you are not acting on our advice.'

'Our friendship requires me to listen to your advice, but not necessarily to do as you suggest.'

Sweyn rarely spoke when Robert and I were at odds over big issues, but this time he intervened.

'Edgar is right, the threat is very real. You must make a move to protect yourself.'

'Thank you, Sweyn, I respect your opinion – and yours, of course, Edgar – but my mind is clear. An invasion will come, it is as certain as the sun rising in the morning. But what will be, will be. When we hear that Henry is building ships, we will start planning. Edgar, we've been together through many battles and have fought men much more fearsome than my little brother. My father managed to invade England by sea and succeeded by the skin of his teeth. It will be much more difficult to invade Normandy and succeed. Don't worry. If Henry does invade, when he's lying dead on the battlefield and I become King, I will install you as my Prince Regent and England will be yours at long last.'

While Robert's promise might have seemed tempting, neither Sweyn nor I thought a victory for Robert a likely result. Henry had shown himself to be very much in his father's mould – unlike Robert, who was his antithesis.

If a shrewd man were to gamble on the outcome of the fight, it was obvious where he would place his wager.

Robert was as stubborn as he was likeable, but Sweyn and I both felt anxious for him. It was almost as if he was hoping Rufus would take the heavy burden of Normandy's dukedom from his weary shoulders.

35. Battle of Tinchebrai

Henry's aggression in Lower Normandy escalated. Bayeux was burned to the ground, Caen was forced to open its gates to him, and then he moved on Falaise. The threat to Falaise, his father's birthplace and home to his now legendary grandmother, Herleve, finally prompted Robert into action; but he did not summon his army, he went to negotiate.

They met midway between Caen and Falaise. After two days of bitter argument, where Henry's naked ambition was all too apparent, the two brothers parted acrimoniously, shouting insults at one another.

Robert seemed to be newly invigorated by the abuse thrown at him and decided on a tactic worthy of the bold strategies of the Princes in the Holy Land. He decided to sail for England with only two dozen loyal supporters, walk straight into the King's Hall at Winchester and get him to see sense by force of argument. No amount of hectoring on our part would convince Robert of the naivety of his plan and so, in late January 1106, we set sail.

Inevitably, the King, although initially shaken by the sudden appearance of his brother, who literally hammered on the doors of Winchester at the break of dawn, was unmoved.

'There is unrest all over Normandy at the stagnant nature of your rule. The sad loss of Sybilla has neutered you; Normandy has always needed strong leadership, and you are not giving it.'

'Henry, you will not provoke me with insults and cruel comments about Sybilla's death. The truth is, we have a treaty, which Edgar, your good friend and mine, negotiated. All I am asking is for you to honour it.'

'My loyalty to my father and my ancestral homeland prevents me from honouring it. I am approached every day by men who beg me to give them leadership.'

'My brother, you are deluding yourself, or engaging in a wicked scheme to serve your own interests. Please let it not be the latter.'

'It is neither; my only interest is Normandy's future security.'

Henry's implacability finally convinced Robert that there was no more to be said.

We took the next tide to Normandy and prepared for war.

Robert's generosity – or, as some would put it, his impotence – in dealing with his brother's threats soon began to exact a telling price. Henry had persuaded many of Normandy's most powerful men that he was a better option for the duchy than its duke. To his dismay, when Robert called for his supporters to join him with their knights, few were forthcoming. Of the most senior men, William of Mortain, the deposed Earl of Cornwall, and Robert of Bellême, Earl of Shrewsbury, were the only ones to hear the rallying call.

On the other hand, King Henry had built up a significant force, far outnumbering Robert's army. He had returned to

Lower Normandy shortly after we had, and immediately began to prepare for battle.

Henry's final provocation, the laying down of the gauntlet, came in September 1106. The King advanced south from Falaise with a large army towards the small settlement of Tinchebrai, part of the lands belonging to William of Mortain. He could have overwhelmed the fortress within the hour, but instead besieged it, as a lure with which to entice us. Count William immediately appealed to Robert for help and we duly rode west, preparing ourselves to withstand the jaws of the trap that had been set for us.

Robert knew the trap was primed and that our prospects were not the best, but several layers of pride were steeling him for the encounter: his Norman ancestry, the legacy of Palestine, and his innate decency which compelled him to behave honourably.

When we arrived, Robert demanded that Henry lift the siege, to which Henry responded by offering Robert an annual pension and a quiet life in exchange for Normandy.

I looked at Sweyn; we were almost tempted to suggest to Robert that he should agree, but then thought better of it. First of all, it was hardly an offer worthy of a noble duke of any stature, let alone that of Robert, and secondly, Henry's promises did not have much of a reputation.

Robert did not even respond to Henry's offer. Instead, he ordered that we make camp and meet to discuss our tactics.

Our scouts had reported on King Henry's disposition. We were outnumbered by about three to one. Robert had his personal squadron, the elite cavalry unit formed by his father – now called the Sybilla Squadron – and a strong deployment of archers and infantry. He would take the centre ground with Hugh Percy, Sweyn and I standing with him. William of Mortain would take the left flank, while Roger of Bellême took the right.

We mustered 300 knights and 3,000 infantry.

King Henry had nearly 1,000 knights and at least 8,000 infantry, many of whom were Englishmen.

Early the next morning, the King took a position to the rear, with his reserves, while Ralph of Bayeux, Robert Beaumont and William II of Warenne led his centre, left and right flanks respectively. Helias, Count of Saint Saens, led Henry's Breton and Manceaux cavalry.

For Robert Beaumont, the highly respected, wily old campaigner, it must have been a particularly poignant moment. Now sixty years old, a lifetime ago he had led the right flank of the army of Robert and Henry's father at Senlac Ridge. Not only that, the date was the 28th of September 1106, forty years to the day since William's army had first set foot on English soil at Pevensey Beach.

This time, Beaumont was on the right flank of the King of England, whose wife was English, whose heir was called Atheling, and whose army contained thousands of English foot soldiers; and he was facing a fight to the death with the Duke of Normandy and his Norman army. Over the years, we had witnessed many strange paradoxes in England. Now we were witnessing another one in Normandy.

Robert did not make a speech before the battle. For the first time in his reign, he raised the baculus of his

Viking ancestors high above his head and bellowed, 'For Normandy!'

Robert's simple but powerful war cry fortified our men, and Henry's first attack was held – but at a fearful price. A second onslaught followed and then a third, until our numbers had been significantly reduced. The battle had raged for less than an hour and already our lines had become ragged and breached in several places. Then Henry unleashed a sustained cascade of arrows into our ranks, causing yet more confusion and heavy losses.

Robert was already in the thick of the fighting, with Sweyn, Hugh Percy and I taking positions to protect his rear and sides, when disaster struck. Robert of Bellême, thinking that the day was lost, turned and fled, leaving our right flank completely exposed.

Henry grasped the opportunity immediately.

He committed his cavalry and ordered Count Helias to charge, letting loose a horde of knights from Normandy's neighbours who had many scores to settle.

Our position was hopeless.

Sweyn turned to Robert and shouted at him, 'We are being overrun; let us get you away before it's too late.'

Hugh Percy and I beckoned to as many of Robert's Sybilla Squadron as we could to form a cordon around him and escort him from the field, but he would have none of it.

'We stand! No retreat!

Moments later, Hugh Percy was unhorsed when his mount took an arrow in its shoulder. He was then beaten to the ground with a huge spiked mace wielded by a

Breton knight; he did not move, and seemed mortally wounded. Robert's horse reared, tipping him off its back, and Sweyn and I dismounted to close ranks around him while the few survivors of his elite cavalry tried to shield us.

We were soon surrounded by a swarm of infantry and knights on horseback, their blades and lances raining blows down on us. I took a heavy blow to the top of my helmet, which brought a painful end to my role in the battle, rendering me unconscious for several minutes.

When I came round, Robert was on his knees with blood streaming down his left arm and face. He was one of only a few of our men left standing in what was a strange calm, disturbed only by the heavy breathing of the living and the moans of the dying.

I could not see Sweyn at first. But then I saw him sprawled in front of Robert, lifeless.

He had taken a Breton lance through his mail and deep into his chest. Blood was still pouring from his wound and forming a pool in the ground beneath him as Robert sank to his haunches and lifted his friend's limp head on to his lap.

I moved to join them, but was again struck from behind, plunging me into darkness once more.

I never saw either of them again.

I was sent to the coast and put on a ship to England. My status as the Queen's uncle saved my life, but I was banished from court, all my lands and money confiscated, save for a small allowance from the King, and I was required, under pain of death, to remain within the boundaries of Northumbria for the rest of my days.

William of Mortain was blinded on the King's orders and confined within the Great Tower in London.

Robert was paraded around Normandy as Henry's vassal, before being sent to England to be incarcerated at the King's pleasure, first in Wareham Castle and then, for a while, in the custody of Roger, Bishop of Salisbury, with whom he got on well. When the King heard of this, he sent him to the much less pleasant environs of Cardiff Castle. Apparently, he was not mistreated or locked in a dungeon, but he was allowed no visitors or any communication with the outside world.

Sweyn, our handsome, brave and noble brother-in-arms, was left lying on the battlefield with Hugh Percy and so many other loyal men, to be stripped of their weapons, armour and clothes and left as carrion for the crows.

He had insisted that Hereward was still alive and found his hero, as he said he would; he had married Adela, so that she could fulfil her dream; and he had avenged Mahnoor's murder. His exploits in the Holy Land were unsurpassed by even the bravest of the Crusaders, and his belief in the ethics of the Mos Militum made him a chivalrous knight of the highest order. His service to Robert and to me was faultless, and he had become a friend and confidant to us both. Perhaps, most importantly, in his brief love affair with Estrith, he had sired Harold, Hereward's grandson, a boy who, one day, may continue the noble legacy of the children of Bourne.

36. Phantom in the Night

Sweyn's death meant that our Brethren still had four living members, but it was unlikely that we would ever see one another again. So, what would our testament be? I have spent a lifetime reflecting on that, concluding that, in the end, it will be the scribes who decide.

The last part of my long story happened just a few months ago, when I had a visitor here at Ashgyll Force. In the intervening years I had heard about his mother's death and had asked the monks at Durham to locate his whereabouts, as I needed to be sure that I could honour a promise I had made many years earlier. However, I had heard nothing in reply.

Then he appeared, like a phantom in the night. I was sound asleep, it must have been three in the morning, and I woke with a start. I could sense a presence in the room and froze, thinking that, at long last, Owain Rheged had tired of my presence and had come for me.

Then a deep, but gentle, voice spoke from the shadows.

'Prince Edgar, don't be concerned. I am Harold of Hereford.'

I peered into the darkness; the moon was bright and casting strange silhouettes. I called out to a figure sitting by the window.

'You mean young Harry? Son of Estrith of Melfi and Sweyn of Bourne?'

'Indeed, sire.'

'Show yourself!'

'I cannot, my anonymity is important to me. I need to tell you some things as a fellow member of the Brethren of the Blood and to obtain your blessing for what I have done and am about to do. My mother made me a full member of our Brethren when I came of age; she said you would be in agreement.'

'I heard that your mother has died?'

'Scarlet fever; it devastated Norwich while I was away. She was a wonderful mentor to me and told me all about the Brethren and your lives together. She was content with her lot, and her work meant everything to her. She took enormous pride in helping the great cathedral grow.'

'Did she give you the casket?'

'She did. That's why I'm here – to thank you for the endowment and the gift of land, and also to seek your permission. Duke Robert is still in Cardiff Castle and no one can see him. You and I are the only members of the Brethren at liberty, and I need your sanction.'

'If I think what you are doing furthers the cause of the Brotherhood of St Etheldreda and our Brethren, then you will have it.'

'I haven't got much time. I leave for Constantinople and the Peloponnese as soon as the winds are favourable. My mother told me where my grandfather's mountain eyrie is. I am going to see it, to spend some time and reflect there. I am sure he is long dead and buried, but I want to be sure he is properly in the ground. I am also going to see the new Emperor, John II, to thank him for his father's very generous legacy.

473

My mother told me he will give me the fabled Talisman of Truth.'

'You don't need my agreement for any of that.'

'I know, but my purpose in coming here is to tell you of a new Brotherhood. When I became a knight, I went to France to serve King Louis VI. There, I met two men of great valour and virtue; we have become great friends. Their names are Hugh of Payens and Godfrey of Saint-Omer; they both served with Geoffrey of Bouillon in the First Crusade. They are much older than me and have become my mentors.'

'I don't recall their names.'

'They remember you and the English contingent, and the exploits of my grandfather, Sweyn, Adela and Edwin. They have formed their own brotherhood. It is a very noble order and they have invited me to join it; it is a great honour. There are only nine of us, and the rest are Normans or Franks. You may have heard their names: André of Montbard, Payen of Montdidier, Archambaud of St Amand, Geoffrey Bisol and two monks, Gondemere and Rosal. We are the Poor Fellow-Soldiers of Christ and of the Temple of Solomon, the Knights Templar.'

'And what is your mission?'

'The King of Jerusalem, Baldwin II, has granted us his church on Temple Mount in Jerusalem, the former al-Aksa mosque, the site of the Temple of Solomon, which gives us our name. We wear the cross of Christ and are sworn to poverty, chastity, piety and obedience in the service of God and our fellow men and are strong supporters of the Mos Militum, the code of chivalry that all knights should follow.'

'It sounds very worthy, but a little strict!'

'It is, but there is so much cruelty and evil in our world we have to be disciplined to resist its temptations. My brother knights will follow me to Constantinople, from where we will travel to the Holy Land.'

'So much time has passed. It is strange to hear your voice now, as a grown man. Be careful in Palestine. I'm sure it's as dangerous now as it was in my day.'

'My mother told me what an inspiration you were to all of them; she was very fond of you.'

'That was kind of her. We were a good team, true brethren.'

Harry's words were very gratifying; they also reminded me of how I had wanted so much more from Estrith, if circumstances had been different. Ah, the wistful memories of an old man!

My eyes were beginning to adjust to the light and I could see the outline of his face. He was like his father – dark of hair and complexion, and tall and willowy. I could not see his eyes, lost in the dark bowls of his eye sockets, but I would have wagered they were warm and dark like Estrith's. I suddenly wondered how Harry knew where my little abode was.

'Tell me, how did you know where to find me?'

'It wasn't difficult. I asked the King.'

I was curious. I knew that Harry was not without funds and knightly status, but that would not normally give him access to the King.

'So, you have access to him?'

'I do. He speaks very highly of you.'

'May I ask how you have access to King Henry?'

'I am part of his bodyguard, what the Saxons used to call his hearthtroop. But I have vexed the King and he searches every shire in the land to hunt me down. That is why there must be no trace of me here. It would put you in mortal peril.'

I was desperate to know more, but realized that Harry's real purpose was to ask me questions, not the other way round.

'I wish you every success in the Holy Land. I have some very vivid memories from the days when we were there; some still haunt me to this day.'

'I have one last question for you. Were you there when my father died?'

'I was.'

'Did he die well?'

'He did; he took a lance intended for Duke Robert. Your father was a very brave man and a noble knight, just like your grandfather. Did your mother tell you about the brave Adela? And Edwin, the man who kept us all together and working as a team?'

'She did, and especially what Adela did for her in Palestine. I have been to her grave in Bourne to thank her, my other "mother". I hope that the order of knights I have joined will be able to emulate the traditions begun at Ely and continued by our Brethren in Palestine.'

'It was my honour to know them all; now I am privileged to meet another knight of Bourne. I wish you well.'

'I will try to live my life as they lived theirs.'

'I have no doubt you will. Go carefully, Harold of Hereford.'

He was a very earnest young man, but I readily gave

him my blessing and as much wisdom about Palestine as I could. I think I must have sounded like Torfida's father in the wildwood, and Hereward atop his mountain – full of talk of truth, virtue and destiny. I suppose I had become a sage. I did give him one piece of firm advice.

'Wherever your destiny takes you and whatever it leads you to do, always remember your past and the legacy you have inherited. It will not only be your guide, it will also bring meaning to your life and to the lives of those who follow you. Your grandfather once told me that that was the message he had learned from the Talisman of Truth. When the Emperor, John Comnenus, passes it on to you, he will help you understand the wisdom of that message.'

I asked Harry to stay so that I could get to know him better, but he insisted that he had to go and, as quickly as he had appeared, he was gone. He did promise to come back with the Talisman one day and to bring news of Hereward's resting place.

Perhaps he will.

When Harry had left, I felt a profound sense of relief. My mission in life had been fulfilled.

A fine young knight was about to embark on his own story, and he carried with him everything that Hereward, the Brotherhood and our Brethren had striven for.

Not only that, I had fulfilled my promise to Hereward to take care of his grandson.

When my time came to join him in the earth, I felt sure that the Wodewose would welcome me, just as he had welcomed my mentor, Hereward, and his own guide, the Old Man of the Wildwood.

Epilogue

Testament

William of Malmesbury, the renowned scribe of England's history, breathes a long, deep breath and adjusts his position to find a more comfortable posture, as he has many times during the long days he has sat listening to the story of the life of Edgar the Atheling, Prince of England. His young cleric, Roger of Caen, yawns; he is overwhelmed by what he has heard in the modest hall of Ashgyll Force and terrified about how much he has to remember.

Twenty years on from the Battle of Tinchebrai, despite the unseemly haste and connivance of his ascendancy, and his subsequent avarice in snatching Normandy from his brother, Henry's reign is largely peaceful and prosperous. Some of the wounds between Englishman and Norman are healing – even so, Prince Edgar is cautious about raking over ashes that are still warm.

'So, there you have it, William of Malmesbury. Do with it as you see fit, but treat us kindly. Perhaps the story is best told after the King is dead. He rules England well, but he still has a vindictive streak, which is never far from the surface.'

William agrees with Edgar; the story is so intimate, it should not be told while the King is alive.

'Your story will stay within the walls of Malmesbury

until the time is right, when the King has been laid to rest. He is nearly sixty now and has not been in good health since the death of his son, William the Atheling.'

'I heard that he drowned off the Normandy coast.'

'He perished on the *White Ship*, dashed on the rocks off Barfleur. They say that he and the crew had been drinking and racing another ship to see which could reach the open sea first.'

'I hear Robert's son, William Clito, is now Count of Flanders and is still harassing the King.'

'Indeed, he is. And to Henry's credit, he does not take any revenge on Robert, who is still alive in Cardiff, or use him as a pawn to persuade Clito to submit.'

'It is astonishing, Robert is seventy-five now. I hope he is as well as I am and not missing Sybilla too much. I wish I could see him; we would have a lot to talk about.'

'I am told that the King used to let him hunt once a week, but he is too old now. His allowance from the King is thirty-five pounds of silver a year – a meagre amount for a royal duke – but he doesn't starve or go about in rags.'

'He deserves better than that.'

To Roger's horror – he had thought their long and exhausting inquisition of Edgar was over – William resumes his questioning.

'What of Estrith, did she ever build that roof?'

'I heard from one of the nuns at Durham that Estrith died a few years ago, during an outbreak of the scarlet fever that killed half the population of Norwich. I don't know about her roof; perhaps they are working on it now.'

'Her father must also be dead. No one can live for ever – not even Hereward.'

'He would be almost ninety, but bear in mind, Robert and I are both in our mid-seventies and still going strong.'

Young Roger, ever keen to impress his abbot with his knowledge of the scriptures, reminds him about longevity in the Bible.

'The Bible tells us that Methuselah lived to be 969, Noah almost as long, and that Moses died at the age of 120. So, Hereward has plenty of years left yet.'

The three men smile at one another.

The scribe of Malmesbury is weary; day after day of revelations and insights have been hard to absorb. He and Roger of Caen have been checking one another's recollections at the end of each day, and every evening until the early hours they have been scratching hurried notes to aid their memory.

What they have been made privy to is a remarkable story of two families, as if in a Greek tragedy: William's powerful, all-conquering Norman family and Hereward's modest, redoubtable English family locked in a bitter struggle over three generations and across a far-reaching landscape. What is more, in Hereward's grandson, recently in the service of William's son, King Henry, the saga still continues.

Edgar the Atheling's long life has been laid bare in minute detail, and now the three men eat a final meal together, drink some wine and mead and savour a few flasks of the dark Pennine beer that Edgar's steward brews for him.

At the end of the feast, William notices a tall, dark woman of about forty, slim and attractive, wearing a light, clinging dress. She slips behind the curtain of Edgar's hall, leading towards his chamber.

The Prince sees that William has noticed the nocturnal guest.

'She is not another phantom, my friend. That is Awel, which means "gentle breeze"; she is a widow from Owain Rheged's tribe. She comes to see me once or twice a week. We have, shall we say, an understanding . . . it gets awfully cold up here, and we keep one another warm.'

Roger of Caen yawns once more, which is the signal for him to make his excuses and retire to his chamber, leaving Edgar and William to indulge in more heavy Pennine beer. Although tired, and much the worse for wear after sampling too many flasks of brew, William still has an appetite for more reflections from Edgar.

For his part, the old prince's prodigious intake of various intoxicating potions is making him melancholy.

'What do you make of my life, master storyteller? You have heard the accounts of many.'

'It is a noble life, well lived and well told, and I am very grateful. You bring great honour to your noble Cerdician lineage.'

'Do you really think that, or are you being kind to an old man?'

'Why would I falsely praise you? You are far too worldly to be deceived by a sycophantic priest at work. Besides, you know in your own heart the weight of your achievements; you don't need me to tell you.'

'I suppose you are right . . . I am content.'

'You should be. Your deeds in the Holy Land, King Henry's Charter of Liberties, the protection of Hereward's family and his legacy – any man should be proud of such things.'

'Thank you, William of Malmesbury.'

'And now, let us drink to Harold of Hereford. May he live a life that all who went before him would be proud of!'

'A good toast. I will drink to that.'

Both men – as many who have drunk too much often do – drain their flasks in deep, satisfying quaffs.

William then gets to his feet and staggers waywardly to his chamber.

Edgar does not stir at all, but descends into a deep slumber in front of the fading fire. Within moments, the widow Awel appears. She summons the steward, and together they help Edgar to his bed.

He will sleep well, the memories of Palestine finally purged, the exploits of an honourable life recorded for posterity.

Late the next morning William, heavy-headed and regretting his excesses, and Roger, brighter and relieved to be going home to Wessex, say their farewells.

They are about to leave Ashgyll Force when Edgar, seemingly none the worse for his intemperance, tells them of some news. He takes a deep breath and looks down, clearly anxious about what he has heard.

'My sergeant returned from Durham this morning. The King has had a shortage of silver for minting for some time now. He has just ordered the royal mint at York to open up the old Roman silver mines on these moors. He is going to build a new settlement at Alston to protect the mines and process the shipments. It is only five miles from here . . . and so, my many years of tranquility in this beautiful wilderness are about to be destroyed by hordes of uncouth miners from all over England and Scotland.'

The old Prince casts a teary eye towards the moors above him, before continuing.

'It will be the end for the wolves and the bears and, of course, for my friends Owain Rheged and the Gul. But nothing is for ever, I suppose.'

'Edgar, don't be too pessimistic. You and Owain have survived for a very long time; your lineages stretch back centuries. I'm sure you will both live out your days in peace.'

'Oh, I don't doubt that, we are both too stubborn to give in yet. But we will be the last of our breed. There's no shame in that – all lineages come to an end, even the mightiest, and the Gul and the Cerdicians have much to be proud of.'

William does not answer; he knows that Edgar is right. He smiles warmly, bows deferentially and kicks his mount eastwards beyond Ashgyll Force towards the ford over the Grue Water.

An hour or so later, as William and Roger begin the climb up Black Fell to traverse the high moors to Appleby, they hear the ominous scream of the Helm Wind. It is cold and gloomy and more like dusk than the middle of the day.

Then, as if the Helm Wind has heralded him, Owain

486

Rheged appears, just as he did on that day over a week ago, a day that now seems a lifetime away.

He is standing on a crag about 100 feet above them, wrapped in a bearskin. He raises his ram's-head staff above his head as a salute and a grant of safe passage through the land of the Gul, England's last vestige of the people of Ancient Britain.

William and Roger halt their horses, and William raises his hand in a reciprocal gesture of friendship.

After all the trauma of their journey to reach Edgar's lair and the long, tiring days and nights hearing his story, Roger is at last at ease.

'Abbott, you were right about this journey. I am privileged to have heard Prince Edgar's account in this mysterious place.'

'So you should be. We have touched three ages of these islands in a heritage that spans hundreds of years. Owain Rheged is a remnant of the people who ruled this land centuries before the legions of Rome came here. Edgar is the last of the Saxons who ruled here after the Romans left. And, my instincts tell me, Harold of Hereford represents the future. He is an Englishman, but one who has embraced Norman ways and thus thickened his English blood. His service in the King's guard would make his parents and grandparents, and all who followed their cause, very proud of him.

'He is the future of these islands. When I am long gone and he is ready to tell his story, you would do well to seek him out and ask him to share it with you.'

Roger of Caen turns round to take one last look at Owain Rheged, but the Druid has gone.

'Thank you, Abbott; perhaps I will come back here too, to see if the Gul survive another generation.'

'Good idea. We'll make a scribe out of you yet.'

Postscript

The motives of Alexius I, the Emperor of Byzantium, in calling for help from the Latin Princes in 1094, were largely met. The Crusade helped him subdue the Seljuk Turks of Anatolia and stabilize the empire in the south and east. He died in 1118.

Following his death, he was succeeded by his son, John Comnenus, whose reign was the high point of a Comneni dynasty noted for the wisdom and justice of its rule. His own tenure as Emperor was so highly regarded that he became known as 'John the Beautiful'.

The Crusades continued for nearly 200 years and, by 1292, numbered nine major expeditions in total. But there were also smaller Crusades, including a Children's Crusade (mostly teenagers and young men) in 1212, where none made it to the Holy Land and few managed to survive crossing the Alps. Some Crusades had other targets, including pagan Balts, Mongols, Slavs, Christian Heretics and Greek Orthodox Christians.

Pope Urban II, the instigator of the First Crusade, died in Rome two weeks after the fall of Jerusalem, but before the news had reached the Holy See.

Robert of Flanders returned to find his realm in chaos. His reputation from the Crusade stood him in good stead and he brought order back to Flanders and lived until 1111.

Gaston of Bearn travelled to Spain, where he lent his siege skills to the fight against the Moors.

Raymond of Toulouse returned to the Holy Land in the ill-fated Crusade of 1101. He eventually turned his attention to creating a Christian enclave in the Lebanese city of Tripoli. He died in the attempt in 1105. The city finally fell in 1109 and his son, Bertrand, completed his father's mission. Tripoli remained a Christian city until 1289.

Stephen of Blois returned home in disgrace. Under pressure from his formidable wife, Adela, daughter of William the Conqueror, he tried to redeem himself by returning to the Holy Land with the Crusade of 1101, where he perished at the hands of the Seljuk Turks.

Bohemond of Taranto, not satisfied with his lordship of Antioch, travelled to the Adriatic in 1105 to mount a campaign, sanctioned by Pope Paschal II, against the Byzantine rule of Alexius I. He was heavily defeated by Alexius at the Battle of Durazzo and was forced to sign a humiliating surrender. He returned to southern Italy a broken man and died in 1111.

It fell to Tancred of Hauteville to consolidate the Christian hold on Antioch. He increased its power to rival even that of Jerusalem. He died in 1112. Even though his successor, Roger of Salerno, nearly lost all that had been gained when his army was destroyed at the Battle of the Field of Blood in 1119, Antioch remained a Christian city until 1260.

Following his bravery during its capture, Godfrey of Bouillon took the greatest prize of all: Jerusalem. But he soon became ill and died in 1100.

Baldwin of Boulogne achieved remarkable success in his avaricious campaign into Mesopotamia in 1097. All cowered before his fearsome Norman knights, and he soon received an invitation from an Armenian named Bagrat to move eastwards towards the Euphrates, where he occupied Turbessel. Another invitation came from Thoros of Edessa, who adopted Baldwin as his son and successor. When Thoros was assassinated in March of 1098, Baldwin became the first Count of Edessa, thus creating the first Crusader city in the east. He ruled the county until 1100, marrying Arda, the daughter of Thoros of Marash. When Godfrey of Bouillon died, Baldwin ceded Edessa to his cousin and rushed south to grab the spoils of Jerusalem. He was crowned the first Christian King of Jerusalem on Christmas Day 1100. His ruthlessness built a powerful Christian domain throughout Palestine and beyond and guaranteed the legacy of the Crusade, until his death in 1118. Edessa remained a Christian city until 1144 and Jerusalem stayed under Christian control until it was taken by Saladin, Sultan of Egypt and Syria, in 1187.

The reign of Henry I brought a period of peace and prosperity in England and Normandy, notable for its judicial and financial reforms. He established the biannual Exchequer to reform the treasury. He used itinerant officials to curb the abuses of power at the local and regional level that had characterized Rufus's unpopular reign. The differences between the English and Norman populations began to break down during his reign, and he made peace with the Church after the disputes of his brother's reign.

But he could not solve the issue of his succession after the loss of his eldest son, William, in the wreck of the White Ship.

Henry's Queen, Edith/Matilda (the niece of Edgar the Atheling and a pure Anglo-Scot) had a great interest in architecture and instigated the erection of many buildings, including Waltham Abbey (interestingly, the resting place of King Harold). She also had the first arched bridge in England built, at Stratford-le-Bow, as well as a bathhouse with piped-in water and public lavatories at Queenhithe. Her court was filled with musicians and poets. She commissioned a biography of her mother, Saint Margaret, was an active queen and, like her mother, renowned for her devotion to religion and to the poor. William of Malmesbury describes her as attending church barefoot at Lent, and washing the feet and kissing the hands of the sick. She also administered extensive dower properties and was known as a patron of the arts, especially music. Matilda died on 1 May 1118 at Westminster Palace; she was buried at Westminster Abbey.

Henry I died on 1 December 1135 at Saint-Denis-en-Lyons (now Lyons-la-Forêt) in Normandy. According to legend, he died of food poisoning, caused by eating 'a surfeit of lampreys', of which he was excessively fond. His remains were sewn into the hide of a bull, to preserve them on the journey, and taken back to England to be buried at Reading Abbey, which he had founded fourteen years earlier. The abbey was later destroyed during the Protestant Reformation. No trace of his tomb has survived.

By the time of King John, Henry's great-great-grandson, much of what Henry had delivered in the Charter of

Liberties became enshrined in Magna Carta. The 'Great Charter' was signed by John in a meadow at Runnymede on 15 June 1215 and became the first milestone on the road to modern democracy.

Empress Matilda (also known as Matilda of England, or Maude) was the daughter and heir of Henry I. Matilda and her younger brother, William Adelin, were the only legitimate children of King Henry to survive to adulthood. William's early death in the White Ship disaster in 1120 made Matilda the last heir from the paternal line of her grandfather William the Conqueror. As a child, Matilda was betrothed to and later married Henry V, Holy Roman Emperor, acquiring the title Empress. The couple had no children. After being widowed for a few years, she was married to Geoffrey, Count of Anjou, with whom she had three sons. Matilda was the first female ruler of England. However, the length of her effective rule was brief, lasting a few months in 1141. She was never crowned and failed to consolidate her rule. For this reason, she is normally excluded from lists of English monarchs, and her rival (and cousin) Stephen of Blois is listed as monarch for the period 1135–54. Their rivalry for the throne led to years of unrest and civil war in England that have been called 'The Anarchy'. She did secure her inheritance of the Duchy of Normandy – through the military feats of her husband, Geoffrey – and campaigned unstintingly for her eldest son's inheritance, living to see him ascend the throne of England in 1154 as Henry II.

Robert Curthose, Duke of Normandy, eldest son of the Conqueror, died in 1134 in Cardiff Castle in his early eighties. He was buried in the abbey church of St Peter, in

Gloucester. The exact place of his burial is difficult to establish – legend states that he requested to be buried before the high altar. The church has subsequently become Gloucester Cathedral.

There is little mention in the historical records of the whereabouts of Edgar the Atheling after the beginning of the reign of Henry I. All that is said by William of Malmesbury, writing in 1025, was that he 'had retired to his estates in England'. There is no record of him ever marrying. Intriguingly, there is mention of an 'Edgar Atheling' in the *Great Pipe Rolls of the Second, Third and Fourth Years of the Reign of Henry II.* It is recorded that 'Edgar Atheling owed money for a donum [Latin: present, gift, offering] taken in Northumberland' before 1157. If this Edgar is Prince Edgar, he would have been 105 years old. It seems unlikely. However, it also seems odd that a man living in Northumbria at this time would carry a name suggesting he was the heir to the English throne – unless he was a twelfth-century Walter Mitty!

It has been written that Hereward of Bourne returned to his mountain eyrie after the Crusade and lived for many years as the 'Old Man of the Mountain'. But the true circumstances of his life or death after the Siege of Ely remain a mystery. Even though he is now known as Hereward 'the Wake', Hereward of Bourne was not given the suffix 'Wake' until many years after his death. The term is thought to come from the Old French 'wac' dog, as in wake-dog, the name for dogs used to warn of intruders.

The present-day Wakes of Courteenhall are directly descended from a Geoffrey Wac, who died in 1150. His son, Hugh Wac, who died 1172, married Emma, the daughter of Baldwin Fitzgilbert and his unnamed wife. That wife, it is supposed, was the granddaughter of either Gunnhild or Estrith in the female line from Hereward and Torfida. It is suggested that her mother had married Richard de Rulos and her grandmother had married Hugh de Evermur, a Norman knight in the service of King William. It is a tenuous link, but a remote possibility.

There are also other claimants, including the Harvard family (the founders of Harvard University) and the Howard family (the Dukes of Norfolk and Earls Marshal of England).

Coronation Charter of Henry I

Also known as the Charter of Liberties, it was sent to every shire in England to mark the King's coronation on 5 August 1100. Although Henry was less than assiduous in following it, it did set a precedent and contained many of the principles that formed the basis of the Great Charter (Magna Carta) of 1215 and put into writing a commitment to the pre-eminence of the rule of law.

Written in Latin in fourteen points, its text translates, in summary, as follows.

1. I, Henry, by the grace of God having been crowned the King of England, shall not take or sell any property from a Church upon the death of a bishop or abbot, until a successor has been named to that Church property. I shall end all the oppressive practices which have been an evil presence in England.

2. If any baron or earl of mine shall die, his heirs shall not be forced to purchase their inheritance, but shall retrieve it through force of law and custom.

3. Any baron or earl who wishes to betroth his daughter or other women kinsfolk in marriage should consult me first, but I will not stand in the way of any prudent marriage. Any widow who wishes to remarry should consult with me, but I shall abide by the wishes of her

close relatives, the other barons and earls. I will not allow her to marry one of my enemies.

4. Any wife of my barons who becomes a widow shall not be denied her dowry. She should be allowed to remarry according to her wishes, so long as she maintains the integrity of her body, in a lawful manner. Barons overseeing the children of a dead baron shall maintain their land and interest in a lawful manner.

5. Common seigniorages taken in the cities and counties, not in the time of Edward I, shall henceforth be forbidden.

6. I shall remit all debts and pleas which were owing to my brother, except those which were lawfully made through an inheritance.

7. If any of my barons should grow feeble, and give away money or other possessions, these shall be honoured, so long as the heirs are properly remembered. Gifts given by feeble barons under force of arms shall not be enforced.

8. If any of my barons commit a crime, he shall not bind himself to the Crown with a payment as was done in the time of my father and brother, but shall stand for the crime as was custom and law before the time of my father, and make amends as are appropriate. Anyone guilty of treachery or other heinous crime shall make proper amends.

9. I forgive all murders committed before I was crowned. Subsequent murders shall stand before the justice of the Crown.

10. With the common consent of my barons, I shall maintain all the forests, as was done in the time of my father.

11. Those knights who render military service and horses shall not be required to give grain or other farm goods to me.

12. I impose a strict peace on the land, and command that it be maintained.

13. I restore the law of King Edward and the amendments which my father introduced upon the advice of his barons.

14. Anything taken from me after the death of my father shall be returned immediately, without fine. If it is not returned, a heavy fine shall be enforced.

Witnesses: Maurice, Bishop of London, and William, Bishop Elect of Winchester, and Gerard, Bishop of Hereford, and Earl Henry and Earl Simon and Walter Giffard and Robert de Montfort and Roger Bigot and Eudo the Steward and Robert, son of Hamo and Robert Malet. At London when I was crowned. Farewell.

Acknowledgements

To my wonderful wife, Lucy, our gorgeous sons Charlie and Jack, my eldest son Adam, his wife, Michelle, and my grandchildren, Sam and Jessica, of whom I am very proud and to all the inspirational friends and outstanding professionals who have made *Crusade* happen.

I could not have done it without you.

Glossary

Anchorite (male)/anchoress (female)

A medieval religious hermit who devoted his or her life to prayer and frugality. Greatly revered by the local community, they often lived in small stone cells built against the walls of churches.

Atabeg

Atabeg, Atabek, or Atabey is a hereditary title of nobility of Turkic origin, indicating a governor of a nation or province who is subordinate to a monarch. The word is a compound of two Turkic words: from ata, 'ancestor', and beg or bey, 'leader, prince'. The title was common during the Seljuk rule of the Near East in the twelfth century. It was also used in Mesopotamia.

Atheling

The Anglo-Saxon name for the heir to the throne.

Baculus

A huge wooden war club, believed to have been carried by the Duke of Normandy as a sort of mace signifying his authority. It may well have been a weapon used in earnest by his Viking ancestors.

Bastide

A fortified settlement of several buildings, or even a small town, often on a commanding hilltop position.

Bezant

A gold coin from the Byzantine Empire.

Bruneswald

The great ancient forest of middle England.

Burgh

The Saxon name for a town or city.

Butescarl

A naval-based elite warrior, the seaborne equivalent of a housecarl and a forerunner of a modern-day marine.

Catapult

Castles, fortresses and fortified walled cities were the main form of defence in the Middle Ages and a variety of catapult devices were used against them. As well as attempting to breach the walls, missiles and incendiaries could be hurled inside, or early forms of biological warfare deployed, such as diseased carcases, putrid garbage or excrement. The most widely used catapults were the following:

Ballista
Similar to a giant crossbow and designed to work through torsion. Giant arrows were used as ammunition, made from wood and with an iron tip.

Mangonel
Designed to throw heavy projectiles from a bowl-shaped bucket at the end of an arm. With a range of up to 1,300 feet they were

relatively simple to construct, and wheels were added to increase mobility. Mangonels are sometimes referred to as 'onagers'. Onager catapults initially launched projectiles from a sling, which was later changed to a bowl-shaped bucket.

Springald

The springald's design was similar to that of the ballista, effectively a crossbow propelled by tension. The springald's frame was more compact, allowing for use inside tighter confines, such as the inside of a castle or tower.

Trebuchet

Trebuchets were probably the most powerful catapult employed in the Middle Ages. The most commonly used ammunition was stones, but the most effective involved fire, such as firebrands and the infamous 'Greek fire'. Trebuchets came in two different designs: traction, which were powered by people; and counterpoise, powered by a weight on the short end of an arm. A simplified trebuchet was known as a 'couillard', where the trebuchet's single counterweight was split, swinging on either side of a central support post.

Cerdic / Cerdician

The dynastic name of the Kings of Wessex, who ultimately became Kings of England, from Egbert, King of Wessex in 820, to Edward the Confessor's death in 1066. The only exceptions were the three Danish kings, Cnut and his sons Harold Harefoot and Harthcnut, between 1016 and 1042. The name reputedly derives from Cerdic, a prince of the West Saxons from *circa* 600, who was an ancestor of Egbert, the first King of England, but he is a figure who may be more myth than reality.

Chain mail

Armour made from linked iron rings (*see* hauberk).

Churchwright

A church builder or architect.

Clito

William, son of Robert, Duke of Normandy, was given the suffix 'Clito'. It is the Latinized equivalent to 'Atheling' – heir to the throne.

Conroi

A squadron, twenty-five strong, of Norman cavalry.

Danegeld

A tribute paid by the Saxons of England to persuade Viking raiders to return to Scandinavia and leave the people unharmed and their goods intact. The first Danegeld was paid in 856 (10,000 pounds of silver) and more was handed over in 991, 994, 1002 and 1007 when King Athelred bought two years of peace for 36,000 pounds of silver. Two more payments were made in 1012 and in 1016 when Cnut the Great became King of England and paid for his invasion fleet with a geld of over 80,000 pounds of silver.

Denier

The denier was a Frankish coin created by Charlemagne in the Early Middle Ages. It was introduced together with an accounting system in which twelve deniers equalled one sou and twenty sous equalled one livre. This system, and the denier itself, served as the model for many of Europe's currencies, including the British pound, Italian lira, Spanish peseta and the Portuguese dinheiro. The British equivalent of the denier was the penny, 240 of which made up one British pound, or 20 shillings. The symbol for both the old denier and the penny used in the United Kingdom and elsewhere was 'd'. The name 'denier' was derived from the name of the Roman coin the denarius.

Destrier

A Norman war horse. The Normans had four designations of horse: a destrier (for use in battle); a palfrey (a good riding horse); a rouney (an ordinary riding horse); and a sumpter (a packhorse).

Faris

An Arab cavalryman, usually carrying a status similar to the European knight.

Fighting Man

The personal war banner of Harold Godwinson, bearing the woven image of an ancient warrior wielding a war club.

Futuwwa

A Sufic (mystical Islamic) term that has some similarities to 'chivalry' and 'virtue'. It was also a name of an ethical urban organization or 'guild' in medieval Muslim realms that emphasized honesty, peacefulness, gentleness, generosity, hospitality and avoidance of complaint in life.

Fyrd

The massed 'citizen army' of the Anglo-Saxon kings before the

Norman invasion. Each local leader held a retinue of chosen companions whose duty it was to protect his lord's life. In return, the lord was expected to share the booty of war with his loyal supporters. The collective of these lords' men formed the king's fyrd (*see also* housecarls).

Garrotte

Strangulation by a ligature around the neck, usually applied from behind. The Byzantines used bow strings. There are examples from antiquity and from many different cultures, the most infamous being the official execution method used in Spain as late as the 1970s. The victim was bound in a chair and a metal band placed around the throat, which was then tightened by a screw mechanism from behind. Sometimes a spike was attached to the screw to hasten death by penetrating the spinal cord.

Geld

Another word for money in Dutch and German ('gelt' in Yiddish), in medieval England it meant tax, or tribute or a ransom – as in Danegeld.

Gonfalon

A small tailed flag or banner, flown from the top of a lance or pole to indicate lordly status, common throughout Europe. It would carry the colours, crest or heraldry of its owner.

Greek fire

The secret weapon of the Byzantine emperors. A sort of ancient napalm, it was invented by a Syrian engineer, a refugee from Baalbek, in the Egyptian city of Heliopolis in 673 AD. The mix of ingredients, a closely guarded secret, was reputedly handed down from emperor to emperor. It has remained a secret to this day, but is thought to be a combination of pitch, sulphur, tree resin, quicklime and bitumen. The key ingredient may well have been magnesium, which would explain why the 'fire' would burn under water.

Hammer-beam roof

A hammer-beam roof allows a span greater than the length of any individual piece of timber. In place of a normal tie beam spanning the entire width of the roof, short beams – the hammer beams – are supported by curved braces from the wall, and further structure is built on top of the hammer beams. The earliest hammer-beamed building still standing in England (built in 1308) is located in Winchester, in Winchester Cathedral Close, next to the dean's garden, and is known as the Pilgrims' Hall, now part of the Pilgrims' School. The roof of Westminster Hall (1395–9) is a fine example of a hammer-beam roof. The span of the hall is 68 feet 4 inches, and the opening between the ends of the hammer beams 25 feet 6 inches. The height from the paving of the hall to the hammer beam is 40 feet, and to the underside of the collar beam 63 feet 6 inches, so an additional height in the centre of 23 feet 6 inches has been gained by the use of hammer beams.

Hauberk

A chain-mail 'coat' worn like a long pullover down below the groin. Hauberks for the infantry were slightly shorter so that the men could run in them, and were split only at the sides. Cavalry hauberks extended almost to the knee and were split front and back. The mail could extend into a hood (ventail), like a balaclava, but had a flap in front of the throat and chin that could be dropped for comfort when not in the midst of battle. Three kinds of mail were used and were progressively more expensive: ordinary ring mail, scale mail and lamellar mail (in which overlapping individual plates were fastened together by leather thongs).

Hearthtroop

The elite bodyguard of kings, princes and lords of the ninth, tenth and eleventh centuries.

Hide

Not a fixed area but an amount of land sufficient to support a family, which became a unit subject to a 'geld' tax. The geld would be collected at a stated rate per hide. After the Norman Conquest, hidage was recorded in the Domesday Book of 1086 and stayed in use until the end of the twelfth century.

Housecarls

The elite troops of the Anglo-Saxon kings, following their establishment by King Cnut in 1016, in the Danish tradition. Cnut brought his own personal troops to supplement the English fyrd (citizen army) when he succeeded to the throne following the death of Edmund Ironside.

Knaar

A traditional Norse ship, a modified form of the Viking longship, but used as a cargo vessel.

Lamellar

Armour made from small iron plates tied together with leather (*see* hauberk).

Latt

A heavy bronze-headed mace favoured by Saracen (Muslim) warriors.

Levunium, Battle of

The most decisive victory of the reign of Alexius I, Emperor of Byzantium. On 29 April 1091, an invading force of Pechenegs was defeated by the combined forces of the Byzantine Empire and its Cuman allies (nomadic warriors of the Eurasian Steppe, related to the Pechenegs). The outcome was a massacre on a terrible scale. The Pechenegs went into battle with their entire families. Few survived; those who did were taken into slavery by the Byzantines.

Mamluk

An Arab soldier, usually an infantryman. Born a slave, he would make his way in life as a professional soldier.

Manceaux

Plural of Manceau, an inhabitant of Le Mans or Maine, the province of France between Anjou and Normandy.

Manzikert, Battle of

Fought between the Byzantine Empire and the Seljuk Turks led by Alp Arslan on 26 August 1071 near Manzikert (modern Malazgirt in eastern Turkey). The devastating defeat of the Byzantine army and the humiliating capture of the Emperor Romanos IV Diogenes brought the empire to the brink of annihilation, destroyed Byzantine authority in Anatolia and Armenia, and allowed the Turks to populate Anatolia.

Mead

An ancient drink, common to many lands. It was a potent and popular concoction in Britain for hundreds of years. It is made from honey, water and yeast. Fruit or spices can be added for alternative flavours. It can be very alcoholic, was thought to be a powerful aphrodisiac and was often given to newlyweds to boost fertility.

Midden

A domestic waste dump for a village or burgh. A word of Scandinavian origin, it is still in use in Scotland and the English Pennines.

Mos Militum

A code of knightly ethics, loosely based on the ancient noble tradition of the Roman aristocracy and the influence of Islamic ethics, such as those of the Futuwwa, which appeared in the late eleventh century and formed the basis of the values of the Age of Chivalry.

Motte and bailey

A motte (a large mound of earth topped by a wooden and then, later, by a stone castle) surrounded by a bailey (an enclosed courtyard, encircled by a fortified wall) was the archetypal Norman fortification, used to subdue and intimidate the defeated Saxons. Most of the medieval castles of England, such as Windsor and the Tower of London, started life as motte and bailey constructions in the 1070s and 1080s.

Muslim

In a historical context, the words 'Muslim' (a follower of the religion of Islam), 'Saracen' (usually applied to the Muslim armies that opposed the Crusades) and 'Moor' (usually applied to the Arab peoples of North Africa and Spain) are often used interchangeably. The word 'Arab' defines the Semitic peoples who originated in Arabia and whose influence spread across the Middle East and North Africa in the seventh and eighth centuries. Sunni and Shia Islam are the two major denominations of Islam. Approximately 80–90 per cent of the world's Muslims are Sunni and 10–20 per cent are Shia, with most Shias belonging to the 'Twelver' tradition (derived from their belief in twelve divinely ordained leaders, known as the Twelve Imams) and the rest divided between several other groups. Sunnis are a majority in most Muslim communities in South-east Asia, China, South Asia, Africa and most of the Arab World. Shias make up the majority of the population in Iran, Iraq, Azerbaijan and Bahrain, and they are the largest religious group in Lebanon (collectively called the Shia Crescent), while Pakistan has the second largest Shia Muslim population in the world. The historic background of the Sunni–Shia split lies in the schism that occurred when the Islamic prophet Muhammad died in the year 632 AD, leading to a dispute over succession that culminated in the Battle of Siffin. Sectarian violence persists to this day from Pakistan to Yemen and is a major element of friction throughout the Middle East. Over the years Sunni–Shia relations have been marked by both cooperation and conflict, often with deadly violence. A period of relative harmony during most of the twentieth century has recently been replaced by conflict. Today there are differences in religious practice, traditions and customs as well as religious beliefs.

Pennon

A small streamer-like flag flown at the top of a knight's lance to signify his status. It would have a combination of one, two or three colours to identify him, his origins or the lord he served.

Plainchant

Otherwise known as 'plainsong', the monophonic melody sung by monks from as early as the eighth century is more popularly known as 'Gregorian chant'.

Purple, The

A term that came to describe the office of Emperor of Byzantium, derived from the imperial purple cloak worn by Byzantine emperors and their Roman predecessors.

Putrid fever

One of the many names – others include slow/camp/ship/jail fever (it flourishes in overcrowded human environments) – for epidemic typhus. The name comes from the Greek 'typhos', meaning hazy, describing the state of mind of those affected. Symptoms include severe headache, a sustained high fever, cough, rash, severe muscle pain, chills, falling blood pressure, stupor, sensitivity to light, as well as delirium. During the second year of the Peloponnesian War (430 BC) Athens suffered a devastating epidemic, known as the 'Plague of Athens', which killed, among others, Pericles. The plague returned twice more, in 429 BC and in the winter of 427/6 BC. Epidemic typhus is thought to have been the cause in each case.

Quarrel

The missile of a crossbow, sometimes referred to as a bolt. Generally shorter and sturdier than an arrow, its name derives from the old French for 'square', arising from the fact that the tip of the quarrel was often made square in order to maximize its killing power. More cumbersome, slower and more difficult to load than a longbow and only effective at short range, it was nevertheless a much more powerful weapon and could penetrate even the thickest medieval armour.

Quran

The Quran, literally 'a recitation', is also transliterated as Qur'an, Koran, Qur'ān, Coran, Kuran and al-Qur'ān. It is the central religious text of Islam, which Muslims consider the verbatim word of God (Allah) and the Final Testament, following the Old and New Testaments. It is regarded as the finest piece of literature in the Arabic language. The Quran is divided into 114 suras of unequal length which are classified either as Meccan or Medinan depending upon their place and time of revelation. Muslims believe the Quran to be verbally revealed through angel Jibrīl (Gabriel) from God to Muhammad gradually over a period of approximately twenty-three years beginning in 610 AD, when Muhammad was forty, and concluding in 632 AD, the year of his death. Muslims further believe that the Quran was precisely memorized, recited and exactly written down by Muhammad's companions (Sahaba) after each revelation was dictated by him.

Rum, Sultanate of

The Seljuk Turk Islamic Sultanate of Rum held sway over most of Anatolia in the years after the disaster of the Battle of Manzikert and the end of Byzantine control of the area. The name 'Rum' was chosen by the Seljuks to signify their inheritance of the legacy of Ancient Rome.

Seax

A short, stabbing sword.

Senlac Ridge, Battle of

Now known as the Battle of Hastings, the decisive battle of William the Conqueror's Norman Conquest of England was fought on Senlac Ridge, also called Senlac Hill, at a place now known as Battle, seven miles north of Hastings, on England's south coast. Known in Old English as 'Santlache' (Sandy Stream), in Norman French it was adapted to 'Sanguelac' (Blood Lake), which was then shortened to Senlac. The ridge was probably higher than it is today, the very top of it being levelled in the building of Battle Abbey.

Shia Muslim

See Muslim.

Sous

'Sous' evolved as a French word from the Roman coin 'solidus', which mutated to 'soldus', then 'solt', then 'sol' and finally 'sou'. No gold solidi were minted after the Carolingians adopted the silver standard; thenceforward, the solidus or sol was a paper accounting unit equivalent to one-twentieth of a pound (librum or livre) of silver and divided into 12 denarii or deniers. The monetary unit disappeared with decimalization and the introduction of the franc during the French Revolution (First Republic) in 1795, but five centimes, the twentieth part of the franc, inherited the name as a nickname.

Strategoi

A commander (general) of a theme (division) in the army of Byzantium (see also 'theme' below).

Sub-regulus

Second in the land; only a king would take precedence over him.

Sunni Muslim

See Muslim.

Surcoat

A long cloth coat, like the long dress of female clothing, worn over a knight's armour. It would often be embroidered with the knight's colours or his heraldic symbols.

Taifa

A series of city states of the eleventh century, including Zaragoza, Cordoba, Seville and Valencia.

Thegn

A local village chieftain of Anglo-Saxon England. Not a great land-owner or a titled aristocrat but the head of a village. Thus, thegns formed the backbone to the organization of Anglo-Saxon life. While serving with the army, usually as part of their service to the earl of their province, they formed a large part of the king's elite fighting force, the housecarls.

Theme

The Byzantine Empire was organized into military districts or themes, which reflected its different nationalities. Themes were responsible for generating their own regiments for the Emper-or's army. In turn, retired soldiers were granted lands in the military theme from which they served. By the end of the eleventh century, there were 38 themes in the Byzantine Empire, each composed of between 4,000 and 6,000 men, giving a stand-ing army of approximately 200,000 men.

Tilt field

A roped-off field used for tilting (jousting). It was also called 'the lists' or 'list field'. Later in the Middle Ages, enclosed spaces were built (tiltyards) and the tilting become a sport as well as a form of military training.

Tithe

Tax owed to a superior in the hierarchy of the feudal system of the eleventh century and later. For example, from a tenant to his lord or the Church, or from landowners to the king.

Trireme

An Ancient Greek galley with three rows of oars, each above the other. A vessel of war on which the oarsmen's strength could produce a ramming speed of significant impact.

Troubadour

A lyric poet composer in a tradition that began in south-west France (Aquitaine, Provence) in the Occitan language in the eleventh century. William IX, Duke of Aquitaine, was the first well-known exponent. Some of his songs have survived. The songs extolled the virtues of Courtly Love, a mix of erotic and heroic sentiments between a knight and his love, a woman who wasn't necessarily his wife. Troubadours came from all walks of life, some of whom were professionals who made a living as strolling minstrels.

Varangian Guard

The elite bodyguard of the emperors of Byzantium for several hundred years. They were extremely well-paid mercenaries who also shared in the booty of the Emperor's victories, thus the Guard could attract the finest warriors. Most were drawn from Scandinavia and were often referred to as the 'Axemen of the North'. Their loyalty was legendary, as was their ferocity. It is thought many of Harold of England's surviving housecarls joined the Guard after Senlac Ridge in 1066.

Verba Novissima

Latin: 'Last words'. In a tradition going back in English law at least 450 years before the eleventh century, to Augustine of Canterbury (St Augustine), the 'last words' spoken by a person prior to their death constituted their 'last will and testament'. They annulled any previous will made by that person.

Villein

The term used in the feudal era to denote a peasant (tenant farmer) who was legally tied to the land he worked on. A villein could not leave the land without the landowner's consent.

Vizier

The senior adviser/minister/counsellor/earl marshal to a caliph. Usually a civilian in a clerical hierarchy. The word is found in Arabic, but also in Persian and Hindi and may be Indo-European in origin.

Woad

A blue dye made from the powdered and fermented leaves of the plant *Isatis tinctoria*, also known as Dyer's Woad. The Celtic tribes of Britain, from before the Roman invasion and beyond, used woad to decorate themselves, both in times of peace and war.

Wyvern of Wessex

A wyvern is a legendary winged creature with a dragon's head and a barbed tail. The wyvern is often found in heraldry. A golden wyvern was the symbol of the ancient Kingdom of Wessex and the early kings of England up to Harold Godwinson. It was thought to have been one of his two banners at Senlac Ridge, the other being his personal standard, the Fighting Man.

Genealogies

The Lineage of Edgar the Atheling

The Lineage of Robert, Duke of Normandy

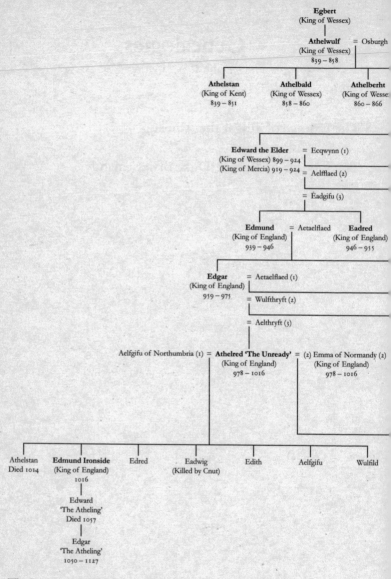

Egbert
(King of Wessex)

Athelwulf = Osburgh
(King of Wessex)
839 – 858

Athelstan   **Athelbald**   **Athelberht**
(King of Kent)   (King of Wessex)   (King of Wesse
839 – 851   858 – 860   860 – 866

Edward the Elder = Ecqwynn (1)
(King of Wessex) 899 – 924
(King of Mercia) 919 – 924 = Aelfflaed (2)

= Eadgifu (3)

Edmund = Aetaelflaed **Eadred**
(King of England)   (King of England)
939 – 946   946 – 955

Edgar = Aetaelflaed (1)
(King of England)
959 – 975 = Wulfthryft (2)

= Aelthryft (3)

Aelfgifu of Northumbria (1) = **Athelred 'The Unready'** = (2) Emma of Normandy (2)
(King of England)   (King of England)
978 – 1016   978 – 1016

Athelstan **Edmund Ironside**   Edred   Eadwig   Edith   Aelfgifu   Wulfild
Died 1014 (King of England)   (Killed by Cnut)
       1016

Edward
'The Atheling'
Died 1057

Edgar
'The Atheling'
1050 – 1127

The Lineage of Edgar the Atheling

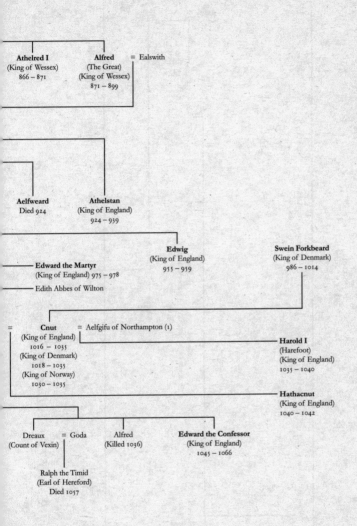

Athelred I
(King of Wessex)
866 – 871

Alfred
(The Great)
(King of Wessex)
871 – 899

= Ealswith

Aelfweard
Died 924

Athelstan
(King of England)
924 – 939

Edwig
(King of England)
955 – 959

Swein Forkbeard
(King of Denmark)
986 – 1014

— **Edward the Martyr**
(King of England) 975 – 978

— Edith Abbes of Wilton

=

Cnut
(King of England)
1016 – 1035
(King of Denmark)
1018 – 1035
(King of Norway)
1030 – 1035

= Aelfgifu of Northampton (1)

Harold I
(Harefoot)
(King of England)
1035 – 1040

Hathacnut
(King of England)
1040 – 1042

Dreaux
(Count of Vexin)

= Goda

Alfred
(Killed 1036)

Edward the Confessor
(King of England)
1045 – 1066

Ralph the Timid
(Earl of Hereford)
Died 1057

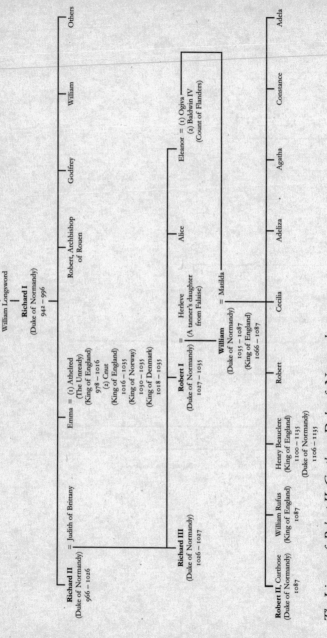

The Lineage of Robert II, Curthose, Duke of Normandy

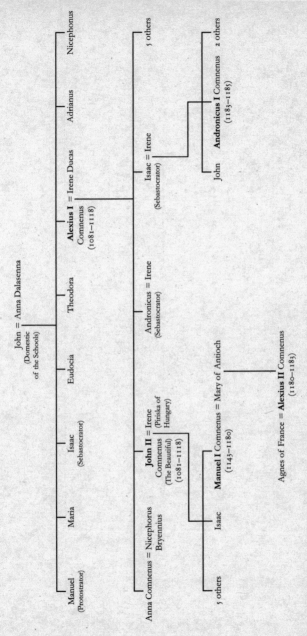

The Lineage of The Comneni Emperors of Constantinople

Maps

N

100 miles

100 km

Abernethy
Dunfermline
Musselburgh Dunbar
Lammermuir Hills
Bamburgh
Alnwick ✕
Hadrian's Wall
Carlisle Newcastle Tynemouth
Gateshead
Alston ✳ Ashgyll ● Durham
Appleby
Sedbergh
Lancaster ● York
Preston

Chester

Bourne ● Norwich
Peterborough
Ely

Hereford
Gloucester
Cardiff Waltham
Malmesbury London Upchurch
Rochester
Wells Canterbury
Winchester Dover
Glastonbury *Senlac Ridge* ✕
Montacute Romsey Arundel
Launceston
Exeter Pevensey
Dartmoor

English Channel

England and Scotland in the 1070s

France, Normandy and Aquitaine in the 1070s

Europe in the 1080s

Norway

Scotland

Ireland

Wales

England

Holy Roman
Empire

Normandy

France

• Geneva

• Turin

Oviedo •

Florence •

Zaragoza •

Rome

Valencia •

Calatafimi/Seges

Maz

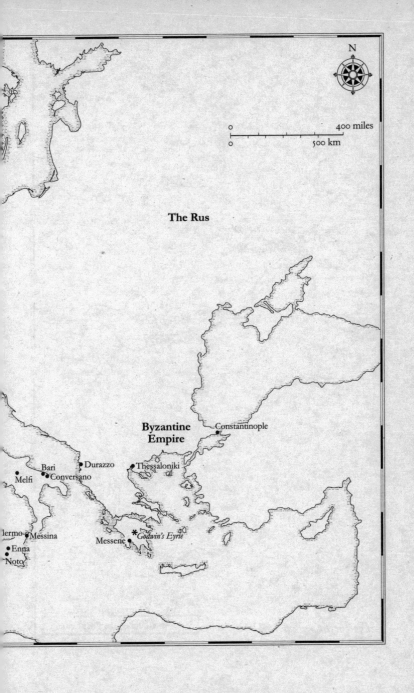

N

400 miles
500 km

The Rus

Byzantine
Empire   Constantinople

Bari   Durazzo   Thessaloniki
Melfi Conversano

lermo Messina
Enna   Messene   *Godwin's Eyrie
Noto

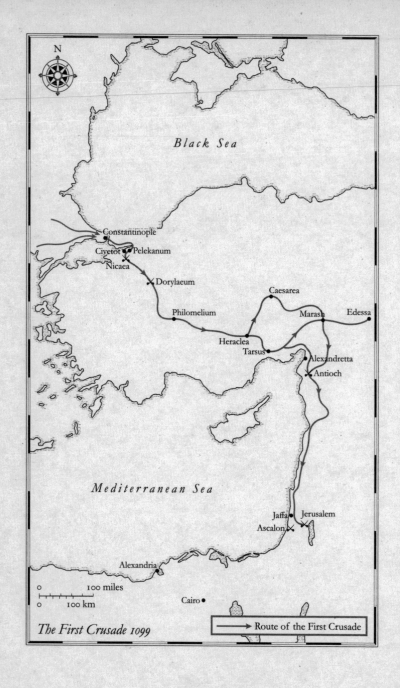

The First Crusade 1099